A CADENCE CREEK
CHRISTMAS

Greenwich Council
Library & Information Service

IN HOUSE
QUALITY
SYSTEMS

Plumstead Library
Tel: 020 8854 1728

Please return by the last date shown

29. 9. 14

26 FEB 2015

Senca
-- JUN 2015

Murray

-- AUG 2015

Matthews

-- SEP 2015

HEATHFIELD

Crundwell
Friar
-- MAY 2016

Leary
-- JUN 2016

-- JUN 2016

-4 OCT 2016

-6 JAN 2018

Thank
You!

To renew, please contact any Greenwich library

Issue: 02	Issue Date: 06.06.00	Ref: RM.RBL.LIS

A CADENCE CREEK CHRISTMAS

BY

DONNA ALWARD

First published in Great Britain 2013
by Mills & Boon, an imprint of Harlequin (UK) Limited,
Large Print edition 2014
Eton House, 18-24 Paradise Road,
Richmond, Surrey, TW9 1SR

© 2013 Donna Alward

ISBN: 978 0 263 24034 4

Printed and bound in Great Britain
by CPI Antony Rowe, Chippenham, Wiltshire

To the Mills & Boon® Romance authors—
my writing family.
You guys are the best.

CHAPTER ONE

TAYLOR SHEPARD FROWNED as she assessed the lineup of men before her. All five of them were big, burly and, with the exception of her brother Jack, looked irritated beyond belief.

"Come on, Taylor, can't we take these monkey suits off?"

Her oldest brother, Callum, pleaded with her. Along with his best man and groomsmen, he'd spent the past half hour trying on various tuxedo styles. Callum, being her brother and, of course, the groom, was the spokesman for the lot.

"If you want to show up at your wedding in jeans and boots, be my guest. I don't think your bride would appreciate that too much, though."

A muffled snort came from down the line. Her head snapped toward the sound and she saw one of the groomsmen—Rhys, if she remembered correctly—struggling to keep a straight face.

"Keep it up," she warned severely, "and you'll be the one trying on a cravat."

His face sobered in an instant.

"This was supposed to be a small and simple wedding," Callum reminded her. "Not one of your massive events."

"And it will be. But small and simple doesn't mean it can't be classy." She pinned him with a stare. "Your soon-to-be wife trusts me. Besides, you need to balance your look with the wedding dress and flower girl dress for Nell." She paused and played her trump card. "They're going to be *beautiful*."

There'd be little argument out of Callum now. All it took was the mention of Avery and his baby daughter and the tough ex-soldier turned into a marshmallow. She thought it was fantastic. He'd needed someone like Avery for a long time. Not to mention how fatherhood had changed him. He had the family he'd always wanted.

She examined each man carefully. "I don't like the red vests," she decreed. She went up to Sam Diamond and tugged on the lapels of his jacket. "And not double-breasted. The green vests, like Tyson's here. The single-breasted jacket like Jack has on, which is much simpler." She smiled up at her brother, easily the most comfortable man in the group. Jack wouldn't give her a moment's trouble, not about this anyway. She got to the last body in the line and looked up.

Dark eyes looked down into hers. A little serious, a little bit of put-upon patience, and a surprising warmth that made her think he had a good sense of humor. She reached up and gave his tie a tug, straightening it. "And not the bolo tie, either. The crossover that Rhys is wearing is classier and still very Western."

Her fingertips grazed the starchy fabric of his shirt as she dropped her hand. It was a negligible touch, barely worth noticing, except the slight contact made something interesting tumble around in her stomach. Her gaze darted up to his again and discovered he was watching her steadily in a way that made her feel both excited and awkward.

Interesting. Because in her line of work she dealt with all sorts of men every day. Rich men, powerful men, men who liked other men and men who couldn't keep their hands to themselves. She knew how to handle herself. Was never tempted to flirt unless it was a business strategy. She was very good at reading people, figuring out their tastes and wants and knowing what methods she needed to use to deliver them.

So getting a fluttery feeling from barely touching Rhys Bullock was a surprise indeed. And feeling awkward? Well, that was practically unheard of. Of course, it could be that she was just very out of practice. She'd been far too busy building her business to do much dating.

She straightened her shoulders and took a step backward. "Okay, now on to footwear."

Groans went up the line.

She smiled. "Guys, really. This will be the best part. I was thinking black boots which we can get wherever you prefer to buy your boots. No patent dress shoes. Put on the boots you wore here so we can accurately measure your inseam for length. Then we'll finish up your measurements and you're done." She made a dismissive sound. "Honestly, what a bunch of babies."

She was having fun now, teasing the guys. They were good men but not much for dressing up. She got that. Their standard uniform was jeans and boots, plaid shirts and Stetsons. Tuxedo fittings had to be torture.

Still, it didn't matter if this was her brother's wedding or a client's A-list party. Or if she was being paid or doing it as a wedding gift. Avery and Callum's day would be exactly what it should be because she'd oversee every last detail.

And if she were being honest with herself, it was a relief to get out of Vancouver for a while and deal with "real" people. It had been exhausting lately. Most of her clients were rich and used to getting exactly what they wanted exactly when they wanted it. Their sense of entitlement could be a bit much. Not to mention the unorthodox requests. She sometimes wondered what sort of reality these people lived in.

As she looked after the ordering details, one of the alterations staff did measurements. Another half hour and they were all done and standing out in the sunshine again. Taylor pulled out her phone and scanned her to-do list for today. She had to drive back to Cadence Creek and meet with Melissa Stone, the florist at Foothills Floral. The final order was going to be placed today—after all, the wedding was less than two weeks away now. All this should have been done a month ago or even more, but Taylor knew there were ways to get things done in a hurry if needs be. Like with the tuxes and invitations. Both should have been tended to months ago but it had merely taken a few phone calls and it had all been sorted. A little out of Callum's budget, perhaps, but he didn't need to know that. She was good for it. *Exclusive!*—her event planning business—had treated her well the past few years.

Still, there was no time to waste. She closed her calendar and looked up.

The group of them were standing around chatting, something about a lodge north of town and what had happened to the rancher who'd owned it. Jack was listening intently, but Rhys was missing. Had he left already?

The bell on the door chimed behind her, and she turned to see Rhys walking through. He looked far more himself now in black jeans and a black, tan and red plaid shirt beneath a sheepskin jacket. His boots were brown and weathered and as he stepped on to the sidewalk he dipped his head just a little and placed a well-worn hat on top. Taylor half smiled. The hat looked like an old friend; shaped precisely to his head, worn-in and comfortable.

"Feel better?" she asked, smiling.

"I'm not much for dressing up," he replied simply.

"I know. None of you are, really. But it's only for one day. You're all going to look very handsome."

"Is that so?"

Her cheeks heated a little. Rhys's best feature was his eyes. And he was tall and well-built, just the way she liked her men. Perhaps it was growing up the way she had. They'd all been outdoor kids. Heck, Callum had joined the military and Jack had been a pro downhill skier until he'd blown his knee out at Val d'Isère.

But Rhys wasn't classically handsome. Not in the way that Tyson Diamond was, for instance. In this group Rhys would be the one who would probably be overlooked. His cheekbones were high and defined and his jawbone unrelenting, giving him a rough appearance. His lips looked well-shaped but it was hard to tell—the closest she'd seen him come to smiling was the clandestine chuckle while they were inside.

But it was the way he'd answered that piqued her interest. *Is that so?* he'd asked, as if he couldn't care one way or the other if anyone thought him handsome or not.

It was quite refreshing.

"I should get going," she said, lifting her chin. "I've got to be back to town in thirty minutes for another appointment. Thanks for coming out. It'll be easy for you from here on in. Weddings do tend to be mostly women's business." At least with these sorts of men...

"Drive carefully then," he said, tipping his hat. "No sense rushing. The creek isn't going anywhere."

"Thanks, but I'd like to be on time just the same." She gave him a brief nod and turned to the assembled group. "I've got to go. Thanks everyone." She put her hand on Callum's shoulder and went up on tiptoe to kiss his cheek. "See you soon." She did the same for Jack. "When are you flying out?"

He shrugged. "I'm going to hang around for a few days. I've got to be back in Montana for meetings on Monday, though, and then I'm flying in the Thursday before the wedding."

"Let's have lunch before you go back."

"You got it. Text me."

With a quick wave Taylor hurried across the parking lot, her heeled boots echoing on the pavement. She turned the car heater on high and rubbed her hands together—December in Alberta was colder than on the coast and she felt chilled to the bone all the time.

She was down to twenty-five minutes. As a light snow began to fall, she put her rental car in gear and pulled out, checking her GPS for the quickest route to the highway.

Three weeks. That was how long she had to decompress. She'd take care of Callum's wedding and then enjoy one indulgent week of vacation before heading home and working on the final preparations for New Year's. This year's planning involved taking over an entire warehouse and transforming it into an under the sea kingdom.

It all seemed quite ridiculous. And because it did, she knew that it was time she took a vacation. Even one as short as a week in some small, backwater Alberta town. Thank goodness her assistant, Alicia, was completely capable and could handle things in Taylor's absence.

She turned on the wipers and sighed. Compared to the crazy demands of her normal events, she knew she could do this wedding with her eyes closed.

If that were true, though, why was she having so much fun and dreading going back to Vancouver so very much?

It was already dark when Taylor whipped out her phone, brought up her to-do list and started punching in brief notes with her thumbs. Her fingers were numb with cold and she'd been out of the flower shop for a whole minute and a half. Where on earth was the frigid air coming from anyway? Shivering and walking toward the town's B&B, she hurriedly typed in one last detail she didn't want to forget. Instead of typing the word "cedar," however, she felt a sharp pain in her shoulder as she bounced off something very big and hard.

"Hey," she growled. "Watch where you're going!"

She looked up to find Rhys Bullock staring down at her, a scowl marking his angular face.

"Oh, it's you," she said, letting out a puff of annoyance.

He knelt down and retrieved her phone, stood up and handed it over. "Hope it didn't break," he said. His tone suggested that he wasn't quite sincere in that sentiment.

"The rubber cover is supposed to protect it. It'll be fine."

"Maybe next time you should watch where you're going. Stop and sit down before you start typing."

"It's too damn cold to stop," she grumbled.

He laughed then, the expulsion of breath forming a white cloud around his head. "Not used to an arctic front? This isn't cold. Wait until it's minus forty."

"Not a chance."

"That's right. You're only here for the wedding."

"If you'll excuse me, I'd like to get out of the cold before my fingertips fall off." She tried to ignore how his face changed when he laughed, softening the severe lines. A smattering of tiny marks added character to his tanned skin. If she had to come up with one word to describe Rhys, it would be *weathered*. It wasn't necessarily a bad thing.

He took a step closer and to her surprise reached into her pocket and took out her gloves. Then he took the phone from her hands, dropped it in the pocket and handed over the gloves. "This will help."

She raised an eyebrow. "That was presumptuous of you."

He shrugged. "Ms. Shepard, I'm pretty much used to keeping things simple and doing what has to be done. If your fingers are cold, put on your gloves."

She shoved her fingers into the fuzzy warmth, her temper simmering. He spoke to her as if she were a child!

"Now," he said calmly, "where are you headed? It's dark. I'll walk you."

Her temper disintegrated under the weight of her disbelief. She laughed. "Are you serious? This is Cadence Creek. I think I'll be safe walking two blocks to my accommodations." Good Lord. She lived in one of the largest cities in Canada. She knew how to look out for herself!

"Maybe I just want to make sure you don't start

texting and walk out into traffic," he suggested. "You must be going to Jim's then." He named the bed and breakfast owner.

"That's right."

He turned around so they were facing the same direction. "Let's go," he suggested.

She fell into step because she didn't know what else to do. He seemed rather determined and it would take all of five minutes to walk to the rambling house that provided the town's only accommodation. To her mind the dive motel out on the highway didn't count. She watched as he tipped his hat to an older lady coming out of the drugstore and then gave a nod to a few men standing on the steps of the hardware. He might be gruff and bossy and not all that pretty to look at, but she had to give Rhys one thing—his manners were impeccable.

The light dusting of snow earlier covered the sidewalk and even grouchy Taylor had to admit that it was pretty, especially in the dark with the town's Christmas lights casting colored shadows on its surface. Each old-fashioned lamppost held a pine wreath with a red bow. Storefronts were decorated with garland on their railings and twinkle lights. Christmas trees peeked through front windows and jolly Santas and snowmen grinned from front yards.

Cadence Creek at the holidays was like one of those Christmas card towns that Taylor hadn't believed truly existed. Being here wasn't really so bad. Even if it was a little…boring.

They stopped at a crosswalk. And as they did her stomach gave out a long, loud rumble.

Rhys put his hand at her elbow and they stepped off the curb. But instead of going right on the other side, he guided her to the left.

"Um, the B&B is that way," she said, turning her head and pointing in the opposite direction.

"When did you eat last?" he asked.

She fought the urge to sigh. "None of your business."

Undeterred, he kept walking and kept the pressure at her elbow. "Jim and Kathleen don't provide dinner. You need something to eat."

She stopped dead in her tracks. Rhys carried on for a few steps until he realized she wasn't with him then he stopped and turned around. "What?"

"How old am I?"

His brows wrinkled, forming a crease above his nose. "How could I possibly know that?"

"Do I look like an adult to you?"

Something flared in his eyes as his gaze slid from her face down to her boots and back up again. "Yes'm."

She swallowed. "You can't herd me like you herd your cattle, Mr. Bullock."

"I don't herd cattle," he responded.

"You don't?"

"No ma'am. I work with the horses. Especially the skittish ones."

"Well, then," she floundered and then recovered, ignoring that a snowflake had just fallen and landed on the tip of her nose. "I'm not one of your horses. You can't make me eat just because you say so."

He shrugged. "Can't make the horses do that, either. Trick is to make them *want* to do what I want." He gave her a level stare. "I'm pretty good at that."

"Your ego isn't suffering, I see."

His lips twitched. "No, ma'am. Everyone has a skill. Smart man knows what his is, that's all."

God, she didn't want to be amused. He was

a bullheaded, overbearing macho cowboy type who probably called women "little lady" and thought he was all that. But she was amused and to be honest she'd enjoyed sparring with him just a little bit. At least he wasn't a pampered brat like most people she met.

She let out the tension in her shoulders. "Where are you taking me, then?" She'd seriously considered ordering a pizza and having it delivered to the B&B. It wasn't like there was a plethora of dining choices in Cadence Creek.

"Just to the Wagon Wheel. Best food in town."

"I've been. I had lunch there yesterday." And breakfast in the dining room of the bed and breakfast and then dinner was a fast-food burger grabbed on the way back from the stationery supply store in Edmonton.

The lunch had definitely been the best meal— homemade chicken soup, thick with big chunks of chicken, vegetables and the temptation of a warm roll which she'd left behind, not wanting the extra carbs.

Her stomach growled again, probably from the mere thought of the food at the diner.

"Fine. I'll go get some takeout. Will that make you happy?"

He shrugged. "It's not about me. But now that you mention it, I think tonight is pot roast. I could do with some of that myself." He turned and started walking away.

Reluctantly she followed a step behind him. At least he didn't have that darned proprietary hand under her elbow anymore. Half a block away she could smell the food. The aroma of the standard fare—fries and the like—hit first, but then the undertones touched her nostrils: beef, bread and baking.

Her mouth watered as she reminded herself that she had a bridesmaid's dress to fit into as well. Pot roast would be good. But she would absolutely say no to dessert.

It was warm inside the diner. The blast of heat was a glorious welcome and the scents that were hinted at outside filled the air inside. Christmas music played from an ancient jukebox in the corner. The whole place was decorated for the holidays, but in the evening with everything lit up it looked very different than it had yesterday at noon. Mini-lights ran the length of the lunch counter and the tree in a back corner had flashing lights and a star topper that pulsed like a camera flash. The prevalence of vinyl and chrome made her feel like she was in a time warp.

Two-thirds of the tables were filled with people, all talking animatedly over the music. Rhys gave a wave to a group in a corner and then, to her surprise, slipped behind the cash register and went straight into the kitchen.

Through the order window she saw him grin at an older woman in a huge cobbler's apron who laughed and patted his arm. Both of them turned Taylor's way and she offered a polite smile before turning her attention to the specials menu on a chalkboard. Takeout was definitely the way to go here. This wasn't her town or her people. She stuck out like a sore thumb.

She was just about to order a salad when Rhys returned. "Come on," he said, taking her elbow again. "Let's grab a seat."

"Um, I didn't really think we were going to eat together. I was just going to get something to take back with me."

"You work too hard," he said, holding out a chair for her and then moving around the table without pushing it in—polite without being over the top. "You could use some downtime."

She shifted the chair closer to the table. "Are you kidding? This is slow for me."

He raised his eyebrows. "Then you really do need to stop and refuel."

He shrugged out of his jacket and hooked it over the top of the chair. She did the same, unbuttoning the black-and-red wool coat and shoving her scarf in the sleeve. She wore skinny jeans tucked into her favorite boots—red designer riding boots—and a snug black cashmere sweater from an expensive department store in the city. She looked around. Most of the men wore thirty-dollar jeans and plaid flannel, and the women dressed in a similar fashion—jeans and department store tops.

Just as she thought. Sore thumb.

When she met Rhys's gaze again she found his sharper, harder, as if he could read her thoughts. She dropped her gaze and opened her menu.

"No need for that. Couple orders of pot roast are on their way."

She put down the menu and folded her hands on the top. While the rest of the decorations at the diner bordered on cheesy, she secretly loved the small silk poinsettia pots with Merry Christmas picks. "What amusement are you getting out of this?" she asked. "From what I can gather you don't approve of me but you do enjoy bossing me around."

"Why would you think that?"

"Oh, I don't know. Because so far you've found fault with everything I say or do?"

"Then why did you come with me?"

"You didn't leave me much choice." She pursed her lips.

"You always have a choice," he replied, unrolling his cutlery from his paper napkin.

"Then I guess because I was hungry," she said.

He smiled. "You mean because I was right."

Oh, he was infuriating!

"The trick is to make them want to do what I want." He repeated his earlier sentiment, only she understood he wasn't talking about horses anymore. He'd played her like a violin.

She might have had some choice words only their meals arrived, two plates filled with roast beef, potatoes, carrots, peas and delightfully puffy-looking Yorkshire puddings. Her potatoes swam in a pool of rich gravy and the smell coming from the food was heaven in itself.

She never ate like this anymore. Wondered if she could somehow extract the potatoes from the gravy or maybe just leave the potatoes altogether—that would probably be better.

"Thanks, Mom," she heard Rhys say, and her gaze darted from her plate up to his face and then to the woman standing beside the table— the same woman who had patted his arm in the kitchen. Taylor guessed her to be somewhere around fifty, with dark brown hair like Rhys's, only cut in an efficient bob and sprinkled with a few gray hairs.

"You're welcome," she said, then turned to Taylor with a smile. "You're Callum's sister. I remember you from the christening party."

Right. Taylor had flown in for that and she'd helped arrange a few details like the outdoor tent, but she'd done it all by phone from Vancouver. "Oh, my goodness, I totally didn't put two and two together. Martha Bullock…of course. And you're Rhys's mother." She offered an uncertain smile. Usually she didn't forget details like that.

Then again the idea of the gruff cowboy calling anyone "Mom" seemed out of place.

"Sure am. Raised both him and his brother, Tom. Tom's been working up north for years now, but Rhys moved home a few years back."

"Your chicken tartlets at the party were to die for," Taylor complimented. "And I had the soup yesterday. You're a fabulous cook, Mrs. Bullock. Whoever your boys marry have big shoes to fill to keep up with Mom's home cooking."

Martha laughed while, from the corner of her eye, Taylor could see Rhys scowl. Good. About time he felt a bit on the back foot since he'd been throwing her off all day.

"Heh, good luck," Martha joked. "I'm guessing groomsman is as close to the altar as Rhys is gonna get. He's picky."

She could almost see the steam come out of his ears, but she took pity on him because she'd heard much the same argument from her own family. It got wearisome after a while. Particularly from her father, who'd never taken her business seriously and seemed to think her sole purpose in life was to settle down and have babies.

Not that she had anything against marriage or babies. But she'd do it on her own timetable.

"Well," she said, a bit softer, "it seems to me that getting married is kind of a big deal and a person would have to be awfully sure that they wanted to see that person every day for the rest of their lives. Not a thing to rush, really."

Martha smiled and patted Taylor's hand. "Pretty *and* wise. Don't see that very often, at least around here." She sent a pointed look at a nearby table where Taylor spied an animated blonde seated with a young man who seemed besotted with her.

"Well, your supper's getting cold." Martha straightened. "And I've got to get back. See you in a bit."

Taylor watched Rhys's mother move off, stopping at several tables to say hello. Her full laugh was infectious and Taylor found herself smiling.

When she turned back, Rhys had already started cutting into his beef. Taylor mentally shrugged and speared a bright orange carrot with her fork.

"So," she said easily. "How'd a nice woman like your mother end up with a pigheaded son like you?"

CHAPTER TWO

TENDER AS IT WAS, Rhys nearly choked on the beef in his mouth. Lord, but Callum's sister was full of sass. And used to getting her own way, too, from the looks of it. He'd noticed her way back in the fall at the christening, all put together and pretty and, well, bossy. Not that she'd been aggressive. She just had one of those natural take-charge kind of ways about her. When Taylor was on the job, things got done.

He just bet she was Student Council president in school, too. And on any other committee she could find.

He'd been the quiet guy at the back of the class, wishing he could be anywhere else. Preferably outside. On horseback.

Burl Ives was crooning on the jukebox now and Taylor was blinking at him innocently. He wasn't sure if he wanted to be offended or laugh at her.

"She only donated half the genetic material,"

he replied once he'd swallowed. "Ask her. She'll tell you my father was a stubborn old mule."

Taylor popped a disc of carrot into her mouth. "Was?"

"He died when I was twenty-four. Brain aneurism. No warning at all."

"God, Rhys. I'm sorry."

He shrugged again. "It's okay. We've all moved well beyond the shock and grief part to just missing him." And he did. Even though at times Rhys had been frustrated with his father's decisions, he missed his dad's big laugh and some of the fun things they'd done as kids—like camping and fishing. Those were the only kinds of vacations their family had ever been able to afford.

They ate in silence for a while until it grew uncomfortable. Rhys looked over at her. He wasn't quite sure what had propelled him to bring her here tonight. It had been the gentlemanly thing to do but there was something else about her that intrigued him. He figured it was probably the way she challenged him, how she'd challenged them all today. He'd nearly laughed out loud during the fitting. He could read people pretty well and she had pushed all the right buttons with Callum. And then there was the way she was used to being obeyed. She gave an order and it was followed. It was fun putting her off balance by taking charge.

And then there was the indisputable fact that she was beautiful.

Except he really wasn't interested in her that way. She was so not his type. He was beer and she was champagne. He was roots and she was wings.

Still. A guy might like to fly every once in a while.

"So," he invited. "Tell me more about what you do."

"Oh. Well, I plan private parties and events. Not generally weddings. Right now, in addition to Callum and Avery's details, I'm going back and forth with my assistant about a New Year's party we're putting together. The hardest part is making sure the construction of the giant aquariums is completed and that the environment is right for the fish."

"Fish?"

She laughed, the expression lighting up her face. "Okay, so get this. They want this under the sea theme so we're building two aquariums and we've arranged to borrow the fish for the night. It's not just the aquariums, it's the marine biologist I have coming to adjust conditions and then monitor the water quality in the tank and ensure the health of the fish. Then there are lights that are supposed to make it look like you're underwater, and sushi and cocktails served by mermaids and mermen in next to no clothing."

"Are you joking?"

She shook her head. "Would I joke about a thing like that? It's been a nightmare to organize." She cut into her slab of beef and swirled it around the pool of gravy. "This is so good. I'm going to have to do sit-ups for hours in my room to work this off."

He rolled his eyes. Right. To his mind, she could gain a few pounds and no one would even notice. If anything, she was a little on the thin side. A few pounds would take those hinted-at curves and make them…

He cleared his throat.

"What about you, Rhys? You said you work with horses?" Distracted by the chatting now, she seemed unaware that she was scooping up

the mashed potatoes and gravy she'd been dili-
gently avoiding for most of the meal.

"I work for Ty out at Diamondback."

"What sort of work?"

"Whatever has to be done, but I work with
training the horses mostly. Ty employs a couple
of disadvantaged people to help around the place
so I get to focus on what I do best."

"What sort of disadvantaged people?" She
leaned forward and appeared genuinely interested.

Rhys finished the last bite of Yorkshire pudding and nudged his plate away. "Well, Marty
has Down's syndrome. Getting steady work has
been an issue, but he's very good with the animals and he's a hard worker. Josh is a different
story. He's had trouble finding work due to his
criminal record. Ty's helping him get on his feet
again. Josh helps Sam's end of things from time
to time. Those cattle you mentioned herding earlier."

Taylor frowned and pushed her plate away.
She'd made a solid dent in the meal and his
mother hadn't been stingy with portions.

"So what are your plans, then?"

"What do you mean?"

She wiped her mouth with a paper napkin. "I mean, do you have any plans to start up your own place or business?"

"Not really. I'm happy at Diamondback. Ty's a good boss."

She leaned forward. "You're a take-charge kind of guy. I can't see you taking orders from anyone. Don't you want to be the one calling the shots?"

Calling the shots wasn't all it was cracked up to be. Rhys had seen enough of that his whole life. Along with being the boss came a truckload of responsibility, including the chance of success and the probability of failure. His own venture had cost him financially but it had been far worse on a deeper, personal level. Considering he now had his mom to worry about, he was content to leave the risk to someone else from here on in. "I have a job doing something I like and I get a steady paycheck every two weeks. What more could I want?"

She sat back, apparently disappointed with his answer. Too bad. Living up to her expectations wasn't on his agenda and he sure wasn't about to explain.

Martha returned bearing two plates of apple pie. "How was it?" she asked, looking at Taylor expectantly.

"Delicious," she had the grace to answer with a smile. "I was trying to be good and avoid the potatoes and I just couldn't. Thank you, Martha."

"Well, you haven't had my pie yet. It's my specialty."

"Oh, I couldn't possibly."

"If it's your waistline worrying you, don't. Life's too short." She flashed a grin. "Besides, you'll wear that off running all over town. I heard you're kicking butt and taking names planning this wedding. Everyone's talking about it."

Apparently Taylor found that highly complimentary and not at all offensive. "Well, maybe just this once."

Martha put down the plates. "Rhys? The faucet in my kitchen sink at home has been dripping. I wondered if you could have a look at it? Consider dinner your payment in advance."

He nodded, knowing that last part was for Taylor's benefit more than his. He never paid for meals at the diner and instead looked after the odd jobs here and at his mother's home.

It was why he'd come back to Cadence Creek, after all.He couldn't leave his mother here to deal with everything on her own. She'd already been doing that for too many years. It had always been hand to mouth until this place. She still worked too hard but Rhys knew she loved every single minute.

"I'll be around tomorrow before work to have a look," he promised. "Then I can pick up what I need from the hardware and fix it tomorrow night."

"That sounds great. Nice to see you again, Taylor. Can't wait to see your handiwork at this wedding."

Rhys watched Taylor smile. She looked tired but the smile was genuine and a pleasant surprise. She had big-city girl written all over her but it didn't mean she was devoid of warmth. Not at all.

When Martha was gone he picked up his fork. "Try the pie. She'll be offended if you don't."

Taylor took a bite and closed her eyes. "Oh, my. That's fantastic."

"She makes her own spice blend and doesn't tell anyone what it is. People have been after her recipes for years," he said, trying hard not to focus on the shape of her lips as her tongue licked a bit of caramelly filling from the corner of her mouth. "There's a reason why the bakery focuses on cakes and breads. There's not a pie in Cadence Creek that can hold a candle to my mom's."

"You seem close," Taylor noted.

She had no idea. Rhys focused on his pie as he considered exactly how much to say. Yes, he'd come back to Cadence Creek to be nearer his mom after his dad's death. She'd needed the help sorting out their affairs and needed a shoulder. He'd been happy to do it.

But it was more than that. They were business partners. Not that many people were aware of it and that was how he wanted it to stay. Memories were long and his father hadn't exactly earned a stellar business reputation around town. Despite his best intentions, Rhys had followed in his footsteps. Being a silent partner in the restaurant suited him just fine.

"We are close," he admitted. "Other than my brother, I'm the only family she's got and the only family here in Cadence Creek. How about you? Are you close with your family?"

She nodded, allowing him to neatly change the subject. "I suppose so. We don't live so close together, like you do, but it's close enough and we get along. I know they were very worried about Callum when he came back from overseas. And they thought he was crazy for buying a dairy farm." She laughed a little. "But they can see he's happy and that's all that matters."

"And Jack?"

She laughed. "Jack is in Montana most of the time, busy overseeing his empire. We don't see each other much. Our jobs keep us very busy. Running our own businesses is pretty time-consuming."

"I can imagine." Rhys had met and liked Jack instantly, but like Taylor, he looked a bit exhausted. Running a big sporting goods chain was likely to have that effect.

Which was why Rhys was very contented to work for Diamondback and spend some of his spare hours playing handyman for the diner and his mother's house. It was straightforward. There was little chance of disappointing people.

Angry words and accusations still bounced around in his brain from time to time. Failing had been bad enough. But he'd let down the person he'd trusted most. And she'd made sure he knew it.

The fluted crust of Taylor's pie was all that remained and she'd put down her fork.

"Well, I suppose we should get going."

"I'm going to have to roll back to the B&B," she said ruefully, putting a hand on her tummy.

"Not likely," he said, standing up, but their gazes met and he was certain her cheeks were a little redder than they'd been before.

He took her coat from the back of the chair, pulled the scarf from the sleeve and held it so she could slide her arms into it. They were quiet now, he unsure of what to say and his show of manners making things slightly awkward. Like this was a date or something. He stood back and grabbed his jacket and shoved his arms in the sleeves. Not a date. It was just sharing a meal with…

With a woman.

Hmm.

"I'm putting my gloves on this time," she stated with a cheeky smile.

"Good. Wouldn't want your fingertips to fall off."

They gave a wave to Martha before stepping outside into the crisp air.

It had warmed a bit, but that only meant that the precipitation that had held off now floated lazily to the earth. Big white flakes drifted on the air, hitting the ground with a soft shush of sound that was so peculiar to falling snow. It draped over hedges and windows, painting the town in fairy-white.

"This is beautiful," Taylor whispered. "Snow in Vancouver is cause for chaos. Here, it's peaceful."

"Just because the wind isn't blowing and causing whiteouts," Rhys offered, but he was enchanted too. Not by the snow, but by her. The clever and efficient Taylor had tilted her head toward the sky and stuck out her tongue, catching a wide flake on its tip.

"I know it's just water, but I swear snow tastes sweet for some reason," she said, closing her eyes. Another flake landed on her eyelashes and she blinked, laughing as she wiped it away. "Oops."

Rhys swallowed as a wave of desire rolled through him. Heavens above, she was pretty. Smart and funny, and while an absolute Sergeant

Major on the job, a lot more relaxed when off the clock. He had the urge to reach out and take her hand as they walked through the snow. Odd that he'd have such an innocent, pure thought when the other side of his brain wondered if her mouth would taste like apples and snowflakes.

He kept his hand in his pocket and they resumed strolling.

It only took a few minutes to reach the bed and breakfast. Rhys paused outside the white picket gate. "Well, here we are."

"Yes, here we are. What about you? You walked me back but now do you have to walk home in the snow? Or are you parked nearby?" She lifted her chin and Rhys smiled at the way the snow covered her hair with white tufts. She looked like a young girl, bundled up in her scarf and coat with snow on her head and shoulders. Definitely not like a cutthroat businesswoman who never had to take no for an answer.

"I live a few blocks over, so don't worry about me."

"Do you—" she paused, then innocently widened her eyes "—live with your mother?"

He laughed. "God, no. I'm thirty years old. I

have my own place. I most definitely do not live with my mother."

Her cold, pink cheeks flushed even deeper. "Oh. Well, thanks for dinner. I guess I'll see you when we pick up the tuxes, right?"

"I guess so. See you around, Taylor."

"Night."

She went in the gate and disappeared up the walk, her ruby-red boots marking the way on the patio stones.

He had no business thinking about his friend's sister that way. Even less business considering how different they were. Different philosophies, hundreds of kilometers between them... He shouldn't have taken her elbow in his hand and guided her along.

But the truth was the very thing that made her wrong for him was exactly what intrigued him. She wasn't like the other girls he knew. She was complicated and exciting, and that was something that had been missing from his life for quite a while.

As the snowfall picked up, he huddled into the collar of his jacket and turned away. Taylor Shepard was not for him. And since he wasn't the type to mess around on a whim that meant keeping his hands off—for the next two weeks or so.

He could do that. Right?

Taylor had left the planning for the bridal shower to Clara Diamond, Ty's wife and one of Avery's bridesmaids. Tonight Taylor was attending only as a guest. In addition to the bridal party, Molly Diamond's living room was occupied by Melissa Stone, her employee Amy, and Jean, the owner of the Cadence Creek Bakery and Avery's partner in business.

In deference to Clara's pregnancy and the fact that everyone was driving, the evening's beverages included a simple punch and hot drinks—tea, coffee, or hot cocoa. Never one to turn down chocolate, Taylor helped herself to a steaming mug and took a glorious sip. Clara had added a dollop of real whipped cream to the top, making it extra indulgent. Taylor made a mental note to start running again when she returned home.

"I hope everything's okay for tonight," Clara said beside her. "It's a bit nerve-racking, you know. I can't put on an event like you, Taylor."

Taylor had been feeling rather comfortable but

Clara's innocent observation made her feel the outsider again. "Don't be silly. It's lovely and simple which is just as it should be. An event should always suit the guests, and this is perfect."

"Really?"

Indeed. A fire crackled in the fireplace and the high wood beams in the log-style home made it feel more like a winter lodge than a regular home. The last bridal shower she'd attended had been in a private room at a club and they'd had their own bartender mixing custom martinis. She actually enjoyed this setting more. But it wasn't what people expected from her, was it? Did she really come across as…well…stuck up?

Taylor patted her arm. "Your Christmas decorations are lovely, so why would you need a single thing? Don't worry so much. This cocoa is delicious and I plan on eating my weight in appetizers and sweets."

She didn't, but she knew it would put Clara at ease. She liked Clara a lot. In fact she liked all of Callum's friends. They were utterly devoid of artifice.

Clara's sister-in-law Angela was taking puff pastries out of the oven and their mother-in-law Molly was putting out plates of squares and Christmas cookies. Jean had brought chocolate doughnut holes and Melissa was taking the cling wrap off a nacho dip. The one woman who didn't quite fit in was Amy, who Taylor recognized as the young woman from the diner the night she'd had dinner with Rhys. The implication had been made that Amy wasn't pretty *and* smart. But she looked friendly enough, though perhaps a little younger than the rest of the ladies.

She approached her casually and smiled. "Hi, I'm Taylor. You work for Melissa, right? I've seen you behind the counter at the shop."

Amy gave her a grateful smile. "Yes, that's right. And you're Callum's sister." She looked down at Taylor's shoes. "Those are Jimmy Choos, aren't they?"

Taylor laughed at the unconcealed longing in Amy's voice. "Ah, a kindred spirit. They are indeed."

"I'd die for a pair of those. Not that there's anywhere to buy them here. Or that I could afford them."

Her response was a bit guileless perhaps but she hadn't meant any malice, Taylor was sure of that.

"I got them for a steal last time I was in Seattle," she replied. She leaned forward. "I'm dying to know. Why is it that everyone else is over there and you're over here staring at the Christmas tree? I mean, it's a nice tree, but…" She let the thought hang.

Amy blushed. "Oh. Well. I'm sure it was a polite thing to include me in the invitation. I'm not particularly close with the Diamond women. I kind of, uh…"

She took a sip of punch, which hid her face a little. "I dated Sam for a while and when he broke it off I wasn't as discreet as I might have been about it. I have a tendency to fly off the handle and think later."

Taylor laughed. "You sound like my brother Jack. Callum was always the thinker in the family. Jack's far more of a free spirit."

"It was a long time ago," Amy admitted. "It's hard to change minds in a town this size, though."

"You haven't thought of moving?"

"All the time!" Amy's blond curls bounced. "But my family is here. I didn't go to college. Oh, I must sound pathetic," she bemoaned, shaking her head.

"Not at all. You sound like someone who simply hasn't found the right thing yet. Someday you will. The perfect thing to make you want to get up in the morning. Or the perfect person." She winked at Amy.

"I'm afraid I've pretty much exhausted the local resources on that score," Amy lamented. "Which doesn't exactly make me popular among the women, either."

"You just need an image makeover," Taylor suggested. "Do you like what you're doing now?"

She shrugged. "Working for Melissa has been the best job I've ever had. But it's not exactly a challenge."

Wow. Amy did sound a lot like Jack.

"We should meet up for coffee before I go back to Vancouver," Taylor suggested. Despite the fact that Amy was included but not quite included, Taylor liked her. She just seemed young and without direction. Heck, Taylor had been there. What Amy needed was something to feel passionate about.

"I'd like that. Just stop into the shop. I'm there most days. It's busy leading up to the holidays."

The last of the guests arrived and things got

underway. Taylor was glad the shower stayed on the sweeter rather than raunchier side. There was no paté in the shape of the male anatomy, no gag gifts or handcuffs or anything of the sort. They played a "Celebrity Husband" game where each guest put a name of a celebrity they had a crush on into a bowl and then they had to guess which star belonged to whom. The resulting laughter from names ranging from Kevin Costner who got Molly's vote to Channing Tatum—Amy's pick—broke the ice beautifully.

The laughter really picked up during Bridal Pictionary, which pitted Taylor against Angela as they attempted to draw "wedding night" without getting graphic. After they took a break to stuff themselves with snacks, they all returned to the living room for gifts.

Taylor sat back into the soft sofa cushions and examined the woman who was about to become her sister-in-law. Avery was so lovely—kind and gentle but with a backbone of steel. She was a fantastic mother to her niece, Nell, who was Callum's biological daughter. Taylor couldn't have handpicked a nicer woman to marry her brother. It gave her a warm feeling, but also an ache in her heart, too. That ache unsettled her a bit, until she reminded herself that she was simply very happy that Callum had found someone after all his troubles. A love like that didn't come along every day.

Her thoughts strayed to Rhys for a moment. The man was a contradiction for sure. On one hand he was full of confidence and really quite bossy. And yet he was satisfied with taking orders from someone else and moving back to this small town with very few options. It didn't make sense.

It also didn't make sense that for a brief moment earlier in the week, she'd had the craziest urge to kiss him. The snow had been falling on his dark cap of hair and dusting the shoulders of his jacket. And he'd been watchful of her, too. There'd been something there, a spark, a tension of some sort. Until he'd turned to go and she'd gone up the walk and into the house.

She hadn't seen him since. Not at the diner, not around town.

Avery opened a red box and a collective gasp went up from the group. "Oh, Molly. Oh, gosh." Avery reached into the tissue paper and withdrew a gorgeous white satin-and-lace nightgown. "It's stunning."

"Every woman should have something beautiful for their wedding night," Molly said. "I saw it and couldn't resist."

Taylor watched as Avery stood and held the long gown up to herself. The bodice was cut in a daring "V" and consisted of sheer lace while the satin skirt fell straight to the floor, a deep slit cut to the hip. It blended innocence with sexy brilliantly.

She took another sip of cocoa and let her mind carry her away for a few blissful seconds. What would it be like to wear that nightgown? She would feel the lace cups on her breasts, the slide of the satin on her thighs. She'd wear slippers with it, the kind of ridiculous frippery that consisted of heels and a puff of feathers at the toe. And Rhys's dark eyes would light up as she came into the room, their depths filled with fire and hunger...

"*Helloooo,* earth to Taylor!"

She blinked and focused on the circle of women who were now staring at her. "Oh. Sorry."

"I was just going to say thank you for the bath

basket, but you were in another world." Avery was smiling at her.

"You're welcome! Goodness, sorry about that. Occupational hazard. Sometimes it's hard to shut the old brain off." She hoped her flippant words were believable. What would they say if they knew she'd been daydreaming about the only groomsman who wasn't married or a relative?

"Right," Amy said with a wide grin. "I know that look. You were thinking about a dude."

Damn her for being astute. Who had said she wasn't smart, anyway?

Melissa burst out laughing. "Were you? Come on, do tell. Do you have some guy hiding away in Vancouver?"

"No!" The word was out before she realized it would have been the most convenient way out of the situation.

Avery came to her rescue, though. "We're just teasing. Seriously, thank you. It's a lovely gift."

She reached for the last present on the pile and removed the card. "Oh," she said with delight. "It's from Martha. I wonder if she's going to part with her coconut cream pie recipe." Everyone laughed. Martha Bullock never shared her pie recipes with anyone. Even Rhys had mentioned that at dinner the other night.

Avery ripped the paper off the box and withdrew a plain black binder. Opening the cover, she gasped. "It *is* recipes! Look!" She read off the table of contents. "Supper Dishes, Breads and Muffins, Cookies, Cakes, Salads, Preserves." She lifted her head and laughed. "No pies."

Excited, she began flipping through the pages when Amy interrupted again. "That's it!" she called out, causing Avery's fingers to pause and the rest of the group to stare at her in surprise.

"That's where I saw you last," Amy continued, undaunted. "It was at the diner. You had dinner with Rhys!"

Six more sets of eyes swiveled Taylor's way until she felt like a bug under a microscope.

"It wasn't a date. We both ended up needing to eat at the same time. We just met outside on the sidewalk and, uh, sat together."

"It sure didn't look that way," Amy answered, a little too gleeful for Taylor's liking. "Now that is news. Rhys hasn't shown up anywhere with a date since…"

She suddenly blushed and turned her gaze to

something over Jean's shoulder. "Well, it doesn't matter how long since."

It was uncomfortably quiet for a few moments until a small giggle broke the silence. Clara was trying not to laugh and failing miserably. Angela and Molly joined in, followed by Jean and Melissa. Even Avery's mouth was twitching. Taylor frowned a little, wondering what the joke could be.

Amy had the grace to look chagrined. "Okay, I know. My track record sucks."

Angela spoke up. "Honey, Rhys Bullock is one tough nut to crack. Someday the right guy's gonna come along."

Amy's eyes glistened. "Just my luck I won't recognize him when I see him."

Everyone laughed again.

Then Avery spoke up. "That's what I thought, too, Amy. Don't give up hope. You just never know." She looked at Taylor. "And I know for a fact that Rhys is smart and stubborn. Sounds like someone else I know. Keep us posted, Taylor."

"Yeah," Clara added, her hand on her rounded stomach. "The old married women need some excitement now and again."

"I swear I bumped into him outside. Literally. Ran smack into him and nearly broke my phone." She brought her hands together in demonstration of the collision. "It was dark, it was dinnertime and we had pot roast. End of story."

But as the subject changed and they cleaned up the paper and ribbons, Taylor's thoughts kept drifting back to that night and how she'd almost reached out to take his hand as he walked her home.

It was such a simple and innocent gesture to think about, especially in these days of casual hookups. Not that hooking up was her style, either. That philosophy combined with her long hours meant she hadn't had time for personal relationships for ages. Not since the early days of her business, when she'd been seeing an investment planner named John. He'd wanted more than a girlfriend who brought work home at the end of a twelve-hour day and considered takeout a sensible dinner. After a few months in, he'd walked. The thing Taylor felt most guilty about was how it had been a relief.

She balled up used napkins and put them in the trash. Time kept ticking. A few days from now was the rehearsal, and then the wedding and then Callum and Avery would be away on their honeymoon and Taylor would move out of the B&B and into their house until Boxing Day, where she planned on watching movies, reading books and basically hibernating from the outside world. It was going to be peace and quiet and then a family Christmas.

Complications in the form of Rhys Bullock would only ruin her plans.

CHAPTER THREE

IT WAS TAYLOR'S experience that if the rehearsal went badly, the wedding was sure to be smooth and problem free. A sentiment which boded well for Callum and Avery, as it turned out, because nothing seemed to be going her way.

First of all, everything was an hour late starting thanks to a winter storm, which dumped enough snow to complicate transportation. The minister had slid off the road and into a snowbank. The car wasn't damaged but by the time the tow truck had pulled him out, the wedding party was waiting and quite worried by his absence. Then Taylor opened the box that was supposed to contain the tulle bows for the ends of the church pews to find that they'd been constructed of a horrible peachy-yellow color—completely unsuited for a Christmas wedding!

The late start and the road conditions also meant canceling the rehearsal dinner that had been organized at an Italian place in the city. Taylor was just about ready to pull her hair out when she felt a wide hand rest on her shoulder.

"Breathe," Rhys commanded. "It's all fine."

She clenched her teeth but exhaled through her nose. "Normally I would just deal with stuff like this without batting an eyelid. I don't know why it's throwing me so much."

"Maybe because it's for your brother," he suggested.

He might be right. She did want everything just right for Callum's wedding. It wasn't some corporate dinner or celebrity party. It was personal. It was once in a lifetime.

God, there was a reason why she didn't do weddings.

"What can I do to help?"

She shrugged. "Do you have a roll of white tulle in your pocket? Perhaps a spare horseshoe I could rub for good luck or something?"

He grimaced. "Afraid not. And you rub a rabbit's foot, not a horseshoe. I'm guessing our plans for dinner have changed."

She looked up at him. He was "dressed up" for the rehearsal—neat jeans, even with a crease down the front, and a pressed button-down shirt tucked into the waistband. His boots made him look taller than ever, especially as she'd decided on her low-heeled boots tonight in deference to the weather. There was a strength and stability in him that made her take a deep breath and regroup. For some reason she didn't want to appear incapable in front of him. "I've had to cancel our reservations."

"I'll call my mom. It won't be as fancy as what you planned, but I'm guessing she can manage a meal for a dozen of us."

"We can't have a rehearsal dinner at a diner."

His lips puckered up like he'd tasted something sour. "Do you have any better suggestions? I guess you could pick up some day-old sandwiches at the gas station and a bag of cookies. You don't exactly have a lot of options."

"It was supposed to be romantic and relaxing and…" She floundered a little. "You know. Elegant."

He frowned at her and she regretted what she'd implied. "What would you do if you were in Vancouver right now?" he asked.

"This kind of weather wouldn't happen in Vancouver."

He made a disgusted sound. "You're supposed to be so good at your job. You're telling me nothing ever goes off the plan?"

"Well, sure it does, but I…"

"But you what?"

"I handle it."

"How is this different?"

"Because it's family."

The moment she said it her throat tightened. This wasn't just another job. This was her big brother's wedding. This was also the chance where she would prove herself to her family. She could talk until she was blue in the face, but the truth of the matter was she still sought their approval. The Shepards were driven and successful. It was just expected. She knew she'd disappointed her dad in particular. He thought what she did was unimportant, and the last thing she wanted to do was fall on her professional face in front of him.

"This isn't Vancouver, or Toronto, or New York or L.A." Rhys spoke firmly. "This isn't a big-city event with a bunch of rich snobs. It's just

Cadence Creek. Maybe it's not good enough for you but it's good enough for Callum and Avery and maybe you should consider that instead of only thinking about yourself."

His words hurt. Partly because he was judging her without even knowing her and partly because he was right, at least about things being simpler here. How many times had Avery said they didn't need anything fancy? Taylor had insisted because it was no trouble. Had she messed up and forgotten the singular most important rule: *Give the client what they ask for?*

"Call your mother, then, and see if there's any way she can squeeze us in."

"Give me five minutes."

The words weren't said kindly, and Taylor felt the sting of his reproof. Still, she didn't have time to worry about Rhys Bullock—there was too much left to do. While the minister spoke to Avery and Callum, Taylor fished poinsettia plants out of a waiting box and lined them up on the altar steps in alternating red and creamy white. The congregation had already decorated the tree and the Christmas banners were hung behind the pulpit. The manger from the Sunday School play had been tucked away into the choir loft, which would be unused during the wedding, and instead she set up a table with a snowy-white cloth and a gorgeous spray of red roses, white freesias and greenery. It was there that the bride and groom would sign the register.

The altar looked fine, but the pews and windowsills were naked. In addition to the wrong color tulle, the company had forgotten to ship the candle arrangements for the windows. This would be the last time she ever used them for any of her events!

Her father, Harry, approached, a frown creasing his brow. "What are the plans for after the rehearsal?"

Taylor forced a smile. She would not get into it with her father tonight. "I'm working on that, don't worry."

"You should have insisted on having the wedding in the city, at a nice hotel. Then the weather wouldn't be an issue. Everything at your fingertips."

She'd had the thought a time or two herself; not that she'd admit it to her father. "This will be fine."

He looked around. "It would have been so much easier. Not that the town isn't nice, of course it is. But you're the planner, Taylor." His tone suggested she wasn't doing a very good job of it.

"It wasn't what Callum and Avery wanted," she reminded him. "And it's their day."

He smiled unexpectedly, a warm turning up of his lips that Taylor recognized as his "sales pitch" smile. "Oh, come now. A smart businessman knows how to convince a client to come around."

Business*man*. Taylor wondered if counting to ten would help. She met her father's gaze. "Callum isn't a client, he's my brother. And he's giving you the daughter-in-law and grandkid you've wanted, so ease up."

Anything else they would have said was cut short as Rhys came back, tucking his cell phone in his pocket as he walked. "Good news. Business is slow because of the weather. Mom's clearing out that back corner and she's got a full tray of lasagna set aside."

It certainly wasn't the Caprese salad, veal Parmesan and tiramisu that Taylor had planned on, but it was convenient. She offered a polite smile.

"Thank you, Rhys." At least one thing had been fixed.

"It's no trouble."

With a brief nod, Harry left the two of them alone.

"Everything okay?" Rhys asked.

She pressed a hand to her forehead. "Yeah, it's fine. Dad was just offering an unsolicited opinion, that's all."

He chuckled. "Parents are like that."

"You've no idea," she answered darkly. "I still wish I knew what to do about the pew markers. There's no time to run to Edmonton for materials to make them, even if it weren't storming. And the candles never arrived, either."

"It doesn't have to be perfect. No one will know."

His words echoed from before, the ones that said she was too good for this town. She dismissed them, because she still had a certain standard. "I'll know."

Clara heard the last bit and tapped Taylor on the shoulder. "Why don't you call Melissa and see if she can do something for the pews with satin ribbon?"

"At this late hour?"

Clara nodded. "Worst she can say is no. I have a feeling she'll try something, though. She's a whiz at that stuff. And I might be able to help you out with the windowsills."

Taylor's eyebrows pulled together. "What do you mean?"

Clara laughed. "Just trust me."

"I'm not in the habit of trusting details to other people, Clara. It's nothing personal—it's just how I work."

"Consider it a helping hand from a friend. You're going to be here before anyone else tomorrow anyway. If you don't like what I've done, you can take it out, no hard feelings." She smiled at Taylor. "I'd like to do this. For Avery. She's like family, you know?"

Rhys's hand touched Taylor's back. It was warm and felt good but Taylor got the feeling it was also a little bit of a warning. "I'm sure Taylor's very grateful for your help, Clara."

Dammit. Now he was putting words in her mouth. Perhaps it could be argued that this was "just family" but to Taylor's mind, if she couldn't manage to get the details of one small country wedding right, what did that say about her business?

Then again, in Vancouver she had staff. She could delegate. Which was pretty much what Clara was suggesting. She was just asking her to trust, sight unseen. And then there was the word "friend." She was a stranger here, a fish out of water for the most part and yet everyone seemed to accept her into their group without question. She wasn't used to that.

"Thank you, Clara," she said, but when Clara had gone she turned on Rhys. "Don't ever answer for me again."

"You were being rude."

Now he was judging her manners?

"Look, maybe Callum and Avery are family but I still hold to a certain standard. This is my job. And it's all carefully planned down to the last detail."

She'd had things go wrong before and it wasn't pretty. She'd been determined never to fail like that again. It was why she dealt with trusted vendors and had a competent staff. She'd pulled off events ten times as complicated as this without a hitch.

Knowing it was like sprinkling salt in the wound.

He put a finger under her chin and lifted it. Considering how abrupt he'd been earlier, the tender touch surprised her. "You don't have to control everything. It'll be fine, I promise. It's okay to accept help once in a while."

"I'm not used to that."

"I know," he said gently. "You're stubborn, strong, bossy and completely competent. But things happen. Call Melissa, trust Clara, pretend to walk down the aisle for the rehearsal and then go stuff yourself with lasagna. I promise you'll feel better."

She didn't like being handled. Even if, at this moment, she suspected she needed it. It was so different being here. More relaxed, laid-back. She was used to grabbing her non-fat latte on her way to the office, not sipping from china cups in a B&B dining room while eating crois-sants. Maneuvering her SUV with the fold-down seats through city traffic rather than walking the two blocks to wherever. Definitely not used to men looking into her eyes and seeing past all her barriers.

Cadence Creek was a completely different pace with completely different expectations.

"Rhys? Taylor? We're ready for the walk-through," Avery called down the aisle, a happy smile on her face. Despite the wrinkles in the plans, Taylor's soon-to-be sister-in-law was beaming.

Well, if the bride wasn't worried, she wouldn't be, either. She looked up at Rhys. "I'll call Melissa when we're done. But if this goes wrong…"

"I expect I'll hear about it."

The other members of the wedding party joined them at the end of the aisle—first Clara and Ty, then Sam and Angela, Jack and Avery's friend Denise, who'd flown in from Ontario just this morning and thankfully ahead of the storm. Rhys held out his arm. "Shall we?" he asked, waiting for her to take his elbow.

She folded her hand around his arm, her fingers resting just below his elbow as they took slow steps up the aisle. It was just a silly rehearsal, so she shouldn't have a tangle of nerves going on just from a simple touch.

At the front of the church they parted ways and while Taylor slyly glanced in his direction several times, he never looked at her. Not once. He focused unerringly on what the minister was saying, and she found herself studying his strong jawline and the crisp hairline that looked as if his hair had been freshly cut.

The minister spoke to her and she jerked her attention back to the matter at hand, but she couldn't stop thinking about Rhys. It wasn't often that Taylor was intimidated by anyone, but she was by Rhys. She figured it had to be because he found her distinctly lacking in…well, in something.

What she couldn't understand was why on earth his opinion should even matter.

The Wagon Wheel was lit up, the windows glowing through the cold and very white night. Hard flakes of snow still swirled through the air, biting against Rhys's cheeks as he parked his truck in front of a growing drift.

They'd all bundled up and left the church a few minutes ago, the procession of vehicles crawling through town to the diner. There was no way they would have made it to the city for dinner. Even with the roads open, visibility was bad enough that there was a tow ban on. The smart thing was to stay put.

Taylor "Bossy-Pants" Shepard hadn't been too happy about that, though. He'd taken one look at her face and seen the stress that came from dealing with things gone wrong. It was a prime example of why he liked his life simple. If things went wrong out at Diamondback, he might get called to work but the worry belonged to Ty and Sam. Besides, his mother kept him plenty busy with things at the diner when she needed help. There were days he wished she didn't own the place. That she'd stayed on as a cook rather than buying it from the last owner. There was too much at stake, too much to lose.

Frigid air buffeted him as he hopped out of the truck and headed for the door, his head bowed down as far into his collar as possible. This storm had been a good one. Hopefully it would blow itself out by morning and nothing would get in the way of the wedding. For one, he only wanted to get dressed up in that tuxedo once. And for another, Callum and Avery deserved an incident-free day.

It was warm inside, and smelled deliciously

like tomatoes and garlic and warm bread. Rhys stamped off his feet and unzipped his jacket, tucking his gloves into the pockets as he walked toward the back corner. His mom had been right. Other than a couple of truckers waiting out the bad roads, the place was empty.

He stopped and looked at the miracle she had produced in a scant hour.

The Christmas tree was lit, sending tiny pin-points of colored light through the room. The heavy tables were pushed together to make one long banquet style set up for twelve, and they were covered with real linens in holiday red. The napkins were only paper but they were dark green and white, in keeping with Christmas colors. Thick candles sat in rings of greenery and berries—where had she come up with those?—and the candles lent an even more intimate air to the setting. But the final touch was the ice buckets on both ends, and the sparkling wineglasses at each place setting.

"What do you think?" His mother's voice sounded behind his shoulder.

"You're something, Ma," he said, shaking his head.

She frowned a little. "Do you think it'll be okay for Taylor? I know she must have had something fancier planned for the rehearsal dinner."

"You've worked a miracle on short notice. And if Taylor Shepard doesn't like it, she can..." He frowned. "Well, she can..."

"She can what, Rhys?"

Dammit. Her sweet voice interrupted him. He felt heat rush to his cheeks but when he turned around she was looking at Martha and smiling.

"Martha, how did you possibly do all this in such a short time?"

"It was slow in here and I had some help." She grinned. "Jean from the bakery sent over a cake—they were closing early anyway and she was happy to help with dessert. It's chocolate fudge."

"And wine?" Rhys watched as Taylor's eyes shone. Maybe he'd misjudged her. Maybe she'd just been stressed, because the snooty perfectionist he expected to see wasn't in attendance just now.

Or, perhaps she understood she was in a sticky place and was making the best of it. He suspected that faking it was in her repertoire of talents. His jaw tightened. When had he become so cynical? He supposed it was about the time Sherry had promised him to stick by his side—until things got dicey. Then she'd bailed—taking her two kids with her. Kids he'd grown very fond of.

You got to see someone's true colors when they were under pressure. It wasn't always pretty. Sherry hadn't even given him a chance to make things right.

He realized his mom was still speaking. "I'm not licensed, so I'm afraid it's not real wine. But the bed and breakfast sent over a couple of bottles of sparkling cider they had on hand and I put it on ice. I thought at least you could have a toast."

To Rhys's surprise, Taylor enveloped Martha in a quick hug. "I underestimated you," she said warmly. "This is perfect."

Martha shrugged but Rhys could tell she was pleased. "Heck," she replied with a flap of her hand. "That's what neighbors are for."

The rest of the wedding party arrived, complete with laughter and the sound of stomping boots. The next thing Rhys knew, he was seated at the table next to Avery's maid of honor, Denise, and things were well underway. Drinks were poured and he found himself chatting to Harry, who was on his other side. The senior Shepard was a very successful businessman, sharp as a tack and charismatic. Rhys could see a lot of his acumen and energy in Jack, the younger son, and the strength and reliability in Callum, the eldest. Rhys noticed that while Harry spoke proudly about Callum's military career and Jack's business, he didn't say much about Taylor's successes.

What about Taylor, then? She had the dark looks of the Shepard men rather than the more fair coloring of her mother, who sat across the table. But her lips were soft and full, like Mrs. Shepard's, and the dusting of freckles came from there, too. When he met Mrs. Shepard's gaze, he saw a wisdom there that he'd glimpsed in Taylor, too. Wisdom and acceptance. He guessed that it must have been hard to be a girl growing up in a household of such strong males. Had she felt pressure to keep up? Or were the expectations lower because she was female? He'd only known her a short time but he understood that she would hate to be treated as anything less than equal to her brothers. And then there was the tension he'd sensed between them at the rehearsal.

To his surprise, Taylor didn't sit at all but donned an apron and helped Martha serve the meal. When she put his plate before him, he looked up and met her eyes. "Thank you, Taylor."

"You're welcome."

She turned to move away but he reached out and caught her wrist. "What you said to my mother, that was very nice."

Her eyes met his. "I meant it. I apologize for my mood earlier. I was stressed."

"And here I thought it was because you didn't like to be told what to do."

Her eyes flashed at him for a second before mellowing, and then her lips twitched. "I do believe you're baiting me. Now stop so I can finish serving the meal."

He watched as she helped put the plates around, smiling and laughing. He'd thought her too proud for serving but she wasn't. She'd do what it took to pull off an event. There was lots of talking and laughing and toasting around the table, but Rhys frowned. Wasn't she going to sit and eat? While Martha tended to the few customers at the counter, it was Taylor who refilled bread baskets and beverages. Once he spied her in a corner, talking on her cell and gesturing with one hand. When Callum stood and offered a toast Rhys could see her in the kitchen, slicing cake onto plates.

Maybe it was her job, but it was her family, too. She was part of the wedding party, after all. And no one seemed to realize she was missing out.

When the meal was over the party broke up. Callum and Avery departed with a wave, in a hurry to get home to their daughter who was with a sitter. Mr. and Mrs. Shepard left for the bed and breakfast and Jack, being chivalrous, offered to take Denise with him, since they were all staying there anyway.

Angela and Clara offered to help tidy up, but Taylor shooed them away. "You've got Sam and Ty waiting and the kids at home. Go. This won't take but a minute anyway. I'll see you in the morning."

They didn't put up much of an argument, Rhys noticed. Clara put a hand on her swollen tummy and looked relieved.

As they were leaving, another group of truckers came in, looking for hot coffee and a meal before calling it a night. Martha bustled around, attending to them—Rhys knew that on a night like tonight, the tips would be generous.

Meanwhile Taylor grabbed a plastic dishpan and was loading up dirty plates.

She'd missed the entire celebration and was left to clean up the mess. He was pretty sure this wasn't in the job description, and he was annoyed on her behalf. Her family had been utterly thoughtless tonight.

He went around to the opposite side of the table and began stacking plates.

"What are you doing?"

Clank, clank. The flatware clattered on the porcelain as he picked up the dishes. "Helping."

"I got this, Rhys."

He took the stack over to her and put it in the dishpan. "Well, you shouldn't."

"Sorry?"

She looked tired. Tiny bits of hair had come out of her braid and framed her face, and her eyes looked slightly red and weary. "Have you even eaten, Taylor?"

"I'll get something later."

Lord, she was stubborn. "There's no one here now to know that this is your job, because I know that's what you're going to say. And you know what? This isn't your job. For Pete's sake."

"Are you angry at me? Because I'm not leaving all this for Martha. It *is* my job, Rhys. When I plan an event, I sometimes have to chip in and help where it's needed. Even if it's taking out trash or clearing dishes or providing someone with a spare pair of panty hose."

"Not this time. And no, I'm not angry at you."

She lifted her chin. "Then why are you yelling at me? People are staring."

He looked over. Martha was pretending not to watch but he could tell she was paying attention. The truckers weren't so discreet. They were openly staring.

He sighed. "I'm angry at your family. They never even noticed that you didn't sit down. Callum gave the toast without you. And other than Clara and Angela, everyone left without so much as an offer to help clean up. If everyone had pitched in…"

"They had more on their minds." Her posture had relaxed slightly. "It's okay, Rhys. Really."

"Will you go eat, please? Let me look after this."

She sighed. "Tell you what. I'll help clear the tables, and then I'll eat while you put the tables and chairs back to where they normally belong. Deal?"

He could live with that, especially since he figured Taylor wasn't one to generally compromise. "Deal."

With carols playing softly in the background, it only took a few minutes to clear the dirty dishes away. Rhys took them to the kitchen while Taylor stripped away the soiled tablecloths and put the centerpieces in a cardboard box. Together they loaded the kitchen dishwasher and then Rhys put a square of leftover lasagna on a plate, heated it in the microwave and poured Taylor a glass of ice water. When it was hot, he added a bit of salad to the side and grabbed a napkin and utensils.

"That smells delicious."

"Sit. Eat. That's an order."

He knew she was tired when she merely smiled and faked a salute as she sat at an empty table. "Yes, boss."

She'd made a good dent in the lasagna by the time he'd pushed the tables back into place and put the chairs around them. Without a word he went to the kitchen and cut a slice of that chocolate fudge cake she'd missed out on. When he took it to her, she held up her hand. "I couldn't possibly."

"Yes, you can. It's delicious."

"I have a dress to fit into tomorrow."

"Which will look beautiful." He put a bit of cake—complete with fudgy frosting—on the fork and held it out. "Trust me."

"Trust you." She raised one cynical eyebrow so brilliantly he nearly laughed. "As if."

He wiggled the fork. She leaned forward and closed her lips around it, sucking the frosting off the tines.

His body tensed simply from the intimate act of feeding her, feeling the pressure of her lips conducted through metal, the way she closed her eyes at the first rich taste. He enjoyed bantering with her. Matching wits. That didn't happen often around here. But it was more than that. There was an elemental attraction at work. Something indefinable that was more than a physical response to her unusual beauty. She was the most capable woman he'd ever met. So why did she seem particularly vulnerable? Especially around her family?

"That's good," she murmured, licking a bit of chocolate from her upper lip.

"I know." His voice was hoarse and he cleared his throat. "Have another bite."

"I shouldn't."

In response he put more on the fork and held it out. She took it, and then he took a bite for himself, feeling adolescently pleased that his lips followed where hers had been. The room seemed more silent now, and he suddenly realized that the last few customers had gone, the music had stopped and Martha was turning out lights.

"Oh," Taylor said, alarmed. "We should go."

Martha peered through the kitchen door. "Was everything all right, Taylor?"

"It was lovely, Mrs. Bullock. Thank you so much."

"Don't thank me. You were the workhorse tonight." When Taylor moved to stand up, Martha flapped a hand. "Take your time. Rhys will lock up, won't you Rhys?"

"Sure thing, Ma." He never took his eyes off Taylor as he answered. They were going to be alone—truly alone—for the first time. Eating cake by the light of the Christmas tree in the corner. The back door through the kitchen shut, echoing in the silence.

"I didn't mean to..."

He shook his head. "I have keys to the place. It's okay. I've locked up plenty of times."

"No, what I mean is..."

She stopped talking, looked into his eyes and bit down on her lip.

She was feeling it, too. There was something. Something that had been lit the moment that she'd threatened to make him wear a cravat. She meant they shouldn't be alone.

She was probably right.

Instead he gazed into her eyes, unwilling to end the evening just yet. "Do you want some milk to go with your cake?" he asked.

CHAPTER FOUR

SHE SHOULD NEVER have had the cake. Or the milk. Or sat around actually enjoying Rhys's company as the night drew on and on and it was close to midnight and she was still so wired the thought of sleep was ludicrous.

Rhys was bossy and annoying and, at times, growly. He was also the only person to have noticed how she was excluded tonight. When she was working a job she tried to be invisible, behind the scenes. Maybe she'd done her job a little too well, then. Because she'd sure been invisible to her family this evening.

It had stung. In her head she knew she was just doing her job but in her heart it had hurt a little bit, that no one had at least asked her to pause and join the celebration. Not even for the toast.

Except Rhys had noticed.

She was getting used to the sight of his face, rugged and far less refined than most of the men she was accustomed to. Rhys wasn't pretty. But as she looked into his eyes across the table, with the lights of the tree reflected in the irises, she realized a man didn't have to be pretty to be sexy as hell.

"It's getting late. I should get back. Tomorrow's a long day." She balled up her paper napkin and put it on her dirty plate.

"You're probably right," he agreed. "I'll just put these things in the sink."

She followed him to the kitchen. "Rhys. Thank you. I know I blew it off before but it did kind of hurt. That they didn't notice, I mean."

He rinsed the plate and left it in the sink since the dishwasher was already running. "No problem."

She gave a short laugh. "Well, at least being away from the table meant I avoided the 'why aren't you married with a few kids yet' speech."

Rhys gave the kitchen a final check. "Why aren't you, by the way? Or aren't you interested in those things?"

She shrugged. "I like kids. My dad tends to think in lines of traditional roles, like who the breadwinner is and who does the nurturing."

"And you don't?"

She lifted her shoulders. "I don't. I think as long as a couple has a division of labor that works for them, then who am I to criticize? I suppose I'll settle down someday, when I have the time. After I've proved myself."

"And how will you know when you get there?"

She looked up, startled. "What do you mean?"

"I mean, how do you measure that? What do you need to check off on a list to consider yourself a success?"

She floundered. There was no list. "I guess I'll just know."

"Or maybe you'll never know. Let me hit the lights."

She thought about his words as she put on her coat. What was her "yardstick" for success? A dollar amount? Number of employees? Acceptance from her family?

She was so afraid of disappointing any of them, she realized. Callum was a decorated soldier. Jack had been an elite athlete before he'd become a businessman. She loved her brothers but it was hard to compete with their overachievements.

It was a bit of a shock to realize that she'd picked

a business where she was behind the scenes, out of the limelight. Where she was protected just a little bit from visibility if she failed.

When had she become so afraid?

Rhys finished up and when they stepped outside she realized just how much snow had fallen—and it was still coming down. Her car was covered and the snowplow had been by, leaving a deep bank right behind her back bumper. She sighed. She didn't even have a shovel, just a brush in the backseat for cleaning off the windshield.

"Come on, I'll take you in the truck," Rhys said, but Taylor shook her head.

"I have to dig it out sometime and I'm due at the golf club by 9:00 a.m. in order to get everything set up for the reception."

"You try driving that little thing out there before the plows make another pass and you're sure to slide off into the ditch." He shook his head. "There aren't even snow tires on it, just all-seasons. I'll take you out there in the morning."

She didn't want to rely on Rhys too much, especially since he seemed very adept at prying into her business. "Jack's rental's a 4x4. I'm sure he'll run me out if the roads are bad."

"Suit yourself." He didn't sound too put out by her refusal, which was a relief. "But for now, you'd best let me take you home."

Home being the B&B. She didn't have a choice. There was no way her car was going to be un-stuck tonight and she really didn't feel like walking through the snowdrifts at this hour.

Rhys unlocked the door to his truck and waited while she got in, then jogged around the front and hopped in the driver's side. He started the engine and let everything warm up for a few minutes while Taylor stared at the clouds her breath was making in the air.

The heater kicked in and the air around her feet began to warm. "Gosh, it's cold. I'm so used to the coast. This is full-on winter."

"Complete with whiteouts and a snow removal system that operates at the speed of a slug." Rhys grinned. "Still, with this good dump of snow there'll be lots of sledding happening over the holidays."

"Sledding?"

"Snowmobiles," he confirmed. "Lots of wide-open space here, but a lot of the guys like to go into the mountains and into the backcountry."

"That sounds like something Jack would love."

Rhys grinned. "He might have said something about coming back for a trip later this winter. If he can drag Callum away from his new bride. I get the feeling that Jack's a little more adventurous than Callum."

"Just in a different way," she replied, rubbing her gloved hands together. "Callum got all the adventure he wanted in the army, I think, and he was ready to settle down. Jack's more of a daredevil. Anyway, hopefully this will let up by the morning so nothing interferes with the wedding."

He put the truck in gear. "Right. Well, let's get you home so you can get your beauty sleep."

It took no time at all, even at crawling speed, to reach the B&B. The front porch light was on and white Christmas lights twinkled through the snow that had settled on the porch and railings. Rhys put the truck in Park and left the engine running.

Taylor faced him; saw his face illuminated by the dashboard lights. The snow on his hair had melted, making it darker than usual, almost black. Who was Rhys Bullock anyway? Horse trainer, sure. And clearly devoted to his mother, which was another plus. But what made him tick? What were his thoughts, his views? What went on in that complicated male mind of his? On one hand he claimed he didn't want to be tied down, but there was no doubt in her mind that he'd put down roots in Cadence Creek. What was that about?

Why on earth did she care?

"I, uh, thanks for the drive."

"You're welcome."

"And for making me eat. And…" She wet her lips. "Well, for noticing what no one else did."

There was an awkward pause as if he were deliberating over his next words. "You don't need to prove anything to your family, you know," he finally said quietly. "As long as you're squared away with yourself, that's all that matters."

Her lips dropped open. How could he possibly know that she'd always felt like she came up short? Her dad was always talking about how the boys made him proud. She always felt a few steps behind. There was something in Rhys's voice, too. Something that said that he was familiar with those words. Like maybe he'd said them to himself a time or two. Why?

"Rhys."

She'd unbuckled her seat belt and for several heartbeats the air in the cab held, as if wondering if she were going to stay in or get out. Their gazes met and things got ten times more complicated as neither of them seemed capable of looking away. Somehow they drifted closer. Closer...

She wanted to kiss him. The notion was strange and wonderful and slightly terrifying. Nothing could ever come of this, but he was feeling it, too. He must be, because she saw him swallow as he blindly reached around and undid his seat belt, his dark gaze never leaving hers. Nothing was holding him back now and still the fear and excitement waved over her, amplified in the small space of the truck cab. She didn't do this. She didn't get personal. And still she had the urge to touch, the desire to explore.

"You're going to have to meet me halfway," he murmured, his voice deep and inviting. There was no doubt now, was there? With those words he'd told her that they were on exactly the same page. The air between them sizzled.

"This is probably a mistake," she answered,

dropping her gaze, breaking the connection. "I should go inside."

She didn't want to, though. And her pulse leaped wildly as he slid across the seat and reached out with his left hand, curling it around her hip and pulling her across the upholstery. "Hush," he said, and then cupped her cheek in that same hand. "We're both sitting here wondering, so why don't we get this out of the way?"

When his lips came down on hers, it stole her breath. Nothing could have prepared her for the warm insistence of his mouth or the reaction rocketing through her body. One taste and the whole kiss exploded into something wild and demanding. She reached out and gripped the front of his jacket and his arms came around her, pulling her so close she was nearly on his lap. A squeak escaped her lips as he looped one arm beneath her bottom and tugged so she was sprawled across his legs, cushioned by a strong arm as the kiss went on and on, her body ached with trembling need and her head was clouded with sheer desire.

Except somewhere in the fog was the understanding that this couldn't go any farther. She pulled away first, shaking with the intensity of their connection. "Wow," she whispered, their limbs still tangled. Despite the truck being left running, the windows had already fogged up as the sound of their breathing filled the cab.

He let out a soft curse. "I didn't expect that," he said, running his hand over his hair. "God, Taylor."

She had to get some of her bravado back or he'd see exactly how rattled she was. "Too much?" she asked innocently.

"Too much?" He gaped at her for a second, but she wasn't fooled. There was a fire in the dark depths of his eyes that was tremendously exciting.

His voice held a rasp that shivered over her nerve endings. "When I was eighteen I would have been digging for the condom in my wallet by now and heading for the privacy of the gravel pit."

She giggled. He had a condom in his wallet? Or did he mean hypothetically? What was most surprising was how badly she wanted to. Wanted him. That if he'd seriously asked she would have actually considered it even though she totally wasn't into casual anything.

It was too much. Too fast. "That sounds romantic," she replied, the words injected with a healthy dose of sarcasm. She pushed off his lap and back onto the seat of the truck.

"I'm not eighteen anymore," he admitted, letting out a breath. "I'd like to think I've learned some finesse since then. And a quickie in the cab of my truck..." He hesitated, let the thought linger.

Would never be enough. He didn't need to say it for her to hear the words. "I'd better go," she said, sliding all the way over to the door and grabbing her purse. Get out before she changed her mind and crawled into his arms again. "This wasn't such a good idea."

"Because I'm a small-town hick, right?"

She frowned, brought up short. Did he really think she was such a snob? "I didn't say that. It just doesn't make sense to start something when I'm only here until Boxing Day. Then I go back to my world and you stay here in yours. Anything else is just fooling ourselves, Rhys, and you know it."

There was a long, awkward silence. "I'll pick you up tomorrow morning and take you to the club," he offered, but his voice was tight, like she'd somehow offended him.

"Jack will take me."

Rhys let out a frustrated sigh. "Will you call if you need anything?"

She squared her shoulders. "I won't. Thanks for the lift. See you at the church."

She opened the door and hopped down, her boots sinking into eight inches of fresh snow. She wouldn't look back at him. He'd know. Know that if he said the right thing or made the slightest move she'd be in the middle of that bench seat, holding on to his arm as he drove out to the pit or wherever people went parking these days, snowstorm be damned. And she never did things like that. In fact, she hadn't been involved with anyone that way since John. Since he'd said all those hurtful things before slamming the door. She'd put all her energy into the business instead.

Without looking back, she started up the walk to the porch. Rhys gunned the engine the slightest bit—did "Mr. Uptight Pants" have a bit of a rebellious side after all?—and pulled away, driving off into the night.

She tiptoed up the steps and carefully opened the door—a single light glowed from the front window but Taylor expected everyone would be in bed. She'd have to apologize in the morning for coming in so late.

"Aren't you a little old to be parking?" came a voice on her right.

She jumped, pressed a hand to her heart. "Jack. What are you doing up?"

"Big brother was waiting for you. What took you so long?"

She recalled Rhys's criticism of her family and felt her temper flicker. "Someone had to stay and clean up."

"Isn't that the owner's job? What's her name? Martha?"

"Rhys's mother, yes. And considering she was a staff of one tonight and still managed to put on a great dinner for us at a moment's notice, I certainly wasn't going to walk out of there and leave her with a mess. Not that anyone else seemed to mind."

He came forward and frowned down at her.

"Touchy," he remarked. "This have anything to do with why you were in Rhys's truck for so long, and with the windows steamed up?"

She didn't want to blush, but the heat crept up her neck and into her cheeks anyway. "That is none of your business."

"Be careful is all I'm saying. He's not your type."

"How would you know what my type is?"

He straightened and it seemed to her that he puffed out his chest. "Oh, I know. You go for the pretty boys who work downtown in two-thousand-dollar suits."

"Men like you, you mean?"

His eyes glittered. "Hardly. You pick guys who aren't a challenge and who don't challenge you. Guys like Rhys Bullock won't let you away with your usual tricks, sis."

She had to keep a lid on her temper before she said something she'd regret. Jack had such a tendency to be cocky and normally she just brushed it off. Tonight it irritated. Could she not do anything right? "Then how convenient for you that he just gave me a lift home after helping me clear away the dishes. Oh, and he reminded me I hadn't had time to eat at the dinner, either, and fixed me a plate. And when we finally went to leave, my rental was completely blocked in by a snowbank so he offered me a drive home. My type or not, Rhys Bullock was very supportive this evening. So you can put that in your pipe and smoke it, Jackson Frederick Shepard."

Unperturbed, Jack merely folded his arms and raised an eyebrow at her.

"I'm going to bed," she announced. "I recommend you do the same. You're taking me to the golf club at eight-thirty so I can be sure it's ready for the reception."

Without waiting for an answer, she swept up the stairs, her pride wrapped around her. It was only when she was settled in her room, dressed in flannel pajamas and curled under the covers that she let down her guard and closed her eyes.

Behind her lids she saw Rhys. And she saw what might have happened—if only they were different people, in a different place and time.

The church was beautiful.

Taylor let out a relieved sigh as she peeked through the nearly closed door leading through the sanctuary. It had taken longer than she'd anticipated, making sure the reception venue was all on schedule and then it had been time to head to Molly Diamond's, where all the bridesmaids were meeting to get ready and have pictures taken. Taylor gave the thumbs-up to the photographer, Jim, who had flown in from Victoria to do the wedding as a personal favor. He was set up at the front of the church, ready for Avery's walk down the aisle.

Taylor's worries about the decorations had been pointless. She wasn't sure how Melissa Stone had managed it, but the end of each pew held a stunning but simple decoration consisting of a red satin bow and a small cedar bough. Not only did it look festive, but the smell was incredible.

And Clara had come through with the sills, too. On each one was a small rectangular plate with three white pillar candles of varying heights. It was incredibly romantic and the warm light radiated through the church. She couldn't have come up with anything more suitable on her own.

With a lump in her throat, she turned to Clara and smiled. "How on earth did you manage that?" she asked. "It's perfect!"

Clara laughed lightly. "I called the owner of the dollar store last night and asked if we could go in early this morning."

The dollar store. Heaven forbid any of her clients ever found out! She gave an unladylike snort and patted Clara's arm. "I swear I need to stop underestimating the women of this town. First Martha with the dinner, then you with the candles and Melissa with the pew markers. I'm starting to feel rather irrelevant."

Avery heard and her face fell with concern. "Oh, don't say that, Taylor! We put this together in such a short time that if it weren't for you we'd be standing in front of the Justice of the Peace and having a potluck. I never dreamed I'd have a wedding day like this. It would never have happened without you."

Taylor's eyes stung. This was so different from anything she'd ever experienced. She hadn't even had to ask for help. Without even knowing her, people had stepped up because it was the right and neighborly thing to do. Maybe Cadence Creek wasn't the hub of excitement Taylor was used to, but never had she ever been made to feel like she belonged so easily. She was starting to understand why Callum was so happy here.

"It was my pleasure, I promise. Now let me check to see what's going on."

Because Avery had no family, they'd decided to forgo the official ushering in of the parents. Instead Taylor's mom and dad sat at the front, with an adorable Nell, dressed in white ruffles, on their laps. Taylor turned her attention to the side door as it opened and the minister and men came through. At last night's rehearsal it had become glaringly apparent that everyone had an escort up the aisle but the bride. They'd made a quick change of plans, and the women would be walking up the aisle alone with the groomsmen waiting at the front.

Taylor's heart beat a little faster as Rhys appeared, looking so very handsome and exciting in the black tux and tie. The men lined up along their side of the altar, with Rhys positioned right after Jack. The pianist began to play Gounod's "Ave Maria," the signal for the women to begin their walk.

"This is it, girls." Taylor quickly got them in order and then took her place behind Angela.

She gave the man at the door a quick nod and it opened, and the procession began.

Clara went first, radiant in dark green, glowing with pregnancy and holding her bouquet in front of her rounded tummy. Then Angela, smiling at her husband at the other end, and then, in the middle of the procession, Taylor.

She stepped on to the white runner, her emerald satin heels sinking slightly into the carpet. She kept slow time with the music, a smile on her face as she winked at her brother who was waiting rather impatiently for his bride. Jack was beside him, grinning like a fool and then...

And then there was Rhys, watching her with an intensity that made her weak at the knees. The smile on her lips flickered until she purposefully pasted it there, but she couldn't deny the jolt that had rushed through her that second their eyes met. Her chest cramped as her breath caught, and then his lips curved the tiniest bit and his gaze warmed with approval. And she was back in the truck last night, feeling his hands on her body and his lips on her lips and she got hot all over.

Then she was in her place, Denise followed and the music changed.

Taylor forgot all about Rhys the moment Avery stepped to the door and on the carpet. Her lace dress was classic and romantic, her solid red rose bouquet perfect. Taylor's throat tightened as she took one quick glance at her brother and found his eyes shining with tears. She couldn't cry. She wouldn't. She never did at these things. But today was different. She knew how Callum had had his heart broken before and how incredible it was that he was even standing here today. Nell stood on her grandfather's lap and everyone chuckled when she bounced and said "Mumm mumm mumm."

Avery reached Callum, and he held out his hand. She took it and they faced the minister together.

The prayers were short and heartfelt, the "I Do's" immediate and clear so that they echoed to the farthest pew. It was when Avery handed her bouquet to Denise and took Callum's fingers in hers that Taylor wished she'd tucked a tissue into the handle of her bouquet.

The vows were simple and traditional, the words solid and true as they filled the candlelit church. "I Callum, take you Avery, to be my wife. To have and to hold from this day forward."

A lump formed in Taylor's throat as she tried to swallow.

"For better or worse, richer or poorer, in sickness and in health."

Taylor took a fortifying breath and told herself to hold it together. But it was so hard, because she could see the look on Callum's face as he gazed into the eyes of his bride. He was so in love. So sure. The promises were the most important he'd make in his life, but they came easily because he loved Avery that much. Taylor had never experienced anything like that. Sometimes she doubted she ever would…if she was actually that…lovable.

Avery's soft, gentle voice echoed them back. "I Avery, take you Callum, to be my husband. To have and to hold, from this day forward."

A single tear splashed over Taylor's lower lashes. She was mortified.

"To love, honor and cherish for as long as I live."

The pair of them blurred as her eyes filled with moisture and she struggled not to blink. The pronunciation was made, there was clapping during the kiss, and then Avery, Callum, Denise and Jack moved to the table to sign the register and wedding certificate. Just when she was sure the tears were going to spill over, a dark figure appeared in front of her and held out a handkerchief.

She didn't need to see the fine details to know it was Rhys. Her heart gave a confused flutter just before she reached out and took the fabric from his hand. The shape of his lips curved slightly before he silently stepped back, and she gave a self-conscious laugh as she turned her head a little and dabbed at her eyes.

She could see again but she didn't dare look at him. A handkerchief—a white one, she could see now, and it smelled like starch and his aftershave. What sort of man these days carried a white handkerchief, for Pete's sake? And why on earth was she charmed by it?

The documents were signed, the minister introduced them as Mr. and Mrs. Callum Shepard and clapping erupted as the bride and groom immediately went to gather their daughter and then swept jubilantly down the aisle.

Taylor swallowed as Rhys offered his elbow. "Shall we?" he asked quietly, smiling down at her.

She tucked her hand in the crook of his elbow. It was strong and warm and she felt stupidly pretty and feminine next to him. "Certainly," she replied as they made their way out of the sanctuary to the much cooler vestibule. They'd form a receiving line there briefly, and then the guests would go on to the golf club for a cocktail hour while the wedding party had pictures taken.

Taylor gave a final sniff and prepared to get herself together. She had the next hour to get through and didn't want smudged makeup or red eyes to mar the photos. The sentimental moments had passed.

What she hadn't prepared herself for was the number of times she'd be forced close to Rhys during the photos; how she'd feel his hand rest lightly at her waist or his jaw close to her hair. By the time the wedding party was dismissed, her senses were so heightened her skin was tingling.

"You want a drive to the club?" Rhys asked, as the groomsmen and bridesmaids gathered by the coatrack.

"Avery said we could all go in the limo that brought us from Diamondback."

"But aren't they doing just some bride and groom photos in the snow first? I guess I figured you'd want to get there and make sure things were running smoothly."

She smiled up at him, making sure to put several inches between them. "You know me too well."

He shrugged. "That part's easy to read. The tears on the other hand? Total surprise." He reached for her coat and held it out so she could slip her arms into the sleeves.

"And yet you were at the ready with a hanky. Impressive." She needed to inject some humor so he wouldn't know how genuinely touched she'd been at the gesture.

He chuckled. "That was Molly's doing. She said that at weddings you never know when a woman might need a hanky. She gave one to all of us."

He brushed his hands over the shoulders of her coat before stepping back. "Didn't think it'd be you, though. You're too practical for that. I guess I figured you'd be thinking two or three steps ahead."

Normally she would have been, and it stung a bit knowing that Rhys only saw what everyone else seemed to see—a woman lacking in sentimentality. But she'd been caught up in the moment just like everyone else. And for the briefest of seconds, she'd felt a strange yearning. Like she was possibly missing out on something important.

"I slipped up," she replied, reaching in the coat pocket for a pair of gloves. "It's just temporary."

She finally looked up into his face. His dark eyes were glowing down at her and whatever other smart reply she'd been about to make fluttered away like ribbons on a breeze. Her gaze inadvertently slid to his lips as she remembered the sound of his aroused breathing in the confined space of his truck. A truck that he was suggesting she get in—again.

This time there would be no funny business. She really should get to the venue and make sure everything was going according to plan. She relaxed her face into a pleasant smile. "I'll accept the drive with thanks. Let me just tell Jack that I'm going on ahead."

"Taylor?" He stopped her from walking away

by grabbing her arm, his fingers circling her wrist. "You should slip up more often. It looks good on you."

Maybe he did see more. She wasn't sure if that was a good thing or not. "I'll tell Jack," she repeated.

"I'll warm up the engine," he answered.

She turned around to find her brother and when she turned back again, a cold gust of wind from the just-opened door hit her like an icy wall.

She had to keep her head about her today. Weddings made people do strange things. It was just as well, then, that she planned on remaining behind the scenes as much as possible.

CHAPTER FIVE

THE RECEPTION WAS going off without a hitch.
When Taylor arrived at the club, the guests were
already circulating and enjoying the cocktail
hour. Platters of crackers, cheese and cold cuts,
shrimp rings, crudités and fruit were set out on
tables close to the bar, where people were lined
up to be served either punch or hot cider.

The place looked lovely. The centerpieces had
been lit—boy, Melissa had really outdone herself
with those. White candles enclosed in glass sat
on real rounds of wood, surrounded by aromatic
greenery and winterberries. Each chair was covered in white fabric, a wide red ribbon around the
back with more cedar and a single pinecone adding a festive, homey touch. The pew markers had
mirrored the design perfectly. She couldn't have
planned it any better. Hadn't, actually. Funny
how some things worked out.

Rhys showed up at her elbow and handed her a cup. "Have something hot to drink."

"I should check the kitchen."

"You should relax. Maybe enjoy yourself."

"I'll enjoy myself later." But she took the mug anyway. The sweet, spicy scent of the cider was too tempting to resist.

"You look beautiful by the way," he said quietly.

Her pulse fluttered again. "Thank you," she answered politely, but inside she glowed. She was used to dressing up, but her style usually ran to the classic and conservative. Tailored fits and solid colors that spoke far more to class, confidence and efficiency than femininity and whimsy. But the dress today made her feel very girly indeed. The bodice was strapless and the lace overskirt to the emerald tea-length gown was far more dainty than she normally wore. Not to mention the gorgeous satin shoes on her feet, or the way her hair was gathered in a low chignon with a few pieces left artfully around her face.

"Do you want something to eat? I can bring you something if you like."

What was she doing? Last night she'd lost her senses, but it was the clear light of day now. Sure, weddings brought out the romantic in anyone but she was smarter than that. This wasn't anything. One kiss in a truck at midnight didn't make them a couple today. Or any day for that matter.

"I can get it myself, you know. You don't have to act like we're a couple just because we're paired up in the wedding party," she answered, making a pretense of scanning the room even though everything was moving along seamlessly.

Her breath squeezed in her lungs as she waited for his reaction. When she didn't get one, she turned to say something only to discover that he'd walked away. He'd gone to the buffet table, and she wondered if he'd stay true to form and simply ignore her wishes. But when he'd put a few selections on his plate, he never even glanced her way. He walked over to the other side of the room, greeting a few guests with a smile.

It made no sense that she felt empty and bereft when he'd done exactly as she'd intended.

Fine. She'd go to the kitchens and check on the dinner prep, and then make sure the sound system was a go for the emcee. That's where she should be anyway. Not trying to impress a stubborn groomsman.

The words had sat on Rhys's tongue but he'd kept them to himself. At a wedding reception was no place to tell her exactly what he thought of her rude response. But he was plenty put out. He'd only been trying to be a gentleman. Sure, he enjoyed pushing her buttons. But after last night...

Never mind that. Even if that kiss had never happened, he would have been courteous to any woman he'd been paired with for the day. That was just plain manners where he came from. But she was too damned independent. Wanted to do everything by herself. Was it to prove she could? She didn't have to prove anything to him. Anyone with eyes in their head could see she was good at her job. She'd pulled this whole event together in a few weeks. That took organizational skills and long hours and, he suspected, a good amount of money. He felt like saying, "I get it. You're successful and you earned it all by yourself."

The contrast between them was laughable. So

why did he bother? He got the feeling she'd never understand his point of view anyway.

He mingled a bit, visiting with neighbors and acquaintances. The Diamonds arrived, and then fifteen minutes after that Avery and Callum followed, along with Denise and Jack and of course, the adorable Nell. His gaze lit on the little girl for a moment, all in ruffles with a tiny green bow in her dark curls. Humph. Taylor probably didn't even want kids. It would take too much time away from her business and important tasks. How much more reminding did he need that she was not for him? Her work was her top priority.

Rhys's heart constricted as he thought of the two little boys he'd grown so attached to. For a while he'd been so focused on saving the business that he'd neglected the people closest to him. Funny how your perspective changed when you lost what you didn't appreciate in the first place.

So why did he kiss her last night? Why had he made an effort today? And why in hell couldn't he stop thinking about her eyes swimming with tears as he handed her a stupid square of cotton during the ceremony?

Sam took the mic and introduced the happy

couple and asked everyone to take their seats. "You, too, Taylor," he added, glimpsing her talking to one of the wait staff by the door. She smiled and gave a little shrug, making people chuckle as she came his way.

Rhys waited. And when she got to his side, he held out his arm.

He could tell her teeth were clenched as she smiled and put her hand on his arm. "You did that on purpose," she accused, smiling brightly.

He smiled back. "Yes, I did. Just to annoy you."

Her eyes sparked. "Why would you do that?"

"Because pushing your buttons amuses me," he replied. "I know I shouldn't." He pulled out her chair with a flourish and noticed her cheeks were flushed. "It's pretty clear where we stand. But I can't resist."

She took up her napkin and gave it a sharp flap before settling it on her lap. "Hmm. I took you for a rule follower. Straight and narrow. Didn't take you as a bit of a scamp."

Once upon a time he'd been far more carefree and less careful. A risk taker. Circumstances had made him grow up in a hurry. "Funny," he answered, taking his seat and retrieving his own napkin. "I never pictured you as the sappy type either, but…"

"Maybe we bring out the worst in each other," she said in an undertone, reaching for her water glass.

"See? We're getting to know each other better. Now I know that you see both fun and sentimentality as flaws."

"You're deliberately twisting my words."

"Be quiet. The minister is going to say the blessing."

He was gratified when she clamped her lips shut—score one for him. After the blessing, Sam took to the mic again, explaining the order of the evening while the salads were served. Even the salads matched the Christmas decor—greens with candied pecans, red cranberries and creamy feta. Her attention to the smallest detail was starting to get annoying.

Staff were on hand at each table to pour the wine, and he noticed that when Taylor's glass had been filled with red, she reached for it immediately and took a long sip.

Maybe he shouldn't bug her so much. She had

a lot on her mind today. He didn't need to add to the stress.

Then again, there was something to be said for distraction. And he did enjoy pushing her buttons. It was a nice break from his self-imposed "dry spell."

"Good wine?" he asked, reaching for his glass.

"One of my favorites, from Mission Hill. Do you like it?"

He did, though he wasn't much of a wine drinker. "It's okay."

"What's wrong with it?"

"Nothing. I said it was okay."

A look of understanding lit in her eyes. "You don't drink much wine, do you?"

He shrugged. "Not as a rule." When would he drink wine? It wasn't like he went on dinner dates or was the kind to chill out at the end of the day with a nice chardonnay. At her distressed look, he took pity on her. "Look, I'm a guy. Most of us around here are beer men, that's all. Which would be totally out of place at this dinner."

"Oh, is it too fancy? I tried to keep it fairly traditional. Nothing that people can't pronounce, that sort of thing, you know?"

Gone was the sharp tongue and sassy banter. She was actually concerned. A few days ago he might have taken her comment differently, like maybe she meant the people of Cadence Creek weren't as sophisticated as she was. But that wasn't it. Her brow was wrinkled in the middle. He knew without asking that she'd tried very hard to come up with a menu that people would like.

"What's the main course?" he asked.

"Beef Wellington, Duchess potatoes, green beans and roasted red pepper."

"Sounds delicious."

"Well, Avery approved it, but then she approved just about everything I suggested." Her eyes widened. "Oh, Rhys, did I railroad her into stuff? Did she feel she couldn't say no?"

"Hey," he said, beginning to take pity on her. "Where is all this doubt coming from? You've said from the beginning that this is your thing."

"It is, but…"

He nudged her elbow. "Why did you pick this as the menu?"

She picked at her salad without eating. "Well, I tried to come up with something that was fancy enough for a wedding, something special, while keeping in mind the guest list. This is a meal for ranchers and, well, regular people. Not crazy movie stars or visiting dignitaries who only eat fish and sprouted grains or that kind of thing, you know?"

"So you tailored the food to the guest list?"

"Of course. I always do."

"Then why are you so worried? Know what I think? I think that for most people this is going to taste like a fancy meal out that's not intimidating, you know? Nothing they can't recognize or need to pronounce in a foreign language."

Their salads were removed and the main course put in front of them. Rhys's stomach growled. He'd only managed a few bites of the salad and the beef smelled delicious.

"I swear I'm not usually like this. Not so insecure."

"Is it because it's Callum?"

"Maybe. Then again, I don't usually do weddings. That's the one day everyone wants utterly perfect. There's more freedom with parties. But wedding days?" She took another sip of wine. Was quiet for a moment. "I screwed one up once."

"You did?" Was Taylor actually going to admit she'd made a mistake? It didn't strike him as her style.

She nodded. "The bride was allergic to strawberries. I'd forgotten. You don't mess with a bride on her wedding day, you know? She had a breakfast for her bridal party. I never thought twice about giving the chef dominion over the menu. I trusted him completely." She winced at the memory. "The wedding colors were pink and cream. The chef added strawberry coulis to the pancake batter. She got hives and her face swelled up like a balloon. Four hours before her walk down the aisle."

Rhys was intrigued. "What did you do?"

"We tried cold cloths, creams…it wasn't until the antihistamine shot that she really started to improve. But the 'getting ready' photos never happened, and she still looked rather pink and puffy in the pictures. Not to mention the fact that she nodded off in the limousine on the way to the hotel and reception because the drug made her drowsy. Not my finest moment as an event planner."

She speared her golden-browned potatoes with

a somewhat savage poke. "I'm telling you, Rhys, you do not mess with a bride on her wedding day."

She looked so fierce he nearly smiled. But there was something else in her expression, too. She didn't like failure, or anything that would reveal a chink in her perfect armor. He wondered why.

"Have you always been a perfectionist?"

She didn't even take it as a slight criticism. "Yes."

"And doesn't that stress you out?"

She shrugged. "Occasionally. As long as I stay organized I'm fine. And I do work best under pressure. It's just now and again something will crop up and I'll chew antacids for a few days."

He wanted to ask her how that could possibly be fun, but they were interrupted as the speeches began. Mr. Shepard welcomed Avery to the family, and then Avery and Callum stood to speak together, thanking their family and friends. They took a moment to thank Taylor for pulling it all together, and Rhys saw her relax a little in her chair. The day was nearly done. The ceremony had gone without a hitch; the reception was lovely and the food delicious. Perhaps she could actually enjoy herself a little during the dancing.

Dessert was served—pastry baskets filled with chocolate mousse and topped with berries and whipped cream. They were almost too pretty to eat, and Rhys noticed that Taylor had slowed down on the wine and accepted a cup of coffee instead.

He frowned. He shouldn't care. Shouldn't bother him that she was wound tighter than a spring or that she was so deliberate in each choice and move. Except he knew now. He knew that there was a vulnerable side. He'd seen it last night when he'd mentioned how her family had ignored her. Whether she acknowledged it or not, she was desperate for her family's approval.

And he knew there was an unpredictable side to her, too, that rarely had a chance to get out to play. Because he was pretty sure that the heavy kissing they'd been doing in the cab of his truck last night had not been planned out and put on a list of pros and cons. It had been spontaneous. And combustible.

When the meal ended, the wedding cake was

rolled in. "Oh, it's stunning," Taylor gasped, leaning forward to see better.

"You didn't know? A detail escaped your notice?"

She laughed. "No one was allowed to see it. Avery's friend Denise did it as a wedding gift. Avery insisted I trust her on this and so I did."

"It bothered you, though, right?"

She tore her gaze away from the cake and slid it up to meet his. "A little," she admitted. "This whole experience has been weird. I've had to give up way more control than I normally do. Usually no detail ever escapes my approval."

"Sometimes it's good to let someone else take the reins."

She chuckled. "Not my style, Bullock."

The cake really was pretty, even Rhys could see that. It looked like three presents stacked on top of each other, each layer turned on a slight angle and alternating red and white. The topper looked like a giant red bow. "What's the bow made out of?" he asked Taylor.

"Fondant," she said, smiling. "Okay, so the only thing to worry about now is the music, and the DJ should be fine, so maybe you're right.

Maybe I can relax." She sighed. "And finally get some sleep."

He wondered if her lack of sleep was to do with the wedding or if she'd been like him last night, staring at the ceiling wondering what it would have been like to finish what they'd started.

It had been a long time since he'd come that close. He certainly hadn't wanted to sow any wild oats here in Cadence Creek. The town was too small. Things got around. And before he knew it he'd be tied down, worrying about what he had to offer a wife, wondering how long it would be before he disappointed her.

No danger of that with Taylor, was there? She wasn't staying long enough for that.

Cheers went up as Avery and Callum sliced into the cake. Nell, clearly exhausted, was curled up in Mrs. Shepard's arms, sound asleep. The wait staff cleaned away the remaining dishes and business at the bar picked up. The show was over. Now it was time for fun.

He looked over at Taylor, who was more relaxed but looking increasingly exhausted. He was starting to wonder if she knew what fun was—or if it was all work and no play with her.

* * *

She wasn't sure how much more she could take.

Rhys was beside her every moment. He smelled so good. Like those peel-away cologne ads in magazines only better, because the scent came alive from the contact with his warm skin. He knew how to push her buttons and she'd started to realize he did it intentionally, trying to get a rise out of her. It was sexy as all get-out, like a strange mating dance that sent her heart racing and blood to her cheeks.

Which was all well and good except she kept feeling her control slipping and the balance of power was not in her favor. She found herself admitting things that she'd normally never dare breathe. Like that wedding story. She never shared that. It was too humiliating! At least she'd stopped before she'd said anything about how that day had ended—with John walking out. Professional and personal failure in one twelve-hour period. Talk about overachieving...

She didn't quite know where she stood with Rhys. It was partly exhilarating and mostly maddening and now, at the end of a very long day, she was feeling a bit off her game.

She decided to take a few minutes to chill out. She'd done her job. Everyone was doing theirs. It would be okay to relax for a bit. Especially when she could watch her brother and brand-new sister-in-law take to the dance floor for their first waltz.

Rhys disappeared momentarily to the bar and she let out a breath. Avery and Callum swept across the parquet as everyone watched, but her gaze slipped away from the floor and to Rhys, who stood chatting to the bartender while he waited for his drink. She swallowed. His tux fit him to perfection, the trousers showcasing long, lean legs that led to a gorgeously tight bottom. He'd taken off the jacket, and the tailored vest over the white starched shirt accentuated the breadth of his shoulders. He wasn't classically handsome, but his physique was as close to perfect as she could imagine.

When he turned back from the bar he caught her staring. She gasped a little as heat snapped between them, even from across the room. Maybe his face would never be in a magazine, but there was an intensity to it, a magnetism, that she couldn't deny.

He was holding two glasses in his hands.

When he got back to the table, he held one out to her. "Here," he said, taking his seat. "You look like you could use this."

"Champagne?"

He grinned, and it lit her up from the inside. "They managed to have a couple of bottles back there."

"You're more of a beer guy."

"It depends on the occasion. And you—" his gaze traveled over her for about the tenth time today "—look like a girl who needs champagne in her hand."

She took the glass.

"To a job well done."

She raised her glass to touch his but he wasn't done.

"And some well-deserved R&R."

That's right. After tonight she was on vacation for a whole week. She wasn't sure if it was a blessing or if it was going to drive her stir-crazy. She wasn't used to being idle.

She sipped at the champagne, the bubbles exploding on her tongue. A waitress stopped at the table, offering small pieces of cake. What the heck. Taylor took one, and so did Rhys. She took a bite. Not straight up chocolate… She closed her eyes. It was lavender. "Holy cannoli," she whispered, taking another sip of champagne, which only intensified the flavors on her tongue. "That is some serious cake."

"You," he said in a low voice, "are killing me here."

She held his gaze. Put a bit of cake on her fork and held it out while the events of the previous night leaped to the front of her mind. "What's good for the goose," she said lightly, offering the cake. "I promise you, this cake is a life-altering experience."

He took it from the fork. "I don't think it's the cake," he answered, reaching out and circling her wrist with his fingers. "Taylor, what are we doing?"

Clapping erupted as Avery and Callum finished their dance. "Now could we have the wedding party on the floor, please?" the DJ called.

Their gazes clung for a brief second as the words sunk in. For all her "you don't have to act like we're a couple" bit, the truth was they *had* been seated together for the reception and they *were* expected to dance together. The other bridesmaids and groomsmen seated along the head table were getting up from their chairs. Rhys held out his hand. "That's our cue."

She put down her fork. For heaven's sake, it was one dance at a wedding. Nothing to get in such a lather over. She'd put her hand in his, the other on his shoulder, and stare at the buttons on his shirt. It would be fine.

Except the moment they hit the parquet, he pulled her close in his arms and the scent that had teased her earlier enveloped her in a cloud of masculinity. Even in her heels—and she wasn't a short girl—he had a few inches on her. His palm was wide and warm and her plan to simply put her other hand on his lapel was a total fail because she remembered he'd removed his jacket and the flat of her hand was pressed simply to his white shirt. And the hard, warm wall of muscle beneath it.

"For goodness' sake, smile," he commanded as their feet started moving to the music.

She looked up into his eyes. He was smiling down at her but rather than feeling reassured she got the feeling that she was looking into the face of the Big Bad Wolf.

CHAPTER SIX

WHOEVER DECIDED THAT slow, angsty songs were appropriate for weddings needed to be shot.

Taylor made her feet move, determined to keep her distance from Rhys as best she could, which was a rather daunting task considering they were slow dancing. It might have been easier if the song choice had been a wedding standard, something she was used to hearing time and again over the years and could dismiss as cliché and trite. But this was something new and romantic, and an acoustic version to boot that only added to the intimacy. Rhys's hand rode the small of her back, fitting perfectly in the hollow just below the end of her zip. The warmth of his touch seeped through the lace and satin to her skin.

During the planning, a wedding party dance had sounded nice. Since Avery didn't have any family, the traditional Groom/Mom of the Bride, Bride/Father of the Groom dances couldn't happen for the second dance of the night. This was Avery's idea of including everyone. Little had Taylor known that something so innocuous sounding would create such havoc.

"This isn't so bad, is it?"

His breath tickled the hair just above her ear and goose bumps popped up over her skin. How could she say how she really felt about it? That it was pure torture being in his arms this way, determined not to touch, wanting to desperately, knowing she couldn't with such an audience watching their every move?

"Not so bad I guess," she answered.

More shuffling steps. Was she imagining it or did his hand tighten against her back, pulling her closer? She swallowed heavily, the nerves in her stomach swirling with both anxiety and anticipation. Oh, God, now his jaw was resting lightly against her temple and his steps were getting smaller.

Her fingers slid over his shoulders as she imagined the smooth, muscled skin beneath the pure white fabric. Each breath caught for just a moment in her chest, making it hard to breathe as the song went on interminably. His fingers kneaded gently at the precise spot of the dimple at the top of her...

They had to stop this. And yet she lacked any will to back away, to put space between them. What she really wanted was to tilt her head so that his jaw wasn't riding her temple but closer to her mouth.

Holy Hannah.

"What are you doing to me, Taylor?"

If he kept talking in that husky voice she was going to have a meltdown right here on the dance floor.

"Nothing," she replied. "I'm not doing anything."

But she was and she knew it. And he wasn't exactly backing off, either.

"You..." Fear crowded her breath. She was getting in way too deep. "You don't even like me. You criticize everything."

"You're not the only one who enjoys a challenge," he replied, his thumb making circles against her tailbone. "You know as well as I do all that baiting was just foreplay."

Melt. Down.

"You're forgetting," he said softly, "who was with you in that truck last night."

She finally braved a look at him. His dark eyes glittered at her and she knew in a heartbeat where this would lead if she let it. The big question was did she want to?

Her body said yes. Her brain was another matter entirely. And while it was a close-fought battle, her brain was still in charge. By a very narrow margin.

"Not going to happen," she said, sounding far more certain than she felt.

"You sure? No gravel pit required. I have my own house, with a nice big bed in it."

Oh. *Oh.*

While that was a temptingly delicious thought, Taylor knew one of them had to be sensible. "I haven't had that much champagne, Rhys. If you're looking to hook up with someone, maybe you can find someone local. I'm sure there are some pretty girls in town who'd be interested."

He lifted his chin and his hot gaze slid away. "I don't date town girls."

"Ever?"

"Ever," he confirmed tightly.

Well. There was a story there, she was sure. But she wasn't about to ask. The farther away from Rhys she could manage the better. She did not want to get involved. A couple of stolen kisses were one thing. Start to probe into his personal life and it was going to get intimate.

"So I'm what? Not hanging around after Christmas, which makes me convenient?"

He let out a short laugh, dropped his gaze to her lips and pulled her close. Her breath came out in a rush as she found herself pressed against his hard length. "Trust me. You are anything but convenient."

The contact rippled through them both until suddenly he released his hold and stepped back. The song ended and a new one began. Other guests crowded the floor as a popular, upbeat song thumped through the speakers.

Taylor stepped back. "Thank you for the dance."

Before he could say anything else, she turned her back on him and went to their table, ready to pick up her purse and go. Except she hadn't brought a vehicle, had she? She'd gone to the church in the limo and to here with Rhys and now she'd have to beg a ride back to the B&B.

Which she'd planned to do with Jack, but she caught sight of him dancing with Amy Wilson, having a good time.

She grabbed her champagne glass and drained what was in it.

Callum and Avery stopped for a moment, happy and glowing. "Taylor, we can't thank you enough," Avery said. "Today was just perfect."

She was relieved to have something to think about other than Rhys. "It was my pleasure. And I did have some help you know. Your florist is a gem and your cake was out of this world. Not to mention Clara saving the day with the church candles." She looked up at Callum. "You've landed in a very nice place, brother."

He winked at her. "I know it. Sure you don't want to hang around a little longer?"

She shook her head. "A nice diversion but not my style. The week of relaxation that I'll get housesitting for you is enough small-town for me, thanks."

"You sure? Seems to me you've made a friend." He raised his eyebrows.

"I'm a big girl. And that's going nowhere, so don't you worry your head about it."

"That's not what Jack says. He said you were necking with Rhys in his truck last night."

This was what she didn't miss about having brothers underfoot. They always thought it was okay to stick their noses in her business under the guise of "looking out for their sister." All of it was a pain in the butt.

"Callum," Avery chided softly, elbowing her husband in the ribs.

"Well, they weren't exactly discreet on the dance floor, either."

Taylor's cheeks burned. "Rhys Bullock is a bossy so-and-so who likes to push my buttons. I'm no more interested in him than...than..."

A hand appeared beside her, reaching for the other champagne glass. She turned on him. "Could you please stop showing up everywhere I am?"

He lifted his glass in a mock toast, totally unperturbed. "I'll disappear somewhere more convenient," he said.

He did, too. Right back to the dance floor. The DJ had put on a faster number and Rhys snagged Amy from Jack and swung her into a two-step.

He turned her under his arm and she came back laughing.

"You're jealous," Callum noted.

"I most certainly am not."

"You're no better at lying now than you were when we were kids. Dad always said the poker face gene passed you by." Callum grinned, but he couldn't possibly know how much the words stung. Another criticism. She never measured up. She was always one step behind her brothers as far as her dad was concerned. One of these days she was going to show her father her accounts and watch his eyebrows go up. Those "frivolous" parties she planned brought in a boatload of cash.

Funny how the idea of that future moment had always seemed so sweet in her mind, but lately it had lost a little of its lustre. It was only a bank statement after all. There had to be more, right? Something more satisfying than the account balance?

"Don't you have cows to milk or something?"

He laughed. "I hired someone to do that today." His eyes twinkled at her. "And you won't have to worry about any farm work, either, while you're at the house. It's all taken care of."

"Good. Because you used to enjoy mucking around in the barns but I'd rather keep my boots nice and clean."

He laughed, then leaned forward and kissed her cheek. "We'll be gone tomorrow before you get to the house. I'll leave the key under the Santa by the door. Make yourself at home and we'll see you on the twenty-third."

She relaxed and kissed him back. "Love you, Callum."

"I love you, too, brat."

They moved off to visit with other guests. Taylor took a turn on the floor with Ty, and Sam, and even once with her father. True to form, he complimented the wedding but in such a way that it made her feel inconsequential.

"You planned a nice little party," he said, smiling at her.

Her throat tightened. Eighty guests, wedding party, church, venue, catering, flowers and all the other tiny details it took to put a wedding together in a ridiculously short amount of time. And it was "little"?

"Thanks," she said, deflated but unwilling to rise to any bait tonight. Not on Callum's day.

"When are you going to stop playing and start putting that business degree to good use?" he asked.

"I am putting my degree to use," she returned, moving automatically to the music. "Just ask my accountant."

"Planning parties?"

"I know you've never understood that. You wanted me to be a fund manager. I'd be bored to death, Dad."

She made herself look into his face as she said it. For a moment he'd almost looked hurt. How was that even possible?

Conversation dropped for a minute or so before Harry recovered and changed the subject, talking nonstop about Nell and how it was wonderful to have a grandchild to spoil. The dance ended just in time—she was starting to worry he was going to ask her when she was going to do her duty and provide some more grandchildren. Her father's opinions were clear enough and pretty much paralleled with what John's had been. Personal and professional failure. And if not failure, at the least disappointment.

When the dance was over Rhys gave her a

wide berth and she attempted to perk up her mood by spending a half hour with the pregnant Clara, chatting about Angela's charity foundation Butterfly House, and the other initiatives the Diamonds were involved in. It was all quite fascinating and before she knew it, the call went up for the single women to gather on the floor for the throwing of the bouquet.

She was not going to do that. Not in a million years.

Except Avery put up the call and every eye was on her. "Come on, Taylor, you, too!" Taylor spied Rhys standing against a pillar, his arms folded smugly as his eyes teased her, daring her to take part in the silly custom. She lifted her chin and ran her hands down her skirt before joining the half-dozen or so women ready to do battle for the mythical status of the next to be married. She wouldn't give him the satisfaction of backing out. Not that she'd actively try to catch it…

When Avery let the bouquet fly, Taylor had a heart-stopping moment when she realized it was heading right for her. Without thinking she simply reacted, raising her hands. But just before the ribbon-wrapped stems reached her, another hand neatly plucked it from the air.

Cheers went up when Amy Wilson held up the bouquet in a sign of victory.

Taylor was really ready to leave now. As she backed off the dance floor, she looked over at her mother, smiling from the sidelines, still cradling a sleeping Nell in her arms. Taylor wondered if her mom knew how much Taylor admired her. It was always her dad in the spotlight, but Taylor knew how hard her mom worked to keep the ship on course. Once, when she'd been about ten years old, she'd discovered her mother in the kitchen, making lists for an upcoming party they were hosting. That was when Taylor understood how, when everything seemed smooth and effortless on the surface, it was because of a well-oiled, well-organized machine running things behind the scenes. The machine, in that case, had been her mother, who handled everything from start to finish and still found time to run the kids to sports and especially Jack to his ski meets.

Maybe her dad was the one with his picture in the business magazines, but it was her mother

Taylor truly admired. Her mother was the reason she'd chosen event planning as her career. Taylor hated how her father minimized the hard work she did, so why did her mother not resent his attitude? Why had it never been an issue for them?

There was another loud shout and Taylor lifted her head to see a stunned Rhys holding the bridal garter. According to tradition, Amy then took the chair in the middle of the dance floor while Rhys slid the garter on her leg. Taylor stifled a laugh. He didn't look too happy about it, especially when the DJ announced that the next dance was for the "lucky couple." Served him right.

As the music started, she headed toward her parents. "I don't suppose you're heading back to the B&B anytime soon, are you?" she asked, kneeling by her mom's chair.

"As a matter of fact, I was just suggesting to your dad that we should take Nell and go. She's staying with us tonight so Callum and Avery can have the place to themselves before they all fly out tomorrow. Poor little mite's had enough excitement for today."

"So has this big mite. I'm beat. Mind if I catch a lift?"

"Of course not, but don't you want to stay at the party?"

Taylor saw Rhys and Amy out of the corner of her eye. For all he said he didn't date local girls, Amy sure was snuggled close to him, her arms wrapped around his ribs and her head nestled into his shoulder. "I'm sure. I've had a long few days and this will pretty much run itself now."

"Get your things then. You did a beautiful job, sweetheart. Proud of you."

The words warmed Taylor's heart. "Thanks, Mom. I had a good teacher."

"Oh, go on."

But Taylor took a moment to press her mother's hand in hers. "I mean it. I don't know that you were appreciated enough for all you did to keep things running smoothly. I should have said this before, but when I started my business you were the inspiration behind it."

"I didn't know that."

"Well, it's true."

Taylor went to pull away but her mom held tight

to her hand. "Mind if I give you a little extra food for thought?"

Surprised, Taylor paused. "Sure."

Susan looked into Taylor's eyes and smiled. "None of it would have meant a thing without your dad and you kids. I know sometimes it looked like I played the dutiful wife…"

"You worked hard."

"Yes, I did, and I enjoyed it. Still, I would have missed out on so much if I hadn't had you kids. I could have gone on and done anything I wanted, you know? And I don't regret my decision for a second. Work is work, but family is forever."

"Didn't it ever bother you that Dad, well, took you for granted?"

Susan laughed. "Is that what you think? Oh, heavens. He wanted you kids, too. Honey, you get so wound up and defensive about this division of labor expectation, but it goes both ways. We did what worked for us. Being home with you three was my choice to make."

"Is this leading to a speech about settling down?"

Susan smiled and patted her hand. "I know better than that."

Taylor let out a breath. "Phew." But after a moment she looked at her mother again. "Mom, maybe I will settle down. When I find the right guy."

"That's a good answer," her mother replied. "Now, let's get going. I want to spend a little more time with my new granddaughter tonight."

Taylor got her coat from the coat check, snagged her purse and checked in with the staff one last time. Her mother was making sure they had all of Nell's stuff—including her car seat—while her dad went to warm up the car. She was just pulling on her gloves when Rhys came up behind her.

"You were just going to leave without saying goodbye?"

She held on to her purse strap. "It's been a long day and I'm catching a ride with my folks."

"That didn't answer my question."

She frowned. "What do you care? You've amused yourself with me a bit for the last few days but the wedding's over, we're not paired up anymore and we can both go about our business."

Rhys stared at her quizzically. "Really?"

"Is there some reason why we shouldn't?"

He looked like he wanted to say something, but

held back. She wondered why. And then got a bit annoyed that she kept wondering about Rhys's state of mind at all. She blew air out her nose in an exasperated huff. "What do you care anyway? You seemed to enjoy having Amy Wilson plastered all over you."

"Jealous?"

She snorted. "Hardly."

He stepped forward until there was barely an inch between them. "Amy Wilson is the last woman on earth I want to be with!"

Silence rang around them, and then, almost as one, they realized someone had heard the entire outburst. Amy stood not ten feet away, her creamy skin stained crimson in embarrassment as humiliated tears shone in her eyes.

"Amy..." Taylor tried, taking a hesitant step toward the woman.

But Amy lifted a hand to halt Taylor's progress, and without saying a word she spun on her heel and disappeared into the women's powder room.

Rhys sighed heavily, let out a breathy expletive.

"Good night, Rhys."

"Taylor, I'm..."

But she didn't listen to the end. She turned and

walked, quickly, toward the exit. She could see the headlights of her dad's rental car as it waited by the front door, saw him helping her mom in the passenger side. She went outside and was met by a frigid wall of arctic air. As she climbed into the backseat, she made a promise to herself.

Tomorrow she was going to stock up on groceries, wine and DVDs. Then she was going to go to Callum's house and as God as her witness, she wasn't going to venture out into the icy cold for the entire week. She was going to be a hermit. No work. No worrying about freezing her tail off.

And especially no men!

CHAPTER SEVEN

TAYLOR ROLLED OVER and squinted at the sunshine coming through the bedroom window.
Why hadn't she thought to close the blinds last
night? Her first full day of vacation and she'd
looked forward to sleeping in. She checked her
watch. It was only eight-fifteen!

She burrowed into the warm blankets and
closed her eyes. Maybe if she breathed deeply
and relaxed, she could fall back asleep. But after
just a few minutes she knew she might as well
get up. She was awake for good now. Besides,
just because she was up didn't mean she had to
actually "do" anything. She could lounge around
in her fuzzy pajamas, drink coffee, read one of
the paperbacks she'd brought along.

Come to think of it, that sounded pretty darn
good. Especially the coffee part. It was going to
be awesome having some peace and quiet. No
ringing phones, no buzzing email, no wedding

plans and especially no Rhys Bullock to get in her way now that the wedding was over.

She was terribly afraid she was going to be bored to tears within forty-eight hours.

She rolled out of bed and shoved her feet into her favorite sheepskin slippers. On the way to the kitchen she pulled her hair back into a messy ponytail, anchoring it with a hair elastic that had been left on her wrist. While the coffee was brewing she turned up the thermostat and chafed her arms. Even the soft fleece of her winter PJs was no protection against the December cold.

She poured her first cup of coffee and, in keeping with the celebratory nature of the week, substituted her usual cream with the festive eggnog she found in the refrigerator.

She was halfway through the cup when she chanced a look out the front window. The mug paused inches away from her lips as she stared at a familiar brown truck. What on earth was Rhys doing here?

As she stared, the man in question came out of the barn. Even with the hat pulled low over his head, she'd recognize that long-legged stride in a heartbeat.

Irritation marred her idyllic morning and before she could think twice she flung open the door and stepped to the threshold. "What on earth are you doing here?"

His head snapped up and even though he was too far away for her to see his eyes, she felt the connection straight to her toes. Stupid girl. She should have stayed inside. Pretended she wasn't home. Not risen to the bait, except Rhys seemed to get on her last nerve without trying. She swallowed thickly, feeling quite foolish but standing her ground as a matter of pride. He hadn't actually baited her at all. He hadn't done *anything*.

Except show up.

"Well?" she persisted.

"I'm doing the chores." His tone said, *What does it look like I'm doing?*

She frowned. Callum had said at the reception that someone had looked after the chores and would continue to do so during his absence. He couldn't have meant Rhys. Rhys had been occupied with the wedding all day on Saturday. She would have noticed if he'd slipped away.

"Why?"

He came closer, walking across the yard as if

he owned the damned place. "Well, I would suppose that would be because Callum hired me to."

"He did not. He hired someone else."

Rhys was only twenty feet away now. "He told you that?"

The wrinkle between her eyebrows deepened. Was that exactly what Callum had said? "He said he hired someone to do the chores during the wedding and during his absence, too."

Rhys stopped at the bottom of the steps to the veranda. "He hired Keith O'Brien on the day of the wedding, because I was in the wedding party."

Oh, hell.

"Why didn't he just hire him for the whole time, then?" She gave a huff that went up in a cloud of frosty air.

"Because Keith left yesterday to go to Fort McMurray to spend the holidays with his family."

"So you're…"

He shifted his weight to one hip, a move that made him look unbearably cocky. "Here for the week," he finished for her, his whole stance screaming *deal with it.*

And then he smiled, that slow grin climbing

up his cheek that was at once maddening and somehow, at the same time, made her whole body go warm. His gaze slid over her pajamas. "Penguins? Seriously?" he asked.

Her mouth dropped open as she realized she was standing in the doorway still in her nightwear. Jolly skiing penguins danced down the light blue pant legs. The navy fleece top was plain except for one more penguin on the left breast.

She stepped back inside and slammed the door.

It was eerily quiet for the space of five seconds, and then her heart beat with the sound of his boots, heavy on the steps, then two more as he crossed the narrow porch.

He was just on the other side of the door. Less than two feet away. He didn't even have the manners to knock. It was like he knew she was standing there waiting for him because he said, in a low voice, "Aren't you going to ask me in for coffee?"

"Humph!" she huffed, taking a step backward and fuming, her hands on her hips. As if. Presumptuous jerk!

"Come on, Taylor. It's cold out here. A man

could use a hot cup of joe. I can smell it, for Pete's sake."

"I hear the coffee is good at the Wagon Wheel. Price is right, too."

Was that a chuckle she heard or had she just imagined it?

Softer now, he answered, "But the company isn't nearly as good."

She shouldn't be persuaded or softening toward him at all. He was used to getting his own way and she wouldn't oblige.

Then he said the words she never thought he'd ever utter. "I'm sorry about the other night."

Damn him.

She opened the door. "Come in then, before you let all the heat out. It's like an igloo in here."

He stepped inside, all six-feet-plus of him, even taller with his Stetson on. She wasn't used to seeing him this way—he looked like the real deal with his boots and hat and heavy jacket.

"You smell like the barn."

"My grandfather would say that's the smell of money."

"Money?"

He grinned. "Yeah. Anyway, sorry. Occupational hazard. Me smelling like the animals, that is. Though usually I smell like horses. They smell better than cows."

She didn't actually mind. While she wasn't interested in getting her own boots dirty, she did remember days on her uncle's farm. The smell was familiar and not too unpleasant.

"Just take off your boots if you're coming in for coffee."

While he toed off his boots she went into the kitchen to get a fresh cup. "What do you take in it?" she called out.

"Just cream, if you've got it," he answered, stepping inside the sunny kitchen.

She handed him the cup and then took a plastic container from a cupboard. "Are you hungry? Avery left a mountain of food, way more than I can eat in a week. This one is chocolate banana bread."

"I couldn't turn that down."

She cut several slices and put them on a plate. "Come on and sit down then."

Before Rhys sat down, he removed his hat and put it carefully on a nearby stool. She stared at him as he sat, pulled his chair in and reached for his coffee cup.

"What?" he asked, pausing with the cup half-way to his lips.

She shrugged. "You can be very annoying. But you have very good manners."

He laughed. "Blame my mom, I guess. So, enjoying your vacation?"

"Well, I've only officially been on holiday for a few hours. Yesterday I slept in, then spent last night hanging with my family. My mom and dad booked a place in Radium for the week and are coming back on the twenty-third for Christmas with Callum and the family. And Jack flew back to Montana this morning for a meeting of some sort. Lord only knows what deal he's cooking up this time. Anyway, I'll probably enjoy my vacation for a few days. And then I'll start going stir-crazy."

Rhys reached for a slice of cake. "You strike me as one of those ambitious, type A personality people."

"You mean I'm driven? Yeah, I guess." She sighed. "I might as well 'fess up. I like being my own boss. Sometimes it's stressful because it's all on me, you know? But I don't like being told what to do."

He began coughing, crumbs catching in his throat. When he looked up at her again his eyes had watered and he was laughing. "Sorry. Stating the obvious shouldn't have been that funny."

"Hey, I know how you feel about it. You think I'm crazy. Most guys are intimidated by it."

"Most guys have a hard time with a woman who is smarter than they are."

She nibbled on her cake. "Careful, Rhys. That almost sounded like a compliment."

He laughed.

"So why aren't you?"

"What?" He tilted his head curiously. "What do you mean?"

"Why aren't you intimidated?"

He smiled again and the dark depths of his eyes warmed. "Oh. That's easy. I said that most guys have a problem with women who are smarter than they are…"

"And you're not most guys?"

"I never said you were smarter than me."

Without thinking, she kicked him under the

table. Her toe hurt but he barely even flinched. "You are an infernal tease!"

"And you love it. Because you like a challenge."

How did he possibly know her so well? It was vastly unsettling.

She picked at her cake another moment or two before putting it down and facing him squarely. "What do you get out of this, Rhys? You and me. We're doing this dance and I'm not sure I see the point of it."

"You mean because we're so different and all?"

She lifted one shoulder. "That's only part of it. We both know that on Boxing Day I'm headed back to my life, so why bother?"

Taylor lifted her gaze to meet his. Something curled through her insides, hot and exciting. This simmering attraction they had going on made no sense. They were as different as water and air. But it was there just the same. This chemistry. Rhys Bullock was exciting. A small-town farm-worker who hadn't the least bit of initiative and she couldn't stop thinking about him.

And yet, maybe the attraction stemmed from his confidence, a self-assurance that he knew who he was and was exactly where he wanted to be. While she didn't quite understand his choices, she had to admit she was the tiniest bit jealous that he'd gained that understanding while she was still trying to figure it all out. He didn't need accolades. Rhys Bullock had the confidence to know exactly who he was. He was comfortable in his own skin the way she'd never been.

"Why you?" He leaned forward a little. "Beyond the obvious fact that you're crazy hot and my temperature goes up a few degrees when you enter the room?"

She suppressed the urge to fan herself. "Rhys," she cautioned.

"You asked. And for what it's worth, I'm not looking for ties and commitments."

"Funny, because you're a pretty grounded guy. I'd kind of expect someone like you to be settled down with two-point-five kids and a dog, you know?"

Something flickered across his face. Pain? Anger? It disappeared as fast as it had arrived. "Start dating in a town this size and suddenly the town gets very, very small. Especially when things go wrong."

"Ah, like that old saying about...doing something where you eat."

He chuckled. "Yeah. Exactly like that. Look, you're a novelty, Taylor. An adventure. A safe one, because in a week's time you're going to be gone."

"So I'm a fling?"

His gaze sharpened. "A couple of kisses hardly constitutes a fling." He took a calm sip of his coffee. "You're an anomaly. You intrigue me. You know how to keep me on my toes."

"I'm glad I'm so amusing."

"Don't act like your feelings are hurt. We both know that the last thing you want is to be ordinary."

"Yeah, well, not everyone appreciates the alternative."

"That's because you highlight every single one of their flaws. You're not always right, but you're committed." He put his hand over hers. "That kind of commitment can take a toll. I can see you need the break."

"Don't be silly. I'm perfectly fine." She looked away, unexpectedly touched by his insight. How could he see what everyone else did not? The whole wedding she'd felt like she was losing her edge. Normally she'd be fired up and excited about the New Year's job, but instead she was dreading it. What on earth was wrong with her?

He squeezed her fingers. "Oh, Taylor, do you think I don't recognize burnout when I see it?"

She pulled her hand out of his grasp and sat back. "I'm not even thirty years old. I'm too young for burnout. Besides, what would you know about the pressures of running a business, with your 'put in your shift and go home' attitude?"

Silence rang in the kitchen for a few seconds. "Okay then." He pushed out the chair, stood and reached for his hat. "I should get going. I have some work out at Diamondback before coming back tonight to do the evening chores. Thanks for the coffee and cake."

She felt silly for going off on him like that—especially when he was right. At the same time, she didn't need to have it pointed out so bluntly. And the way he'd spoken so softly and squeezed her fingers? Argh! The sympathy had made her both angry and inexplicably tearful.

"Rhys, I..."

"Don't worry about it," he said evenly, going to the door and pulling on his boots. "I'll see you later."

He was gone before she had a chance to do anything. To take back the snippy words. She'd judged him, when she knew how it felt to be on the receiving end of such judgment.

She turned her back to the door and leaned against it, staring at the Christmas tree, fully decorated, standing in the corner. She couldn't even muster up a good dose of Christmas cheer.

Maybe Rhys was right. Maybe she was a little burned out. But she couldn't just take off and leave things. She had clients and commitments. She had employees who were counting on her for their livelihoods.

One week. Somehow she needed to recharge during this one week. With a heavy sigh, she went to the kitchen, retrieved her coffee and headed back to the bedroom. Coffee and a book in bed was as good a start as she could come up with right now.

Rhys was glad of the physical labor to keep him going. He'd been up early to head to Callum's for chores, then to Diamondback, and now back at Callum's for the evening milking. Plus he hadn't been sleeping well. He'd had Taylor on his mind. Something had happened between them as they'd danced at the wedding. Then there was this morning in the kitchen. Lord, how he loved bantering with her. She was quick and sharp and it was like a mating dance, teasing then pulling away. Except that when it got a little too honest she ran scared and the game was over.

It was fully dark outside as he finished tidying the milking parlor and went to the stainless sink to wash his hands. What was she doing now? Having dinner? A bubble bath? His fingers paused for a moment as that idea saturated his consciousness, crowding out any other thoughts. He imagined her long, pale limbs slick with water and soap, tendrils of hair curling around her face from the steam rising from the bath.

Not dating came with a price. It was like anything else, he supposed. Deny yourself long enough, and temptation was nearly too much to bear. And Taylor Shepard was tempting indeed.

But he knew what she really thought of him.

That fact alone would keep him from knocking on her door again.

He shut off the tap. He knew a damn sight more about running a business than she thought. His livelihood and his mother's future were tied up in the diner. And he knew the pain of failure, too. It wasn't even a matter of his savings. It was a matter of trying to make things right for employees. Creditors. Putting himself last, and scraping the bottom of the barrel to keep from declaring bankruptcy. The unfortunate part was that he hadn't just messed things up for himself. It had messed up Sherry's life. And by extension, that of her kids.

He rubbed a hand over his face.

Never again. Punching a clock made for a lot less stress in the end. Taylor had no right to judge him for it.

He shoved his gloves on his hands and stepped outside into the cold. His feet crunched on the snow and he was nearly to his truck when the front door to the house opened.

"Rhys?"

He turned. His breath formed a frosty cloud as he saw her standing in the circle of porch light, her arms crossed around her middle to keep warm. Her long braid fell over her shoulder again, neat and tidy. Just once he'd like to take that braid apart with his fingers and sink his hands into the thick softness of her hair.

"You need something?" he called out.

There was a slight hesitation. "I… Do you want to come in for a few minutes?"

Hell, yes. Which was exactly why he shouldn't.

"It's been a long day, Taylor." He put his hand on the door handle.

"Oh."

That was all she said. Oh. But he was just stupid enough to hear disappointment in her voice as well as a recognition that it wasn't about the long day at all.

He closed his eyes briefly. This was very likely going to be a big mistake. Huge.

"Maybe just for a minute."

She waited for him, though she had to be nearly freezing by now. She stepped aside as he climbed the steps and went inside to where it was warm. He heard the door shut behind him and fought the urge to turn and kiss her. The desire to take her in his arms was so strong it was nearly overwhelming. Whatever differences they had, the connection between them was undeniable. It made things very complicated.

"Did you need something?" he asked. "I'm pretty handy if something needs fixing."

Taylor slid past him into the living room. He noticed now that the tree was lit up, a beautiful specimen glowing with white lights and red and silver decorations. A few presents were beneath it, wrapped in expensive foil paper with precise red and green bows. "Tree looks good."

"Avery did it before she left."

"I didn't notice it this morning."

She met his gaze and he'd swear she was shy. "It looks different when it's lit up."

"So do you."

He shouldn't have said it. Keeping his mouth shut had never been much of a problem for him before. But there was nothing usual about Taylor, was there? She provoked all kinds of unexpected responses.

"About this morning," she said quietly. "I asked you in tonight because I owe you an apology."

He didn't know what to say. Taylor didn't strike him as the type who apologized. Or at least—

came right out and said it. He recalled the night of the rehearsal dinner, and how Taylor had told Martha that she'd underestimated her. She'd expressed the sentiment in a roundabout way when talking to Rhys. But not a full-on apology.

She came forward and looked up into his eyes. "I was overly sensitive this morning, and I said something I shouldn't have. It's not up to me to judge your life choices. Everyone makes their own decisions for their own reasons and their own happiness. I don't like it when people do it to me, and I shouldn't have done it to you."

He'd respected her intelligence before, admired how capable she was. But this was different. Taylor had a lot of pride. Making a point of saying she was sorry took humility.

"It's a bit of a hot-button with me," he admitted. "I tend to be a bit sensitive about it."

"Why?" She cocked her head a little, and the motion made him smile.

"It's a long and boring story," he said lightly.

"I bet it's not. Which is why you're not talking."

He couldn't help it, he smiled back. It might be easier to stay away if he didn't actually *like* her—

but he did. She was straightforward and honest and made him laugh.

"Listen," she said, her voice soft. "I made cannelloni for dinner and there's enough to share. Have you eaten yet?"

Her lips had some sort of gloss on them that didn't add much color but made them look shiny and plump. He swallowed and dragged his gaze from her mouth back to her eyes. "Um, no."

"Take your boots off, then, and come inside. I promise that I won't poison you."

She said it with one eyebrow raised and her lips curved up in good humor.

He questioned the wisdom of hanging around, and then his stomach rumbled. As Taylor laughed, he took off his boots and left them by the door.

"Bathroom's through there, if you want to wash your hands. I'll dish stuff up."

When he arrived back in the kitchen, the scent of tomato and garlic seduced his nostrils. "That smells so good," he commented, pausing in the doorway.

She'd only left on the under-counter lighting, which cast a warm and intimate glow through the room. A cheery red and green plaid tablecloth covered the table, and she'd lit a couple of stubby candles in the middle.

Suddenly he wondered if he'd fallen very neatly into a trap. And if he actually minded so very much.

"Do you eat like this every night?" he asked casually, stepping into the room.

Taylor blushed. "Confession time, I guess. I planned dinner a little late because I was hoping you'd say yes." She placed a glass casserole dish on a hot mat on the table, then added a bowl of salad and a bottle of white wine. "I thought I'd have some wine, but if you'd prefer something else?"

"Wine is fine. Just a single glass, though." He was trying to decide what he felt about her admission that she'd planned dinner with him in mind. "You wanted me to come to dinner, and yet this morning you were pretty mad about seeing me here."

She hesitated, wine bottle in hand. "You complicate things for me. But I was here today at loose ends, no work to do, no one to talk to. It seemed lonely to eat here alone and I didn't want to go into town again."

"So I'm a chair filler."

"I decided to stop being annoyed with you and enjoy your company instead." She finished pouring the wine.

When she was seated he sat, and reached for the cloth napkin. "What do you do in Vancouver, then? I mean, at meal times?"

It occurred to him that maybe she didn't eat dinner alone. A beautiful woman like her. It was stupid to think she wasn't taken, wasn't it?

She took his plate and served him a helping of the stuffed pasta. "I usually pick up something on my way home. Or I get home so late I just grab something quick in front of the TV before hitting the bed."

"This pace must be a real change for you."

"A bit. Different, but not entirely unwelcome, actually."

She added salad to his plate and handed it back. "I'm very good at what I do, Rhys. I've built the business from the ground up and I'm proud of it. But sometimes I do wonder if I'm missing out on something."

He nearly bobbled his plate. "You're joking, right?"

"Not really." She sighed. "Of course, it's entirely possible I just need a vacation. I haven't taken any time off in a while."

"Since when?"

She served herself and picked up her fork. "Nearly three years. I took a very brief four-day trip to Hawaii. A few days of sun, sand and fruity drinks with umbrellas."

"Four days isn't much time."

"It was what I could manage. It's not like punching a clock and putting in for two weeks of holiday time."

"I know that." He tasted his first bite of cannelloni. Flavor exploded on his tongue—rich, creamy cheese, fresh basil, ripe tomatoes. "This is really good, Taylor. I never knew you could cook."

"My mom taught me."

"Your mom? Really? She strikes me as a society wife. Don't take that the wrong way," he warned. "Your mom seems very nice. But I kind of see her as someone who, I don't know, has things catered. Who outsources."

Taylor nodded. "Sometimes. But growing up— we weren't hurting for money, but we didn't have household staff, either. Mom kept us kids in line, helped with homework, decorated like Martha Stewart and cooked for her own dinner parties. At least until we were much older, and Dad's firm was on really solid ground." She speared a leaf of lettuce. "I learned a lot about my event planning biz from my Mom. She's an organizational whiz."

"Hmm," he mused. "Seems we have something in common after all. While my old man was out taking care of business, my mom held down the fort for me and my brother. I've never met another woman who could make something out of nothing. She worked at the diner during the day, but she was always helping my dad with his ventures."

"What did he do?"

Rhys shrugged. "What didn't he do? He sold insurance for a while, a two-man operation here in Cadence Creek. When that didn't fly, he was a sales rep for some office supply company, traveling all around Alberta. He sold used cars after that if I remember right."

And a bunch of other jobs and schemes that had taken him away more than he was home, and never panned out as he'd hoped. Time and again he'd moved on to something newer and shinier, and financially they'd gone further and further in the hole.

"Sounds industrious," Taylor commented easily, reaching for the wine and topping up her glass.

"Yeah, he was a real go-getter," Rhys agreed, trying very hard to keep the bitterness out of his voice and not doing such a great job. He'd loved his dad but the legacy he'd left behind wasn't the greatest.

She put the bottle down carefully and frowned. "You aren't happy about that, are you?"

He focused on his pasta. "Dad was full of bright ideas and a little fuzzier on the execution. It was my mom who kept her feet on the ground and really provided for us kids. Problem was, every time Dad moved on to something better, he usually left some damage in his wake. Debts he couldn't pay and employees out of a job. It didn't get him the greatest goodwill here, you know? We were lucky that everyone loved my mom. Otherwise maybe we would've been run out of Cadence Creek."

"Surely it wasn't that bad," Taylor said, smiling.

"I know I wasn't supposed to hear, but one day I was passing by the hardware store and I heard these guys outside talking. They called him 'Big Man Bullock' and not in a nice way."

He couldn't look at her. For some reason that single memory had shaped him so much more than any other from his childhood, good and bad. In that moment he'd decided he would never be like his father. Never. Only for a while he had been. He'd let so many people down. It was his biggest regret.

"So that's why you don't want to own your own business? You don't want to fail like your dad did?"

Rhys nodded and stabbed some salad with his fork. "That's exactly why. You said it yourself— you're responsible and can't just take off on a whim. You have other people relying on you." His throat tightened and he cleared the lump away. "You mess up and it's other lives you're affecting, not just your own. I would never want anyone to speak about me the way they were speaking about him that day. My brother and I both left home after high school. It was two less mouths for my mom to try to feed, to be honest."

Silence hummed through the kitchen. It hadn't turned out to be a very pleasant conversation after all. All it had done was stir up things he'd rather forget.

"Well," she said softly. "You're back in Cadence Creek now, and the diner is the heart of this town, and your mom is fabulous. You're steady and reliable, Rhys. There are worse things." She patted his hand. "You don't have to live down your father's reputation. That was his, not yours. You came back to help your mom. Not everyone would do that."

She seemed so sure that she said the right thing as she smiled again and turned back to her meal.

Rhys's appetite, though, shriveled away to nothing as he picked at his food. She had no idea, none at all. Yes, he'd come back when his father died because Martha had needed him. And he'd gone against his instincts and done what she'd asked of him because she was his mother and he couldn't stand the thought of disappointing one more person. He wondered what Taylor would say if she knew he'd gone from one bad venture into immediately investing in another?

He'd come back to Cadence Creek with his tail between his legs. He was more like his old man than anyone knew.

And he hated it.

CHAPTER EIGHT

THEY RETIRED TO the living room after dinner. Taylor made coffee and insisted they leave the dishes. She'd need something to keep her busy tomorrow anyway. Besides, Rhys had turned surprisingly quiet. She wondered what that was about.

"You okay?" she asked, offering him a short-bread cookie.

"Sure, why wouldn't I be?" he responded, taking one from the plate.

"I don't know. You got quiet all of a sudden. After we talked about your dad."

She looked over at him. Despite his relaxed pose, his jaw was tight. "Rhys," she said gently, "did you feel like it was your job to look after everyone after he died?"

"Why are we talking about this?" He shoved the cookie in his mouth, the buttery crumbs preventing him from saying more. But Taylor waited. Waited for him to chew and swallow and wash it down with a sip of coffee.

"Because," she finally answered, "it seems to me you could use a friend. And that maybe, since I'm not from Cadence Creek, I might be a logical choice."

Confusion cluttered his eyes as they met hers. "Do I strike you as the confiding type?"

She smiled. "Maybe you could make an exception. This once."

He seemed to debate for a while. Taylor pulled her knees up toward her chin and sank deeper into the cushions of the sofa, cradling her cup in her hands. How long had it been since she'd spent an evening like this, with a warm cuppa in front of a glowing tree? No files open, no cell phone ringing. Just a rugged cowboy and coffee and cookies.

Simple. And maybe it would bore her in a couple of days, but for right now it was quite heavenly.

"I had my own business once," he confided, staring into his cup. "I had an office based in Rocky Mountain House. I'd wanted to start something away from Cadence Creek, away from my dad's reputation. I was determined to make a go of it, the way he'd never been able to."

She got a sinking feeling about where this was headed. "What kind of business?"

"Feed supplements," he said simply. "I had an office, a couple of office staff and a few reps other than myself who traveled the area to the various ranches. For a while it was okay. Then I started losing money. It got to a point where I wasn't even drawing a salary, just so I could pay my staff. I fell behind on the office rent and we shifted it to run from my house."

His face took on a distant look for a few seconds, but then he gave his head a little shake and it cleared. "It wasn't long before I knew I had to shut it down or declare bankruptcy. Since I didn't want the mark on my credit rating, I closed my doors. My final accounts owing paid my back rent and wages and I got a job as a ranch hand. I got to bring home a paycheck while my employees had to file for Employment Insurance since I laid them off. They had families. Little kids. Mortgages."

"But surely they didn't blame you!"

He shrugged, but the distant look was back.

"A million times I went over what I might have done differently, to manage it better. The jobs I took—working the ranches I used to serve—kept a roof over my head. When my dad died, I quit. Sold the house and moved back here to help my mom."

He opened his mouth and then suddenly shut it again.

Intrigued, she unfolded her legs and sat forward. "What were you going to say?"

"Nothing," he answered, reaching for another cookie from the plate on the coffee table.

"You were going to say something and stopped." She frowned. There was more to this story, wasn't there? Something he didn't want to talk about. Something about coming home.

"You're nosy, you know that?"

She grinned. "I'm a woman. We don't let anything drop."

"You're telling me." He sighed. "Look, let's just say I wasn't a big fan of my mother buying the diner. Running a small business is tough and she's worked hard her whole life. She's over fifty now and working harder than ever."

"You wished she had stuck with working her

shift and going home at the end of the day. Leaving the stress behind."

"Yes."

She understood. He'd felt terrible when his own business had failed. He'd seen the bad reaction from people when his dad had failed. He wanted to spare his mother any or all of that. She got it. She even admired him for his protective streak.

"Some people aren't satisfied with that, Rhys. I wasn't. I wanted to build something. I wanted to know I'd done it and done it on my own. But I understand where you're coming from. I'm responsible for my employees, too. It's a big responsibility, not just financially but morally. At least for most people, I think, and if not it should be. People need to look at their employees like people and not numbers. Even if I wanted to make a change, I know I'm not the only one to consider."

"You thinking of changing?"

The question stirred something uncomfortable inside her. "Nah, not really. Like I said—I'm just overdue for a break, that's all."

She liked it better when they were talking about him. She put her hand on his knee. "You help her a lot, don't you? Around the diner. Fixing things and whatever needs to be done."

He looked away. "Of course I do."

"And you don't get paid."

He hesitated. "I'm not on the payroll, no," he said.

"You're a good man, Rhys."

She meant it. The things he said made perfect sense and only served to complicate her thoughts even more. She was enjoying the downtime too much. She hadn't truly loved the work for a while now, and she was finally admitting it to herself. Sometimes it felt pointless and frivolous, but every time she considered saying it out loud, she heard her father's voice proclaiming that very thing. She was just stubborn enough to not let him be right. Damn the Shepard pride.

Every time she thought about making a change, she was plagued by the realization that it wasn't just her who would be affected. Her employees needed wages. Her landlord was counting on her rent. Suppliers, caterers... All of that would trickle down, wouldn't it? Walking away would be just about the most selfish thing she could do.

They were quiet for a few minutes, until Rhys

finally spoke up. "This business of yours, you've had to fight hard for respect, haven't you?"

"I'm sorry?"

"With your family. Your father's hugely successful, Jack's running what can only be considered an empire and Callum, while way more low-key, has fulfilled the family requirement for a spouse and grandchild. Must be hard standing next to that yardstick."

"I'm doing just fine, thank you." Indignation burned its way to her stomach, making it clench. She wanted to be able to tell him he was dead wrong. Problem was she couldn't.

"Hey, you don't have to tell me that. You're one of the most capable women I've ever met. But seeing your family at the rehearsal dinner, I got the feeling that you had to work just a little bit harder for the same recognition."

"You're a guy. You're not supposed to notice stuff like that."

She put her cup down on the table and folded her hands in her lap.

His voice was low and intimate as he replied, "I only noticed because I can't seem to take my eyes off you whenever you're around."

And there it was. The acknowledgment of whatever this was. Attraction. Curiosity. Carnality.

"I thought we weren't going to do this," she said softly. She kept her hands folded tightly in her lap to keep them from going where they wanted to go—on him. "I'm only here for a few days."

"Then there's no danger. We both know what's what. We're going in with our eyes wide open."

She looked up at him and was caught in his hot, magnetic gaze.

"Since that night in my truck, I can't stop thinking about you," he murmured, reaching out and tucking a piece of hair behind her ear. "I've tried. God knows I've tried." His fingers grazed her cheek and before she could reconsider, she leaned into the touch, the feel of his rough, strong hand against the sensitive skin of her face.

"Are you seducing me, Rhys?" His thumb toyed with her lower lip and her eyes drifted closed.

"With any luck." He moved closer, leaning forward slightly so she began to recline against the cushions. "We're adults," he stated. "We're both wondering. It doesn't have to go any deeper than that."

Tentatively she lifted her hand and touched his

face. "Usually I'm the confident one who goes after what she wants."

He smiled a little, his gaze dropping to her lips. "You don't want this? I could have sworn you did."

"I didn't say that," she whispered, sliding deeper into the cushions.

"That's what I thought." His voice was husky now, shivering along her nerve endings. He leaned closer until he was less than a breath away.

The first kiss was gentle, soft, a question. When she answered it his muscles relaxed beneath her hand and he pressed his mouth more firmly against hers. Her pulse quickened, her blood racing as he opened his mouth and invited something darker, more persuasive. His hand cupped her breast. Her fingers toyed with the buttons of his shirt. He sat up and stripped it off, leaving him in just a T-shirt. She expected him to reach for the hem of her sweater but instead he took it slow, braced himself over top of her and kissed her again. His lips slid along her jaw to her ear, making goose bumps pop out over her skin and a gasp escape her throat.

"I'm in no rush," he whispered just before he

took her lips again, and they kissed, and kissed, and kissed until nothing else in the world existed.

Taylor's entire body hummed like a plucked string. Rhys felt so good, tasted so good, and it had been too long since she'd felt this close to anyone. Yearning and desire were overwhelming, and his leisurely approach had primed her nearly to the breaking point. The words asking him to stay were sitting on her lips when he softened his kiss, gently kissed the tip of her nose, and got up off the sofa.

She felt strangely cold and empty without his weight pressing upon her. Maybe he was going to hold out his hand and lead her down the hall, which would suit her just fine. If he could kiss like that, she would only imagine his lovemaking would be spectacular and...thorough. She swallowed roughly at the thought and got up, ready to take it to the next step.

Except he was reaching for his coat.

Her stomach dropped to her feet while heat rushed to her face. "What...? I mean where...?" She cleared her throat, crossed her arms around her middle, feeling suddenly awkward. "Did I do something wrong?"

He shoved his arms into the sleeves but wouldn't meet her gaze. "Not at all. It's just getting late. I should go."

She wasn't at all sure of herself but she lifted her chin and said the words on her mind anyway. "For a minute there it kind of looked like you weren't going to be leaving."

For a second his hand paused on the tab of the zipper and the air in the room was electric. But then he zipped his coat the rest of the way up. "I don't want to take things too fast, that's all."

Too fast? Good Lord, she was leaving in a matter of days and he was the one who'd said he couldn't stop thinking about her. She wasn't innocent. She knew where this sort of make-out session was headed. And he was putting on the brakes without so much as a warning? Just when she thought she understood him, he did something else that made her wonder who the heck he was.

"What happened to 'we're both grown-ups'?"

Now he had his boots on. One moment they were sprawled on the couch and the next he couldn't get out of there fast enough. What in heaven's name had she done wrong?

"Let me take a rain check, okay?"

This night was getting stranger by the minute. "Rhys?"

He took a step forward and pressed a kiss to her forehead. "It's fine, I promise. I'll see you tomorrow."

Right. Because he'd be here twice. Great.

Still dumbfounded, she heard him say, "Thanks for dinner." Before she could wrap her head around what was going on he was out the door and headed for his truck. He didn't even let it warm up, just got in, started it up and headed out the driveway to the road.

What had just happened?

In a daze she gathered up the cups and the plate of cookies and took them to the kitchen. She expended her pent-up energy by washing the dishes and tidying the supper mess, and then went back to the living room to turn off the Christmas lights, still reeling from his abrupt change of mood.

His cotton shirt was still lying on the floor in a crumpled heap. He'd been in such a hurry to leave he'd forgotten to pick it up. She lifted it from the floor and pressed it to her nose. It smelled of soap and man and aftershave, a spicy, masculine scent that, thanks to the evening's activities, now elicited a physical response in her. Want. Need. Desire.

She stared at it while she brushed her teeth and washed her face. And when she went to bed, she left the penguin pajamas on the chair and instead slid into Rhys's soft shirt. Having the material whisper against her body was the closest she was going to get to Rhys. At least tonight!

But the week wasn't over yet. And she was pretty sure he owed her an explanation.

Rather than drive into Edmonton to shop, Taylor decided to explore the Cadence Creek stores for Christmas gifts. After her conversation with Rhys about running a small business, she felt the right thing to do was to buy local and support the townspeople who made their livelihood here. For Avery and Callum, she bought a beautiful evergreen centerpiece for their table from Foothills Floral. The craft store sold not just yarn but items on consignment, and she bought Nell a gorgeous quilt in pink and blue with patchwork bunnies in each square. The men were a little harder to buy for, but she ended up being delighted at the silversmith, where she purchased both her father and Jack new tie clips and cuff links, the intricate design a testament to the artist's talents.

While she was browsing the handcrafted jewelry, a particular display caught her eye. Beautiful hammered and sculpted silver pendants on sterling chains shone in the morning sunlight. She picked one up, let the weight of it sit on her fingers, a delicate horseshoe with tiny, precise holes where nails would go. She smiled to herself, remembering asking for a lucky horseshoe at the wedding and how Rhys had informed her that a rabbit's foot got rubbed for luck.

He'd amused her, even then when she'd been her most stressed.

She let the pendant go and moved on. She still had her mother's gift to buy and then the groceries for Christmas dinner.

At the drugstore she picked up a gift set of her mother's favorite scent, and hit the grocery store for the turkey and vegetables needed for dinner, loading everything in the trunk of her car. She must have done okay, because the bags nearly filled it to capacity.

The last stop was the bakery, where she figured she could grab something sweet and Christmassy for the holiday dinner and maybe sit and have a coffee and a piece of cake or something.

Anything to avoid going to the Wagon Wheel. She was too afraid of running into Rhys, and she had no idea what to say to him. Sleep had been a long time coming last night. This morning he'd been by early to do the chores, and was already gone when she'd finally crawled out of bed.

The first thing she noticed as she went inside was the welcoming heat. Then it was the smells—rising bread and spices and chocolate and vanilla all mingled together. Browsing the display, she immediately decided on a rich stollen, her mouth watering at the sight of the sugar-dusted marzipan bread. She also ordered a traditional Christmas pudding which came with a container of sauce and instructions for adding brandy.

They were going to have a traditional Christmas dinner, with all of them together for the first time in as long as Taylor could remember.

She was just sitting down to a cup of salted caramel hot chocolate and a piece of cherry strudel when Angela Diamond came in, her cheeks flushed from the cold. She spotted Taylor right away and came over, chafing her hands together and smiling. "Well, hello! I didn't expect to meet you in here this morning."

"I thought I'd do a little shopping before the honeymooners get back. It's hungry work."

"Amen. I like to cook but my talents can't compare to the goodies in here. Do you mind?" She gestured to the chair across from Taylor.

"Of course not! I'd love the company."

Angela sat and took off her gloves. "God, it's cold. I wish a Chinook would blow through and warm things up a bit. What are you having? It looks good."

Taylor laughed. Angela was quite chipper this morning. "Hot chocolate and strudel."

"I'll be right back. I need something decadent."

Angela returned shortly with a cup of chocolate and a plate holding an enormous piece of carrot cake. "I'll tell you a secret," she confided, leaning forward. "Since Avery joined forces with Jean, the quality has gone way up. The specialty in here used to be bread and that's it. Now it's everything."

"I bought a Christmas pudding," Taylor admitted. "It's the first time we've all been together in a long time. I'm thinking turkey and stuffing and the whole works this Christmas." She took a sip of her hot chocolate.

"When are Callum and Avery back?"

"The afternoon of the twenty-third."

"And when do you head back to Vancouver?"

Taylor sighed. "Boxing Day."

Angela put a piece of cake on her fork. "Sounds to me like you're not too excited about it." She popped the cake in her mouth.

"I should be. I've got a ton of work to do and not much time to do it in. Big New Year's party happening. I've left most of the work to my assistant. She's very capable, thank goodness."

"You're not enjoying the project?"

Taylor brushed a flake of strudel pastry off her sweater. "I've been doing this for a while now. When I started, some of the unorthodox requests I got were exciting. And I really liked being creative and working under the gun. But lately—"

She broke off. She really *was* having doubts, wasn't she? And then there was the conversation with Rhys last night. How could she even flirt with the idea of walking away when so many people depended on her?

"Lately what?" Angela asked.

"I think I'm getting jaded or something. Most of the events seem so extravagant and pointless."

"You're looking to create something meaningful."

Taylor put down her mug. She'd never quite thought of it that way. "I suppose I am. This party on New Year's Eve? It's just some rock star throwing cash around and showing off, you know? And it'll be fun and probably make some entertainment news and then it'll be gone twenty-four hours later and no one will remember. Weeks of planning and thousands of dollars for what?" She sighed. "It lasts for a few hours and then it's gone like that." She snapped her fingers.

For a minute the women nibbled at their treats. Then Angela spoke up. "You don't have to give up the business to make a change. Maybe you just need to switch the focus."

"What do you mean?"

Angela shrugged easily, but Taylor knew a sharp mind at work when she saw one. Angela had single-handedly started her own foundation for helping battered women. She was no light-weight in the brains or in the work department, and Taylor knew it would be smart to pay attention to what Angela said.

"Say, for instance, there's a non-profit looking to hold a fund-raiser. The board of this foundation is pretty on the ball, but organizing social events is not where their strongest talent lies."

"You're talking about the Butterfly Foundation."

Angela smiled. "Well, yes, in a way. But we're small. We wouldn't have enough work to keep you going. But there's the housing organization that helped build Stu Dickinson's home after they lost their things in a fire. And many others in any part of the country you choose. I think you'd be very good at it, Taylor."

The idea was interesting, and to Taylor's surprise she didn't dismiss it right away. That told her something.

Angela put down her fork. "Look, I was a social worker before I started Butterfly House and the foundation. I was good at my job but I was frustrated, too, especially as time went on. I'm still using much the same skill set, but I finally started doing something I'm really passionate about—helping abused women get back on their feet. Anyway, think about it. We're going to be planning something for later this spring. I'll give you first crack at the job if you want it. Get your feet wet."

"Thanks," Taylor replied, her mind spinning. "But I can't just up and walk away from what I've built, you know?" It certainly wasn't as easy as putting in two weeks' notice and going on her way.

"Of course." Angela checked her watch. "And I've got to go. I'm picking my son up from a play date in twenty minutes. But I'm really glad we ran into each other."

"Me, too."

Angela got up and slid her gloves back over her fingers. "And merry Christmas, Taylor. To you and your family, if I don't see you again."

"You, too. Say hi to Molly and Clara for me."

After Angela was gone, Taylor sat at the table, her hot chocolate forgotten. Angela had been so right. What was missing from Taylor's job was meaning. It was why she'd been so flustered

about things not being perfect at the wedding—
it had been important to her on a personal level.

Right now she did a job because she was paid
good money to do so. And she had enjoyed the
challenges that went along with the position of
being sought after. But at the end of the day, all
she had left was the satisfaction of a challenge
met. She hadn't given anything back. What Angela suggested, an event like that had the power
to make ripples throughout communities, a difference in peoples' lives. It would matter; last longer
than a single night. Wouldn't that be amazing?

And then Taylor thought of her staff, and her
leases, and the fact that they, too, had lives, and
bills to pay.

Maybe Rhys was on to something after all.
Maybe working nine-to-five was way easier. He'd
just learned his lesson faster than Taylor, that
was all.

But then, he'd been forced to shut down his
company. As Taylor stood and put on her coat
again, she let out a long breath. She didn't have
that worry. Her company was well into the black.
And as long as they stayed there, she was sure
she could find an answer.

CHAPTER NINE

RHYS HOVERED AT the door to the barn, wanting to go to the house, but hesitating just the same. He'd been an idiot last night. It had all been going great. He hadn't even minded talking about the past so much. Maybe Taylor was right. She was an outsider and completely impartial, and it made a difference. She certainly hadn't judged.

But it hadn't just been about talking. Oh, no. Every time he was around her the sensible, cautious part of his brain shut off. The physical attraction was so strong and sitting alone, in front of the tree, with the cozy lighting and the way her eyes shone and her hair smelled...

Yep. He was an idiot. There'd been no room for logic. Just justification for doing what he wanted rather than what was smart.

He'd been ready to take it to the next level when warning bells had gone off in his head. At first it was knowing that he was on the verge of losing control and pushing his advantage, which he made a practice of never doing. Taylor wasn't as ready as she thought she was. It was in the sweetness of her kiss, the tentative way she touched him, the vulnerable look in her eyes. And just like the horses he worked with, he knew she had to be sure. She needed to come to him.

Except she hadn't, not this morning. He'd hung around for a while, hoping to see her at the window or door, but nothing, and he'd been due for work at Diamondback and couldn't stay forever. Now he'd finished the evening chores and the lights were glowing at the house and still there was no sign of her. His hasty exit had probably hurt her feelings, he realized.

But there'd been a second issue, too, and one equally if not more important. He'd known exactly where things were headed and abruptly realized he had absolutely no protection. He was a guy who was generally ready for any eventuality, and he should have had a clue after the way the passion had exploded between them while parked in his truck. But he hadn't. And if he'd let things go any further, he might have been very irresponsible. Might have lost his head and let his body override his brain. He wanted to think he wouldn't, but he wasn't exactly objective when it came to Taylor, for some reason.

So he'd pulled the pin and gotten out. And not exactly gracefully.

It wouldn't happen again. A condom packet was nestled in his back pocket. He'd driven out to the gas station on the highway to buy it, because this town was so damn small that it would be just his luck that he'd be spotted at the drugstore and the rumors would start.

He told himself that the condom was just a contingency plan. He could get in his truck and go back home, or…

Resolutely he left the barn and latched the door behind him, and with his heart beating madly, took long strides to the house. He made no secret of his approach, his boots thumping on the steps and he knocked firmly on the door. Whether this went further or ended, some decisions were going to be made right now. He had to stop thinking of her like some nervous, inexperienced filly, afraid of her own shadow. Taylor Shepard was the most self-assured, confident woman he'd ever met. She knew her own mind.

The door opened and anything he'd considered saying died on his lips.

She looked stunning. She'd left her hair down, the dark mass of it falling in waves past her shoulders. Her jeans hugged her hips and legs like a second skin and the red V-neck shirt was molded to her breasts, clinging to her ribs and giving her the most delicious curves he'd ever seen.

"It's about time you got here," she said softly, holding open the door.

He didn't need any other invitation. He stepped inside and, with his gaze locked with hers, kicked the door shut with his foot. She opened her lips to say something but he caught her around the waist and kissed her, erasing any words she might have uttered. When he needed to come up for air, he released her long enough to shed his jacket and boots.

"Hello to you, too," she said, her voice rich and seductive. "Not wasting any time, I see."

"I'm done wasting time. Aren't you?"

The moment paused as her gaze held his. "I think I am, yes."

It was all the encouragement he needed. As a saucy grin climbed her cheek, he chuckled. And then he reached out, threw her over his shoulder in a fireman carry and headed for the hallway as her laughter echoed off the walls.

It was still dark in the bedroom but Taylor's eyes had adjusted to it and she could see shadows cast by the moonlight streaming through the cracks in the blinds. The dark figure of the dresser, a small chair, a laundry basket.

Rhys, snuggled under the covers beside her, his hair flattened on one side where he'd rested against the pillow.

Her heart slammed against her ribs just looking at him. Not in her wildest dreams had she been prepared for last night. Any impression she'd had of him as…well, she supposed ordinary was as good a word as any…was completely false. He'd been an exciting lover, from the way he'd taken control and carried her to the bedroom, to how he'd managed to scatter their clothes in seconds, to how he'd expertly made love to her.

She swallowed thickly. It had been more than exciting. It had been much, much more. He'd been physical yet gentle, fun yet serious, and he'd made her feel things she'd never felt before in her life. She'd felt beautiful. Unstoppable. Completely satisfied. And in the end, rather than skedaddling home as she expected, he'd pulled up the covers and tucked her securely against him.

She'd felt cherished. More than she'd ever imagined, Rhys Bullock was turning out to be someone very, very amazing. Someone who might actually have the power to chase away some of the ghosts of the past.

His lashes flickered and his lips curved the tiniest bit. "You're staring at me, aren't you?"

Heat climbed her cheeks but she braced up on her elbow and rested her jaw on her hand. "Maybe."

"I can't blame you. I'm really quite handsome."

Her smile grew. Had she really ever thought him plain and unremarkable? There was a humor in the way he set his mouth, the way his eyes glowed that set him apart, wasn't there? And then there was his body. She'd had a good look at it now—all of it. There was nothing plain about Rhys.

"Your ego knows no bounds."

"I'm feeling really relaxed this morning." He opened his eyes. "Why do you suppose that is?"

She dropped her gaze for a moment. "Rhys…" she said shyly.

"Is it okay I stayed all night?"

Her gaze lifted. "Of course it is." She preferred it. Things had happened so quickly. They'd touched and combusted. At least by him staying she didn't get the feeling it was only about the sex.

Which was troubling because there really couldn't be anything more to it, could there?

His hand grazed her hip, sliding beneath the soft sheets. "It was good."

She smiled, bashful again because they were still naked beneath the covers. "Yeah, it was."

For a few minutes his hand lightly stroked and silence filled the room. Taylor wished she could abandon all her common sense and simply slide into his embrace again, but being impulsive wasn't really her way. Last night she'd waited for him. She'd wanted this. But now? It was how to go on from this moment that stopped her up.

"Listen, Rhys…"

"I know what you're going to say." His voice was husky-soft in the dark. "You're going to say there's only the weekend left and Callum and Avery will be back and you'll be going to Vancouver."

Nervousness crawled through her belly. "Yeah, I was going to say that."

"Since we're both aware of that, the way I see it we have one of two choices."

She couldn't help but smile the tiniest bit. Rhys was used to being in charge. Even now, he was taking control of the situation. When they'd first met it had grated on her last nerve. But now not so much. It was kind of endearing.

"Which are?" she asked.

"Well, I could get out of bed and get dressed and do the chores and we could say that this is it. No sense going on with something that's going to end in a few days anyway."

"That sounds like a very sensible approach."

"Thank you."

She might have believed him, except his fingers started kneading the soft part of her hip. She swallowed, trying to keep from rolling into the caress. "And the second?"

"I'm glad you asked. The second option, of course, is that we enjoy this for however long it lasts and go our inevitable separate ways with the memory of the best Christmas ever."

"Not as sensible, but it sounds like a lot more fun."

"Great minds think alike."

The smile slid from her face as she turned serious, just for a moment. "Do you think it's possible to do that?" she whispered.

Dark eyes delved into hers. "I'm not ready to say goodbye yet. I don't see as we have much choice."

She slid closer to him until they were snuggled close together, skin to skin. She hadn't counted on someone like Rhys. She'd thought she'd come here, watch her brother get married, recharge, go back to her life. Instead she was...

She blinked, hoping he didn't notice the sudden moisture in her eyes. She would never say it out loud. Couldn't. But the truth was, she suspected she was falling in love. She recognized the rush. The fear. The exhilaration. Something like that only happened once in a while, and it had been a long, long time for Taylor. It wasn't just sex. She had real feelings for Rhys. Saying goodbye wasn't going to be easy.

"Can I ask you something?"

"Sure." He, too, braced up on an elbow, more awake now.

"Why did you leave so fast the other night?"

"Oh, that." He smiled, but it had a self-deprecating tilt to it that she thought was adorable. "Truth is, things were happening really fast. And you caught me unprepared."

That was it? Birth control? She suppressed a giggle, but a squeak came out anyway. "You could have just said that," she chided. "Instead of rushing out like you couldn't stand being near me another moment."

"Is that what you thought?" His head came off his hand.

"Maybe."

He leaned forward and kissed her lightly. "Nothing could be further from the truth. If I was in a hurry, it was because I was in danger of not caring if I had a condom or not."

Her heart turned over. She wondered if he realized how much he truly tried to protect those around him.

"Now, as much as I'd like to repeat last night's

performance, I've got cows that need to be milked," Rhys said quietly.

"And then what?" She lifted her chin and looked into his eyes. The dark light was turning grayer as the night melted into day, highlighting his features more clearly.

"It's Saturday. I'm not due at Diamondback. I'm not expected anywhere, as a matter of fact."

"Then come back in for breakfast," she invited. "I'll make something good."

"You got it." He slid out of bed and she watched as he pulled on jeans and a T-shirt. He turned and gave her a quick kiss. "Look, I'll be a while. Go back to sleep."

"Okay."

He was at the doorway when he turned and looked back at her. "You look good like that," he said softly, and disappeared around the corner while her heart gave a little flutter of pleasure.

They had the weekend. She rather suspected a weekend wouldn't be nearly enough.

After breakfast Rhys went back home to shower and grab fresh clothing. In his absence Taylor also showered and did her hair and put on fresh makeup. She vacuumed the rugs and tidied the kitchen and wondered if he'd bring his things to stay the night. When he arrived again midmorning, he carried a bag with him containing extra clothes and toiletries.

Seeing the black case brought things into rather clear perspective. Their intentions were obvious. There was no need for either of them to leave the house now.

After a rather pleasurable "welcome back" interlude, they spent the rest of the day together. Rhys helped Taylor wrap the presents she'd bought the day before, cutting tape, tying ribbon and sticking a red and gold bow on top of her head while making a lewd suggestion. She made soup and grilled cheese and the long awaited Chinook blew in, raising the temperature and softening the snow. They went outside and built a snowman, complete with stick arms, a carrot for a nose, and rocks for the eyes and mouth. That event turned into a snowball fight, which turned into a wrestling match, which ended with the two of them in a long, hot shower to ward off any damp chill.

He did chores. She made dinner. They curled

up in front of the television to watch a broadcast of White Christmas while Rhys complained of actors feeling the need to sing everything and Taylor did a fair impression of the "Sisters" song. And when it was time, they went together to Taylor's room.

By Monday morning Taylor's nerves were shredded. The weekend had been nothing short of blissful but in a few hours Callum would be home and her time with Rhys would be over. There was no question in her mind—her feelings for Rhys were real.

But what hope did they have? He would never be happy living in a city like Vancouver, and she could tell by the way he spoke and how he'd acted since they'd met that he wanted to stay close to his mother to look after her. She realized now that his desire to hold a steady job rather than being the boss was all about taking care of his family. What she'd initially seen as complacency was actually selfless and noble. From what she could gather, his need to care for Martha was, in part, a way to make up for the instability in her past.

He'd hold things together the way his father never had—no matter how well-intentioned.

Despite Angela's ideas, Taylor couldn't see any way to avoid going home either. She had commitments and responsibilities at *Exclusive!* This was nothing new. She just hadn't expected that even the thought of leaving him would cause the ache she was feeling in her chest right now.

"Hey," he said softly, coming up behind her. She was standing at the kitchen window, looking out over the fields. "You look like you're thinking hard."

"Just sad the weekend's over, that's all."

"Me, too."

She turned to embrace him and noticed his bag by the kitchen door. "You're leaving already?"

"It's Monday. I'm due back at Diamondback, remember? I should have been there an hour ago."

Right. His job. Time hadn't stood still, had it? "You're working today?"

"And tomorrow."

Emptiness opened up inside her. This was really it then. She might not even see him again before her flight out on the twenty-sixth.

"Rhys..."

"Don't," he said firmly. "We both knew what this was from the start."

Dread of losing him sparked a touch of anger. Was she so easy to forget? So easy to leave—again? "And you're okay with that? Just a couple of days of hokey pokey and see you later, it's been fun?"

He gripped her upper arms with strong fingers. "We weren't going to do this, remember?"

"Do what?"

"Get involved."

"I am involved. Up to my neck, as it happens."

"Taylor."

He let go and stepped back, his dark eyes clouded with confusion. He ran a hand through his hair. "I should never have come back. I should have left well enough alone."

"You didn't. We didn't. I don't know how to say goodbye gracefully, Rhys."

To her chagrin she realized tears were running down her face. She swiped them away quickly. "Dammit," she muttered.

He came closer, looked down at her with a tenderness in his eyes that nearly tore her apart. "Hey, we both knew it would come to this. My life's here. Yours is there. You have *Exclusive!* to run."

Yes, yes, the damn business. When had she started resenting it so much? Even a quick check of her email on her phone this morning had made her blood pressure spike. She couldn't ignore reality forever. Didn't mean it didn't stink, though.

"Thanks for the reminder." She stepped back, wished she had something to occupy her hands right now.

Rhys frowned. "Look, Taylor, we both know you're competitive and a bit of a perfectionist. I like those things about you. I really do. But I also know that the drive and determination that made you so successful is going to keep you in Vancouver until you set out to do what you've wanted to achieve."

"Even if what I'm doing isn't making me happy?"

It was the first time she'd come right out and said it.

His frown deepened. "The only person who can decide that is you. But I'll caution you right now. Letting go of that goal isn't easy. There are a lot of things to accept. And I'm not sure you'd be happy walking away."

"And if I did walk away, would you be here waiting?"

Alarm crossed his features. She had her answer before he ever opened his mouth, didn't she? Oh, she should have listened to what he'd said ages ago when they'd first kissed. She was different from local girls, and she was low risk because she wasn't staying. The idea of her not going was scaring him to death.

"Look, Taylor..."

"No, it's okay," she assured him. "You're right. This was what we agreed and I don't have any regrets." That, at least, was the truth. She didn't regret the last few days even if there were mixed feelings and a fair bit of hurt. They'd been magical when all was said and done. And Rhys Bullock would be a nice memory, just like he said.

He came forward and tilted up her chin with his finger. "I know I'm where I belong. I learned my lessons, had my failures and successes. You're not there yet, that's all."

She pulled away, resenting his attitude. What did he know? She had her own failures, but she was glad now that she'd kept the baring of her soul to one messed up wedding and not the disaster that was her last relationship. "You're leaving anyway, Rhys. I'd appreciate it if you weren't patronizing."

The air in the room changed. There was a finality to it that had been absent only moments before. Rhys went to the doorway and picked up his bag. Silently he went to the door and pulled on his boots and jacket. When he was ready he looked up and met her eyes. "I don't want to leave it this way," he said bleakly. "With us angry at each other."

"I'm not angry," she said quietly. "I'm hurting, and the longer you stay, the worse it is."

He stepped forward and pulled her into his arms for one last hug. "Hurting you is the last thing I wanted to do," he murmured in her ear. "So I'll go." He kissed the tip of her ear. "Take care, Taylor."

She swallowed against the lump of tears and willed herself to stay dry-eyed. "You, too, Rhys. And Merry Christmas."

He nodded and slipped out the door. The milder temperatures of the Chinook had dipped slightly and she could see his breath in the air as he jogged down the steps and to his truck.

She shut the door, resisting the opportunity to give him one last wave.

They'd set the ground rules. Leaving was supposed to be easy. It definitely was not supposed to hurt this much.

CHAPTER TEN

CALLUM AND AVERY arrived back home, happy and tired from their trip and with tons of pictures from Hawaii. Taylor found herself bathing Nell after dinner while Callum checked on the stock and Avery started to make a dent in the mountain of laundry from their luggage. When Taylor suggested she go back to the B&B for the next few nights, Avery insisted she stay. "The couch pulls out. Please, stay. I've missed having a sister around."

Taylor had no good argument against that so at bedtime the cushions came off the sofa and the mattress pulled out. Avery brought sheets from the linen closet. "Sorry it's not as comfortable as our bed," she apologized.

A lump formed in Taylor's throat. Memories she wished she could forget crowded her mind, images of the last few nights spent in the master bedroom. This morning she'd stripped the bed and put the sheets in the washer. Rhys's scent had risen from the hot water and she'd had to go for a tissue.

"Taylor, are you okay?"

"Fine," she replied. "Hand me that comforter, will you?"

Avery handed it over while putting a pillowcase on a fat pillow. "Callum said Rhys did fine with the stock. Did you see him much while he was here?"

Taylor met Avery's innocently curious gaze, watched as her expression changed in reaction to Taylor's. "What's wrong? Did something happen with Rhys?"

Taylor focused on tucking the bedding around the mattress. "Of course not."

"Taylor." Avery said it with such meaning that Taylor stopped and sat down on the bed.

Avery came over and sat beside her. "I saw you dancing at the reception. And Callum said Jack said something to him about you and Rhys kissing in his truck the night of the rehearsal. There's something going on between you, isn't there?"

"Not anymore," she replied firmly. She wondered if she sounded convincing.

Callum came through to the kitchen carrying an empty baby bottle. "Hey, what's going on?"

Avery looked up at him. "Girl talk. No boys allowed."

Taylor saw her brother's expression as he looked down at his wife. He was utterly smitten. Having someone look at her that way hadn't been so important even a month ago. Now it made her feel like she was missing out on something.

"Who am I to get in the way of my two favorite girls?" he asked, then looked down at the bottle with a stupidly soft expression. "Well, two of my three favorites anyway."

Callum knew where he belonged. He was contented, just like Rhys. So why was it so hard for her to figure out?

"I'll leave you ladies alone, then. Gotta be up early anyway."

When he disappeared back around the corner, Avery patted Taylor's arm. "Wait here," she commanded, and she skipped off to the kitchen. She returned moments later carrying two glasses of wine. "Here," she said, handing one to Taylor. "Sit up here, get under the blanket and then tell me how you managed to fall in love with Rhys Bullock within a week."

"How did you know?" Taylor asked miserably.

Avery laughed. "Honey, it's written all over your face. And as an old married woman, I demand to know all the details." She patted the mattress. "Now spill."

Christmas Eve arrived, along with Callum and Taylor's parents and Jack, back from Montana bearing presents and a strained expression. His trip hadn't gone all that well, as the manager for his corporate retreat business had been in an accident, leaving no one to run things at his Montana property. He was going to have to go back down there right after Christmas instead of taking the break he'd planned.

But nothing kept Jack down for long, and as they all gathered in Callum's small house laughter rang out in the rooms.

"I wish we had room for everyone here," Avery mourned.

"The bed and breakfast is lovely, don't you worry," Susan assured her. "And Harry and I have a surprise for you. We're taking you all out for Christmas Eve dinner."

A strange sort of uneasiness settled in Taylor's stomach. Please let her say it was out of town and not at the diner...

Susan went on happily. "You two just got back from your honeymoon and you're hosting us all tomorrow for Christmas. Tonight someone else is going to worry about the cooking. It's all arranged. Martha Bullock is doing up a prime rib for us and then we'll go to the Christmas Eve service."

Oh, God. The Wagon Wheel? Really?

Taylor pasted a smile on her face. "Surely the diner closes early on Christmas Eve?"

Harry shrugged. "Mrs. Bullock said it would be no trouble, especially for just the six of us."

Avery caught sight of Taylor's face and jumped in. "What a lovely thought. But really, we can have something here. There's no need..."

"Are you kidding?" Jack interrupted. "Prime rib? I've been living on sandwiches for a week. I'm so there."

Avery looked over at Taylor. What could she

say? Besides, there was no guarantee that Rhys would be there. It was Christmas Eve after all.

She gave a short nod. "Sounds good to me," she answered, trying to inject some enthusiasm into her voice. This great Shepard family Christmas wasn't going to be brought down by her bad mood.

During the afternoon everyone brought out their presents and put them under the tree, which was a major source of frustration to Nell, who got sick of the word *no* as she crawled through the living room and pulled herself up on the chair next to the decorated spruce. She went down for an afternoon nap and everyone relaxed with a fresh batch of one of Avery's latest creations— eggnog cupcakes—and hot spiced cider. It was supposed to be perfect. Magical. And instead Taylor could only think about two things—the work waiting for her back in Vancouver, and how much she missed Rhys.

Jack pulled up a footstool and sat beside her, bringing his mug with him. "You're awfully quiet today. What's going on?"

She shrugged. "Too long away from the city, I guess."

He nodded. "Can I ask you something?"

"Sure." Jack and Taylor were the most alike in her opinion. He tended to see the big picture in much the same way that she did. And they were the ones still single now, too.

"Are you happy, sis?"

The question surprised her. "What do you mean?"

He raised an eyebrow. "I recognize the look on your face."

Oh, Lord. If he guessed about Rhys she was going to wish for the floor to open up and swallow her.

"I saw it when I first got here, when you were planning the wedding," he continued. "How's business?"

"Booming," she replied.

"And how do you feel about that?"

She met his gaze. "What do you mean?"

Jack hesitated for a minute. "A few years ago, remember when the company expanded? New franchises opened up, and Shepard Sports launched south of the border. It was all very exciting, right?"

"Dad was ready to burst his buttons with pride."

"I wasn't. It was everything I'd worked for and yet...do you know what ended up making me happiest?"

Curious now, she leaned forward. "What?"

"The property I bought in Montana. The corporate retreat and team-building business. The sporting goods, well they're like numbers on a page. Units in and out. Sure, we do some special work with schools and organizations and that sort of thing. But it's just selling. The team building stuff, though, it's about people. I like that. I like meeting different people and finding out more about them. I like seeing groups come in and leave with a totally different dynamic. They come in and push themselves in ways they don't expect, which was the very best thing I liked about competing."

"That's really cool, Jack."

"I know. And because of it, I can look at you and see that what you're doing isn't giving you that same buzz. Something's missing."

"I've been doing some thinking," she admitted. "But you know what it's like. The bigger you get the bigger the responsibility. You can't just pull up and abandon what's already there."

Jack nodded. "There's always a way. And anyway, you've got good people working for you. You've been gone quite a while and everything's run in your absence, hasn't it?"

It had. Sometimes a little too well. Even when trouble popped up, a quick email giving her assistant the green light to solve the problem was all it took.

"Just think about it," Jack said. "Responsibility or not, there's no sense doing something if you're not happy at it."

"Thanks," she answered, taking a drink of cider. She was glad he hadn't assumed her reticence was caused by a man. That would have been a whole other conversation. Then Avery called her to the kitchen to taste Susan's recipe for cranberry sauce and the afternoon passed quickly.

They arrived en masse at the Wagon Wheel at six on the dot. A sign on the door stated that Christmas hours went to 5:00 p.m. on the twenty-fourth and closed on Christmas Day and Boxing Day. Just as she thought, Martha had stayed open for their family and Taylor was a bit upset at her parents for requesting it. Martha had family of her own, probably had plans too.

Inside was toasty-warm and two tables were pushed together to make plenty of room for the six of them plus the high chair for Nell. Nell was dressed in soft red pants and a matching red velour top with tiny white snowflakes on it. After her nap she was energized, tapping a toy on the tray of the high chair and babbling at the blinking tree lights. Taylor was laughing at her antics when a movement in the kitchen caught her eye. It was Rhys, dressed in one of Martha's aprons, taking the roast out of the oven to rest.

He was here. Her stomach tangled into knots and her mouth felt dry. They hadn't seen each other or spoken since the morning they'd said goodbye. From the strained expression on his face, he wasn't too happy about tonight, either. As if he could sense her staring, he looked up and met her eyes across the restaurant. She looked away quickly, turning to answer a question of her mother's about the upcoming event her company was planning.

Martha brought them all glasses of iced water and placed a basket of hot rolls in the center of the table. That was followed by a fresh romaine salad with red onion, peppers and mandarins in a poppy seed dressing that was delicious. Rhys stayed in the kitchen, out of everyone's way. The fact that he seemed to be avoiding her stretched her nerves taut, and by the time the main course was served she was a wreck.

Martha had outdone herself. Glazed carrots, green beans with bacon, creamy mashed potatoes and puffy Yorkshire pudding and gravy complemented the roast, followed by a cranberry bread pudding and custard sauce. By the time the plates were cleared away, Taylor was stuffed to the top. Her father checked his watch. "Seven-fifteen. We'd better get going," he announced. "The church service starts in fifteen minutes."

Everyone got up to leave, reaching for coats and purses and gloves. Everyone but Taylor. They really didn't see, did they? She'd bet ten bucks that Martha and Rhys probably wanted to go to church, too. According to Callum, most of the community showed up at the local Christmas Eve services. And the Bullocks were going to be stuck here cleaning up the mess instead of enjoying their holiday.

"Taylor, aren't you coming?"

"I'll be along," she said lightly. "You go on without me."

Avery gave her a long look, then a secret thumbs-up. Taylor returned a small smile, but it was quickly gone once the Shepard crew hit the door.

She went back to the table and started clearing dessert plates and coffee cups.

Martha hustled out from the kitchen. "Oh, heavens, girl, don't you worry about that! You head on to church with your family."

"What about you? Aren't you planning to go to church?"

Martha looked so dumbfounded that Taylor knew she had guessed right. "If I help it'll get done faster and we can all make it."

"Bless your heart."

"Where's Rhys?" Taylor looked over Martha's shoulder into the kitchen.

"He just took a bag of trash to the Dumpster out back. I swear I don't know what I'd do without that boy. He always says we're in this together, but he's got his own job." She handed Taylor the bin of dirty dishes and briskly wiped off the tables. "It was more than enough that he invested in this place for me. He's supposed to be a silent partner, but not Rhys. He thinks he needs to take care of me."

Taylor nearly dropped the pan of dishes. Silent partner? But Rhys was so determined to stay away from owning a business. How many times had he gotten on her case about it? And this whole time he was part owner in the diner and just neglected to mention it?

For the briefest of moments, she was very, very angry at him. How dare he judge her? And maybe he hadn't exactly lied, but he hadn't been truthful, either.

She remembered pressing him for something he'd been going to say. Now she got the feeling he'd almost let his stake in the diner slip while they'd been talking, and caught himself just in time.

"Rhys is part owner of the diner?"

Martha looked confused. "He didn't tell you? I mean, he doesn't say much about it, but I thought the two of you…" Her cheeks flushed. "Oh. I've put my foot in it."

Taylor shook her head. "Not at all. We're not…"

But she didn't know how to finish that sentence. They weren't together but they weren't *not* together, either.

"I'm sorry to hear that," Martha said quietly, putting her hand on Taylor's arm. "You've been real good for him these last few weeks. And I think he's been good for you, too. You smile more. Your cheeks have more color. If I'm wrong tell me to mind my own business."

"You're not exactly wrong."

"He's needed someone like you, Taylor. Not that he's said a word to me about it." Her lips twitched. "He's not exactly the confiding type. Bit like his father that way."

Taylor knew that Rhys probably wouldn't like that comparison.

"My husband had his faults, but he always meant well. And he loved his family. I wish you were staying around longer, Taylor. You're a good girl. Not afraid to work hard. And I can tell your family is important to you."

She was perilously close to getting overemotional now. "Thanks, Martha. That means a lot to me. And Rhys is a good man. I know that. I'm sorry things can't work out differently."

The back door to the kitchen slammed and he came back in. A light snowfall had begun and he shook a few flakes off his hair. Their gazes met again and she fought to school her features. She should be angrier that he hadn't been totally honest, but instead all she could think of was how he had said he didn't want his mom to own the place. He'd gone against his own instincts and wishes to make her happy, hadn't he? Did Martha realize what a personal sacrifice he'd had to make?

They couldn't get into this now, if for no other reason than Martha was there and she should talk to him about it in private.

She marched the dishes into the kitchen. "Should I put these in the dishwasher?"

"What are you still doing here?"

"Helping. I thought you and your mom might like to go to the service."

"Then maybe you shouldn't have requested a private dinner after we closed."

Guilt heated her cheeks at his condemning tone. "I didn't know about that until it was a done deal.

Avery even suggested they do something at home but my parents insisted."

"Really? It kind of struck me as exactly the kind of thing you'd be comfortable asking for. You know, like when you're planning an event and you just 'make things happen.' Right?"

"Are you really that mad at me, Rhys?" She tried to muster up some annoyance, some justifiable anger, but all she felt was a weary sadness.

He shoved a cover on the roaster and placed it—none too gently—in the commercial fridge. "I don't know what I am. I know my mom is tired and was looking forward to a quiet Christmas Eve. Instead she ended up here after hours."

"None of the staff would stay?"

"She insisted they go home to their families. It's their holiday, too." His voice held a condemning edge that made her feel even worse.

He really was put out and honestly she didn't blame him. She hurried to put the dishes in the dishwasher while Martha put the dining room back to rights. "So you helped."

"Of course I did."

Yes, of course he did, because this wasn't just Martha's diner but his, too. "I'm sorry, Rhys. My parents didn't think. What can I do now? Can we still make it to the church?"

"Run the dishwasher while I finish up these pots and pans. We'll be a little late, and not very well dressed, but we'll get there."

Martha bustled back into the kitchen, either too busy or simply oblivious to the tension between Rhys and Taylor. "My goodness, you're nearly done in here. Rhys, let's just leave the sweeping up and stuff until Boxing Day. It's always slower then anyway."

"If that's what you want."

Martha grinned. "Well, what I want is to get a good dose of Christmas carols and candlelight, followed by a double dose of rum in my eggnog."

Taylor laughed. "Get your coat while I start this up."

Martha disappeared into the office. Rhys frowned at Taylor. "Why did you stay? You could have gone on with your family and been there with time to spare."

She shrugged. "Because tonight isn't about just my family. There are other people to consider, too." She tilted her head to look at him. "Why didn't Martha just say no when my father asked?"

What little softening she'd glimpsed in his expression disappeared as his features hardened. "Your father offered a Christmas tip she couldn't refuse."

Taylor winced. Her dad, Jack, her—they were all used to getting what they wanted. It simply hadn't occurred to her father that Martha would say no. And it wasn't that he was mean or unfeeling. Of course he would consider it fair to properly compensate Martha for the inconvenience.

But she rather wished he hadn't inconvenienced the Bullocks at all. It would have been more thoughtful.

"I'm sorry, Rhys. Can we leave it at that and get your mom to the church?"

His gaze caught hers for a prolonged moment. In that small space of time she remembered what it was to hear him laugh, taste his kiss, feel his body against hers. It had happened so fast, and now here they were, as far apart as ever. Trying to keep from being hurt any more than they already were.

"You'd better get your coat. You can drive over with us."

She rushed to grab her coat and purse and by

the time she was ready Rhys was warming up Martha's car and Martha was shutting off the lights to the diner and locking the door. The parking lot at the church was packed and inside wasn't any better; the only seats were on the two pews pushed against the back wall. Taylor spied her family, several rows up, but the pew was full from end to end. She squeezed in with the Bullocks, sitting on one side of Rhys while his mother sat on the other. As the congregation sang "The First Noel" she realized that while everyone here was dressed up in their best clothes, Rhys wore jeans and Martha wore her standard cotton pants and comfortable shoes from work.

It didn't seem fair.

They turned the pages of their hymnbook to "Once in Royal David's City." It was less familiar to Taylor, and Rhys held out the book so she could see the words better. Their fingers never touched, but there was something about holding the book together that healed the angry words of before. When they finally sat down, Taylor took advantage of the hushed scuffle. "I'm sorry," she said, leaning toward his ear. "I really am."

The minister began to speak and she heard the

words "Let us pray," but she couldn't. Rhys was staring down into her eyes and she couldn't look away. Not now. She wanted to tell him how much she hated the way they'd left things. Wanted to ask him why he'd never told her the truth about the diner. Wanted to kiss him and know that she hadn't just imagined their connection. Instead she sat in a candlelit church that smelled of pine boughs and perfume, the fluid voice of the minister offering a prayer of thanks for the gift of Christmas, and wondered at the miracle that she'd managed to fall utterly and completely in love for the first time in her life.

Her lower lip quivered the tiniest bit and she looked away. What was done was done.

And then Rhys moved his hand, sliding it over to take hers, his fingers tangling with her fingers. Nothing had really changed, and there was a bittersweet pain in her heart as she acknowledged the truth of that. At least he wasn't angry at her anymore.

During the sermon Taylor looked around at the people gathered to celebrate the holiday. Her big brother cuddling a sleeping Nell in the crook of his arm. Her parents sat in between with Jack

on the other side and Amy Wilson beside him—
an odd surprise. There was the whole Diamond
clan—Molly, Sam, Angela, Clara, Ty, the kids.
Melissa Stone and her fiancé, Cooper Ford, sitting with two older couples she assumed were
their parents. Many others she recognized as
guests from the wedding. Business people, pro-
fessionals, ranchers. Ordinary folks. This was
real. This was life. Not the glammed-up high-
paced craziness she was used to living in. Somehow, between Clara's sunny generosity, Angela's
steady advice and Martha's ready acceptance
she'd managed to become a part of this town instead of remaining on the fringes, where she usually made it a policy to stay.

She'd changed. And she couldn't find it within
herself to be the least bit sorry.

As if she could sense her thoughts, Angela Diamond turned in her seat and caught Taylor's eye.
She smiled and turned back around.

For the first time ever that she could remember, Taylor had no idea what to do next.

An usher brought around a box with tiny white
candles in plastic holders. As the service ended,
the choir started with the first verse of "Silent

Night" as the minister went along and lit the first candle on the end of each pew. The congregation's voices joined in for the second verse as Rhys leaned over a little and let the flame from his candle ignite hers. Soon they were all standing with their candles, singing the last verse as the piano stopped playing and there was no sound but two hundred voices singing the age-old carol a cappella.

It was the most beautiful Christmas tradition Taylor had ever seen.

And when the song ended, everyone blew out their candles, the minister gave the benediction and a celebratory air took over the sanctuary.

In the midst of the confusion, Rhys leaned over. "Are you staying at the house or the B&B?"

"At the house." She waved at someone she only half recognized and smiled. "Callum and Avery insisted. I got the sofa bed."

Rhys's dark complexion took on a pinkish hue. She shouldn't have mentioned sleeping arrangements.

"Can I drive you home?"

"What about your mom?"

"I'll take her now and come back for you."

She wasn't at all sure what she wanted. She had no idea where things stood or even where she wanted them to stand. And yet they both seemed determined to play this out for as long as possible.

"I'll wait."

He gave her a quick nod and turned to Martha. The older woman had clearly decompressed during the service, and now she looked tired. It didn't look like Rhys was going to have much fight on his hands, getting her to leave.

There was a lot of socializing happening in the vestibule. Avery and Callum were working on getting Nell into her snowsuit without waking her up and the other three Shepards were putting on their coats and wishing a Merry Christmas to anyone who stopped by and offered a greeting. Susan saw Taylor and frowned. "You don't have your coat on! We're nearly ready to leave."

"I'll be along a little later."

"But you didn't bring your car."

Callum joined the group, a blurry-eyed, half-awake Nell fully dressed and snuggled into his shoulder. "We ready to go? Santa will be along soon."

"I was just telling Taylor to get her coat."

Taylor let out a breath and smiled brightly. "I've got a lift home, actually. No worries. You go on ahead."

"A lift home?"

"Rhys is going to drive me."

"I just saw him leave with his mother."

Taylor resisted the need to grit her teeth. "He's coming back."

Harry stepped in. "Rhys. He was one of Callum's groomsmen, right? Is there something going on there?"

Avery looked panicked on Taylor's behalf and Callum's brows were raised in brotherly interest but it was Jack, bless him, who stepped in, Amy Wilson hanging back just a bit, as if she was uncertain whether to join the group or not. "Hey, Dad, I've been meaning to ask you something about a new property I'm interested in buying."

The topic of a property investment was enough to lure her father away and Taylor relaxed. "Don't worry," she said to her mother. "We'll be right behind you."

"You've got your phone?"

Taylor laughed. "Of course."

"We'll see you in a bit, then." She hurried off in the direction of Jack and Harry. Avery came over and gave her a hug. "We're off, too. Good luck."

"Thanks."

As Avery and Callum walked away, Taylor heard Callum say, "Good luck? What do you know about this, wife?"

The vestibule thinned out until there were just a handful of people left. Jack got their parents on their way and came back for Amy, offering her a lift home. They'd just turned out of the lot when Taylor saw Rhys pull back into the yard in his truck.

Her boots squeaked in the snow as she crossed the parking lot, opened the door and hopped up inside the cab. She wasn't sure what to say now, so silence spun around them as he put the truck in Drive and headed out of the parking lot.

"I'm sorry I was so hard on your family." He finally spoke when they hit the outskirts of town.

"Don't be. You were right. About a lot of things."

"Such as?"

"Such as this is exactly something I probably

would have done. Like you said, I make things happen. That's my job."

"I shouldn't have said that, either."

She chuckled then. "Boy, we can even turn an apology into an argument. We're good."

He laughed, too, but it didn't do much to lighten the atmosphere in the truck.

"So you're really going day after tomorrow."

"Yeah."

More silence.

It was only a short drive to the farm. Taylor longed to ask him about the diner but didn't want to get in another argument and she sensed it would be a sensitive subject. Besides, what did it truly matter now? It really didn't change anything.

The damnedest thing was that she did want something to change. And she couldn't figure out what or how. She just knew it felt wrong. Wrong to leave here. Wrong to say goodbye.

"You've got a couple days off from Diamondback?"

"Yeah," he answered. "Actually Sam suggested we all take Friday off, too, so I don't actually have to be back to work until Monday. I thought

I'd sneak Mom to Edmonton one of those days, let her take in some of the Boxing Week sales."

"You're good to your mom, Rhys. She appreciates you, you know."

"Someone has to look out for her. She's my mom. She doesn't have anyone else."

It made even more sense now, knowing he had a stake in the Wagon Wheel. "You're very protective of the people you care about."

"Is that a bad thing?" He slid his gaze from the road for a moment.

"On the contrary. It's one of the things I l…like most about you."

Yeah, she'd almost said "love." She took a deep breath. This would be a stupid time to get overly emotional, wouldn't it?

They turned onto Callum's road. "The thing is, Taylor…"

"What?"

He frowned. "You're competent. Everyone can see that. You're confident and successful and clearly you know how to run a business. I don't know why you feel you have to prove yourself. Why you have this chip on your shoulder."

"Sometimes I ask myself the same thing, Rhys."

She turned in her seat. "Remember the time you said that most guys were intimidated by smart women? You had something there. There's a lot I don't know and more I'm not good at, but I'm not stupid. I've never understood why I should hide that fact just because I'm a woman."

"So you push yourself."

"Yeah. I guess if this trip has shown me anything, though, it's that I don't need to try so much. That…" She swallowed, hard. "That there are things more important that I've maybe been missing out on. In the past I haven't paid enough attention to personal relationships." She sighed. "I've made my share of screw-ups."

"Figuring that out is a good thing, right?"

"To be honest, it's been a little bit painful."

They pulled into Callum's driveway. Rhys parked at the far side, giving them a little space away from the house, and killed the lights.

"Sometimes the best lessons we learn are the ones that hurt the most."

She laughed a little. "Helpful."

But he reached over and took her gloved hand in his. "I mean it, Taylor. My mother told me once that we rarely learn anything from our successes, and the best teachers are our failures. It hurts, but I have to believe it always comes out better on the other side." He squeezed her fingers. "I wish you didn't have to go."

She wanted to say "me, too," but it would only make things worse, wouldn't it? Why wish for something that wasn't going to happen?

"Right. Well. Before you go in…I uh…" He cleared his throat. "I saw this earlier in the week and…"

He reached into his pocket and held out a small rectangular box. "Merry Christmas."

"You got me a present?"

"It's not much."

"Rhys, I…"

"Don't open it now, okay? Let's just say goodnight and Merry Christmas."

She tucked the package into her purse. "Merry Christmas," she whispered, unbuckling her seat belt.

She looked up into his face. How had she ever thought it wasn't handsome? It was strong and fair and full of integrity and sometimes a healthy sense of humor. Before she could change her mind she pushed against the seat with one hand, just enough to raise her a few inches so she could touch her lips to his. The kiss was soft, lingering, beautiful and sad. It was the goodbye they should have had yesterday morning. It filled her heart and broke it in two all at the same time.

"Goodbye, Rhys."

She slid out of the truck before she could change her mind. Took one step to the house and then another. Heard the truck engine rev behind her, the creak and groan of the snow beneath the tires as Rhys turned around and drove away for the last time.

She took a few seconds on the porch to collect herself. She didn't want her family to see her cry or ask prying questions. She had to keep it together. Celebrate the holiday the way she'd intended—with them all together and happy. And if she had to fake it a little bit, she would. Because she was starting to realize that she'd been faking happiness for quite a while now.

She was just in time to kiss Nell good-night; to sit with her family and share stories of holidays gone by. Jack arrived and added to the merriment. After her brother and parents left for the B&B, she stayed up a little longer and chatted with Callum and Avery before the two of them went down the hall hand in hand. No one had asked about Rhys, almost as if they'd made a pact to spare her the interrogation. But as she finally burrowed beneath the covers on the sofa bed, she let the emptiness in. Because in the end she was alone. At Christmas. And her heart was across town, with Rhys.

CHAPTER ELEVEN

CHRISTMAS MORNING DAWNED cool and sunny. Taylor heard Callum sneak out just after five to do the milking; she fell back to sleep until Avery got up and put on coffee around seven. With Nell being too young to understand it all, there was no scramble for presents under the tree. Nell slept late after the busy night before, and Avery brought Taylor a coffee then slipped beneath the covers with her own mug.

Taylor looked over at her sister in law. "I think I would have liked having a sister if this is what it's like. Jack and Callum's idea of this would be to count to three and jump on the bed and see if they could make me yell. Extra points if they left bruises."

Avery smiled. "It was like this for me and my sister. I'm really glad you're here, Taylor. It's been so very nice."

"I'm glad I came, too."

"Even though it's bothering you to leave Rhys?"
Taylor nodded.

They sipped for a moment more before Avery took the plunge. "Did you fall in love with him? Or was it just a fling?"

Taylor curled her hands around the mug. "It would be easier to say it was a fling."

"But it wasn't?"

She shook her head.

Avery laughed. "I don't know whether to offer my congratulations or my sympathy."

"What do you mean?" Taylor looked over at her. "Do I look happy about it?"

"Yes. And no. You light up when you talk about him, you know."

No, she hadn't known. Damn.

"Falling in love is a bit of a miracle, don't you think? So that's the congrats part. And the sympathy comes in because I can tell you're confused and that's not easy."

"I live in Vancouver."

Avery nodded. "When I met Callum, I lived in Ontario. My life and job were there."

"But you could quit your job. It's different when you own your own venture. It would be harder for you now, with your bakery business, wouldn't it?"

"Difficult, but not impossible."

Taylor let out a frustrated sigh. "Avery, I get what you're saying. I do. But I've spent years building this business and my reputation. I've known Rhys less than a month."

Avery smiled softly. "I know. If you didn't have the business in the way, what would you do?"

See where it leads.

The answer popped into her mind with absolute ease. But it wasn't just up to her. "Rhys never once asked me to stay or hinted at anything past our…"

"Affair?"

Taylor blushed.

Avery finished her coffee. "It's that serious, then."

"Look," she said, frustration in her voice. "Last night he said he wished I didn't have to go but that's not the same thing as asking me to stay or when I'm coming back."

"Why would he ask when he's sure of the answer? Have you given him any reason to think you would stay? Told him how you feel?"

She hadn't.

"Only because I'm positive nothing could come of it except our being hurt even more. Besides, there's a good chance he doesn't feel the same way. He told me straight out that he liked me because I was a challenge. That I was low risk because I was leaving anyway."

Avery snorted. "Oh, my God, that's romantic."

Taylor couldn't help it. She started laughing, too. "I'll be fine, Avery, promise. I just need to get back to a normal schedule. And first we have a Christmas breakfast to cook. You're the whiz, but I'm happy to be your sous-chef today."

"Deal," Avery said.

Babbling sounded from the second bedroom and Avery grinned. "Let me get the princess changed and fed first."

While she was gone and the house was quiet, Taylor snuck out of bed and got the box from her coat pocket. She didn't want to open it when anyone else was around. Sitting on the bed in her pajamas, she carefully untied the ribbon and unwrapped the red foil paper.

Inside the box was a necklace—the very same horseshoe necklace she'd been admiring at the silversmith's the other day. She lifted it gently and watched the U-shaped pendant sway as it dangled from the chain. How had he known it was just what she liked? It was simple but beautiful. When she went to put it back in the box, she heard a strange ruffle when her fingers touched the cotton padding. Curious, she moved it out of the box and saw the folded note hidden beneath.

For all the times you need a horseshoe to rub for good luck. Merry Christmas, Rhys.

He remembered, but he'd hidden the note, as if he didn't want her to find it right away. As if—perhaps—he'd meant her to discover it after she was home again and it would remind her of the time they'd spent together.

She didn't know whether to laugh or cry.

She tucked the necklace back in the box. She wouldn't wear it today, not when everyone was around. She didn't want any more questions about her relationship with Rhys. She just wanted to keep this one thing private, like a secret they shared. Cherished.

But she thought about it as the rest of the family arrived, breakfast was served, presents were opened. And when there was a lull, she took the necklace out of her bag and tucked it into her pocket, where it rested warmly within the cotton.

An hour or so before dinner, it all got to be too much so she excused herself and bundled up for a short walk and some fresh air to clear her head. She was partway down the lane when a dull thud echoed on the breeze. She turned around to see her dad coming down the steps, dressed in Callum's barn coat and a warm toque and gloves. "Hey, wait up," he called.

She had no choice but to wait.

When he reached her they continued walking, the sun on the snow glittering so brightly that Taylor wished she'd put on her sunglasses. "It's been a good day," Harry said easily, falling into step.

"We haven't all been together like this in a long time." Taylor let out a big breath. "It's been good."

"Yes, it has."

Silence fell, slightly awkward.

"Taylor, I've gotten the impression you're not completely happy. Are you okay?"

Her heart clubbed. "What gave you that idea?"

"Your mother pointed out a few things. And

then there's this Rhys guy. You seem half miserable, half thrilled about it."

She huffed out a laugh. "That about sums it up."

"Is it just this guy? Or is it work, too?"

She frowned. "You don't have to sound so hopeful about it. I know you don't like what I do and you'd love to see me settled with kids like Callum."

There. She'd come right out and said it.

Harry let out a long sigh. "I haven't been very fair. Or put things the right way."

Her feet stopped moving, as if they had a mind of their own. "What?"

She looked up at him, suddenly realizing why his eyes seemed so familiar. They looked like hers.

"I don't hate what you do. I resent it a bit, that's all."

"I don't get it."

Harry started walking again. "Callum joined the military instead of going to college. It wasn't my first choice, but when your son says he wants to serve his country, it's a hard thing to find fault with. Then with Jack…we both knew he couldn't ski forever. But after his accident and after the scandal…" There was a telling pause. "When he came to me asking to help him start Shepard Sports, I couldn't say no. It was good to see the light in his eye again. He could have died on that hill."

"What does this have to do with me, Dad?"

"I built my company from the ground up, Taylor. Neither of my boys were interested in finance. But you…you weren't just my last chance to pass it on to one of my kids. I could see the talent in you. You're good at making money, maybe even better than Jack. And you weren't interested in the least in the market or fund management or anything I do."

"You wanted me to work for you?"

"With me. Eventually."

"I thought you thought what I do is stupid."

He stopped walking again. "I was jealous of it."

"You never said anything."

"I kept hoping you'd come to me. I didn't want to pressure you."

"Instead you just made me feel like a disappointment." She wasn't holding anything back today. Maybe Rhys's way of plain speaking was rubbing off.

"I know. And I'm sorry. The truth is that you should do what makes you happy. I can't put my wishes on you kids. I'm proud of all of you for being strong and smart enough to make your own way."

"Even if it's planning frivolous parties?"

He chuckled. "I've seen your mother work her magic enough times at our small functions to know that a big event takes massive planning. You've got a talent, Taylor. And again, I'm sorry that my selfish pride took away from that."

They turned around and headed back, the house waiting for them at the end of the lane, snowbanks curling along the driveway and the remnants of her snowman listing lazily to one side. Her father's approval meant a lot. But she was also realizing that his validation wasn't everything. Her restlessness and drive wasn't about proving herself. It was about looking for something that was missing. It was about meaning, not accomplishment.

"I wish I could tell you that I could join the firm, but I need something that makes me excited to get up in the morning, Dad. I know fund management isn't it. I'm sorry, too. I wish you'd told me sooner."

"All I've ever really wanted for my kids is for them to be happy. If you're not, I want to know if there's anything we can do to help."

"Oh, Daddy." She stopped and gave him a hug, warmth spreading through her as he put his strong arms around her and hugged her back. "Thank you for that. I've got to figure it out on my own, that's all."

"Well, anything worth having is going to take a lot of work. If it was easy it wouldn't mean half so much. And none of my kids are quitters."

"No, we're not."

"You'll figure it out," he assured her. "Now, let's get back. I'm getting cold and I swear I can smell the turkey clear out here."

Taylor walked beside her father, feeling like a weight had been lifted. And yet a heaviness remained, too. Because their conversation hadn't offered any insight into what she should do about her current situation. So much for her creative, problem-solving mind. All she could see right now was a massive New Year's party that needed finalizing and about a dozen employees who were counting on her to keep their lives afloat. Where could she and Rhys possibly fit into that?

No stormy weather or mechanical failures had the grace to delay her flight, so bright and early on Boxing Day Taylor took the rental car back to the depot and walked into the departures area of the airport. Her feet were heavy and her stomach felt lined with lead as she tugged her suitcases behind her. She should be glad to be going home to her apartment, her regular routine, familiar things. Her muffin and coffee from the café around the corner each morning. Walks in Stanley Park. Warmer temperatures. Shopping. Work.

It would be good. It would be fine.

After she checked her bags she went through security and to the gate, even though she had nearly an hour to spare. She checked her phone, going through the email that was waiting for her attention. There was a rather frantic one from her New Year's client, and Taylor's blood pressure took a sudden spike. It was only five days to the party and the construction of the aquariums was delayed. He'd emailed her on Christmas Day, for heaven's sake. Like she could—or would—have done anything during that twenty-four hour period. People did celebrate holidays, she thought grumpily. Even workaholics.

Her fingers paused over the keypad. Was that what she was? A workaholic?

She scanned through the rest, knowing she should cool off before responding, and saw an urgent reply from her assistant, Alicia. Everything was under control. The aquariums were set to be delivered on the morning of the thirtieth, the fish would come a day later when the tank conditions were at the proper levels, and everything else was on schedule.

Taylor let out a breath. Why had she even worried? Alicia could handle anything their clients dished out. She never panicked and she was incredibly resourceful. Heck, Taylor wasn't even really needed.

She put the phone down on her lap as the thought sunk in.

She wasn't really needed.

The truth should have been obvious before. She was great at her job. She knew how to make the impossible happen. It stood to follow that she'd train her staff the same way. Alicia had been her right-hand girl for three years. She'd managed smaller events on her own. This party was probably the biggest challenge they'd had in a while and all Taylor had done was been available by email simply to confirm or approve changes in plan. Alicia had done the grunt work. She and her team had put it together.

And yet Taylor couldn't just walk away. She owned the business after all.

Suddenly her conversations with family came back with disturbing clarity. *What you're doing isn't giving you that same buzz,* Jack had said. *Something's missing.* And he'd gone on to say that what had given him the most fulfillment was his corporate retreat business. That it was more than just buying and selling. That it was about people.

An even bigger surprise was how her father had taken her aside yesterday afternoon. Just before they'd gone inside, he'd added one little addendum to their conversation. "I want you to know that I couldn't have done what I have all these years without your mother. Without all of you. Don't let life pass you by, sweetheart. Build your business with people you trust, but build your life with people you love."

People you trust. People you love.

The solution was so clear she couldn't believe it had taken her so long to put it together.

Even though it was still a statutory holiday, she scanned through her directory and found the number she was looking for. A quick call later and she was heading to the gate desk where two service agents had just arrived.

"I need you to pull my bags, please," she said, holding out her boarding pass.

The first agent came to the desk. "I'm sorry? This is the flight to Vancouver, leaving in forty minutes."

"Yes, and I checked in and this is my seat, 12F. But I'm not going to be leaving on it, so I need you to pull my bags."

"Miss." She checked the boarding pass. "Miss Shepard. We're going to be boarding in about fifteen minutes."

"I'm not going to be on it." She tried to stay calm and smiling. "And if I'm not on it, you're going to have to pull the bags anyway, right?"

"Yes, but…"

"I don't even care if I take them with me now. I can come back to get them. I don't care if my ticket can't be refunded." Her smile widened even as the agent's expression grew more confused. She leaned forward. "Would it help if I told you I fell in love and decided I can't leave after all?"

The confused look morphed into sentimental amusement. "You're absolutely sure you're not boarding this flight?"

"I've never been more sure of anything in my life."

"It might take a while. You'll have to pick them up at baggage services." She sent Taylor a wink. "I'll call down."

"Thank you! I'm sorry for the trouble. And Merry Christmas!"

"Merry Christmas," the agent returned, picking up the phone. "And good luck."

CHAPTER TWELVE

RHYS PUT THE BROOM back in the storage closet and began running hot water for the mop bucket. He'd left Martha in bed with a cold; she'd insisted on getting up and coming with him to give the diner a good cleaning but he'd convinced her to stay in bed since she'd be needed when they opened tomorrow. Knowing she'd likely change her mind, he'd made sure to give her a good dose of cold medicine. She'd be asleep for a good few hours, getting some much deserved rest. He could mop the floors and do up the bank deposit without any trouble.

If only he could stop thinking about Taylor as easily. That last kiss she'd given him had been so sweet—a bit shy and a bit sad. He knew he had no choice but to let her go, but it was killing him. She'd awakened something in him that was unexpected and he didn't know how to make it go back to sleep. At least a dozen times in the past thirty-six hours he'd grabbed his car keys, ready to drive over to Callum's and tell her he wasn't ready to let what they had end. But he'd put the keys back on the hook every time. It already hurt to let her go. To prolong it would only make it worse.

Something made him shut off the water, a persistent thump that came from out in the main part of the restaurant. Frowning, he stuck his head out of the kitchen and called out, "We're closed!"

He'd nearly pulled his head back in when he saw the red boots.

His heart gave an almighty *whomp*.

She was supposed to be gone. Her flight was supposed to have left almost an hour ago. Maybe he'd been mistaken about the boots?

He slowly stepped through the kitchen door and into the front of the diner. There was no question, they were red boots. The only red boots like them he'd ever seen in Cadence Creek. Most of her body was hidden by the gigantic pine wreath hanging on the door, but he saw her long legs and the tails of her soft black and red coat.

He smiled as she knocked again, harder.

"Rhys, I know you're in there. Your truck is parked right outside."

His smile widened. God, he loved it when she got all impatient and bossy.

"I said we're closed."

There was a moment of silence. Then her voice came again, mocking. "Don't be an ass. Open the door."

He rather thought he could play this game all day. Except he did really want to see her. And find out why she was still here.

"Rhys!" she commanded. "It's freezing out here!"

He couldn't help it, he burst out laughing, half in surprise and half in relief that he actually got to see her again. He went forward and turned the lock back. Gave the door a shove and then there she was, standing in the snow, her dark hair in the customary braid and her eyes snapping at him from beneath a black hat, one of those stylish things women wore in the winter that wouldn't ruin their hair.

"Hello, Taylor."

She stepped inside, reached up and swiped the hat from her head and shoved it in her pocket. "Hi."

"I thought you were leaving today."

"I was."

He locked the door again and faced her, his pulse leaping as he registered the fact that she'd used past tense. "Wait. Was?"

She nodded.

"Your flight get canceled or something?"

"Nope."

"I don't understand."

For several seconds Taylor remained silent. "Do you have any coffee on or anything?" she asked. "I'm freezing."

She was stalling, and the only reason she'd do that was that she was nervous. "I put a pot on when I got here. Have a seat."

She went to one of the lunch counter stools and perched on it. He added the right amounts of cream and sugar to her cup and handed it over. "It's probably not as good as mom's."

"Where is she, by the way?"

"Home in bed with a cold."

"Oh, I'm sorry to hear that." Her face seemed to relax a bit, though—was she glad they were alone? He was still confused as hell. She was insistent on coming in but now that she was here, trying to get anything out of her was about like working with a pigheaded colt who refused to be bridled. Trying on the patience. Once he got the bit in her mouth she'd be just fine, he realized. It was just figuring out what to use to lure her in, make her explain.

"You're probably wondering why I'm here," she said softly, looking up at him with wide eyes.

Feelings rushed through him as he held her gaze. Pain, because prolonging the inevitable was torture of a special kind and they'd done it twice now. Hope, because for some reason she was here and not crossing thirty thousand feet over the Rockies. And tenderness, because he knew now that beneath the dynamo that was Taylor Shepard was one of the most caring, generous people he'd ever met. At the very least he could admit to himself that he'd fallen for her. Hard.

"The thought crossed my mind," he replied.

"I forgot to give you your Christmas present," she said, reaching into her handbag. "I apologize for the poor wrapping job."

She held out a thin plastic bag that bore the logo of one of the airport gift shops.

Amused, he reached inside and pulled out a key chain with a fuzzy fake rabbit's foot on the end.

"Someone told me that you rub a rabbit's foot for good luck." Her voice was barely above a whisper.

It was then he noticed the horseshoe hanging around her neck, just visible in the "V" of her coat and sweater. She was wearing his Christmas present. That pleased him more than it probably should.

"Do you think I'm in need of some good luck?"

She put down her coffee cup but not before he noticed her hand was trembling the slightest bit. She was nervous. So was he. He had no idea what this all meant but he got the feeling they were standing on the edge of something momentous. Somewhere he'd never wanted to be again. Until now.

"Why don't you try rubbing it and find out?" she suggested.

He felt like a fool, but she was here, wasn't she? He'd indulge her. He rubbed the tiny faux-fur foot.

"Ok, Luck," he said when he was done, spreading his arms wide. "Here I am."

She got up from the stool, went around the counter, and grabbed onto his shirt, just above where he'd fastened the last button. "And here I am," she whispered as she tilted up her head and kissed him.

His arms came around her by sheer instinct, pulling her against his body into the places where she fit so well. There was relief in holding her in his arms again, passion that ignited between them every time they touched. She tasted good and he kissed her back, loving the feel of her soft lips against his, the sleek texture of her mouth, the way she made the tiniest sound of pleasure when he nibbled on her lower lip.

"You're right," he murmured. "It *is* lucky."

She smiled against his lips, but then pulled away a little and simply rested in his arms, her head nestled in the space between his shoulder and neck. A lump formed in his throat. Whatever he'd said over the last few weeks, he'd been a liar. There was nothing easy or casual or temporary about his feelings for her. They were very, very real. It wasn't all physical. The way they were embracing now was much, much more than that. What a mess.

"Why didn't you tell me about the diner?" Her voice was slightly muffled against his shirt but he heard her just the same. It was not what he expected her to say.

"What?"

She pushed back out of his arms and met his gaze. "This place. Why didn't you tell me you were part owner?"

Nothing she could have said would have surprised him more. "Who told you that?"

"Your mother. Though I don't think she meant to. It slipped out the other night."

"It's not a big deal."

"It's a very big deal." She frowned, a cute little wrinkle forming between her eyebrows. "For all your talk about not wanting to own your own business, not wanting to be the boss. Heck, you even said you hadn't wanted your mother to buy this place."

"I really didn't want her to buy it. But she was determined. Once my mother gets something in her head…"

"Sounds like someone else I know. And you invested because?"

He frowned. "If I hadn't invested all the money I'd gotten for my house in Rocky, she would have mortgaged herself to the eyeballs to have it. As it is, this place is free and clear in another four years."

"You did it to protect her."

"Of course I did. I couldn't stop her from taking the risk, but at least I could help cushion the fall."

"You did it thinking that you'd never see your money back."

He remembered the heated discussions he'd had with his mother about taking such a big step. In the end he'd had no choice. Money was just money. This was his mother and Rhys knew he had to look out for her. "I did it knowing that was a very real possibility, yes. And not because I didn't think she could do it. I just know from painful experience how many small businesses fail. She'd already lost enough over her lifetime. Her whole nest egg went into buying it, plus Dad's life insurance money. If the diner went under, she'd lose everything."

Taylor must think him an idiot. He'd made a business decision for reasons that had very little to do with business.

"You did it for your mother."

"I know it was foolish. But she's my mom."

"And the job at Diamondback?"

"Security. The best way to take care of her, to protect her, was to minimize financial risk. At least I bring in a regular paycheck that I, or rather we, can rely on."

Taylor reached out and pressed her hand to the wall of his chest. "You are a dying breed, Rhys Bullock. You protect the people you love no matter what. There's nothing foolish about that. What about your brother?"

"He's been gone too long, I think. He's off doing his own thing. He just said, 'Whatever she wants.'"

It had been Rhys who'd come home and helped his mom through those first days of grieving. Who'd met with lawyers and bankers. There had been no way he was going to let her go through that alone.

Taylor squeezed his hands. "Let me guess, Martha insists on you taking your share of the profits."

"Of course. I draw out the same percentage of profit as I initially invested."

He didn't quite like the keen way she was looking up at him. Like she could see right through him. He wasn't exactly lying…

She lifted one eyebrow. "You use the profits to pay down the loan, don't you?"

Busted. "Perhaps."

"And your house?"

He met her gaze. If she was after the whole picture, she might as well have it. She could probably still catch another flight today.

"Rented." Because by using all his equity he'd had nothing left for a down payment.

"And Martha doesn't know. She thinks you own it?"

He nodded. "That's right. You're looking at a full-time ranch hand with a rented house, truck payment and not a scrap in savings."

"So that's why you didn't tell me? Pride?"

She was here. Things were bigger between them than he'd ever planned. "No, not just pride. There's more. You know I never wanted to be like my dad. I was so determined that I'd do better. That no one would suffer because of my mismanagement."

"But someone did?"

He nodded. "Her name was Sherry. She had a couple of kids. She was my office manager—and my girlfriend."

"Oh, Rhys."

"I let them down so completely," he explained. "She blamed me, too. For losing the business. For putting her out of a job when she had the children to support. For..." He cleared his throat. "For breaking her heart."

"So you carried that around, on top of losing the business?"

"She depended on me. I can't blame her for being angry." He ran a hand over his hair and looked in her eyes, feeling miserable. "So you see I don't have a lot to offer in the way of brilliant prospects."

She took his hand. "That's not true! You work hard and you put the ones you love first. You made your mom's dream come true. You're strong and honest and loyal. You've got two strong hands and the biggest heart of anyone I've ever met." Her smile widened. "Know what else you've got?"

"What?"

"Your ace in the hole. Me."

* * *

Taylor gazed up at him, filled with admiration for the man he'd become. He really had no clue, did he? Rhys was self-assured, knew his place in the world. But he didn't understand how extraordinary he was.

"You? Come on, Taylor," he said, pulling away a little. "Look at you. You're successful. Your business is profitable enough to keep you in designer boots and who knows what else. We're as different as night from day."

"Not as different as you think. Just so happens that we're peas in a pod, you and me. I was in a relationship a while ago, too. At the same time as that wedding story I told you about—remember the bride with the allergy? I was so upset about that. I mean disproportionately freaked out. John accused me of being cold. Of caring more about the business than I did about our relationship. The thing is he was right. And so your little digs about proving myself really hit a nerve. I was at a crisis point and he bailed. You weren't the only one who thought you were incapable of making a personal relationship work, and I really wasn't interested in risking myself like that again, you know?"

"He was an idiot."

She smiled at Rhys's blind loyalty. "No, he was honest. And the truth is, I didn't invest enough in our relationship. Probably because I didn't love him. I loved the idea of him. But not him. The idea of losing him didn't make me lose sleep. It didn't break my heart or make this heavy pit of despair settle right here." She pressed her fist to her stomach. Her voice lowered to a whisper. "Not like it felt about an hour and a half ago while I sat in Edmonton airport wondering how I could ever be happy if I left you without telling you how I feel."

His lips dropped open. He hadn't been expecting that. Neither had she. Neither of them had expected any of this.

"Do you really think I care about your bank statement? Truly? When have I ever given the impression that my goals are about making money?"

He shook his head. "You haven't," he admitted. "It's always been about proving yourself, meeting challenges."

"That's right." She tugged on his hand. "Come sit down. I want to run something by you."

"Me? Why?"

"When we first met, you told me that a smart person knows their strengths, do you remember? My dad taught me that a smart person also sees the strengths in others. I want your honest to goodness opinion about something. Will you help?"

"Of course."

They sat side by side on the stools, swiveled so they were facing each other and their knees were nearly touching. Rhys wasn't just some ranch hand. He had a lifetime of experiences to draw upon and she trusted his judgment. "Do you think I could keep the event planning business in Vancouver going and branch out into something else that excites me personally? Can I do both?"

Possibility hummed in the air. Rhys sat up straight and tall. Neither of them were rushing through to the end of the conversation. They'd been through enough to know that what was said today was constructing the foundation of wherever they went from here. It deserved to be built with care and attention. "It depends. What are you thinking?"

"Angela put the idea into my head before Christmas. I mentioned that I'm getting tired of the here today, gone tomorrow scene. Remember when I was so stressed about the rehearsal dinner and you said it was because the event meant something personal to me? You were right. But you know what? The satisfaction from planning Callum's wedding was greater than I expected, too. She said what I want is to create something meaningful, and suggested I help plan an upcoming fund-raiser for the Butterfly Foundation."

"That's a great idea!" Rhys smiled at her. "The Diamonds have done a really great thing with that charity. I know they'd appreciate the help."

"What if I took it a step further and used my expertise to work for lots of charities and non-profits? I love what I do and I'd still have the challenge of that, but I think I'd feel like I was doing something important, too, you know?"

"How could you do that and still keep the Vancouver business going? You'd be spreading yourself pretty thin."

"By promoting my assistant. She can do it.

She's handled this party on her own since I've been here and it's been one of the most challenging projects we've ever done. She's built her own team. I'd still own the company, and I'd still be involved, of course. But in a different way. Kind of like Jack is with his business. He's far more hands-on with his team-building stuff than with the sporting goods."

"Would you set up the new venture from the same office?" he asked. "It would cut down on expenses."

He hadn't put the two together. The two of them and the business change. "This might come as a surprise, but I was thinking about running it from here."

"From Cadence Creek?"

He sounded so surprised she faltered. Had she possibly misread the situation? "Well, yes. It's close to Edmonton, not that far to Calgary, and an easy flight to Vancouver or even Toronto. I have family here. And..." She looked down at her lap. She was so confident when it came to her work and capabilities, but when it was personal she wasn't nearly as sure of herself. John's words—*Incapable of what it takes to maintain a relationship*—still echoed in her head. Even though she didn't really believe them, they'd left their mark just the same. "I guess I thought you might like it if I were around."

"Taylor."

She couldn't read what emotion was in his voice other than surprise. Embarrassment flooded through her as she felt quite ridiculous. The old insecurity came rushing back. What if the problem was really her? What if she wasn't lovable? She'd spent so much time trying to be strong that it had become a shell around her heart.

"Of course, it's okay if you don't. I mean, we did agree that this was a short-term thing, and I don't want you to feel pressured."

His hand touched hers as it sat in her lap. She stared at it for a long moment, watched as his fingers curled around hers, firm and sure. Her heart seemed to expand in her chest, filled with so much emotion she didn't know what to do with it all. She drew hope from the simple touch. Felt wonder at the newness and fragility of it all. And there was fear, fear that this couldn't all be real and that it would disappear at a moment's notice.

She put her other hand over his, tentatively,

until she couldn't bear it any longer and she lifted their joined hands, pressing them to her cheek as her eyes closed, holding on to the moment as long as she could.

Rhys lifted his right hand, placed it gently along the slope of her jaw, his strong fingers whispering against the delicate skin there. "Taylor," he murmured, and she opened her eyes.

He was looking at her the way she'd never imagined any man would ever look at her. Wholly, completely, his lips turned up only the slightest bit, not in jest, but in what she could only think of as happiness. His eyes were warm, and looked on her with such an adoring expression she caught her breath. The pad of his thumb rubbed against her cheek, and he pulled his left hand from her grasp. He placed it along her other cheek, his hands cupping her face like a precious chalice, and he slid closer, so slowly it was sweet torture waiting for his lips to finally touch hers.

She thought the sweetest moment had to be in that breathless second when his mouth was only a fraction of an inch away, and all the possibilities in the world were compacted into that tiny space. But she was wrong. Sweeter still was the light touch of lips on lips, soft, tender and perfect.

"You're staying?" he asked, his voice barely a whisper in the quietness of the diner.

"I'm staying," she confirmed.

He pressed his forehead to hers and she slowly let out her breath as everything clicked into place.

"I tried not to fall in love with you." Rhys lifted his head, smiled, and patted his lap. She slid off the stool and onto his legs, and he put his arms around her, strong and secure.

"Me, too. I kept telling myself it was a fling. But I couldn't get you off my mind. You're bossy and you drive me crazy, but you're loyal and honorable and you…"

She broke off, feeling silly.

"I what?"

He gave her a jostle, prompting her to finish her sentence. "It's corny." She bit down on her lip.

"I don't care. What were you going to say?"

She leaned against his shoulder. "You make me feel treasured."

He tilted his head so it rested against hers. "And you make me feel invincible."

She smiled, the grin climbing her face until she chuckled. "I'm glad."

His smile faded as his face turned serious. "I won't let you down."

"You couldn't possibly."

He kissed her again, more demanding this time, and when he lifted his head her tidy braid was well and truly mussed. "Hey," she said, running her fingers through his hair. "Now that I'm going to be here on a permanent basis, we can take all the time we need to fall in love."

"Honey, I'm already there."

She smiled. "Me, too. But I want to enjoy being this way a little longer. Is that okay?"

"Look at me. I'm in no position to argue."

She kissed him again, thinking that she could happily stay that way forever when he gave her braid a tug.

"Hey," he said. "I know we're taking our time and all that, and I don't mean to rush, but what are you doing New Year's Eve? Do you have plans?"

She nodded slowly. "I do have plans, as a matter of fact."

"Oh." Disappointment clouded his voice.

"I think I'd like to spend it right here, in your arms. If that's okay with you."

"That's more than okay. And the night after that, and the night after that."

She snuggled closer. "I don't know what the future holds. Changes are coming, adjustments and transitions are going to be made. But I know one thing for sure. You're my anchor, Rhys. Somehow you make everything right simply by being. And for the first time, I don't have to have all the details sorted and everything planned to the last item. Things will fall into place. And do you know how I know?"

He shook his head.

"Because I didn't plan for you. And you were the best thing of all."

He kissed her hair. "I love you, Taylor."

"And I love you."

And that was all she really needed to know.

* * * * *

Mills & Boon® Large Print

March 2014

MILLION DOLLAR CHRISTMAS PROPOSAL
Lucy Monroe

A DANGEROUS SOLACE
Lucy Ellis

THE CONSEQUENCES OF THAT NIGHT
Jennie Lucas

SECRETS OF A POWERFUL MAN
Chantelle Shaw

NEVER GAMBLE WITH A CAFFARELLI
Melanie Milburne

VISCONTI'S FORGOTTEN HEIR
Elizabeth Power

A TOUCH OF TEMPTATION
Tara Pammi

A LITTLE BIT OF HOLIDAY MAGIC
Melissa McClone

A CADENCE CREEK CHRISTMAS
Donna Alward

HIS UNTIL MIDNIGHT
Nikki Logan

THE ONE SHE WAS WARNED ABOUT
Shoma Narayanan

0214 Rom LP

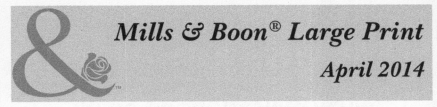

Mills & Boon® Large Print

April 2014

0314 Rom LP

Discover more romance at

www.millsandboon.co.uk

- ❤ WIN great prizes in our exclusive competitions

- ❤ BUY new titles before they hit the shops

- ❤ BROWSE new books and REVIEW your favourites

- ❤ SAVE on new books with the Mills & Boon® Bookclub™

- ❤ DISCOVER new authors

PLUS, to chat about your favourite reads, get the latest news and find special offers:

- Find us on facebook.com/millsandboon

- Follow us on twitter.com/millsandboonuk

- ❤ Sign up to our newsletter at millsandboon.co.uk

Preface

The ancients knew seven wonders of the world, among which were the Pharos of Alexandria, the Colossus of Rhodes, and the pyramids of the Nile. The pyramids still exist: their dimensions are such that they withstood the ravages of time. Neither nature nor human hands have been able to destroy them.

Why did the Greeks speak of the "wonders of the world?" They admired the great cultural monuments of their age because of the importance in their culture of marrying artistic vision with the architectural skill necessary to create such enormous structures.

The "Wonders of the World" were wrought with human hands. This book adopts this same criterion for selecting its wonders of today's world. The technological advance of humankind though has brought with it a threat to the natural magnificence of this world. Hence we also feature the national parks and nature reserves established on every continent to protect the natural wonders of nature which are at least as important as those monuments to our modern technology.

Both natural and cultural monuments are listed by UNESCO as monuments that humankind must strive earnestly to protect, but this book ranges wider than the UNESCO list because there are many examples of architecture and landscape that do not have a world cultural heritage designation. Such inclusions by us that UNESCO omits are the Eiffel Tower in Paris, the Manhattan skyline, prehistoric cave paintings of Lascaux, and the limestone cliffs of Rügen.

There are a great many wonders in our world and therefore the choice is of necessity subjective. Travel with us through these pages to visit one hundred of the most magnificent wonders on earth.

The publisher

Contents

The forgotten Machu Picchu

The ancient Inca settlement in the Peruvian Andes was discovered in 1911

PERU
Machu Picchu

SOUTH AMERICA

Pacific
Ocean

Atlantic
Ocean

ROUTE

Flight from Lima to Cuzco,
train to Machu Picchu

BEST TIMES

June–October

ALSO WORTH SEEING

Ruins from the
Sacsayhuaman Inca
settlement near Cuzco

On the eastern side of the Andes in Peru, where the mountain river Urubamba flows to the Amazon basin, the American explorer Hiram Bingham made the most important discovery of his career on July 24, 1911. He was searching for relics of the Inca culture which was destroyed by the Spanish *conquistadores* in the sixteenth century. After climbing a steep mountain wall at one of the many bends in the river, the young history professor from Yale finally reach a mountain path at about 7,500 feet that was surrounded by large rocks and not visible from the valley. The entrance had been blocked by an earthquake many years earlier. The many walls draped with foliage and high tiered terraces sug-

gested a large city had once stood there.

In the center of the temple complex

Bingham named his discovery Machu Picchu which means "Old Top" in the Quechua native American language. Research later showed that this indeed was a former Inca settlement which had been intentionally built in an inaccessible place in an effort to hide from the plundering conquistadors who had already conquered the Inca capital of Cuzco, only 75 Miles away to the northwest. In the years following Bingham's discovery, archaeologists uncovered the overgrown temple and palace whose walls were

magnificently constructed from granite blocks.

At what was obviously the center of the settlement stands the temple complex and here at the highest point there is a terrace carved from the granite with spiral steps hewn from granite leading to it. The archaeologists identified a monolith as an *Intihuatana* or sacred stone of the Incas, that "captures the sun." Similar structures of rock were used by the Incas as a sun dial, which was central to their cult of the sun.

Not far from the Intihuatana, archaeologists found three well-preserved walls of a sun temple with an altar formed from three slabs of rock. Another important structure within the palace is the *Torreón*, a half

round tower with sacrificial altar, beneath which is a pit that Bingham dubbed the "King's Mausoleum." Close by they found 142 skeletons, mainly of women who were probably *Ajillas* as the maidens were known who were selected for the sun cult. There are other parts of the settlement that are more simply constructed and were probably inhabited by soldiers and workers. A large open area, now known as *Plaza Principal*, was probably a meeting place for festivals such as the winter solstice.

The hundreds of tiered terraces that lead upwards to the city itself were cultivated for crops such as potatoes, corn, and other vegetables in small fields enclosed by rocky walls. It is thought the soil for these was brought up over sixteen hundred feet from the Urubamba valley. Calculations show that the fields could produce sufficient food for ten thousand people.

The Incas built the settlement of Machu Picchu on a mountain path and so well hidden by rocks that the conquistadors did not find it. Stairways and tombs were hewn from rock, like the "King's Mausoleum" bottom left. Other buildings are constructed of stone dressed to fit precisely without use of mortar (bottom right).

The mysterious giant pictures of Nazca

Why were they etched in the desert 1,500 years ago?

Strange grooves in the desert created by unknown hands are one of the biggest archaeological mysteries in South America. They were formed about fifteen hundred years ago over an area of about 200 square miles between the present-day towns of Nazca and Ica in southern Peru. Some grooves run straight across the flat plains of the Peruvian pampas, while others form huge designs on the high planes and steep surrounding hills. These can only be recognized as giant drawings from the air.

Drawings of huge creatures

These geometric forms were first discovered in 1939 by the American cultural historian Paul Kosok during an exploratory flight.

The observations that Kosok made inspired the German mathematician Maria Reiche to devote her life to studying these patterns in the desert. She discovered that once these grooves in the yellow sand of about eight inches deep and at least three feet wide were cleared of their covering of red earth they became much more apparent. By this means scientists exposed a drawing of a condor that is more than 390 feet wide. The drawing had to be photographed from the air to reveal its subject. Later other creatures were uncovered such as a spider with legs of over 130 feet and other giant depictions of humans, fish, cacti, and flowers.

Most of these drawings are etched as a single line, which sometimes runs for hundreds of yards or even miles across the desert. The survival of these ancient etchings is due to the good fortune of the local climate and geography. Very little rain falls in the Pampa de las Figuras between Nazca and Ica and the area is shielded against sandstorms by the line of mountains running along the

coast to the west and by spurs of the Andes to the east.

What is so striking about these etchings—apart from their size—is both the accuracy of the drawings and the artistic flair with which they have been performed. Similar designs, attaining the same aesthetic standard, are also found in the ceramics of the Nazca culture that flourished in southern Peru between the fourth and fifth centuries. This makes it certain that Nazca artists also created the desert etchings.

Astronomical drawings

Quite how the early Peruvians—from before the time of the Incas—were able to make these drawings which they could not oversee at a single glance remains a mystery.

It is certain that they used ropes to help them draw straight lines and circles but no-one has provided a complete explanation of the meaning or purpose of these drawings. Most scientists agree that they are astronomical drawings and Maria Reiche believes they are accounts of cosmic observations. One of the grooves she discovered leads straight to spot at which the sun sets in the southern hemisphere during the June solstice. Other lines that are not precisely parallel relate to the different points at which the sun sets during the solstice for the years 300 through to 650 of our calendar. Even with these theories the mystery remains as to the cultural significance of these drawings. This gives plenty of scope for the imagination such as the Swiss writer Erich von Däniken, who believes these drawings are signals to and landing strips for aliens.

Most of the drawings made in the Nazca desert 1,500 years ago by unknown artists can only be seen from the air. The etching on the right is of a bird.

Riches amidst poverty

Havana is still the jewel of the Caribbean despite its decline

No one agrees on the origin of the name Havana or La Habana for the Cuban metropolis but all Habaneras agree that they know not of a more beautiful city. Even though the beauty has faded and crumbling since it was the richest colonial city in the Caribbean, Havana is still very impressive.

Old Havana is protected by St. Christopher

The virtues of Cuba's beauty were first extolled when Christopher Columbus discovered the island on October 28, 1492. He noted in the ship's log: "This island is the most beautiful ever seen by human eye." Spanish colonists established their first settlement in 1515, which they traditionally called Villa de San Cristobal de la Habana but four years later they moved because of the climate to a first-class natural harbor to the north that is today's Havana. Historians suspect the name "La Habana" refers to the Ciboney tribal chief Habaguanex who ruled over the western part of Cuba at that time. Another legend refers to a beautiful Arawak woman who cried out "Habana!" with arms outstretched while the Spanish ship was anchoring.

In the sixteenth century another pretty native woman became the wife of the Spanish governor, who failed to return from a voyage up the Mississippi. The legend has it that the woman peered out to sea for her returning husband for so many years that she eventually became blind. She is immortalized in bronze as "Girradilla", decorating the bell-tower of El Castillo de la Real Fuerza.

The old fortress of La Fuerza was of little strategic significance—it was the headquarters of the Spanish governors—but came into its own in the twentieth century as a tourist attraction on the edge of the old city, where the greatest collection of Spanish colonial buildings in the Caribbean are to be found. The lively Old Havana, La Habana Vieja, with its artistically decorated facades, archways, old wells, and hidden courtyards, was declared a

world heritage site by UNESCO in 1982. Extensive renovation saved it from the threat of decay and buildings that had already deteriorated were restored to their original condition.

Palaces, traders' houses, and churches evidence the wealth of Havana through the seventeenth and eighteenth centuries when Spanish ships laden with gold and silver used Havana as a refuge on their voyages home. Cuba also flourished from the sale of its sugar cane, rum, and cigars.

The attractive old town is a blend of Spanish architecture with the bright colors and forms of the Caribbean. The cathedral of San Christóbal, with its pillared frontage has clear signs of late baroque Italianate influences. The glazing bars are reminiscent of the wrought-

iron talents of Andalusian blacksmiths and there is a trading house as grand as a mosque. Given the parlous state of Havana's other old quarters, the restoration of the historic city center seems wholly inadequate. Havana is in desperate need of economic growth to enable the tremendous damage that

dictators of the right and the left have inflicted on such beautiful avenues as the Carenas Boulevard. In cheerful bars such as Bodeguita del Medio, many people will raise their Daiquiris to toast the hope that this may soon happen.

Old Havana has the largest collection of Spanish colonial architecture in the Caribbean. They are a magnificent assortment of fine churches, noble palaces, and traders' houses. The historical quarter—known as Habana Vieja—with its narrow alleys and cozy cafés, has been significantly restored in the past few years.

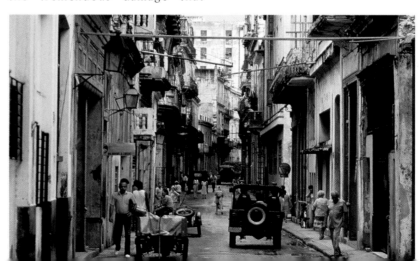

At the wells of Itza

Traces of the Mayas and Tolteks on the Yucatan peninsula

MEXICO

Chichén Itzá

Pacific Ocean

ROUTE

Almost 75 miles (120 km) east of Merida and Cancun

BEST TIMES

October–January

ACCOMMODATIONS

Hotel Mayaland, Villas Arqueológicas

ALSO WORTH SEEING

Mayan cities on Yucatan peninsula: Coba, Tulum, and Uyma

It was night, with only the light of the moon penetrating the darkness of the jungle as the amateur American archaeologist Edward Herbert Thompson climbed the one hundred foot pyramid of Chichén Itzá for the first time in the late nineteenth century. Then, the Mayan city to the north of the Yucatan peninsula was a crumbling mass beneath a covering of green foliage. Shadows of enormous great buildings of stone—temples, palaces, colonnaded galleries, and superbly crafted walls—could be seen above the tree-tops which the researcher inspected more closely the following morning. Discovering the people behind the construction of the city was to become Thompson's life's work.

The name of this city of Chichén Itzá predates Columbian times, harking back to the Mayan civilization and language in which it means "at the well of Itza." The Itzas are thought to have been people of noble birth who established a new religious metropolis here within the first centuries of the first millennium AD. Following them the Mayans flourished here until the fourteenth century when the city was conquered by the Tolteks who added their architectural style to that of the Mayans. Hence Thompson was looking down on the remnants of

two South American civilizations from the top of the pyramid in the moonlight.

Later archaeological digs by the American uncovered a processional avenue twenty feet wide and almost one thousand feet long, paved with red bricks. This leads from the edge of the ruins to a natural limestone basin about two hundred feet across and more than 130 feet deep that is half full of water. Thompson was certain this had been a sacrificial well about which he had read in the notes of a sixteenth-century Spanish missionary who reported that virgins were thrown into the well of Chichén Itzá at times of great

drought to appease the rain god. Thompson's investigation was meticulous. Jewelry which appeared to have broken when the sacrifices were made was recovered from the well. Jade was also found, together with clay pots, and gum copal, from which the Mayans made incense.

In the observatory

Together with two professional divers, the maritime archaeologist also recovered human remains which were probably from sacrifices. These were not solely of young women but also included skeletons of boys and men. The circumstances surrounding their deaths is difficult to ascertain. Were they thrown into the well by priests or did they jump willingly in the hope their sacrifice would make the rain god Chac more benevolent towards their people?

Perhaps it is this kind of unanswered question which draws masses of tourists to see Chichén Itzá today with the impressive structures uncovered and carefully restored in the past decade. There is much to see here beneath the burning sun of the Yucatan peninsula. Like Thompson you can climb to the top of the stepped pyramid that was built by the Mayans and which is surmounted by a temple of the Tolteks. There are also frightening monuments with feathered serpent deities that have enormous jaws and tails that point towards heaven. There are many tombs, the remains of a hall of a thousand columns, and more than seven areas for playing ball games. Here teams once competed by trying to throw a rubber ball through a ring of stone. One of the principal attractions is an elevated dome that is built on two

stone terraces. This acted as an observatory for the Mayans. A spiral stairway leads to three openings in the tower of the observatory. These apertures align precisely with points at which the sun and moon set and have enabled archaeologists to reconstruct a system with which the Mayans drew up their calendar.

The most dreadful building at Chichén Itzá is the Tzompantli—skull platform—of about two hundred feet by forty feet. This rectangular building has the appearance of a large sarcophagus and the reddish brown walls are decorated with a relief of four rows of a skull design. Archaeologists believe this represents the severed heads of enemy captives that were kept in the inner part of the Tzompantli.

The tablet at the center of Chac Mool— one of the Mayan deities— shown top left, was probably used to receive hearts as offerings. Tourists climb the stepped pyramid, top right, surmounted by a Toltek temple. Below is one of the courts at which inhabitants played an ancient ball game.

Where people became gods

The ancient town of Teotihuacán remains a Mexican mystery

NORTH AMERICA

Teotihuacán

MEXICO

Pacific Ocean

SOUTH AMERICA

ROUTE
Sited 31 miles north of Mexico City; bus from metro station Indios Verdes

BEST TIMES
October–January

GOOD FOOD
Restaurant in culture center

ALSO WORTH SEEING
Acolmen convent, pyramid at Place Tenayuca

Three questions for a quiz game. Who commissioned the building two thousand years ago of the first important metropolis of the Americas? What is that city called? What do you call the people who lived there? The answer to all three questions is that nobody knows. The city in question is an impressive array of pyramids that was probably already abandoned and derelict before the Aztecs started a new settlement around the start of the fourteenth century just thirty-one miles to the south that became Mexico City.

Sun pyramid as tomb

The Aztecs kept the neighboring ghost town as a mythical burial ground and gave it the name by which it is still known today: Teotihuacán. This means "Where the people became

gods." The latest archaeological discoveries suggest that the history of Teotihuacán dates back to before the beginning of our first millennium. Around 100 BC the unknown builders started construction of a city laid out like a chess board at an altitude of over 7,500 feet. There was a temple complex, a processional avenue flanked with palaces, and wide residential areas. The city grew so big that it eventually spread over more than seven square miles.

The residents of Teotihuacán completed their most important building in the first century BC. For this they moved and carried in millions of tons of soil to form a large volcano-like cone that is the Pyramid of the Sun. The pyramid's base is similar in size to the Cheops pyramid at 728 feet by 738 feet but it is only half the height at 206 feet.

The Pyramid of the Sun is crowned by a temple that has survived centuries of erosion and earthquakes. This was probably used within the Meso-American civilization for a cult of the sun. This assumption is based on the alignment of the structure with the point on the horizon where the sun sets at the summer solstice. The name of the Pyramid of the Sun therefore appears to be entirely appropriate. A similar but smaller building with sides about 138 feet shorter is known as the Pyramid of the Moon. This building, which has no temple, has withstood the elements for that past two thousand years.

In the first century AD the people of Teotihuacán also built the Quetzalcoatl temple in the form of a pyramid. Giant stone heads of the feathered serpent deity Quetzalcoatl

and the rain god Tlaloc projected from the top of the temple. The archaeology suggests that large parts of the city consisted of living quarters where workers and craftsmen lived. From one of these *barrios* it appears tools and weapons were made of obsidian—a glass-like volcanic crystal that is extremely hard. Objects of earthenware and gold exhibit craftsmanship of the highest order. The city flourished and became both a religious and trading center in the first and second centuries, at which time the population of Teotihuacán had reached around 150,000. The walls of their religious buildings and palaces were magnificently decorated with frescos and images of their deities. Superb stone-carved masks were decorated with turquoise, obsidian, red mussel shells, and mother-of-pearl.

In the course of the next two centuries Teotihuacán fell into ever-increasing decline. Perhaps this was

due to the felling of the surrounding forests which created a steppe-like landscape and conditions which coincided with long periods of droughts, causing famine. One can imagine that the starving population rebelled against the priests and rulers and many left the city in search of better living conditions. By 750 the first metropolis of the western hemisphere was completely deserted and the buildings gradually became buried beneath sand and wind-blown

soil. The man-made mountains of the pyramids soon took on the appearance of real mountains.

It took the tourism of the twentieth century to bring the hustle and bustle of life back to Teotihuacán.

View from the Pyramid of the Moon shows the sacred heart of Teotihuacán, surrounded by further pyramids. The Avenue of the Dead leads past a number of smaller tombs to the Quetzalcoatl. The 206 ft high Pyramid of the Sun can be seen at the top left of the main photo. It was built in the first century BC.

The place where the clouds are born

The Iguaçu Falls are the world's mightiest

If you drifted silently in a boat along the upper reaches of the Iguaçu River—through the Brazilian jungle—you would at first hear nothing but the screeches of monkeys and the shrieks, whistles, and strident song of exotic birds. Eventually though above this you would hear the distant sound of thunder, coming ever nearer until it is deafening. It is time to turn back before the sound gets any closer.

Through the Devil's Gorge

The hellish thundering is created by the Iguaçu Falls at the border of Brazil, Paraguay, and Argentina where the river plunges 230 to 260 feet across a crescent of basalt escarpment two miles wide. The clouds of vapor that rise from the spume cause lush vegetation on islands in the river as water races through the Devil's Gorge before the Iguaçu gasps its last breath as it merges with the Paraná River. This is not just another waterfall but a legion of cataracts, with twenty-one major falls and some 250 lesser ones. Huge veils of mist rise up, often with the myriad colors of the rainbow. The native Guarini people who inhabit the area call this "the place where the clouds are born." They bury their dead here.

The Brazilians celebrate the *Saltos do Iguaçu* as they call the falls, as one of the world's greatest wonders, in which Niagara Falls could easily be lost. The Iguaçu Falls are three times wider than Niagara and the 111 million gallons of water which passes over the falls every minute is more than two and a half times the flow at Niagara. The Spanish name for the falls is *Cataratas del Iguazú*. The Iguaçu River (also Iguazú and Iguassú) flows inland from the Serro do Mar away from Brazil's Atlantic coast. Much of the 820-mile course of the river is navigable until it reaches its confluence with the Paraná, which is 2,300 miles long.

The remote location of the falls in the flora-and-fauna-rich rain forest has retained its natural splendor. Small areas on both the Brazilian and Argentine side of the falls have been designated as nature reserves.

From the tourist hotels sited at the borders of the three countries it is possible to watch the unusual behavior of swallows that build their nests in rocks behind the Iguaçu's curtain of water. This protects them from predators. During the day one can observe large flocks of swallows wheeling above the torrents as they catch insects to feed their young before returning to their brood with their catches.

Rare butterflies

The many different butterflies provide further colorful visual splendor in this tropical paradise. They can be seen everywhere: bright blue, yellow, white with red spots, and many other magnificent colors. At least the butterflies are less at risk here of being captured by native butterfly hunters who earn a living from selling these beautiful butterflies which are close to extinction elsewhere. Giant species with wingspans of almost eight inches are so sought after in the area around the falls that they are threatened with extinction.

ROUTE

Flights from Buenos Aires, São Paulo, and Rio de Janeiro

BEST TIMES

November–March

ACCOMMODATIONS

Hotel das Cataratas (next to falls) and Hotel Rodovia das Cataratas (17 miles)

ALSO WORTH SEEING

Itaipu, the world's largest hydro-power station (book through hotels and travel agents)

There are 21 major and 250 lesser falls at the borders with Brazil, Argentina, and Paraguay spread across a crescent of 2 miles and plunging 260 ft into the Devil's Gorge

A lot of ice in Patagonia

Wild natural beauty at the southern tip of the inhabited world

SOUTH AMERICA

ARGENTINA

Pacific Ocean

Patagonia

Atlantic Ocean

ROUTE
To San Carlos Bariloche by air from Buenos Aires to El Calafate, entrance to nature reserve Los Glaciares and Torres del Paine from Buenos Aires via Rio Gallegos

BEST TIMES
October–March

ACCOMMODATIONS
Hotel Llao-Llao (one of Argentina's best) on lake Nahuel Huapi near San Carlos Bariloche, where there is also more budget accommodation

A large block of ice that has broken away floats in the wild sea like some giant claw of a predator. Anyone who comes too close will be irretrievably lost for this is close to the notorious Cape Horn, where the great storms of the Southern Ocean collide with those of the Pacific and Atlantic. The wilderness of Patagonia was first reconnoitered by air in the 1920s by the German adventurer Gunther Pluschow in his "Silver Condor" aircraft.

This wild tip of Argentina and Chile got its name from the Portuguese seafarer Ferdinand Magellan who dubbed it Patagonia because of the *patagones* or big feet from the tracks they discovered everywhere. These tracks were made by the primitive footwear of the native Tehuelche people which they made from *guanacos*' skins (a type of llama).

The Cordillera a boundary

Neither Magellan or the British naturalist Charles Darwin (in 1834) found the summit of the Cordillera particularly attractive. Darwin recorded that "an infertility curse lies over this land." The German aviator-explorer Pluschow on the other hand found the richly tinted landscape very exciting. His descriptions started to fuel the eventual growth in interest in tourism to this far-flung corner of our planet with its fiords, glaciers, primeval forests, semi-deserts, seal islands, and largest sheep pastures in the world.

Patagonia extends over 1,242 miles from the Colorado wells to Cape Horn. The eastern part is Chilean while the less mountainous and more extensive western part is Argentine. The ice encrusted mountains running from north to south form the boundary between the two countries. In Argentina parts of Patagonia consist of steppe-like

plains across which strong icy winds blow, but despite this harsh climate the land is fertile and supports around twenty million sheep. Admittedly more than twelve acres of land are needed per sheep, but land is plentiful in this part of the world. The woolly flocks share the land with the native guanacos and nandoes (the Patagonian ostrich).

On the mountainous Chilean west coast rainfall is much more abundant and everything is covered in greenery. The northwestern part of these mountains resemble the European Alps, leading to the name of "the South American Switzerland." Milking cows graze Alpine meadows and there are also "Alpine" views and farms that resemble

buildings in the Black Forest and Swiss chalets. In common with the Alps there is also the panorama of snow-capped mountains.

Further south the mountains that form the border are covered with the largest ice sheet of the world except for that at the two poles. Continuous heavy snowfall has formed twice the depth of ice here that is found in Iceland. This is why such enormous glaciers have formed here, threading their way to the lower land. On the Chilean side the glaciers feed regular crops of new icebergs into the sea while on the Argentine side enormous glaciers of blue ice thunder downwards, leading to severe flooding. The largest of the Patagonian glaciers, the Perito

Moreno, surges continuously forward with a two-and-one-half-mile-wide and 230-foot-high wall of ice into the two elongated crescents that are the lake known as Lago Argentino.

The Moreno Glacier has left a memorial to Gunther Pluschow untouched. He died nearby when his Heinkel seaplane crashed in the Lago Argentino on January 28, 1931. His last flight had been over the ice sheets, swamps, mountainous seas, and glaciers of Patagonia.

Three views of Patagonia: the summit of Cerro Fitzroy (11,072 ft.) above is considered one of the five most difficult peaks to scale by mountaineers. The Moreno glacier (left) pushes a 2½-mile-wide and 230-foot-high wall of ice into the Lago Argentino. A vast steppe-like landscape characterizes the southeast of Patagonia.

Highway to adventure

The Pan-American Highway runs from Alaska to the southern mountains ranges of Argentina

NORTH AMERICA
Atlantic Ocean
Panamerica
Pacific Ocean
SOUTH AMERICA

ROUTE

By well-equipped and well-maintained vehicle from the highways of the U.S. and Canada. Take important spare parts, replacing them en route could prove very expensive. By boat or air around the missing portion through the Darien Gap

BEST TIMES

Ideally a year-long journey but aim to travel from the north during spring and be in the south by December

The northern part of the Pan-American highway is the Alaska Highway that was constructed during World War II to help defend the most northerly state of the U.S.

The Pan-American Highway appears in travel guides as an "ideal" road to adventure. The famous (and infamous) highway is not a single road but interconnecting series of roads from the Alaskan Highway in the far north of the U.S. through the Inter-American Highway of Mexico and Central America into South America on the final leg of the Pan-American route. Depending on the starting point and route chosen, the trip can be from over 15,000 to around 28,000 miles.

The original intention of North and South American countries in the nineteenth century was to construct a Pan-American railroad. At a joint conference at Santiago, Chile in 1923 preference was given for a Pan-American freeway, known in Spanish as *Carretera Interamericana*. The U.S. contributed its western coastal freeway to the project, but it was difficult to complete an unbroken link through the difficult terrain of Central and South America, with much of the proposed route running through swamp and tropical rain forest. Part of the proposed highway between eastern Panama and Colombia has still not been constructed and may never be because of both political and environmental issues.

Also passable in winter

The main extension of the Pan-American Highway was made by the U.S. with the building of the Alaska Highway. This was constructed in 1942 in a matter of months to make it easier to defend the northernmost state of the Union in the event of a Japanese invasion. Since then civilians have also benefited from this highway that is also passable in winter, linking Alaska across Canada with the North

American coastal road Highway 101 that forms part of the Pan-American route. In his book *Panamericana*, Roland E. Jung describes a journey by car in forty-two days from Alaska across the Equator to Tierra del Fuego.

The Swiss motoring writer Peter Ruch took five months on a motorbike along the highway on a similar journey traveling about 15,500 miles. The high-points for Ruch were the enormous Matanuska Glacier in Alaska, the wild landscape of the Fraser Valley in Canada, attractive Mexican towns such as Guadalajara and Putzcuaro, the Mayan ruins of Copan in Honduras, the old colonial town of Cartagena in Colombia, and the snow-covered peaks of volcanoes to the east of the highway in Chile.

The journey's toll

Most travelers along the Pan-American Highway find that they pay a high price in order to see its beauty. The searing heat or biting cold, mechanical problems, blocked side roads, unbelievably high tolls apart from bribes to corrupt police and other officials, together with some hatred and envy of foreigners all make the journey a major challenge.

But the lure of adventure continually draws people to it. Clemens Carles, who was born in Germany, did the journey in the opposite direction on a cycle. He started his epic mountain bike adventure at Ushaia—the southernmost town in South America— and pedaled north towards the polar circle and the Arctic Ocean. He more or less followed the line of the Pan-American Highway—apart from

an excursion to the east to view the Iguaçu Falls on the borders of Brazil, Paraguay, and Argentina.

His journey took him through eighteen different countries and was filled with all manner of trouble, political unrest, robberies, torrential rain, and copious amounts of bureaucratic wrangling. Close to exhaustion on a worse than usual road in Columbia the German cyclist wrestled his way through the jungle of the Darien Gap to Panama. It took Clemens three years to complete his journey which he has since recalled in books and articles.

When he finished the journey the odometer on his mountain bike read 44,620 kilometers (27,725 miles).

In the north of Chile the Pan-American Highway follows route CH 11 that links Chile across the Andes with Bolivia. Between Big Sur and Morro Bay in California the route follows Highway A1 for splendid panoramas of the Pacific coastline. The total length of the Pan-American is up to about 24,800 miles, depending on the route chosen.

Manhattan, the city of all cities

Manhattan's skyscrapers acclaim the New Yorker's zest for life

NORTH AMERICA

USA

New York

Pacific Ocean

ROUTE

Bus from JFK Airport to Grand Central Terminal

BEST TIMES

April–June and September–October

OPENING TIMES

View locations: Empire State building – daily 9.30 a.m.–11.30 p.m.

ALSO WORTH SEEING

Statue of Liberty, Long Island, Hudson River Valley

Manhattan was once just a small settlement. However, right from the outset, the town on Manhattan Island between the Hudson and East Rivers was a melting pot of people of many racial backgrounds. In 1524 Giovanni da Verrazano, a Florentine in the service of the French king Francis I, landed in what is now New York Bay. The Englishman Henry Hudson, who worked for the East India Company also landed there in 1609, but the first colony was founded in 1624 when Dutch settlers established New Amsterdam on Manhattan Island. By 1643 the colony numbered about five hundred persons, who spoke eighteen different languages. The settlement was taken over by the English in 1664, who renamed the town for the English king's brother, the Duke of York. In 1788 New York became the capital of the eponymous state, which was the eleventh of the initial thir-

teen states of the United States. Two years later the city was easily the largest in North America with 31,131 inhabitants. The city spread from the island of Manhattan to the mainland so that a bridge was urgently needed. In 1883, the newly built Brooklyn Bridge was at that time the longest suspension bridge in the world. The bridge linked the island of Manhattan with Brooklyn and Queens to form Greater New York City.

The golden apex of the Fuller Building, erected in 1929.

These days Manhattan is a city of two faces: one is hectic and glittering with busy streets, bars, cinemas, theaters, museums, galleries, cheap stores, and classy boutiques, the other is a commercial center trying to turn that extra buck, usually way way up above the street level. Since the end of the nineteenth century Manhattan has increasingly been shaped by office blocks, rising ever higher into the sky to maximize returns on the enormous cost of land there. This has made Manhattan the world capital of skyscrapers.

The peaks were decorated

Ever-higher buildings were made possible with the advent of the steel-frame of girders that enabled increasing numbers of storeys to be piled one on top of another. The style with which some architects executed such miracles is part of what makes Manhattan so exciting. The Flatiron Build-

ing of 1902 is a particularly fine example of the sculptural form that can be created with a building. In the 1930s architects returned from Europe with decorative motifs which they used to embellish their skyscrapers. Such an example is the General Electric Building of Cross & Cross. The apex of this office complex was decorated by them with a fine Gothic tracery of red bricks, enriched with glazed earthenware. The most famous building of them all—though no longer the tallest—the Empire State, is embellished with an Art Deco facade that reveals architecture as an aesthetic art form.

When skyscrapers started to be built in other cities, Manhattan developed the "international style" as this European-influenced but essentially American architecture was described. An architect who is now regarded as the "grand old man" of skyscrapers built his first at this time. He is Philip Johnson who gained his first international recognition in 1958 for the Seagram Building that he designed with his colleague Mies van der Rohe. Twenty years later in 1978, the architectural team of Hugh Stubbins & Associates set new standards with the forty-six-storey Citicorp Center that has become a striking feature of the Manhattan skyline with its four gigantic towers high above Lexington Avenue with the arresting peak at an angle of forty-five degrees. The following year Johnson returned to start construction of the first post-modernist skyscraper for AT&T. The office block, in the form of a Chippendale chest, was completed in 1983. Johnson dared to experiment with different forms and set new standards that freed architecture from a rigid set of aesthetic "rules."

Until their tragic destruction in September 2001, the twin towers of the World Trade Center dominated the skyline of Lower Manhattan.
The Chrysler Building (above) is exuberantly decorated in Art Deco style.

The "thundering water"

Niagara's cliffs are a spectacular backdrop to adventure

NORTH AMERICA

NIAGARA FALLS

USA

Atlantic Ocean

Pacific Ocean

ROUTE

Internal flight to Buffalo, New York. Daily shuttle flights from Toronto. By road from Toronto or New York

BEST TIMES

June–August

ACCOMODATION

Hotels and motels in all price categories. Book well in advance

ALSO WORTH SEEING

Trips on the "Maid of the Mist", hovercraft trips on the Niagara River, and helicopter flights over the falls

Every minute around forty-five million gallons of water cascade over the 164 feet high horseshoe escarpment of the Niagara Falls from Lake Erie to Lake Ontario. The two lakes are linked by the Niagara River. A heavy mist is always present above the abyss and conceals the tourist boat "Maid of the Mist" from which thousands of people clad in multi-hued rainwear each year get a grandstand view of the magnificent natural spectacle.

Native Americans called the world's most famous waterfall "the water that thunders." The falls are situated on the border between the United States and Canada and are actually two cataracts: the Horseshoe Falls in Canada and the American Falls in the U.S. Between them they are a Mecca for tourists, seekers of Dutch metal, and a magnet for those planning suicide. Charles Dickens was so impressed by the awesome power the falls reveal of nature and wrote: "It was as if I had left the earth and cast a glance in heaven." His fellow countryman Oscar Wilde on the other hand—commenting on the flourishing marital tourism—observed: "The Niagara Falls are the biggest disappointment of American married life."

Ice from Lake Erie

Few people can tear themselves away from the spectacle. The sound of the water tumbling can be heard from some way off and closer you can actually feel the ground vibrate. The Niagara Falls are most impressive at the start of spring when the Niagara River transports great floes of ice from Lake Erie that tumble over the falls with a great crashing sound to form a great barrier of ice.

The main tourist season starts in May with 35,000 people per day at the peak and around thirteen million in total visiting the cataracts each year. Not everyone comes to look, some come to be seen because the falls are such a spectacular stage backdrop for those who wish to perform. Many have attempted to ride the falls in a boat while others have tried barrels such as the mad Englishman Charles Stephens. This father of eleven allowed himself to be thrown over the Falls tied to an oak barrel. Niagara only relinquished his arm, still tied to the lid of the barrel.

Border skirmishes on the banks

The main drama here in earlier times was between soldiers. When America joined in war with its British colonial masters in 1812, the Americans quickly seized the town on the Niagara peninsula and the banks of the falls that were in the British province of Canada. It took two years before the governor of Upper Canada, Isaac Brock was able to force the Americans to retreat. There are a number of historical monuments on the western bank of the Niagara River that remind us of this conflict, which gave the Canadians their first sense of a separate identity from America.

There are twin cities of Niagara Falls on both sides of the border but nobody really cares today whether the thundering water falls on American or Canadian soil although people still hunt for relics of the British colonial past.

After a visit to the Falls a drive around the wine region and the beautiful landscape of the peninsula, or through the attractive town center of Niagara on the lake are a must. This was once the capital of Upper Canada and the town is still very traditional and decidedly British in style.

The road from which tourists can watch the spectacle of Niagara Falls is on the waterfront. The panorama (left) shows the grandeur of the landscape.

The American Dead Sea

The size of the Great Salt Lake depends on the rain

NORTH AMERICA

Salt Lake City
USA

Pacific
Ocean

ROUTE

Flight to Salt Lake City from throughout U.S. San Francisco to Salt Lake City is about 750 miles

BEST TIMES

April–June,
September–November

OPENING TIMES

Visitor Center at Great Salt Lake City State Park on Antelope Island open 9 a.m.–5 p.m.

ALSO WORTH SEEING

Salt Lake City: Temple Square (entry for Mormons only), Pioneer Trail State Park

The lake, sixty-two miles long and around thirty miles wide, covers a large area of the northern part of the state of Utah but it is a fraction of the size it once was. This inland sea was almost 20,000 square miles and once stretched far into Nevada and Idaho. There is a very real risk that America's dead sea—the Great Salt Lake—may shrink still further because the inflow from the Bear River, Weber River, and Jordan River that rise in the Wasatch mountains and the Rockies is no longer sufficient to replenish the water in the lake.

Once the lake was almost one thousand feet deep but today it is barely sixteen feet in depth. Changes in inflow and evaporation have caused the level to drop at a rate of about two feet each year. Any sudden change in the level of water entering the lake immediately effects the size of the lake because the banks of the lake are so shallow. The lake is regarded as a sensitive climatic indicator because a loss of just two feet in depth results in a loss of almost one hundred square miles of surface area. This is why the lake expanded to more than 2,300 square miles in the wet 1980s but was a mere 965 square miles in the much drier years of the 1960s.

The Mormons, who colonized this area and made Salt Lake City the capital of both their land and the state of Utah, have never concerned themselves much about the volume of their "holy" lake. It was here that their prophet Brigham Young heard God's call on July 24, 1847 in which he was told how life was to be led in this "holy" community. Today's Mormons still adhere to strict codes established by their founder and their temple complex is still the center of the city, with its population of 160,000.

Railroad crosses the lake on a dike

The lake posed a major problem for those building the railroads across America and for a long time it stood in the way of the great east–west route New York–Chicago–Omaha–Cheyenne–Ogden–San Francisco. The Union Pacific line through Utah between Ogden and Lucin could not be linked directly until the Lucin Cut-

off was built between 1902 and 1904 to carry the railroad over the lake on a dike. This runs for more than twelve miles across the lake.

Despite the high salinity of the water in the lake—which can be as high as twenty-seven percent—there is life in the lake; not in the water, but on islands in the lake where bison and pelicans have found refuge from people. Since the 1950s, large quantities of cooking salt have been recovered from the lake—over 165,000 tons each year. At Grantsville on the southern shore a flourishing industry has sprung up producing chemical salts from the bed of the lake.

The lake has found a wide range of other uses from early on. The salt flats were soon used by the U.S. Army as a testing ground for new vehicles and this lured privateers here too which soon resulted in the creation of the "Bonneville Speedway". This seemingly endless flat track has been the scene of many world speed records. The track is marked with a black line in the salt but if no records are planned, or if heavy rain has washed out the markings then anyone can use the speedway. In a country that is so strict on speeding on the highway the salt flats are a great draw for those seeking the thrill of speed.

The Great Salt Lake was once much bigger—stretching way into Idaho and Nevada. The reduced flow of water into the lake these days is not enough to compensate for evaporation. The salt industry (below) benefits though and the car industry tests new automobiles here. The salt flats are often used for attempts at the world speed record.

Grand Canyon National Park

The Colorado River creates a glimpse of our earth's history

ROUTE
Flights from Los Angeles and Las Vegas to Grand Canyon. By road: 81 miles north from Flagstaff, Arizona on Arizona 64

BEST TIMES
South rim closed October–May. Extremely hot at the height of summer

ACCOMMODATIONS
Grand Canyon National Park Lodges

ALSO WORTH SEEING
Canyonlands National Park, Utah

The steep walls of the Grand Canyon glisten colorfully as if lit by the sun. The strata revealed by the Colorado River's erosion expose the history of the earth

The Grand Canyon is 217 miles of territory from another world. In 1898, the Scottish writer John Muir wrote of the Grand Canyon: "Its architecture is so unworldly, it is as if one has landed on an extinct place on another planet. A play of nature, wonderful, bizarre, huge. Unbelievable colours, dramatic contrasts, the intense aromas of nature, the deadly silence."

The Colorado River has carved its way through rock for more than ten million years, revealing the history of our earth as recorded in the strata in the canyon's walls. The wonderful natural spectacle was created by the river but its beauty has been preserved by the low rainfall of Arizona. If there was more the superb colors of the canyon walls would have been washed away.

The gorge is more than a mile deep

The magnificence of the Grand Canyon does not impress from a distance. It is just a chain of rocks, like so many others between Utah and Arizona, until one nears the rim of the canyon and looks into its depth. The best vantage point is Desert View. Only then do you see layer upon layer of glowing shades of red that form a stark contrast with the ponderosa pine forest. This inverted mountain is growing downwards through the flow of the shimmering ribbon of silver at its base: the Colorado River.

The river's current has dissected a cross-section through the earth's crust, as if with a scalpel, allowing us a glimpse into millions of years of the

Panoramic view of the Grand Canyon. The Colorado flows at about 12 m.p.h., tumbling throug

earth's history. The geology spans many eras but the canyon is also impressive for its sheer size. It is more than one mile deep and the Colorado River which formed it transports around 44,000 tons of soil through the canyon each day much of which is deposited lower down. This has caused the Clen Canyon to form through deposits of around 800,000 tons of sediment. The canyon bottom can reach temperatures as high as 113°F (45°C) in summer—as high as the deserts of Mexico—while it is a more comfortable 75°F (24°C) outside the canyon.

The first Europeans to see the canyon were a group of Spanish led by Francisco Vasquez de Coronado in 1540 exploring the territory of the

60 rapids in its course.

Hopi native Americans. The canyon was an unbridgeable obstacle for them. The most spectacular section of the canyon became a National Park in 1919, covering an area of over 1,900 square miles.

Around 30,000 people visit the view points each day during the main season (about four million each year). These are scattered around the gorge and there are also places where it is possible to descend into the canyon. One of the most popular places for holiday snapshots is Hopi Point, a protruding rock platform from which you can see from west to east.

Today some five hundred Havasupai native Americans live in the bottom of the gorge. This tribe came here in the twelfth century as a refuge and one of the attractions of a visit to their reservation is the chance to see the three emerald green waterfalls from which the tribe derive their name—"people of the green water." The Havasupai have been able to ward off all attempts at infringement into their gorge during the course of their history. There were plans to lay a railroad across their land in 1889, intentions for a Christian chapel in one of the canyon walls with a lift, and proposals in 1961 for developers to build an eighteen-storey hotel into the south wall. The people of the green water are resigned to such attempts, but then they have been patiently dwelling in the Grand Canyon for eight hundred years.

View points like these attract 30,000 visitors each day in season.

The Golden Gate Bridge

A technical miracle spanning San Francisco Bay

NORTH AMERICA

USA

• **San Francisco**

Pacific Ocean

ROUTE

Buses for Golden Gate, change Market Street/corner 7th Street for Golden Gate Bridge

BEST TIMES

September–October

ACCOMMODATIONS

Sherman House, 2160 Green St. (Victorian villa with view of Alcatraz and the bridge)

ALSO WORTH SEEING

Golden Gate Park, Alcatraz, Fisherman's Wharf, View from Telegraph Hill

Bridge builder Joseph Baermann took on a battle against the elements with the construction of a suspension bridge across San Francisco Bay. He had to cope with the tides of the Pacific Ocean, the furious storms that can batter America's west coast, and the risk of earthquakes and he triumphed over all of them. The final rivet of the project Americans consider as the "seventh wonder of the world wrought by human hands" was driven on May 27, 1937: San Francisco's Golden Gate Bridge was finally completed.

The Golden Gate is the strait at the entrance to San Francisco Bay that separates the bay from the Pacific Ocean. The promoters of the bridge decided to raise steel towers of 745 feet on either side of the strait on which to attach thick steel cables to support a suspension bridge. The bridge is 9,186 feet long with a central span of 4,200 feet. The bridge deck needed to be 220 feet above the surface of the bay to enable ships to pass through.

Risk of collapse during construction

Construction of the bridge started in 1933 and ran into immediate difficulties. The first attempts to form a foundation for the southern pylon on a platform three hundred feet below water failed because of the strong tidal flow. During one of San Francisco Bay's notorious fogs a ship rammed a work platform and sank. Soon after this three huge blocks of concrete needed for the foundations and some construction equipment fell into the sea. Storms in the fall swept away more equipment, and workers suffered from sea-sickness.

One especially hazardous operation was the stringing of the thirty-six inch thick cables that are made up of 27,000 separate strands of wire. There was a continuous risk of collapse because of gusts of wind or carelessness so a safety net was rigged part-way through the operation. This act saved the lives of nineteen men who fell. These nineteen workers who survived the fall formed the "Halfway to Hell Club." The bridge builders Ed Murphy and Ed Stanley wanted the final rivet to be driven on May 27, 1937 to be one of gold but the golden rivet was too soft and it broke, disappearing into the depths. Therefore the final rivet to be hammered home was of steel, like the countless others in this million ton structure. The opening of the bridge was celebrated for many days and tens of thousands of pedestrians crossed the new construction.

The Golden Gate Bridge quickly recovered its investment. In the early years an average of four million motorists crossed the bridge each year. Half a century later in 1987 ten times as many were using the bridge. This does not include the many pedestrians and joggers who cross toll free while enjoying one of the world's most amazing vistas.

The Golden Gate Bridge has withstood the risks that Baermann had to overcome, such as bad weather, and the passage of time, and remains in reasonable condition despite all the pessimistic predictions. Severe storms can cause the road deck to sway considerably. During World War II the R.M.S. Queen Elizabeth passed through the strait laden with troops with barely forty inches to spare between her funnels and the bridge deck.

The world's most famous suspension bridge also attracts those

with suicide on their mind. More than a thousand people have jumped from the bridge. When fogs rolls in from the Pacific only the towering pylons can sometimes be seen rising out of the mist. Another ethereal character to the strait is lent by the water organ of the Golden Gate Yacht Club which automatically pipes to announce the turn of the tide.

The Golden Gate Bridge—built between 1933 and 1937—saves motorists driving between San Francisco and Marin County from a long detour. The bridge is 9,186 feet long with a central span of 4,200 feet. The height of the deck above the sea varies from 216–236 feet, depending on the tide.

The mammoth trees of America

Sequoias grow 440 feet high and live for thousands of years

NORTH AMERICA

USA
**Sequoia
National Park**

*Pacific
Ocean*

ROUTE

From Los Angeles via
Interstate 5 to Bakersfield,
Highway 99 and 63 to
Visalia, Highway 198 through
the Sequoia National Park.
Total journey 218 miles

BEST TIMES

June–September (closed in
winter)

ACCOMMODATIONS

Giant Forest Lodge, Grant
Grove Lodge, motels at Three
Rivers

ALSO WORTH SEEING

Kings Canyon National Park
(northern neighbor to
Sequoia N.P.), Yosemite
National Park (125 miles to
the north)

Fur trappers were the first people who claimed to have seen giant redwoods with trunks as thick as an elephant. They swore they had seen such trees with their own eyes and this was the God's honest truth. These trees were on the western escarpment of the Sierra Nevada. They should have kept quiet about them for soon lumberjacks were felling great swathes of these trees.

The giant Californian redwood or "big tree" is known to scientists as *Sequoiadendron giganteum* and is related to the swamp cypress. They can reach heights of 440 feet. Some of the enormous trees that were felled were three to four thousand years old. Their lumber ended up as dance floors or bowling alleys. Two of the largest specimens were auctioned to be exhibited as wonders of the world.

The survival of the remaining "big trees" in Southern California is due to the activity of a few men who established the Sequoia national Park in 1890 against the wishes of the lumber industry. The Giant Forest area became the showpiece of the National park to the north of Los Angeles. It was here that the native American Monachi brought the cattle breeder Hale Tharp in 1858. He moved into the burnt out trunk

The tallest trees in the Sequoia National Park are between 2,500 and 3,000 years old and more than 260 feet high. If allowed to continue to grow they will live for several thousand years more. These mammoth trees do not die of old age but when the roots can no longer support the 100-plus tons of their trunks, or when destroyed by fire.

of a sequoia, bought a piece of ground, and then refused to sell despite offers of huge sums until the government took over the land to form a national park.

There is a thrilling walking trail through the middle of this forest of mammoths, the Congress Trail. Taken at an easy pace it takes about two hours to complete. You will see that the trees are just as those fur trappers described them: as tall as church spires, and as thick as an elephant. The name sequoia is derived from Cherokee Chief Sequoyah who drafted the native American alphabet from which the botanists took the name. An individual tree is also named for him and others are named for prominent politicians and generals of United States history.

Drive straight through the tree

One particularly large example is known as General Sherman of the Union army during the civil war of 1861–1865 who decisively won the final victory for the Union against the Confederates with his troops. The celebrated sequoia known as "The Largest Living Thing" is 2,500–3,000 years old with a diameter of its trunk at the base of more than 102 feet. The trunk reaches upwards to almost 275 feet and the diameter of the upper trunk is more then thirty-six feet. It has been calculated that the tree contains 52,477 cubic feet of lumber, weighing about 1,384 tons.

Trees of a similar size can be found in the two neighboring national parks. In Kings Canyon National Park the tree known as General Grant—Union commanding general and one-time president—is just over 267 feet tall with a trunk that is just over 107 feet in diameter. In Yosemite National Park you can admire the Grizzly Giant that is about 2,700 years old and about 210 feet tall. Close by this specimen is a tree with a tunnel bored through its trunk large enough to allow buses to pass through after the tree fell in 1968.

Chambord: a dream turned to stone

This château on the Loire became the model for grand absolutist architecture

ROUTE

From Paris on the A10 via Orléans to Mer, then cross the Loire and take D112 to Chambord (distance 94 miles). Closest rail stations at Mer and Blois

OPENING TIMES

Daily from 9.30 a.m.–4.45 p.m. or 6.45 p.m. depending on time of year

ALSO WORTH SEEING

Châteaux on the Loire, including Blois and Orléans

When a power conscious ruler, inveterate womanizer, and unstoppable visionary builds himself a hunting lodge then it must be something very special. Francis I (1494–1547) created a dream in stone when he built Chambord. It is a splendid work of fantasy, like a tale from the *Thousand and One Nights*. When the Holy Roman Emperor Charles V visited this most pompous of all royal hunting lodges in 1539, with its 440 rooms, eighty-three stairways, and overall dimensions of 512 feet by 384 feet, it moved him to state: "Chambord is the paragon of the works of art humans can create."

Francis I, king of France, was constantly at war with the Habsburgs for control of Europe and developed his desire for a Renaissance châteaux while campaigning in Italy. It was important for him that he and his hunting friends should be as well cared for as they were at court. The southwest of the Sologne was considered the best location for such a château because the king could indulge his passion for hunting there. The area then was filled with wild boar and deer and remains one of the best places for hunting in France to this day. Since the site chosen for the palace was marshland, building it was more of a nightmare

than a dream, and when a plan to divert the Loire proved unsuccessful an entirely new river bed was dug at Cosson. It was essential to the king that the beauty of the château be reflected in water.

The plans for the château were drawn by Italian architects with the medieval style of French castle as their starting point. A monumental tower was sited in a large square structure to mimic the *donjon* or lookout tower of earlier settlements. This central feature remains the heart of the château today. A roof terrace is reached by means of a stairway, but not just any stairway. Part of the wonder of Chambord is this truly

royal entrance through the *escalier meridional*. It is believed that the plans for this were drawn by Leonardo da Vinci. It is certainly true that Francis persuaded the original "Renaissance man" to come to the Loire and a love for architecture is one of the many things for which the master was renowned. Double helix stairways spiral in opposing directions, with deep windows that enable you to see both ascending and descending visitors without them meeting one another. This part of the château is also said to represent the globe, while rooms on one floor are grouped in a Grecian circle.

Revolutionary plunder

The roof terrace was designed for festivities. The château served as the pedestal to the roof terrace rising above it like a giant centerpiece, with 365 chimneys, hundreds of spires, capitals, lanterns, and bell towers.

People partied on the roof, played games there, walked around beneath parasols, got drunk, or looked out for returning hunting parties to see if they had been successful.

Francis I did not live to see his château completed. His successors reluctantly continued with the building of it, but it was Louis XIV who added some sparkle to Chambord when he rediscovered the place during the construction of his palace at Versailles. The French revolutionaries of 1789 were opposed to the grandeur of Chambord and they plundered the château of its furniture, wall hangings, and paintings. Under state ownership and stewardship efforts have been made to restore Chambord's decaying glory, partly funded by tourism. A visit to Chambord is an absolute must for anyone visiting the Loire.

The Loire was diverted so that Chambord's beauty could be reflected in it when the château was built between 1519 and 1537. Francis I was inspired by the palaces of the Italian Renaissance. The enormous building has 440 rooms, 83 stairways, and is the largest of the châteaux of the Loire. The imposing towers and turrets emphasize the building's grandeur and enclose a roof terrace where elaborate court parties were held.

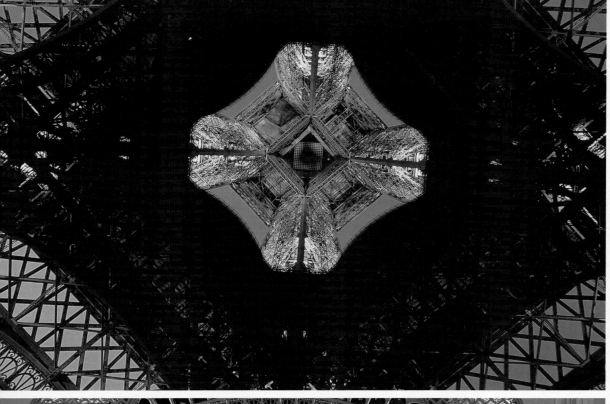

The Eiffel Tower: the best-known face of Paris

The most important structure of the 19th century looks out across Paris

ROUTE

Hakeim (Metro line 9), Trocadero (line 6), Champs de Mars/Tour Eiffel (RER)

OPENING TIMES

Daily 9.30 a.m.–11 p.m. (9–midnight July–August)

FOOD

Restaurant Jules Verne (2nd floor)

ALSO WORTH SEEING

Arc de Triomphe, Notre-Dame, Sacre-Coeur, The Louvre, Pompidou Center, The Pantheon

There was a struggle at first. As soon as it became known there were plans to build a 984 foot tower in the center of Paris for the World's Fair of 1889 architects, artists, and politicians got the "Petition of 300" together. This warned of disfigurement to the capital and described the plans to build what they described as a "pitch-black chimney" as a "fraud like ugliness." The tower was built in spite of these protests and subsequently contributed much to the fame of both France and Paris.

The initial plans were made by Maurice Koch, a technical assistant employed by Alexandre Gustave Eiffel's (1832–1923) engineering and construction company. Eiffel, a descendent of German immigrants from the Eiffel region, was awarded the lucrative contract for the World's Fair when his company won the architectural competition held by the department of commerce.

Champs de Mars building site

The city of Paris provided an old training ground on the banks of the Seine, known as the Champs de Mars, as site for the new structure and the foundations were established in 1887. Eiffel had four huge concrete anchors, each fifty feet by twenty-six feet, set in the natural gravel bed of the waterside site to carry the burden of the four "elephant legs" and the entire weight of the tower of some 10,700 tons. Erection of the steel work started on July 1, 1887 to a carefully prepared plan. Workers had to join together twelve thousand separate pieces that were then partially assembled at an ironworks in Clichy.

It was an amazing puzzle which Parisians watched rise before their gaze. Eiffel's planning was so sound that he used a surplus crane to

construct the lifts which take people to the viewing platforms at heights of 187, 377, and 899 feet above the ground.

As the tower grew higher it cast its shadow across Paris like a sun dial but the vociferous group of protesters got smaller and smaller. The vast majority of Parisians were now acclaiming and admiring the apparent elegance of the edifice with its web-like structure which enables this colossus to give an impression of delicate tracery in spite of its significant mass.

When the tower was completed on time on March 31, 1889, and Eiffel had the French tricolor run up at a height of 985 feet 10 inches, newspapers celebrated the tower as a "triumph of the modern industrial culture" and as a grand secular counterpart to the Sacre-Coeur— that other elevated monument that can be seen from much of Paris.

From the highest observation point it was possible not just to see all of Paris but on a clear day to see far into the countryside surrounding the city.

Monument of the Revolution

For the opening of the World's Fair in 1889 the steel structure that quickly became known as the Eiffel Tower was illuminated with ten thousand gas lamps which competed with the fireworks display for the Fair.

Gustave Eiffel declared that for him the tower was a monument to the French Revolution of 1789 which created the conditions for "the century of industry and technique," which was so emphatically celebrated at the World's Fair.

In addition to great renown, the *Tour Eiffel* brought great financial rewards to its creator. The company owning the tower earned more than the construction costs in the first

year alone. The Eiffel Tower quickly became the "trade mark" of Paris and has helped to make Paris one of the most popular city destinations for tourists. In 1929 a radio mast was added to the top of the tower, followed in 1935 by a television transmitter, increasing the height of the tower to 1,052 feet. There is a laboratory, meteorological station, equipment for air traffic, and a small apartment on the top platform. Eiffel once used the apartment.

The original height of the Eiffel Tower was 984 ft but it is now 1,052 ft with its television antenna. The original weight of 10,700 tons was reduced by 1,477 tons after renovation. Some five million people visit the tower each year, which is the city's biggest attraction and its world "trade mark."

Palace of the Sun King

Versailles' pomp was created to reflect the power and glory of Louis XIV

ROUTE

12½ miles SW of Paris. Fast RER train to Versailles Rive-Gauche

OPENING TIMES

May–September 9 a.m.– 6.30 p.m.; October–April 9 a.m.–5.30 p.m. (closed Mondays)

ACCOMMODATIONS

Trianon Palace, Boulevard de la Reine (luxury); Hotel de Clagny, Impasse de Clagny (budget)

Louis XIII had a hunting lodge built in the wilderness-like landscape of Versailles. This was a simple brick-built building of three wings that was surrounded by water. His son Louis XIV had many fond boyhood memories of this château and so he chose it as a refuge where he could conduct his affair with Mademoiselle de la Valiere. The outside of the château was adorned for him with all manner of finery and he had the interior modernized and added a separate new wing.

When Louis XIV decided to make the château his palace and to move the court there from Paris in 1668, he needed much more space in which to hold court and give recep-

tions and grand state occasions. Therefore, Louis Le Vau was commissioned to give the new palace a scale more becoming such a royal purpose. Further embellishments in the form of the grand exterior windows were executed by the architect Jules Mansart ten years later in order to further enhance the brilliance of *Le Roi Soleil*—the Sun King—as Louis XIV was now known.

A triumph of obsession

The palace had to be grand by design with "scale, design, and beauty which would remain throughout the centuries as a testimony to the self-esteem of the most powerful king in Europe," and in this it certainly succeeded. It was a tremendous testimo-

ny to the power of Louis XIV. His court at Versailles in 1682 numbered twenty thousand, at least five thousand of which lived in the palace itself, which has 1,300 rooms heated by fires from 1,252 chimneys. The stables alone can house 2,500 horses and two hundred coaches. The Sun King's power was not solely reflected by the palace but by his ability to constantly succeed in throwing ever-increasing sums into the project against wide opposition. Former people of great influence such as his Chancellor of the Exchequer who were opposed to further extravagance were dishonored. Even natural obstacles could not stand in the way of the king's obsession.

Duc Louis de St. Simon described Versailles as: "A glum, meager place,

without view, no forest, no water, and even without firm foundation because the ground here consists of quicksand and morass, and inside there is a serious lack of fresh air." The king merely laughed at such criticism and had his soldiers reclaim the swamp, plant mature trees, and dig miles of ditches to provide water for both wells and fountains.

A complete work of art

The completed work of art became what the garden historian Wilfried Hansmann described as: "The most tremendous edifice of all architecture and garden history of the Occident." The importance of the green surroundings to the palace for Louis is revealed in the instruction given to the garden designer André Le Nôtre to design a king's garden "such as the world has never seen before." From this point onwards the extension of the grounds surrounding the palace became the main priority above all other building work.

While Mansart was decorating the interior of the palace with marble, gold, and silver— the Sun King received messengers and envoys from every point of the compass while seated on a silver throne—and created a Hall of Mirrors in which the magnificence was multiplied, Le Nôtre was enhancing the garden with walkways, vistas, fountains, rills, ponds, garden sculpture, and an orangery. The culmination was the creation of the royal villas known as the Grand and Petit Trianons. Queen Marie Antoinette, for whom the Petit Trianon was built, described it as "the merriest message of Versailles."

Versailles, seen from the gardens. The architect Jules Mansart was instructed to "build a palace of which the dimensions, design, and beauty would remain throughout the centuries as a testimony of the self-esteem of the most powerful king in Europe." Mansart furnished the interior with marble, gold (see Mars salon left with its gilt ceiling), and silver, while the famous garden designer André Le Nôtre created a garden with walkways, vistas, fountains, ponds, garden statuary, and an orangery as testimony to the power of "Le Roi Soleil."

Stone Age paintings in the caves of Lascaux

Galloping horses, deer, ibex, and buffalo inhabit the rock walls, showing animals once commonplace

In the French province of Dordogne, seventeen-year-old Marcel Ravidat and his three friends literally fell upon an amazing discovery. Looking for a place to bury a dead donkey, they were told by a woman farmer of an unusual hole beneath a fallen spruce. The tree seemed to be set well into the ground and so the boys took matches, and oil lamp, and a terrier named Robot and went in search of treasure. They found the hole close to the river Vezere and the terrier jumped in the hole followed by Marcel. Then, the ground beneath the three boys' feet gave way and swallowed them up. At the bottom of the hole the shocked friends saw the light of a match held by Marcel and heard him call to them to join him. So they continued further down into the cave, feeling their way along the walls of the dark tunnel until they reached a chamber about sixteen feet high. In the flickering light of the oil lamp they discovered something quite remarkable. A red horse was drawn on the cave wall between the horns of two bulls. This chamber has become known as the "Bull Chamber."

Doll person

The abbot, Henri Breuil, the leading French expert on cave paintings, who was called in by the boys' teacher, immediately realized that this was a major discovery. The boys had stumbled across the largest collection of Paleolithic art that has ever been found. A pair of tunnels lead from this first small chamber that the boys discovered into larger areas with domed ceilings. The entire cave is around 460 feet long with walls with so many colorful drawings, such as depictions of animals, that they overlap. The abbot studied the galloping horses, deer with detailed antlers, fifty-foot-long bulls, ibex, and buffalo, most of which were painted in ochre, red, or black. Amid all these portrayals of animals there is only one of a human, but this is drawn as if by a child. Like a child's doll the figure is seen lying at the bottom, arms outstretched with a bird in

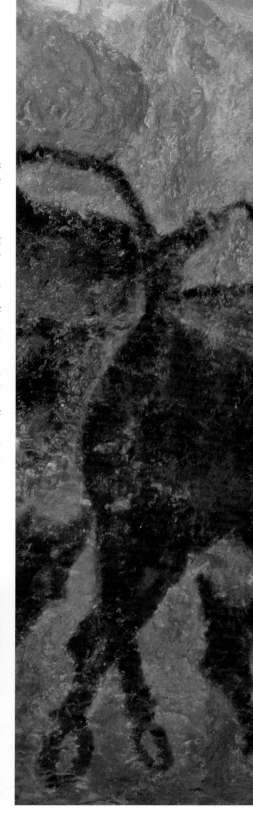

a branch drawn below it and a buffalo and running rhinoceros shown above in the same type of still life style. Could this be a hunting scene that is depicted?

Abbot Henri Breuil thought the paintings to be about eighteen thousand years old. His estimate proved to be fairly accurate. Modern research now places them at about fifteen thousand years ago. At this time most of present-day Germany lay beneath a sheet of ice while the south of France was savanna with only a few trees. Horses, buffalo, reindeer, and thick-skinned rhinoceros roamed the open grass land, and Stone Age hunters had learned how to kill them with spears

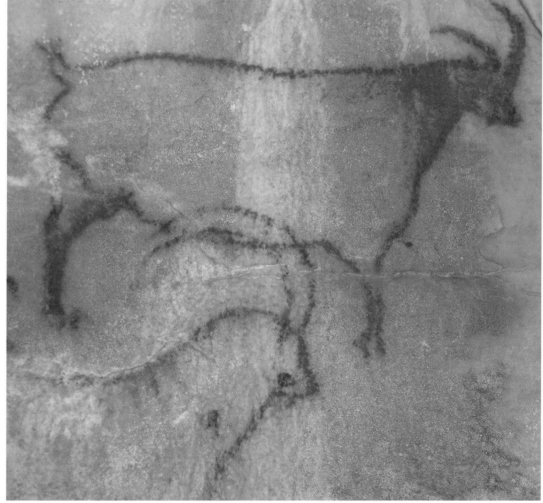

20000 year old cave paintings - ibexes along with illustrations of footprints.

tipped with sharpened stones. The reason for the cave paintings remains a mystery and the subject of much debate. Did these budding Michelangelos want to portray their prowess at hunting, as many have suggested? If this is the case then why are there so few drawings of reindeer which were the principal prey? Perhaps the drawings have a mystical purpose of which we know nothing and the cave was used for rituals.

After the discovery at Lascaux, wall paintings were also discovered elsewhere, particularly in the valleys of the Vezere and throughout the Dordorgne, in the Perigord, along the Rhine, at the foot of the

Pyrenees, and the Cantabrian Mountains. The most recent discovery was on the coat near Marseilles, where the cave is 118 feet under water. A discovery had been made at Altamira in Spain in 1879 but the authenticity of this was doubted for some time because it was felt that prehistoric man could not be capable of such creativity.

Risk of colors fading

The discovery at Lascaux in the summer of 1940 was not made public until several years after the event because France had just been occupied by the Germans. The find was made known eight years later and people visited the cave in their hundreds. A road was

built to make the cave more accessible and to protect the paintings from the vapor exhaled by the visitors, hermetically sealed doors were installed and a climate control system. But despite all this the colors of the paintings began to fade. Paintings which had survived for thousands of years began to deteriorate rapidly. Today the 35,000 visitors each year have to be content with reproductions because the originals are no longer exposed to public gaze.

Modern man had never before seen such a collection of art from the Stone Age as was revealed at the cave in Lascaux. Paintings of buffalo, giant bulls, horses, and cat-like predators adorn the walls of the cave in the Dordogne.

The divine art of Chartres Cathedral

Notre Dame regarded as the supreme example of Gothic architecture

ROUTE

Via A10/A11 for 52 miles SW of Paris

ACCOMMODATIONS

Hotel Le Grand Monarque, Place Epars

FOOD

Restaurant La Truie qui File, Place Poisonnerie

ALSO WORTH SEEING

Church of St. Pierre, Musée des Beaux-Arts (Museum of Fine Art)

Medieval art achieved its zenith in the form of Gothic architecture. The Cathedral of Notre Dame (Our Lady) at Chartres in turn is regarded as the supreme example of Gothic architecture as a divine form of artistic expression. By the time of its building in the twelfth and thirteenth centuries all the building techniques established over the preceding centuries came together in a magnificent form that achieved superb optical effects and delightful proportions.

For the first time tall buttresses provided support and the slabs of walls were broken up and decorated with stained glass windows, the size of which had earlier been impossible. Chartres was the first cathedral to have three large rose windows, each of more than forty-two feet in height. These were points of concentration of this new divine form of art. For the first time too there were three huge naves decorated with many life size statues of earlier rulers and saints. All this created a different atmosphere for

the worshipper. Opulent jewels and expensive finery were replaced with colorful beams of light from the windows, which believers regarded as the "light of Christ."

Pilgrimage to the "holy raiment"

The dimensions of the cathedral were a great novelty too. The vaulting above the nave for the first time soared to a height of more than one hundred feet. The great importance of Chartres was that it possessed the most important relic of the Virgin

northern slopes of the Prescelly Mountains and the large "altar stone" is thought to come from Pembrokeshire, both in Wales.

Astonishing feat of transport

Some of these stones appear to have been brought to Stonehenge from quarries more than 180 miles away. They probably rolled the stones on timber until they were able to move them by raft across the sea and perhaps also up the River Avon until they once were more transported over the ground on rollers. Great ingenuity must also have been used by the people who built this monument in order to lift the massive stones into position and then to cap them with massive stone lintels. The name Stonehenge refers to the "hanging stones" but archaeologists refer to all these Neolithic circular monuments as a *henge*.

There was no serious study of Stonehenge until the seventeenth century when the British antiquarian John Aubrey discovered fifty-six pits, now known as the "Aubrey holes," containing human bones and charcoal in the inner bank. Who these people were and why they were buried at what must clearly have been such an important site is shrouded in as much mystery as much else about Stonehenge.

It is believed that Stonehenge was built for ritual purposes. It is possible that Stone Age people paid homage to the sun, as did many early civilizations, possibly treating the sun as a god who created life. Computer models suggest the monument is capable of predicting the summer and winter solstices, the vernal and autumnal equinoxes, and eclipses of both the sun and moon and also acts as a calendar.

Huge blocks of sandstone from Wales, weighing about 28 tons were used for part of Stonehenge's structure, placed upright as sarsen stones and capped with lintels.

Kings and Queens of England were crowned in Westminster Abbey

Memorial tablets relate the history of an island race

ROUTE

Westminster subway station (Circle/District Line)

OPENING TIMES

Main entrance, nave and transept: 8 a.m.–6 p.m. (more limited times for access to the choir and royal tombs)

FOOD

Ye Olde Cheshire Cheese, 145 Fleet Street (prominent pub of 1665)

ALSO WORTH SEEING

St. Paul's Cathedral, British Museum, Victoria & Albert Museum

In 1700 a knight of the realm exclaimed: "Good God, I do not want to be buried in Westminster Abbey. They bury idiots there." Perhaps the culprit, Sir Godfrey Kneller, was a bit of a republican for apart from the handful of poets, philosophers, and scholars the Collegiate Church of St. Peter at Westminster, as the abbey is officially titled, is also the burial place of English monarchs. But even its role of burial place for the great and the good is dwarfed in significance by the abbey's close association with the throne itself. The coronation of every English king or queen since William the Conqueror crowned himself there at Christmas 1066 has taken place at Westminster Abbey.

Built over five hundred years

When the English state split with Rome it kept the existing churches within the new Church of England. The abbey church was built and has survived under royal patronage to be one of the most beautiful of medieval churches.

A legend surrounds the origins of the abbey. The Anglo-Saxon king Sebert is said to have founded an abbey on the spot in the seventh century. It is certain that there was indeed a Benedictine abbey at what is now known as Westminster in the late tenth century for which Edward the Confessor (1042–1066) had an abbey church built. The name, that is also borne by a borough of London and the British parliament building (Westminster Palace), means nothing more than an abbey church, or minster, located to the west of the City of London–the old, historic heart of today's metropolis. Edward's church was inaugurated in December 1065 and eight days later the king died and was laid to rest in his new church.

Westminster Abbey as it stands today was largely fashioned in two phases. In 1245, Henry III wished to display his power and status by constructing a new royal church at Westminster to rival the great Gothic cathedral that was being built at Reims. The second major work was instigated one hundred years later by Richard II. His master builder was the architect of Canterbury Cathedral, Henry Yevele, who is largely responsible for the important adaptations in a style known as Early English Gothic.

Three hundred years later the outer stone cladding was renewed by Sir Christopher Wren who rebuilt much of the city of London after the Great Fire of London in 1666, and whose most important work is St. Paul's Cathedral in the city. A further one hundred years later—a building period therefore spanning five centuries—the twin Gothic towers were completed, that are such a key feature of the abbey.

In the usual manner, the basic form of the building is in the shape of a cross, 512 feet long by two hundred feet. The height above the nave at 115 feet is the highest in Britain. The abbey has largely retained its simplicity and remains in good condition in spite of a few minor changes and some restoration in the nineteenth century.

The vast majority of those who visit this house of God each year do not come for any religious purpose but for the mass of different memorials to "the great and the good," honoring members of the English aristocracy, major statesmen, scholars, and those from the arts. Some four hundred different memorials are reminders of our transitory time on earth but also shed some light on the history of the British.

A magnificent nave

A French traveler and historian clearly disliked much of the abbey, London, and the English weather but managed a word of praise for the abbey's magnificent nave, along which kings and queens have trod in procession. In his diary for 1872, Hyppolite Taine observes: "Westminster Abbey: a beautiful nave. Curious Gothic architecture. It is the only kind suitable for this climate. It is spoiled by the jumble of forms and abundance of sentimental statues, but is quite in keeping with this depressing weather."

Westminster Abbey was to rival Reims Cathedral. Its Early English Gothic style is the work of Henry Yevele who also built Canterbury Cathedral. Immediate left are the twin towers. Opposite page: the vaulted ceiling of the nave.

Scotland's Royal Mile

The medieval street that links Holyrood Palace to Edinburgh Castle

ROUTE
By air: direct to Prestwick (Glasgow) or via London to Edinburgh

BEST TIMES
May–July, September–October

OPENING TIMES
Castle (April–October): daily 9.30 a.m.–5 15p.m.; Holyrood House: check with Tourist Information as times vary due to royal state visits

ALSO WORTH SEEING
Calton Hill (view point), Royal Botanical Garden

Daniel Defoe described Edinburgh's Royal Mile as perhaps the longest and most beautiful street in Britain, if not the world when he visited in 1706. Both the buildings and their inhabitants impressed him.

The name Royal Mile has a curious ring to it. Houses and people have been crowded into this part of the capital city since the sixteenth century. In 1558, the population of Edinburgh was eight thousand. A hundred years later it had grown to around sixty thousand—who all lived in or around the Royal Mile.

Edinburgh was the first European city to build apartment blocks, known there as tenements. In the seventeenth century, buildings of seven to eight floors were commonplace and ten to twelve floors not unheard of. The highest rise dwelling from this era was of fifteen storeys.

But the name Royal Mile relates to the property of the crown not the people. This is the street of the Scottish royalty that runs from Edinburgh Castle to the Palace of Holyrood House, where the present Queen spends time each summer. The Royal Mile consists of a number of streets: Castle Hill, Lawnmarket, High Street, and Canongate.

A road steeped in history

The Royal Mile is a road that is steeped in the often bloody history of Scotland and of the British Isles, from the medieval castle on its hilltop that looks down upon the city to the Palace of Holyrood House at the other. It was here that the Catholic Scottish queen, Mary Stuart, who brought the influence of the French court to Edinburgh, was pursued with implacable hatred by the dark Protestant reformer John Knox, founder of the Church of Scotland. He was known by

the people as "Killjoy" somewhat appropriately. Knox lived a short distance away from Mary Queen of Scots, between the palace and Edinburgh's principal church of St. Giles—on the steps of which drunken Scots have been known to fight one another at Hogmanay (New Year's Eve) —and further up the street is the Tollbooth, court and prison where Mary Stuart's supporters, such as the Marquis of Montrose and the Duke of Atholl lost their heads. Mary herself was beheaded in England.

Other bloody deeds linked to the Royal Mile are the murder of Mary's secretary Rizzio by her jealous husband Lord Darnley and the infamous "Black Dinner" of 1440. The host, Sir William Crichton, served roast ox for his guests and then had them murdered. The unfortunate dinner guests were Crichton's rivals for Scottish power, the sixth Earl of Douglas and his brother.

Today this historic thoroughfare is overrun with tourists who often shuffle past places of great significance in blissful ignorance. The Palace of Holyrood House was originally the guest house of Holyrood Abbey, rebuilt in its present form in the seventeenth century for Charles II. Parts of Edinburgh Castle on the other hand date back to Viking times. Visitors today, whose imagination is caught by the tragic story of Mary Queen of Scots, press to see the small room in which she gave birth to her son who became James I of England and James VI of Scotland, uniting the English and Scottish crowns. Her claim to the English throne was barred because she was Catholic, but when Queen Elizabeth died without an heir Mary's son was the natural successor. Her son's name has adorned the authorized bibles of the Protestant church for centuries.

The Royal Mile has recently witnessed happier times when Queen Elizabeth II left Holyrood Palace to open the first Scottish Parliament since the eighteenth century.

The Palace of Holyrood House was rebuilt for Charles II in the seventeenth century as a home for Scottish monarchs. Today is has largely become a focus of interest in the tragic story of Mary Queen of Scots. Mary's distant relative, Queen Elizabeth II, spends a little time here each year. The unicorn (far left) in the entrance hall is a blazon from the coat of arms of Mary Stuart. The historic apartment houses or tenements of the Royal Mile (left) are early examples of high-rise living.

Green hopes, icy white reality

Greenland, the largest island in the world, retains a primeval icy nature

Greenland

Atlantic Ocean

ROUTE
By air from Ottawa or Copenhagen

BEST TIMES
June–September (winter clothing necessary)

ACCOMMODATIONS
Overnight accommodation is scarce. Pre-booking is essential.

The indigenous people of Greenland call it Kalaallit Nunaat or "human hand" in their native Inuit (Eskimo) and yet there are few human hands on this island that is the world's largest. The population of this autonomous part of the Kingdom of Denmark is 57,000. Most of the island lies north of the Arctic Circle. The entirely inappropriate name of Greenland (Grønland in Danish) was given to the island more than a thousand years ago as a marketing trick by the rapacious Viking, Eric the Red, in order to attract colonists. He managed to persuade four hundred people to colonize the island, taking wives and children, equipment and cattle. Their Viking prows reached the shores in the summer of 986, landing at what is now Ericsfjord, close to Narssarssuarq where flights from the original mother country land. It was here that the first settlement in this inhospitable land was established.

From north to south the island is about 1,650 miles long but has a total of just over ten miles of paved road. More than four-fifths of Greenland is covered by permanent ice cap with a maximum depth of about eight thousand feet. When seen from the air Greenland mainly looks white and cold, like the North Pole. Standing on the ice cap one can see outcrops of basalt mountains breaking through the ice to reassure

one that this ice is founded on solid ground unlike the ice sheet at the North Pole.

The green land that Eric the Red promised is a thin strip of land at the coast and this is where Greenlanders live in small settlements. The coast, which is deeply indented with fjords, makes visiting a major undertaking. The only means of travel between the capital of Nuuk (Godthab) to the provincial town of Ivittuut is only

Four-fifth of Greenland is covered by a layer of ice (3 km thick)

possible by air or by sea. One fifth of the population of Greenland lives in Nuuk.

From Eskimo to Inuit

Over time, the Viking population merged with the native Inuit peoples until there were no authentic Norsemen left. Soon after Greenland was rediscovered by Europeans, the Danes took possession of the island in 1721, ruling almost continuously for more than 250 years until 1979, when the colony became autonomous. Greenland has prospered since going its own way, with a freely elected parliament of twenty-seven members and a government with six ministries. The Royal Greenland Business Association, that had previously governed the island economy was replaced by the Kalaallit Nuerfiat enterprise. Greenland pulled out of the European Community following a referendum because of disputes over fishing quotas. Today Greenlanders are eagerly developing their own cultural identity. Because of this Greenlanders do not like themselves or their language to be termed Eskimo, rather Inuit, in

common with people of related ethnic origin in Canada, Alaska, and Siberia. They do welcome the benefits of western civilization in the form of hospitals, radio stations, and schools and they tolerate the American air bases that have existed there since the start of the Cold War. Life here is governed strictly by the time of year and though much of life is still largely traditional, such as hunting for seals in a kayak, modern vessels are used to fish for crab, trout, and cod. Enlightened animal rights activists have recognized the legitimacy of the traditional Inuit seal hunt. The principal source of income is derived from the commodity which the people of Greenland have in abundance but for which they have little use: icy wilderness. The sheer scale and magnificence of the landscape, astonishing geysers, and mountains of at least 13,000 feet lure increasing numbers of tourists to the island who want to breathe the pure Arctic air, see musk oxen, and Arctic foxes. They are also tempted into buying Inuit souvenirs made of rope and enjoying a Greenland *smörrebröd*. By the time these travelers have returned

home they will have learned the most important word used in Greenland: imaga meaning something like "maybe." This word is used widely, especially when weather conditions prevent flights back to the "civilized" world, as occurs often. This happens so frequently that all Greenland airports have a stopover hotel. The record delay is for Kangerlussuaq (Sandre Stromfjord)—which is rated as an airport usable in all conditions— where a group of tourists once had to wait three weeks before they could leave the island. The locals insist this kind of thing really only happens in winter.

Enormous icebergs that have broken away from the northern coast of Greenland, close to the North Pole form a majestic backdrop to the huts of the native Inuit. The icebergs can be seen at closer quarters on boat trips through the fjords.

When Iceland's geysers boil and blow

Hot springs are an astounding natural spectacle

ICELAND
Reykjavik
Atlantic Ocean

EUROPE

ROUTE
By air to Reykjavik

BEST TIMES
June–August

ALSO WORTH SEEING
Gulfoss Falls, Jökusárgljufur
and Skaftafell Nature
Reserves, Hot Spa at
Hveravellir

Around sixty-five million years ago the earth's crust rent apart between Greenland and Scandinavia. Magma from the bowels of the earth flowed to the surface where it was cooled by the sea. As the process continued, mountains of basalt formed that grew higher and higher until about sixteen million years ago they emerged, hissing and steaming from the deep as volcanoes. Thus Iceland was born. The processes that gave birth to this island continues to the present day. The occupants of this volcanic island reap benefits from and face risks with their life above the cauldron.

At the "hot spot"

The continents of the Americas and Eurasia have been drifting apart for millions of years by about an inch each year. Iceland was formed when a rift opened that allowed magma to emerge through the fault. This accounts for Iceland's fascinating geological history.

Iceland is still one of those "hot spots" in the world where large volumes of lava are spewed from the earth. In the case of Iceland one of the stranger factors is that this is mainly beneath the massive ice sheet of the Vatnajökull Glaciers covering 3,204 square miles, making them the largest expanse of ice within the European Community. This is not usually the place at which to witness Iceland's volcanoes erupting, but the danger is ever present and made apparent from time to time. When eruptions occur here large quantities of ice are melted. Some experts predict that much of the fertile southwestern part of Iceland will eventually be flooded and force the population to evacuate.

Volcanic activity does have some benefits though. The heat of the earth's core there means that groundwater temperatures at a depth of just over 3,000 feet reach 536°F (280°C) and this provides energy for generating electricity, and is piped to homes and greenhouses for heating. This means that even the sidewalks are heated in the capital of Reykjavik to keep them free from ice in winter. The blue lagoon of cooled water at the Grindavik power station is used as naturally heated thermal baths for therapeutic purposes that permit comfortable outdoor bathing. The constant volcanic activity brings another benefit to the islanders: they attract tourists. Iceland's hot springs and geysers have brought an important cash crop of tourism to

land that is otherwise of no economic value.

The thermal springs of Haukadalur with its enormous geyser, about sixty or so miles east of the capital, is one of the most visited natural phenomena of Iceland, even if the springs do now seem to be less active. The geyser once spurted a jet of steam almost two hundred feet into the air every hour. This has been happening since 1294 but its performance is now less dependable.

Hot springs at Strokkur

Tourists are more reliably catered to by the geyser at the hot springs at Strokkur which spouts about eighty feet into the air every ten minutes. After the brief shower of rain following this display the surface of the pool is calm except for a few wisps of steam on the surface. Then suddenly the water starts to boil and a large bubble of vapor forms until the moment when the bubble bursts as steam and hot water surges skywards once more. The water in the pool at this moment is 206.6°F (97°C). There are some thirty geysers in Iceland's interior but few are as attractive as Strokkur.

The blue springs of Hveravellir about 44 miles further north are also worth a visit, located between the glaciers of Hof and Langiökul, at a height of almost five hundred feet above sea level. The hot springs here bubble and fume but beware, the ground beneath your feet is brittle, especially where covered in yellow deposits of sulfur or white lime. The water here can cause severe burns.

The thermal springs of Haukadalur with their main geyser of Strokkur are one of Iceland's main tourist attractions. At regular intervals Strokkur sends plumes of boiling water and steam high into the air. The pool of water then becomes calm again as if nothing had occurred, except for a few wisps of steam. Suddenly the water starts to boil and bubbles erupt from the depths, breaking through the boiling water to shoot eighty feet into the sky. This impressive show happens every ten minutes.

Where Swedish queens learned to dream

Drottningholm Castle is the "Versailles of the north"

Drottningholm, the "Versailles of the north" is something of a fairy-tale castle. Not just because this is considered the finest baroque palace in northern Europe but because it was the scene against which love stories were played out that caught the imagination of the people. The palace on the island of Lovön is also one of the few important places in history where women held sway. In

1662, Queen Hedwig Eleonora, widow of Carl Gustavus X, gave orders for a new palace to be built at Drottningholm, the Queen's island. This was to be built on precisely the same spot where exactly one hundred years earlier the Polish born Queen Caterina Jagel Ionica had resided. One hundred years after this, came yet another woman who ordered the expansion and renovation of the palace. This was Ulrike,

the sister of Frederick the Great and wife of the Swedish king Adolphus Frederick, who not only added an impressive new side wing but was also responsible for the splendor with which the many rooms were redecorated.

Classicism in blue and gold

In 1771, Ulrike's son Gustavus III assumed the throne. He is known as the initiator of Sweden's "golden age,"

and the style of the era was also named after him: Gustavian—a French and Italian inspired classicism that was characterized by the use of blue and gold in decorating the houses of royalty and the aristocracy. The arts and sciences flourished under this monarch and theaters were added to the royal palaces, so that Gustav was also known as the "theater king."

Bourgeois queen

Sweden was less fortunate with Gustav's descendants. The state imported the Napoleonic general Jean-Baptiste Bernadotte in 1810, made him dauphin, and then crowned him in 1818. His queen was a former love of Napoleon, Bernardine Eugénie Dési-

rée, daughter of a merchant known as Clary. It is her sad and moving story that is related in the novel *Désirée*.

The present lady of Drottningholm was also born a commoner. She was born in Germany as Sylvia Renate Sommerlath until she married the Swedish king Carl XVI Gustavus. She too had a former love and her story evokes great sympathy for the royal house in Sweden. Queen Sylvia, who lives in the south wing of Drottningholm, is more at home with the art and history of Sweden than many of her acquired countrymen and women. The palace's library is a favorite place for this cultural queen.

Drottningholm also has a room in full-blown rococo style by the

Swedish master Jean Eric Rehn created for Gustavus III, and parts of the gardens are in the English landscape style that contrasts with the formal beauty of the baroque French-style. These are further bequests to Drottningholm by that artistic monarch.

The palace's theater was inaugurated in 1766 and thirty of the original sets still exist. Performances of opera and ballet herald summer each year. The biographer of King Gustavus wrote: "Life was loved and lived in good taste," at "fairy-tale Drottningholm castle." Clearly, it was not only commoner queens Désirée and Sylvia who found their dreams of becoming queen come true.

The front of the royal palace of Drottningholm looks out onto the gardens. It displays a happy blend of baroque and rococo. The castle's history is closely linked to the queens who have lived here. Queen Hedwig Eleonora had it built in 1662; Queen Ulrike had it expanded and redecorated; Queen Désirée tried to forget her native France here, and Queen Sylvia now organizes happy family parties here.

Moscow sparkles again

Restorers now rule the Kremlin and Red Square

ROUTE

Subway stations: Biblioteka Imeni Lenina and Borowizskaya (Kremlin), Plosjsjad Revoljoesji (Gum, Red Square)

BEST TIMES

May–June, September

ACCOMMODATIONS

Baltsjoeg Kempinski (luxury class) near Kremlin, Intourist (medium class) in city center

ALSO WORTH SEEING

Pushkin Museum, Trejakov Gallery, Kolomenskaye summer residence, Ostankino Castle

Entrance to the Kremlin: the Gate of Resurrection. Deep religious belief has survived ideology.

The eternal struggle in Russia between the church and state ended in favor of the church—at least so far as the architecture of Moscow is concerned. The golden crosses and domes of the Jesus the Savior Cathedral that were blown up on the orders of Stalin in 1932 once more dominate the view of the inner city. The cathedral has been rebuilt.

For hundreds of years the capital of the vast expanses of Russia was little more than a fortress or *kremlin* but the settlement kept expanding in a series of rings around the inner fortifications. Today in addition to this citadel with its defensive walls there are large avenues, a railway, the old city quarters, the Bolshoi Theater, the enormous cathedral of St. Basil, and Red Square.

City behind walls

The Kremlin retained the basic form it acquired during the reign of Czar Ivan III in the late fifteenth century. The Russian word *kremlin* has an identical meaning to the English word *citadel*. This citadel has a triangular ground plan that covers about seventy-four acres on a hill

overlooking the Moskva or Moscow River. Ivan brought in architects from Italy and commissioned them to build palaces and churches around the Kremlin, but to Russian precepts. His successors later added chapels, churches, cloisters, an arsenal, several palaces, theaters, imperial mansions, and buildings for the administration of government. All these were within the Kremlin so that today the Kremlin has the appearance of an entire city within walls.

But the Moscow and Kremlin one sees today is a mere shadow of its former self, for the city had to be rebuilt after its brief occupation of thirty-nine days by Napoleon's Grande Armée in 1812.

Remains of the old city can still be found at the center of the rebuilt one. Red Square has stood alongside the Kremlin, at the heart of this settlement on the Moskva River since the early Middle Ages. People congregated here to hear the edicts of the czar or witness the execution of his enemies. And today the body of Lenin, founder of the Soviet Union, lies at the foot of the Kremlin wall, visible in a glass sarcophagus as an embalmed tourist attraction. Tourists come from all over the world to gaze at the impressive palaces that were built within the tall walls of the Kremlin.

When Moscow was rebuilt, theaters, museums, and even shops in the classical style were added. The

three huge galleried floors of the Gum department store were built on the perimeter of Red Square in 1856. There is also the somewhat pretentious delicatessen named Gastronome Number One, of 1910. The Bolshoi Theater opened its doors in 1856. Moscow's first subway or metro started running in 1935. Its opulent and palatial stations are a tourist attraction in their own right, heavily influenced by the German Bauhaus style of architecture. A classic example of this genre is the Soviet Laborers Club built in 1929.

At the present time the 850-year-old city is virtually the largest construction site in Europe. Reconstruction and restoration is mainly concentrated on churches and buildings that were destroyed or severely damaged under Communist rule. One of the men charged with the task of guardian to Russia's heritage, Victor Bulochnikov, says that the renaissance of the Russian state requires the restoration of its cultural heritage. It is expensive heritage for the cost runs into many millions in any currency.

The Kremlin or citadel. What makes the Moscow Kremlin so important is that a major capital city grew up within its walls, complete with churches and palaces. The golden domed Archangel Cathedral (left, shows interior) is within the Kremlin, the Cathedral of St. Basil is just outside.

Beautiful St. Petersburg

The city on the Neva is Russia's "window to the west"

Of the major grand-style cosmopolitan cities of the world, St. Petersburg is the youngest of them all, more recent than New York for example. True, there are more recent cities such as Brasilia, but these have been built using modern construction techniques and town zoning. By contrast St. Petersburg is very much an eighteenth-century style city in which baroque and classical architecture dominates. Russia's "window on the west" was created by a mix of German, French, and Italian architects. Historians cannot agree if that description should be attributed to Peter the Great, the Italian writer Francesco Algarotti, or the Russian writer Pushkin.

St. Petersburg sprawls over more than forty islands and these are further subdivided by small rivulets and canals into about one hundred smaller ones. At first sight it seems absurd to build a city on such a river delta, but this provided Peter the Great, who was constantly moving his place of residence, with additional security. Its modern virtue is that this has resulted in one of the finest cities in Europe, with ever changing vistas.

Rastrelli's palaces

At the heart of the city is the baroque Winter Palace which Peter the Great's daughter Elizabeth had built for her by her favorite architect, Bartolomeo Rastrelli. The enormous palace was completed in eight years. It remains impressive with its 1,057 rooms, 1,945 windows, and 117 staircases. Rastrelli joined the court of Peter the Great when he was just sixteen. Once Peter's daughter Elizabeth became Czarina he came into his own. The Smolny Monastery and five baroque palaces that he built in St. Petersburg led to his being dubbed Rastrelli the Magnificent.

The city on the river Neva owes its great beauty to Catherine the Great, who conscripted a great army of architects. Only one of the major palaces that she had built during her reign—the Taurist Palace—was built by a Russian architect, Ivan Starov. Catherine depended on foreigners for all the rest. The Hermitage and the art academy were built by the Frenchman Vallin de la Mothe, while the Italian Giacomo Quarenghi undertook the Hermitage Theater and the Academy of Science. The Czarina wrote: "Building is a sickness, just as dipsomania is." The best example of this "sickness" of hers is the Alexander Palace in Tsarskoye Selo, which experts consider is by far Giacomo Quarenghi's finest work for

St. Peterburg's finest church is that of The Savior, with its gold leaf embellished domes. Below is one of the many fascinating stairways in the Hermitage.

the empress. The colorful Catherine Palace, ornamented with golden domes, is from Elizabeth's reign. Catherine merely asked the Scottish architect Charles Cameron to "clear up and decorate the interior." The Scot did so with great enthusiasm and use of unusual materials for those days—malachite, bronze, agate, colored glass, and marble.

Hermitage: a temple to art

The palaces and cathedrals that resulted from these imperial crazes for building provide a costly setting for the jewel in their midst: the new Hermitage. This building in the classical style was built between 1839 and 1852 and houses one of the largest art collections of the entire world. Each year more than three millions visitors admire a tiny portion of its works of art which includes many famous paintings.

Novgorod, the cradle of Russia

The St. Sophia Cathedral is an impressive display of former power

ROUTE

By air to St. Petersburg and train to Novgorod

BEST TIMES

June–August

ACCOMMODATIONS

Beresta Palace Hotel, Intourist

ALSO WORTH SEEING

Home of Dostoyevsky (Staraya Russ, Lake Ilmen)

Although the name of the city of Novgorod means "new city" it is actually as old as Russia itself. Founded in the tenth century, the name implies there must have been an earlier settlement on the site, which was perhaps established by the legendary Rurik in the ninth century. Novgorod is north of Lake Ilmen, about 119 miles from St. Petersburg. The city has long been divided by the Volkhov River which flows into Lake Ladoga, where it links with other waterways including one to the east.

It is these waterways to which Novgorod owes its economic position, which has made the city a powerful center of cultural richness for over five hundred years that is unique in Russia.

Vladimir I (The Holy) who reigned from 978–1015 was ruler of Novgorod before he gained control over all the Russian peoples and moved to Kiev to rule his wider realm. The freedom-loving people of Novgorod did not take kindly to being subjects of Kiev, but the wealthy mercantile city managed to retain a degree of autonomy from Russian authority. From 1136 the true power was in the hands of the major landowners or Boyars and their bourgeois government which appointed the governor. Novgorod by this time had achieved a status unique in Russia: a free republic known as Novgodrodskaya.

The Boyar rule was checked though by the Russian alliance with the Orthodox church. In 988, Vladimir I had elevated Orthodox Christianity to the status of state religion. Conversion to Christianity was slow with the people of Novgorod, many of whom still worshipped the ancient Slavic god of thunder, Peroen, and it was also bloody. Eventually an archbishop was appointed to reside in the Novgorod kremlin who was also a representative of the general assembly.

Mural by Theopanes

Novgorod's kremlin, known as Detines ("strong boy") is sited in the west of the city and the left bank of the Volkhov. Five onion-domed towers rise up above the sturdy walls of the citadel of limestone. This is the St. Sophia Cathedral, the finest and largest building within the citadel. It was built between 1045 and 1052 and has managed to withstand change and retain its simple and austere appearance. A number of characteristics of what was to later become recognized as a

"Novgorod style" are already evident in this early brick-built church: the enormous scale and dominance of powerful and heroic forms over quaint and poetic motifs.

The facade of the cathedral is not embellished. Little remains of the ancient murals of the interior. The oldest and most valuable icon, the eleventh century St. Peter and St. Paul icon, is now in the Novgorod museum with many other icons from Novgorod. These have long been greatly valued for their high artistic merit.

In the fifteenth century this city state had 150 churches and monasteries. Many of these were commissioned by families, mercantile associations, and the bourgeois, so that they are less ostentatious than buildings erected by royal decree. The city had buildings such as the Yuriev Monastery, capped with domes in the form of military helmets, the church of St. Peter and St. Paul in Kosjevniki, and the Christ the King Cathedral with its superb

frescoes that dominated the city for centuries. Byzantine artist Theophanes created murals in 1378 regarded as among the best of their age.

In 1570, terrible slaughter by Ivan the Terrible brought an end to Novgorod's political power. During World War II the Germans inflicted

considerable damage on both the population and to the city's churches and art treasures. Many of these monuments were carefully restored after the war, including the golden and silver domes of the churches of Novgorod, giving them back the old Russian charm.

Gold embellishes the main dome and silver the lesser ones of the Cathedral of St. Sophia (top left). The principal churches of the city were built in 1045–1052 and retain their sober and austere appearance. The blue-gold onion domes of the smaller church (top right) is like a smaller version of the cathedral. The unusual 16th century wooden church dedicated to the Virgin Mary (left) stands in an open air folk museum.

City of the stones that speak

The inner city of Krakow is the history of art in stone

One does not need to be a poet to call Krakow the city of the "stones that speak." For this city—the medieval heart of which was largely untouched by the destruction of World War II—contains a wealth of magnificent architecture in the form of patrician homes, palaces of the nobility, more than one hundred churches and cloisters, one of the oldest universities in the world, and the residence of Polish kings. Few places can boast such a collection of gems from the Middles Ages, through the Renaissance, to the baroque era. This is why Krakow was the first Euro-

pean city to be added to UNESCO'S list of world cultural heritage sites.

Krakow did not gain its charter as a city until 965 but was nevertheless already a well-known trading settlement on the Vistula River and an important center for Catholic missionaries. Krakow became a bishopric and then capital of the divided realm of the Piast dynasty that ruled Poland in 1039. The Piasts erected the Royal Wawel Castle and a cathedral on the nearby Wawel hill. Polish kings were crowned and buried at the cathedral until the eighteenth century.

In 1241 the city was invaded by the Tartars and razed to the ground, but under the Piast Duke and later King Boleslaw and his successor Casimir III, the city was rebuilt with great vigor. The new city was constructed in a checkerboard plan with the large Rynek square at its center as market place, and it developed into one of the leading cities of late medieval Europe. In 1364 the University of Krakow was founded, the first in Poland and one of the world's oldest. Nicholas Copernicus, the famous astronomer, studied here with thousands of other students. In the fifteenth century, the

Mary's Cathedral that features two hundred gilt carvings in lime wood. Stoss was engaged on this project for ten years. At thirty-six feet by forty-three feet, this is the largest Gothic altar in Europe and also the most important example of late Gothic altars.

A city in decline

Krakow's golden age was from 1506 to 1572 when Kings Sigismund I and II invited Italian painters and architects to their court and commissioned them to rebuild the Royal Wawel Castle in the finest of Renaissance styles. With designs by the architect of the Tuscan court, Bartolomeo Berecci, the Sigismund chapel was created, which is the most important example of Renaissance architecture in Poland. An impressive collection of fine furniture and paintings, and the famous Flemish Arras tapestries can be visited by means of an Italianate arcade reaching three storeys high. The royal treasure chamber contains valuable examples of the goldsmith's art and royal regalia, such as the coronation sword, dating from 1320.

Krakow remained the center of Polish culture after the Polish king moved to Warsaw in 1596 but lost its significance. The ultimate horror was during the German occupation of 1939–1944, when the Nazi "governor general" Hans Frank took control. Krakow's large Jewish community of the Kazimierz district, which had contributed much to the city's history of art and culture, was deported to concentration camps and annihilated. It is fortunate that Nazi plans to explode mines beneath the city and eradicate it totally were foiled.

The unequal towers of St. Mary's Cathedral soar above the patrician mansions of Rynek. Built in the 13th century, the Rynek Square was the trading center for textiles from throughout the world. This is still where the city comes to life, especially in the cool of the summer nights.

university was attended by some 10,000 foreign students, which is an astonishing number for the times.

In 1439, Krakow joined the Hanseatic League, specializing as a trading center for textiles from throughout the world, and it became the leader in this activity. The Rynek Square still has a textile house and cloth halls more than three hundred feet long that are known as *Sukiennice*.

Flourishing trade made both the bourgeois and aristocratic Krakow patricians rich so that both classes built stately mansions close to the market place. The inner courtyards of many of these still survive. Generous patronage attracted both artists and artisans from Germany and Bohemia, including Veit Stoss from Nuremberg, the principal sculptor of the late Middle Ages who created the tripartite altar for the St.

The Belvedere Palace in Vienna

Bureaucrats now rule where emperors once held court

North Sea

EUROPE

AUSTRIA

Vienna

Mediterranean

ROUTE

Nearest subway station is
Herrengasse (U3)

OPENING TIMES

Riding School and chapel
closed July–August

FOOD

Coffee houses, legendary Café
Hawelka (Sacher Torte),
Dortheergasse 6

ALSO WORTH SEEING

Stephan Cathedral, Schön-
brunn Palace, Hundertwasser
Haus, The Prater (giant Ferris
wheel) for the views

The Austrian emperor Leopold I complained he would rather live in a desert than his Belvedere Palace. The Viennese named him the "Turkish hare" after he fled the city during the Ottoman siege of 1683. The city was regained from the Turks by an alliance with the monarchs of Saxony, Bohemia, Bavaria, and Poland which restored the seat of the empire. When the Turks withdrew they left behind not only the secret of good coffee but also so many damaged buildings that on his return the Habsburg emperor created an

entirely new baroque city. Part of this grand architectural endeavor was Belvedere Palace.

The Belvedere Palace is a mixture of styles of different periods, now extending to 2,583,000 square feet if one includes the various buildings of the complex and the Belvedere Park that originate from the original thirteenth-century fortifications. The oldest portion of the Belvedere is the Schweizer Hof that was started by King Ottokar II of Bohemia. The name refers to the Swiss guard that Maria Theresa had billeted here.

Extensive library

All that remains of the Gothic building of Ottakar is the apse of the palace chapel. From the Renaissance, the stables and Amalia wing survive. Baroque splendor is displayed in the chancellor's wing and the winter riding school where the gray Lippizaner horses of the Spanish Riding School and their riders now show off their prowess. The library, with its grand reception room, was designed by the leading baroque architect, Joseph Emanuel Fischer von Erlach.

Building continued until the start of the twentieth century because it

The grounds of the Belvedere Palace extend to 2,583,000 square feet. (Left) The baroque domes of the old Belvedere Palace. (Above) Carriage ride through the Belvedere Park. Today the Belvedere is home to 5,000 bureaucrats of the Austrian government and several cultural and scientific institutes.

was deemed essential to reflect the importance of the empire. An Imperial forum was added as two wings alongside the main avenue but only one was completed. It bounds the Heindeplatz, named in memory of the successful Austro-Hungarian generals Prince Eugene and Grand Duke Carl. A curious but fine mixture of borrowed ideas and styles occurred at the behest of Habsburg rulers during Austrian history. They represent an astonishing labyrinth of power play, intrigue, and display of vanity.

Chancellor's seat

Perhaps the grandest moment during these power games was the Congress of Vienna in 1814–1815 when the borders of Europe were redrawn following Napoleon's defeat. The feet of hundreds of diplomats, messengers, and chancellors scurrying across these floors will have added to their smooth sheen. The elite of European nobility were also present in the Austrian capital and they spent their time enjoying the city.

Perhaps less illustrious is the present day use of these buildings. Some five thousand bureaucrats now work in the Belvedere Palace in the Ministry of Foreign Affairs which occupies much of the space. The Austrian chancellor has his official chambers in the Leopold wing, where Maria Theresa and her son Joseph II once lived.

Despite this the Belvedere Palace is still a center of culture and science. Scientific institutes, the National Library, and an anthropology museum are all housed here. In addition, visitors to the Belvedere may take in the imperial silver collection or the Augustinian chapel, which contains silver urns holding the hearts of the Habsburg rulers from 1618 to 1878. However, the main attraction by far is the equestrian display of dressage as performed by the Spanish Riding School.

The Vienna Court Castle – from poor fortress to pompous residence

Benedictine monastery of Melk

One of Europe's finest baroque buildings overlooks the Danube

North Sea

EUROPE

AUSTRIA **Melk**

Mediterranean

ROUTE

A1, Melk exit or by boat along the Danube from Vienna or Krems

OPENING TIMES

Daily May–September 9 a.m.–6 p.m. April and October until 5 p.m. Tours every hour

FOOD

Castle restaurant in Lubberegg, Emmersdorf

Halfway between Vienna and Linz, rock outcrops rise up along the Danube which have always attracted the interest of those in power. Stone Age chieftains built their clan settlements there, the Romans used them for their forts, and the Hungarian tribes turned them into a buffer against Bavaria. This area is known as Medelike in Niebelungen song and flourished as Melk in the tenth century under the Duke of Bebenberg when it formed the Eastern Mark and cradle of Austria. Melk's enduring fame though is due to the Benedictine monks who built one of the finest monasteries of Europe on this plateau.

It was in 1089 that Duke Leopold II founded a monastery within his stronghold at Melk and had a mausoleum built for St. Coleman, the Irish prince who got no further on his pilgrimage to Jerusalem than Stockerau, where he was tortured to death as a suspected spy. In the twelfth century, the Babenbergers donated their entire estate at Melk to the Benedictines who expanded the monastery, supported ecclesiastical reform, and made Melk into an important religious, clerical, and artistic center in Lower Austria.

In the fifteenth century, the abbey was one of the wealthiest in the Catholic church. During the Ottoman incursion of 1683, the fortified monastery, almost two hundred feet above the Danube, was beleaguered but not taken. The widely talented Benedictine, Berthold Dietmayer, was the abbot who had the former fortress and monastery demolished in 1700 and appointed the gifted Jacob Prandtauer of St. Pöltener to erect new cloisters on a grand scale. The rich and colorful form of high Austrian baroque was fashionable at this time with the royalty and

aristocracy along the Danube, but Prandtauer was determined to outdo all these previous efforts. He created a west front, facing toward the Danube, that rises up behind a terraced approach on the rocks, "like a huge organ sitting on a mountain," as it was later described. Two elegant towers complete the facade. The 1,050-foot-long monastery was completed in 1736, ten years after Prandtauer's death. The building is aligned along an east-west axis and it encloses a number of inner courtyards.

It is difficult to describe the abundant richness that the building displays to visitors. Artisans, sculptors, painters, and plasterers led by Prandtauer and his successors, created a work of baroque art that is impressive in its scale and the extent of the variation in its fantasy. The architectural forms are like individual notes in music that together form chords, revealing a symphonic feast for the beholder.

One reaches the Prelate's Courtyard via the Benedictine Hall. The courtyard's seclusion is underscored by a marble fountain. The 210-foot-high dome of the monastery church surveys the entire monastery. A marble hall for festive receptions is a baroque masterpiece of spatial arrangement, and in the library, the goddess of reason exhorts humanity to emerge from barbarism with brightly colored ceiling frescos by Paul Troger.

A further surprise awaits the visitor in the basilica-like monastery church, with its vaulted ceiling, magnificent side columns, elegant clerestory and upper friezes, painting of architectural detail in gold, brown, green, and ochre, and the play of light beneath the cupola and on the decorated chapel. The high altar is covered with generous golden swags and the lesser altar contains a sarcophagus with the remains of St. Coleman, the martyr of Stockerau.

The main hall of the monastery library is a spiritual and inspirational treasure house containing some 80,000 books and 2,000 ancient manuscripts, many of them superbly illuminated in the spirit of St. Benedict, who intended that "God should be adored in all things."

The Benedictine monastery at Melk (left) was built anew between 1702 and 1736. It is built in Austrian high baroque and located on a rock outcrop above the Danube. It is one of the most exquisite of architectural masterpieces. The entire monastery, grouped around a series of inner courtyards, extends for 1,050 feet. From the entrance to the great Prelate's Courtyard (right) there is a fine view of the 210-ft.-high cupola of the monastery church.

Prague and the Charles Bridge

Following history's traces: across the Moldau to the Hradcany

ROUTE

Closest subway (line A)
Starometska

ALSO WORTH SEEING

The fortress of Hradcany with
St. Vitus Church, old town
hall, Tyn Church, Powder
Tower, Wencelas Square, old
Jewish cemetery

It is not often that a bridge marks the true center of a city. One such exception is the Charles Bridge that connects east and west Prague. From the Charles Bridge you can see the Hradcany and the Lesser Town on one side of the river and the inner Old Town and New Town on the other. Every road in Prague leads to the Charles Bridge as there is no other way to cross the Vltava (Moldau).

In 1357, Emperor Charles IV laid the foundation stone for the sandstone bridge that is 820 feet long, thirty-three feet wide, and supported by 126 arches. Its predecessor, the Judith bridge, had been damaged during a flood. The new crossing is modeled on the German bridge at Trier. The construction of the replacement bridge, that was to become world famous, was entrusted to Peter Parler, a young man of twenty-seven, who later designed the St. Vitus Church in Prague which is a foremost example of Gothic architecture.

During the Thirty Years War much of the architectural detail of the bridge was heavily damaged by Swedish artillery—especially the sides of the bridge. Nevertheless the bridge remains a superb example of secular Gothic architecture and an artistic homage to its noble Bohemian patrons. In one of his poems Berthold Brecht begins: "Three emperors are interred in Prague..." as he writes of the fickle fate of history. Parler has captured the three kings in stone on the eastern side of the bridge tower in the inner city. Charles IV, Wencelas II The Holy, and Charles' son, Wencelas IV. Researchers were astonished to discover the closeness of the likeness, and the bust of the emperor is particularly impressive. The pose of the bust is very imperial and examination of the skull has shown that even an injury gained through exercise has been reproduced.

Collection of saints

The bridge is especially famous for its collection of thirty saints on its balustrades. Many of the patron saints have today been replaced with reproductions. Exhaust fumes from the city seem to be particularly harmful for saints. A special place was reserved for St. Nepomuk, a martyr who was leader of a counter-reformation movement during the Thirty Years War. To this day he is revered as the "true defender of the faith."

The fortress of Hradcany and the mighty St. Vitus Church of the 14th century form the impressive skyline of the Lesser Town of Prague. It can be reached via the Charles Bridge. In 1357, the Emperor Charles IV laid the foundation stone for this sandstone bridge that is 820 feet long, thirty-three feet wide, and supported by 126 arches. It is based on a German bridge at Trier. Peter Parler at age 27, was entrusted with the construction. He was later the architect of the fine Gothic St. Vitus Church.

Saints or heretics, kings or communists, the Charles Bridge has always been at the center of Prague's history. The Bohemian kings were crowned on this bridge, and the followers of John Huss massed on the side of the Lesser Town during the Hussite uprisings of 1420. In 1620, Friedrich von der Pfalz, the "winter king," fled across the bridge after losing the battle for the white mountain, where his Protestant army was defeated by Habsburg troops. In 1649, the students of Prague defended the old inner city against the advancing Swedish army and two hundred years later the struggle was for independence from Austria. Today only long streams of tourists, from every corner of the world, jostle with each other on the bridge. The Charles Bridge has become a place to promenade and a meeting place for artists and musicians, forming a great open-air theater.

Dresden's merry Zwinger

Once a place of pleasure, today a home for the arts

North Sea

Dresden

GERMANY

EUROPE

Mediterranean

ROUTE

By air to Frankfurt, local flight to Dresden-Klotzsche, transfer with airport city bus; A4 and A13, exit Dresden-Abstatt to Dresden Nord

ACCOMMODATIONS

Kempinkski Hotel Taschenbergpalais at the Taschenberg; Astron, Hansastrasse 43 (medium class in northern Neustadt)

FOOD

Cafe Kreutzkamm, Altmarkt 18 (famous since 1825)

ALSO WORTH SEEING

Loschwitz and Weisser Hirsch city quarters, boat trips with Wesser Flotte on Elbe, sandstone rocks on the Elbe

The pavilion is supported on columns and decorated with stucco (bottom right). The rounded arches inspired Gottfried Semper when he built the art gallery in 1847–1854, which also houses the armory of August the Strong (bottom left).

For those with an understanding of German, the name of the Zwinger Palace in Dresden tends to mislead. This was a place where August the Strong, Elector of Saxony and King of Poland, held extravagant feasts. Yet a close study of the Zwinger's history reveals the name's origin. This was once the outer ward of fortifications. The sort of space where wild animals were often kept; hence, the name *zwinger* which means "cage" or "arena". The building in front of the Luna Bastion was significantly changed in 1700 and turned into a place for enjoyment of life.

Built with sandstone from the Elbe

Even though the first new building on this site for August the Strong was a wooden amphitheater built specifically to celebrate the visit of August's cousin, King Friedrich IV of Denmark to Dresden in 1709, the name Zwinger was kept. The king's love of orange trees, which were such a costly status symbol at the time, prompted the Elector to build an orangery. The landscape architect Matthaeus Daniel Poppelmann created two bower galleries between 1710 and 1712, with one on each storey, where the sensitive orange trees could be nursed through the winter.

This though was merely the overture to the building activities with which August left his mark. The architect and sculptor Balthasar Permoser left his own strong imprint. He surrounded the natural dais of the Zwinger, where parties were held, with a series of baroque buildings that can stand comparison with examples of this style anywhere. Dresden's baroque is characterized by its lightness of touch and playfulness, while retaining symmetry that ensures the impression of seclusion in harmonious surroundings is maintained. The area that was enclosed according to Permoser's design measures 380 feet by 7,600 feet.

The pavilion, which was completed in 1718, is not just the most important building of the Zwinger Palace, it is also a high point in European architectural history. The elegant contours create an illusion of

motion and Permoser's busts of gods and heroes are woven into the Elbe sandstone like costly swags. The architecture strives to rise above the impressive central facade, rising upwards towards the figure of Hercules Saxonicus, bowed under the weight of the globe on his shoulders, that crests the pavilion's roof.

Building on the eastern side of the Zwinger was started by the master builder Poppelman in the same year, and he was pressed for time. The feast to end all feasts was planned for Dresden for September 1719 when the Elector and Prince Friedrich August, son and heir of August the Strong, married the Grand Duchess of Austria, Maria Joseph, daughter of the emperor. August the Strong had two bowered galleries built at great haste on the eastern side in repetition of those on the west. Galleries had already been extended and a crown gate added in 1714 to mask the view of the moat of the stronghold. By these means three sides of the Zwinger were enclosed.

August the Strong died in 1733 and the Zwinger fell into neglect after his death. The days of great court feasting were over. The opulent ornamentation was no longer fashionable and it was even considered that they should be removed. As early as 1728 a pavilion was used to store the collections built up by the art-loving Electors and also a museum of porcelain that is only surpassed in art-historical terms by the harem of the Topkapi palace in Istanbul.

The Zwinger Palace is still a center of the arts. From 1847 to 1854 an impressive art gallery was built by the architect Gottfried Semper, occupying space within the Zwinger next to the theater. In common with other buildings it was reduced to rubble in February 1945 by warfare. The entire complex of buildings has been restored to its former glory in a long running program of rebuilding and restoration. The gallery contains masterpieces such as those of Rembrandt, Dürer, and Rubens plus more than 350 works by Italian artists, including Raphael's "Sistine Madonna."

The pavilion at the Zwinger Palace was completed in 1718 and is the most important of the Zwinger' buildings, an important monument of European architecture. Relief molding and sculpture are woven into the masonry like expensive swags.

Wattenmeer National Parks

Unique environment created by the tides of the North Sea coast

North Sea
Waddenzee
GERMANY
EUROPE
Mediterranean

ROUTE

By train from Hamburg to Westerland

BEST TIMES

May–September

ALSO WORTH SEEING

Walking on the Wattenmeer between Föhr and Amrum; seal crèche at Frederiksoog

Many holiday-makers on their first visit to the North Sea coast ran enthusiastically towards the sea only to find it was not there. Instead they were confronted with miles of grayish mud flats. Known in German as Wattenmeer and Dutch as Waddenzee, the wat or wad merely means shallows or mud flats. The pull of the moon that causes the tides to ebb and flood sees this area along the coast of Friesland (Dutch and German) flooded at high tide and dry at low tide. Because the area is so flat the tide ebbs a very long way. This is an extremely important environment for all manner of species but especially for birds. A large part of the German Wattenmeer is protected as the Lower Saxony, Hamburg, and Schleswig-Holstein National Parks.

The special environment of these areas is not solely restricted to the shallows and mud flats themselves. The dunes, beaches, and islands are also an important part of this unique natural world.

The Schleswig-Holstein part of the Wattenmeer was declared a national park in 1985 covering an area from the German-Danish border to the mouth of the Elbe.

Mud flats, sand banks, and mixed flats

The flats are not one homogenous type of mud/sand mixture but vary depending in part on certain conditions. The more sheltered an area is, such as in the lee of an island, the flatter it will be and the greater is also the surface area covered at high tide. Water will also ebb away less quickly. In such places a more glutinous type of mud-flat occurs. Where the current is stronger, one finds larger sand banks and in between these two sets of conditions

Although the Wattenmeer mud seems devoid of life it is home to countless species.

the bed of the sea is a mixture of mud and sand. In addition to the tide there are other factors which affect the formation of the flats and banks. These were formed off the coast of Denmark through thousands of years of silting up with the deposit of sediment. In North Friesland great expanses of reed beds and marshland formed where there was shelter of sand dunes. When the sea level rose at the end of the last Ice Age these areas were flooded and covered with fertile soil. In places where the land was only flooded occasionally— during the big spring tides—sandy beaches and salt flats formed. Certain types of hardy plants took root there, depending on the distance from the sea.

Although at first glance the Wattenmeer does not appear very hospitable and rather devoid of life, nothing could be further from the truth. Two thousand different species of animals live on these flats. The flats are teaming with life and at low water it is even possible to hear the activities of the myriad collection of worms, snails, mussels, and crabs searching for food. This is a land of plenty for these creatures. On average there are over six million algae per square inch here. Worms and crabs in turn are prey for countless other creatures of the Wattenmeer, from fish to seals.

One of the most popular tourist activities on the Wattenmeer are the trips to the sand banks where seals

haul themselves out or breed and the areas where millions of gulls, terns, oyster-catchers, eider ducks, and geese congregate. Special protection areas are designated to guard these birds from disturbance. Fishing is permitted in the National Parks and is the cause of constant conflict between the fishermen and environmentalists.

The government says that the protection of nature has to be balanced with economic interests but the principal threat to the Wattenmeer is from pollution by oil slicks from North Sea shipping.

A kind of system can be detected from the air: larger channels and smaller ones drain the Wattenmeer. Where water flows slowly mud-flats are formed, where it floods and ebbs quickly sand banks are created. These are the preferred haul-out spots for seals.

Mother of all churches

Cologne Cathedral is one of Germany's most important religious buildings

The Cologne Cathedral and the Wallraf-Rtichartz Museum/ Museum Ludwig (left)

Cologne Cathedral is the symbol of Cologne and perhaps the architectural monument of Germany that is best-known world wide. In the Middle Ages it was already being described as "the mother of all churches." From the mid-nineteenth century it was elevated to a kind of national shrine. When the final act of construction took place in 1880, with the placing of a cross on the south tower, it was 632 years since the foundation stone had been laid.

The first Gothic cathedral was already in existence in France when the government in Cologne decided to replace their old cathedral dating from the fourth century with a new building. The laying of the foundation stone was delayed though because of the transfer of the Shrine of the Three Magi—said to contain the remains of the three kings who visited the infant Jesus—from Mailand to Cologne. This turned Cologne into one of the best-known places of pilgrimage in the west.

No building for 250 years

The master builder Gerhard and his successor Arnold took the cathedral at Amiens as their model for the choir and tripartite transept. The five-part nave was based upon a predecessor of Cologne Cathedral of the twelfth century. In September 1322, Archbishop Heinz von Virneburg was able to consecrate the choir even though the rest of the building was far from complete. A wooden partition closed off the nave to the west and masons were busy constructing a south tower. According to the thirteen-foot-long plans which still exist, the tower was to be proportional to the overall length of the cathedral: 492 feet high to the length of 1,640 feet. On the north side from 1410 onward work was underway on the transept which was provided with magnificent stained glass in 1508. The typical Gothic flying buttresses were for the first time extensively embellished.

But building ceased in 1560. Some argue this was because of the spirit of the times. A more pragmatic age began in which people were more inclined to consider their earthly life than look toward heaven, and they were more interested in exploring and conquering the earth, with less time for church buildings on such a grand scale. At this time about ninety percent of the planned cathedral was available for services and a provisional wooden roof enclosed the interior above the arcades.

Cologne Cathedral continued with a shadowy existence until the nineteenth century. During the French Revolution it even served as a fodder store for the French cavalry and was then promoted to the humble role of diocesan church. In 1815, when Cologne became Prussian territory, all Germans hoped construction work would start again. King Frederick IV did advocate the establishment of a national shrine and in 1842 he laid the foundation stone for the front of the south transept. Under the leadership of Zwirner and Voigtel the cathedral was now completed in thirty-eight years. The two final master builders took the medieval plans and elevation drawings as their starting point. Their work is a masterpiece of late Romantic architecture, showing both care and historical awareness. Zwirner improved on the plans with a southern transept that is a masterpiece of Neo-Gothic architecture.

The most impressive of all though is undoubtedly the cathedral's west front. The north tower at 516 feet four inches is just 2½ inches higher than its southern neighbor. When one enters the cathedral there is an overview of the slender lofty heights of the central nave, 390 feet long. Among Cologne Cathedral's most significant art treasures is the Gero Cross. This tenth-century crucifix is one of the oldest in the west.

The Shrine of the Three Magi was eventually sited behind the main altar after World War II when the damage to the interior was repaired. The shrine, which was made in the twelfth century, is regarded by experts as one of the most significant pieces of goldsmith's art from the Middle Ages.

Cologne Cathedral is still a construction site today because pollution is harmful to the materials from which it is built. Residents of Cologne have come to terms with the constant restoration and scaffolding. For, they say, when the cathedral is complete, the world will end.

North Sea
Cologne EUROPE
GERMANY
Mediterranean

ROUTE

By air to Cologne, via Frankfurt; or by regular trains to the Köln Dom station

OPENING TIMES

Daily 6.30 a.m.–7 p.m.

FOOD

Früh am Dom (traditional brewery) Am Hof 12–14

ALSO WORTH SEEING

Archbishop's Diocesan Museum, Wallraf-Richartz Museum, Romanesque churches, city hall (rathaus)

The twin spires of Cologne Cathedral soar majestically. The northern tower is 516 ft 4 in, just 2½ in higher than its neighbor. The facade is the largest of all Christian churches. Flying buttresses (top right) are customary for Gothic architecture. Of the three portals, only the St. Peter portal on the south is medieval. The other two and their sculpture are from the 19th century. The statue of St. Christopher (bottom) adorns the nave.

Bavaria's rococo jewel: the Wieskirche

The pilgrims church that is a magnificent example of full-blown German glorification

North Sea

GERMANY

Wieskirche

EUROPE

Mediterranean

ROUTE

From Munich A95/E5 to Oberau, B23 then signs for Wies

OPENING TIMES

Daily May–September 8 a.m.–7 p.m. Closes 5 p.m. in winter

ALSO WORTH SEEING

Rococo Church of St. John the Baptist, Steingaden; Hohenschwangau, Neuschwanstein, and Linderhof castles near Fuessen

It all started with a miracle in June of 1718 when a local farm girl, Maria Lory placed a wooden statue in her room and prayed before it. The statue depicts Christ being scourged. This Scourged Savior was carried through the Upper Bavarian village of Steingaden during processions on Good Friday but no-one had noticed anything special about it before. Soon though the farm girl from the meadows reported miraculous cures and the flagellated figure of Christ was said to shed tears.

The message spread to the devout and soon so many pilgrims came that the abbot of Steingaden, Hyazinth Gassner, decided to build a fitting sanctuary for the miraculous statue. The work began in 1745 and was completed nine years later. When the church was dedicated it was one of the finest examples of Bavarian high rococo style, standing in a pastoral and gently sloping landscape at the foot of the Alps.

Divine view of heaven

Abbot Gassner was not to witness the realization of his dream, for he died soon after construction of the church began, but the work was continued under his successor, Abbot Marian Mayer, apparently without begrudging the cost. Initially eight thousand marks were reserved for the building costs, but the actual cost eventually ran to 180,000 marks. Under pressure from the elector of Bavaria, Max II, abbot Mayer surrendered his office but was permitted to continue supervision of the building of the church through to its completion. The builder was Dominikus Zimmerman, while his brother, Johann Baptist, was responsible for the frescos and stucco work. Both had already established their names before this masterpiece was created.

Dominikus Zimmerman's concept for the pilgrimage church was as an oval central form with more sober outer walls. An adjacent choir was to display the miraculous Scourged Savior statue. This was customary practice for places of pilgrimage at the time, enabling people to file past the object of veneration. The master builder gave special consideration to the harmonious relationship between forms and the interplay of color and light. Twenty tall windows flood the interior with light.

Eight pairs of columns support the great expanse of vaulted ceiling that is surrounded with detailed plaster work. The ceiling represents the divine heaven and it acts as a setting for a precious gem. The ceiling frescos are in the form of a trompe l'oeil, yielding a series of surprises for the viewer. At the center of heaven is Christ the Savior, seated on a rainbow—symbolizing a link between man and God— offering his divine grace to humankind.

Angels float through the heaven in a manner that is both joyful and inspiring. The Day of Judgment has not yet arrived, the throne of the judge of the world is vacant and the gate to paradise is closed. The message repeatedly impressed on pilgrims is that those who live by faith and in humility will experience the Savior's grace.

Because of the unrestricted view, it is possible from the main nave of the Wies church to look at its sacred heart, the twin altars and gracious image of the Scourged Christ. Reliefs and moldings together with allegorical frescos in confusing proliferation seem to form a rhythm through the space. Where Johann Baptist Zimmerman created color harmony with use of white, blue, and gold in the main nave, he has added the warm red glow of marble columns beside the statue of grace. This symbolizes Christ's blood shed for us, for our salvation.

The magnificent Wieskirche was only rediscovered and recognized as the great work of art that it is in the 1920s. Since that time it has become not just a renewed place of pilgrimage but a major tourist attraction. Although the frescos have survived superbly, the church needed extensive restoration between 1985 and 1990. The breath of so many tourists had affected the colors.

The master builder Dominikus Zimmerman kept the exterior of the Wieskirche relatively simple. Inside, it is one of the most elaborate examples of high Bavarian rococo. Tall windows flood the colorful frescos and the ceiling trompe l'oeil—that depicts heaven—with bright light.

Spain's Moorish palace

The Alhambra is one of the best examples of secular Islamic architecture

Granada is one of the finest examples of a multi-cultural society. Muslims, Christians, and Jews lived together in peace in the small kingdom of Granada for 250 years. Eventually, under Isabella of Castile, Christian fundamentalists ousted the Moors in 1492 and prohibited freedom of worship.

The Alhambra Palace rises up in front of the snow-capped mountains of the Sierra Nevada like a memory of a lost dream. This building ranks alongside the Taj Mahal in terms of secular Islamic architecture. The fragrance of the flowers, the coolness of the marble, the gurgling water in the fountains and rills all transport visitors back to the oriental style of life in Spain, to a rich Moorish heritage which flourished in Andalusia in the thirteenth and fourteenth centuries.

The Calat Alhambra or red castle crests one of the foothills of the mountain range which rise at their eastern end to a summit of 11,483 feet. To the west, at the foot of the mountains, lies Granada. The Alhambra's outward appearance owes much to the fortified wall which encloses the hill. The Moorish palace is found behind this wall. From below one first sees the Alcazaba, the oldest section of the Alhambra, jutting out above the city like the prow of a ship.

Home of the Nasrite kings

This home of the Nasrite kings is the only Moorish palace in the west. Its system of defensive walls and towers encloses separate buildings and a series of pavilions and courtyards. Various sources of diffused light penetrate into every corner of these spaces. The plants on the outside of

the buildings are continued inside by decorative moldings in stucco. Cooling water from fountains flows through the living quarters. This creates a unity between nature and the man-made structure. Standing at the back of one of the inner hallways the landscape is seen as a series of images framed by richly ornamented window casements. Conversely when viewed from outside the architecture acts as a setting for the fountains, flowering jasmine, and cypresses. Gardens have always been special for the Moors. They remind them of the quiet pleasures promised by the Koran as a reward for devotion. Perhaps this is why the Christian conquerors changed them beyond recognition. High above the Alhambra though there is El Generalife, a building with the most exciting and delightful Arabian gardens to be found in Spain.

Decorative exteriors are not part of the Moorish tradition. Ornamental display of wealth is something reserved for the intimacy of inner parts of the building. Hence the sober simplicity outside contrasts starkly with the overwhelming beauty within. Inside the palace both the floor and apparently weightless columns are of marble while the ceilings are decorated with coffers and woodcarvings.

The palace itself falls into three areas: the Mexuar Palace was originally reserved for administrative and judicial matters, the Myrtle Court, with its magnificent pool in which the columns are reflected, was favored for official audiences. At the center beneath the Tower of Comares is the Ambassadors' Hall where the sultan sat enthroned in a room with windows down to the floor. The Lion Court and adjacent buildings were reserved for the sultan's private life and for his family and harem. At its center are twelve lions supporting a fountain of white marble bearing an inscription which seems the essence of Moorish architecture: "Let your eyes mingle with the flowing and the still water and marble, and we know not which of them guides you."

Amid this oriental magnificence is the palace that the Holy Roman emperor and Habsburg monarch Charles V built on this plateau in astonishing harmony. The fine detail of the Arab buildings contrast strongly with the powerful forms of massive masonry of 206 feet in length. In 1526, Pedrom Machuca, a student of Michelangelo, designed this example of high Renaissance architecture but sadly the work was never completed and Charles V never lived there.

The interior of the palace is richly adorned with stalactite arches, colonnades, and elaborate stucco ornaments. In the Lions Court twelve of the beasts support the marble fountain (left). High above the Alhambra the colorful and delightfully fragrant gardens of El Generalife are cooled by water in the most beautiful Arab garden on Spanish soil.

113

Doric columns in Segesta

A temple to the Elimi's gods where sheep graze on Sicily

The inhabitants of Segesta in Sicily are recorded in ancient history primarily as the implacable enemies of neighboring Selimunte, a trading town. Various treaties with the rulers on the mainland were interspersed with bloody wars. Eventually only remnants of the town remained and the ruins of the Doric temple of Segesta.

Around three thousand years ago the Elimi lived in the limestone hills of Calatafimi in northwest Sicily. Legend has it that they had fled the burning Troy, led by the Homeric hero Aeneas, whose sons or cousins founded Rome. The refugees selected the mountain of Monte Barbaro for their fortified settlement of Segesta from where their look-outs could keep an eye on the entire area and the Gulf of Castellemare. It was there that the first homes and public buildings were erected, and perhaps a few small temples.

Following the Greek way

Most of the town in the mountains is now nothing but ruins and much of it still has to be excavated by archaeologists. Remains of fortifications and a few derelict watchtowers suggest the place was protected by a double wall. The Elimi theater is relatively well preserved and its seats hewn from rock offer a view to the Mediterranean.

The colonists built their first grander temple around the sixth century BC, behind the walls of their stronghold. Its outer wall measures 272 feet by 154 feet but it is unknown to which particular gods the Elimi offered their sacrifices. A century later construction was begun on the famous Elimi temple on the western side of Segesta. Its classic Doric styling is reminiscent of Grecian temples although these builders were not Greeks. It is assumed a Greek architect played an important role in the project.

The temple dominates the hilly landscape today as far as the road to Trápani, and although it was never finished, the temple still appears a

In the fifth century BC, the Elimi built a Doric temple behind the walls of Segesta. A Greek architect may have supervised the construction.

The temple of Segesta owes its beauty to 36 slightly tapered columns. It is not known to which deity the temple was dedicated. It is assumed the roof was never completed.

model of perfection. The superstructure in the form of a Doric metope frieze is supported on thirty-six Doric columns that taper slightly towards their capitals. There is no sign of an entranceway or an altar and is thought likely work had to be suspended before completion.

The Elimi and the Greeks maintained close cultural relations. This is apparent from various sections of wall that have been uncovered in the ruins of Segesta, with inscriptions dating from the fifth century BC. The lettering is Greek but the language is not.

Segesta's decline began around the fifth century BC when a series of border feuds occurred with their neighbors of Selimunt. In 409 BC, the Elimi, aided by the Carthaginians, attacked Selimunt, razed it to the ground, and killed more than sixteen thousand inhabitants. The following year an allied force from Syracuse recaptured Selimunt but it soon fell

again to Carthage and never regained its former glory. All that remains in evidence are a number of reconstructed temples.

For a long time the people of Segesta were dependent on the Carthaginian town of Panormos (Palermo) until it became Roman. Ultimately the city was severely damaged by the Vandals and other marauding tribes. The survivors fled, and the city deteriorated rapidly. Only the impressive Doric columns remain as a memory of the Elimi.

In recent years the theater of Segesta has once again seen performances. Classic dramas are enacted every other year in this third century BC amphitheater.

Pompeii emerges from its entombment

A city frozen in 79 AD and preserved beneath volcanic lava

North Sea

EUROPE

ITALY

• **Pompeii**

Mediterranean

ROUTE

International flights to
Naples; by car A1 or N18 to
Herculaneum and Pompeii;
station: Circumvesuviana

BEST TIMES

April–June,
September–October

ACCOMMODATIONS

Hotel Vesuvio, Via Partenope
45, Naples

ALSO WORTH SEEING

Naples: National
Archaeological Museum; San
Gennaro cathedral

The catastrophe that overcame the Bay of Naples started in the morning of August 24, 79 AD. A noise like a tremendous thunderclap rolled down Mt. Vesuvius. The entire top of the mountain had blown apart and was venting a dark cloud and spewing forth fire. Soon a storm of rock and ash descended from the darkened sky and a surge of molten lava headed from the flanks of the volcano towards the valley.

The first place to be overcome was the small seaside resort of Herculaneum. A torrent of muddy water, earth, and lava surged through the homes, suffocating man and beast, and ultimately covering the town beneath a sixty-five-foot-thick layer that turned to rock. The 100,000 or so citizens of Pompeii on the southeastern flank of the volcano seemed to be more fortunate. Only a continuous drizzle of ash fell there and the fiery lava flow headed in a different direction.

Those on the paved streets of the city took shelter in their villas, shops, temples, and bath houses but wherever they hid they were caught in a death trap. The drizzle of ash soon changed to small volcanic rocks, mixed with larger chunks of pumice. The stench of sulfur pervaded the entire city, reaching to every corner in which people sheltered, suffocating every breathing creature.

Two days later the smoke and dust clouds cleared and the sun shone brightly above the Bay of Naples, but Pompeii had vanished. The once wealthy provincial city was covered by a gray mass. The city had repaired the damage from the previous eruption a few years earlier but now its entombed population were soon covered by new grass and forgotten.

Treasure hunters discover civilization

Time passed. More than fifteen centuries later, treasure seekers started to take an interest in the buried city. A few statues were found at the site of Herculaneum but the mass of rock covering the site was difficult to

penetrate. Matters were more favorable at Pompeii for it was buried beneath a more fragile covering of ash, small volcanic stones, and pumice.

In 1748, during the first archaeological excavation that had been commissioned by royalty, the diggers chanced upon an astonishingly well-preserved Pompeiian villa with walls covered with murals. Marble and bronze statues of their gods were recovered and a market hall for selling produce and wine was uncovered.

The most pitiful findings relate to the people whose lives were abruptly ended by the eruption and its poisonous cloud of sulfur. One group that had been surprised by sudden death were gathered for a funeral meal. Others had fled, laden with their most treasured possessions but been overtaken by the poison lurking everywhere.

Other finds reflect a sensuous life style which authorities long kept under wraps. A sign was found in the shape of a penis, pointing to a brothel. A mosaic in the Casa del Fauna depicts a satyr engaged in love play with a naked nymph. Discoveries included a sculpture more than 160 feet high, that was painted red, of a vigorously erect phallus. It is clear that such erotic art was an important part of their Bacchus cult, while scholars suggest that representations of penises on the outside walls of their homes were intended to ward off the evil eye.

After 250 years of increasingly more methodical excavation, Pompeii has risen again from the ashes of Mt. Vesuvius like a phoenix, to provide us with a unique insight into city life around the time of Christ.

One of the main streets buried in 79 AD by the volcanic eruption. Cart tracks are worn into the paved street. The main walls of the houses were left standing and murals like that at the bottom left were preserved. People became mummified where they died, as the family shown at the bottom right.

Residence of the Pope

The Vatican contains more art treasures than any other building in the world

North Sea

EUROPE

ITALY

Rome, Vatican

Mediterranean

ROUTE

Bus line 64 to Piazza San Pietro (St. Peter's Square), subway line A to Otttaviano Station (about 300 yards N of Vatican)

BEST TIMES

Easter, April–June, September–October

OPENING TIMES

St. Peter's: daily 7 a.m.–7 p.m., winter to 6 p.m. Public audiences with the Pope on Wednesday, usually at 11 a.m. Requests to the Prefetturia della Casa Ponificia, Tuesdays 9 a.m.–1 p.m.

When the Roman emperor Constantine the Great embraced Christianity in the fourth century, he also established the basis for the political power of the Roman Catholic church, headed by the Pope. Constantine gave the Lateran Palace to the Christians as a residence which still belongs to the Vatican. This was where the Popes lived until 1308. Constantine also established the palace church of San Giovanni in Laterano. To this day it is the papal cathedral and the highest ranking church of Catholicism.

It was not until 1377 that the papal palace of the Vatican was developed on the hill on the right bank of the Tiber known as the Mons Vaticano. Construction of the Sistine Chapel began in 1473. The papal residence was built in the sixteenth century, designed by Raphael. At this time one of the most historically significant popes, Julius II, started collecting and exhibiting works of art, laying the foundation of today's treasury of Vatican art that is of inestimable value.

More than a thousand different rooms of every size

Art now became wholly associated with these holy places. The Sistine Chapel is richly decorated with the work of Sandro Boticelli and Pietro Perugino. From 1508 to 1512, Michaelangelo created the famous paintings depicting the story of creation which have recently been superbly restored. In 1541, *The Last Judgement* on the altar wall was completed. At present the Vatican, with its thousand plus rooms and a library of about 60,000 manuscripts, houses more art treasures than any other building in the world.

Surrounded by this beauty, the pope lives in and rules the world's smallest state or *Stato della Città del Vaticano*, the fragmentary remains of what was once a vast Roman Catholic empire. The Vatican City measures a mere 108 acres, with St. Peter's Square at its heart, and a population of about one thousand. In the Lateran charter, Italy guaranteed the independence of this church state which has its own "army" —the Swiss Guard—a mint, railway station, radio station broadcasting in thirty-five languages, and its own daily newspaper, the *Osservatore Romano*.

At the very center of this minuscule state is St. Peter's Square and the eponymous church, first built in 326 on the grave of Peter the apostle.

In the early sixteenth century, the artistic Pope Julius II had an enormous new basilica built to replace the original. It was designed by Bramante. St. Peter's can hold 60,000 people in its 15,708 square yards of space and took 120 years to build (1506–1626) before this enormous basilica was completed.

The 433-foot-high dome was designed by Michaelangelo. The basilica was regarded as a miracle of architecture. The most famous artists of the day contributed to both the church and its surroundings. The colonnaded crescent which encloses the forecourt, its columns, pylons, and life-size sculptures of various saints is by Giovanni Lorenzo Bernini, who also designed the installation of the eighty-two-foot-high Egyptian needle at the center of St. Peter's Square and the canopy above St. Peter's altar. Michaelangelo's *Pieta* appears in the right-hand side nave of the church. At the entrance to the principal nave, one is reminded that this is where Pope Leo III baptized Charlemagne and crowned him as Holy Roman emperor. The church's need for buildings has vastly outgrown the tiny Vatican state and there are palaces to be found elsewhere in Rome plus three patriarchal basilicas and the pope's summer residence at Castle Gandolfo.

St. Peter's Square and the administrative buildings of the Vatican State. Bernini, who designed the square's colonnades, also arranged the 82 ft-high-needle in the center of the square. The Vatican's greatest treasures are 60,000 manuscripts, housed in the beautiful Bibliotheca Palatine (below view of library and mural).

ROUTE

International flights to Peretola airport, Highway A3 and A11. Restricted access for vehicles to the inner city

OPENING TIMES

Uffizi: Tuesday–Saturday 9 a.m.–7 p.m.; Sunday to 2 p.m. Closed Mondays

ACCOMMODATIONS

Porta Rossa, Via Porta Rossa 19 (central, one of Italy's oldest hotels)

Florence: cradle of the Renaissance

Under the Medici the capital of Tuscany reached sublime cultural heights

Human beauty soon fades, but art endures, wrote the Tuscan poet Francesco Petrarch (1304-1374). No other city impresses us with this wisdom so strongly as Florence. Its astonishing richness of truly great architecture, sculpture, paintings, manuscripts, bronzes, and masterpieces of the goldsmith's art is simply incredible.

Here, on the banks of the Arno River, surrounded by green hills, an Etruscan settlement existed as early as 200 BC. As a Roman colony one hundred years later, the still small town was named Florentia, suggesting it was blossoming. Changing fortunes brought a succession of rulers to Florence until its citizens deprived the nobility of all their privileges in the thirteenth century and established the first citizen's republic, in which the bourgeois and well-intentioned merchants held sway. Ultimately though, the Medici family drew all power unto themselves.

The Medici were merchants and bankers who brought great commercial prominence to the city. However it was their role as patrons of the arts that led to an incomparable blossoming of creativity. Through their patronage, some of the Tuscan capital's most important buildings came into being, the first public library in Europe opened its doors, science and the arts were advanced, and great works of art collected. Great minds were able to develop in Florence, like those of Brunelleschi, the painter and sculptor Michaelangelo, and the universal genius Leonardo da Vinci.

One of the most attractive routes through Florence of the Middle Ages and Renaissance leads from the south bank of the Arno across the old bridge known as the Ponte Vecchio. This spanned the river in 1342 and by the sixteenth century goldsmiths had established their workshops and shops on either side of the bridge. Pedestrians jostled shoulder to shoulder among the continuous line of precious objects for sale. Just one corner of the bridge was not built upon, and this provides a view of the warren of alleyways, palaces, churches, and towers of the inner city.

The octagonal baptistery that was once the Cathedral of John the Baptist has stood here since the eleventh century, with its green and white marble and bronze doors that are heavily encrusted with reliefs. Immediately below the baptistery the 351-foot-high dome by Brunelleschi of the Santa Maria del Fiore reaches skywards. This church was completed in the fifteenth century.

Collection of masterpieces

One day's sightseeing is not sufficient to see the inner city of Florence. One must take time to look properly at the San Lorenzo Church built by Brunelleschi and embellished with sculpture by his contemporaries Michaelangelo and Donatello. There are Renaissance palaces to be admired such as the Palazzo Medici-Ricardo with its inner courtyard, and the crenellated fortified tower of Palazzo Vecchio, complete with its murals, painted ceilings, grand halls, and sculpture.

In the famous Uffizi Gallery the visitor can admire one of the most significant collections of paintings anywhere in the world, with ancient sculpture displayed alongside masterpieces by the leading European artists. And within the Palazzo Pitti, built in the fifteenth century to a Brunelleschi design, there is the Palatini Gallery with works by Titian, Rubens, Raphael, and many other masters from the Medici collection.

The French poet Guy de Maupassant took special pleasure in gazing upon Titian's naked *Venus*, but after many visits to the museum he was "exhausted from looking, as a hunter of the hunt." And his very sensitive German colleague Rainer Maria Rilke reported after touring Florence: "Wandering through the network of quaint alleys I had to tear myself away. I could take no more."

Three images of Florence: painted ceilings in the Venus Hall (below) of the Palazzo Pitti, which holds one of the largest art collections in the city; the rich facade of the Santa Maria del Fiore (consecrated 1467) with 269-ft campanile of the 13th century; and the Ponte Vecchio, which has spanned the Arno since 1342. Goldsmiths built their studios and shops on the bridge.

Monasteries perched on pinnacles

Greek monks found solitude on the peaks of the Metéora

In Greek, *metéoros* means "raised up." And this is precisely how we find the monasteries in the Metéora Mountains of Greece. Monks built their refuges atop pinnacles of rock that tower up to a thousand feet above the Pinios River. When dusk covers the valley as the sun has almost disappeared, or when the morning mist still hovers over the peaks, the monasteries appear to be floating amid veils of white gossamer.

Hermits were drawn to the mountain peaks northwest of Thessalia as early as the ninth century. The caves at the foot of these mountains provided adequate shelter and made it possible to meditate without being disturbed. Using ladders, some of them climbed to crevices in the sandstone higher up, cast away the ladder, and fasted and sought the presence of God through self-castigation and ecstasy.

Serbian incursions into Byzantine Thessalia in the fourteenth century prompted the construction of the first settlements and monasteries in virtually inaccessible places on rocky ledges and mountain peaks. The monks used ropes or lashed ladders together to carry the materials up to the site, and later they hauled both men and materials up in nets or large baskets.

No admission to woman

One of the first monasteries in the Metéora Mountains was that of Agios Stéfanos (St. Stephen), established in 1332 by the Byzantine emperor Andronicus III. After Thessalia was conquered by the Serbs in 1340, who were also Orthodox Christians like the monks, building activities grew apace. Abbot Athanasius, named after Mt. Athos and nine fellow believers, started in 1356 to build a monastery on the highest pinnacle of *Platos Lithos* or the "Broad Stone." The most prominent monk of this community was the Serbian heir-apparent to the throne, John. In common with the others he had to obey a very strict regime, particularly the injunction forbidding woman to the cloisters. If a woman offered food, it could not be accepted, even if starvation was the result.

During the long period of Ottoman rule, which began in 1420, large and small monasteries continued to be added to the pinnacles. In 1438 monks built the small monastery of Hagai Triada on a narrow ledge of rock with sheer drops. The building of red sandstone against the dark rock is a pleasing

sight. The monastery and its fresco decorated chapel is reached by means of a steep flight of steps hewn from the rock. This is the route used by thieves in 1979, when they stole a number of priceless icons.

By the sixteenth century there were twenty-six monasteries on the Metéora Mountains. The Turks levied high taxes and appropriated land to resettle refugees of Greek origin from Asia Minor. Eventually this weakened the economic position so much that many of the monasteries were abandoned and became derelict. During the nineteenth century, only seven of them were still inhabited. Monastic life halted almost completely during World War II because Thessalia became a battlefield, firstly through the advance and then retreat of German troops and then through the civil war between the Communists and anti-Communists.

In the mid 1960s, monks started to live again in those monasteries that had not been damaged beyond repair. In the meantime one of them is now exclusively reserved for nuns. The abbots of these monasteries have accepted tourism as a major source of income and easier means of reaching the monasteries have been created to facilitate this.

The abbots no longer shun or debar female visitors, but women are expected to wear skirts that cover their legs.

North Sea

EUROPE

GREECE

Metéora Monasteries
Mediterranean

ROUTE

E75 to Larisa, N6 to Kalampáka (237 miles NW of Athens/125 miles SW of Thessalonika)

BEST TIMES

May–June, September–October

ACCOMMODATION

Hotel Amalia, Kalampáka (2 miles from monastery)

ALSO WORTH SEEING

Témbli valley 62 miles E, mountain village of Makrinitsa, 75 E in Pilion Mountains

Monks once more live in mountain-top monasteries such as Russanú (left) and Haga Triada (right). Tourists can visit.

The Acropolis–Athens' holy mountain

The Parthenon was once a treasury and then a powder magazine

ROUTE

By air to Athens. Ten minute walk from central Sindagma Square

BEST TIMES

May–June, September–October. Severe air pollution in midsummer

ALSO WORTH SEEING

National Archaeological Museum, the inner city of Plaka, view from Likavitos Hill

The Acropolis or "high city" of Athens is situated on a limestone outcrop 512 feet high. This formed a natural stronghold, complete with its own wells. The Mycenaean kings settled here in the early thirteenth century BC and were the first to build a palace on the hill associated with the goddess Athena, daughter of Zeus, surrounding it with an enormous wall.

When the Mycenaean monarchy was abolished the palace became a temple during the seventh century BC. The first major new buildings on the site—the old Parthenon or temple of Athena and the pre-Parthenon—were started in the sixth century BC. A century later the buildings of the Acropolis took the form we know today.

Athens was frequently conquered and subject to different rule and during the Middle Ages it became a fortress once again. The Acropolis

knew Catalan and Frankish dukes and regents as residents and the Turks too, until in 1687 a Luneburg artillery officer brought this to an end. Serving in the army of Doge Morosini of Venice, who were beleaguering the Turks in occupation of the Acropolis, he landed a direct

hit on their powder magazine and blew up the Parthenon.

After this severe damage the Parthenon became a source for souvenir hunters on the grand tour. The British diplomat Lord Elgin ran a booming business in artifacts from his base in Constantinople. This

Scottish lord purchased large parts of the fallen buildings, parts of which went in 1809 to the British Museum in London where they are known as the "Elgin Marbles." Until her death, the famous Greek actress Melina Mercouri pleaded with Britain for their return as Greek minister of culture. Greece continues to press the British, who produce evidence of their "legitimate purchase."

Goddess of gold and ivory

The entire area of the Acropolis was declared an archaeological monument as early as 1854, but it was not until 1977 that an archaeological reconstruction of the structures on the site began. Since that time each of the buildings of the Acropolis has been reconstructed. Those parts that are missing were carefully recreated in marble and fixed into place with stainless steel pins. It is an expensive effort to restore the most important collection of historical monuments in Europe.

The Parthenon is the primary image of the Acropolis. This ruin, surrounded by columns, is the finest building from ancient civilizations still existing. Today's Parthenon or Temple of Athena was completed in 438 BC as a place to house the treasure chests of the Attica Sea League and from the former Athena temple within the stronghold of the Acropolis. An almost forty-foot-high statue of the goddess Athena in gold and ivory cost more than the building itself. Its gold alone weighed more than a ton. In the fifth century BC this priceless Athena disappeared somewhere in Constantinople. Smaller marble copies are now in the National Archaeological Museum in Athens. In the sixth century the Parthenon served as a church for the Athenians, and in the thirteenth century, the Holy Roman emperor dedicated it to Catholicism. In 1640, the Ottomans turned the classical edifice into a mosque.

Whoever ruled Athens, and no matter how badly the Parthenon suffered in terms of plundering, fire, or war, the Greeks continued to regard the Acropolis with its Parthenon as the home of the goddess Athena.

No other ancient building was as well furnished with sculpture and reliefs as the Parthenon and no other ancient building was dedicated to just the one goddess. The achievements of the goddess Athena were depicted on the front wall in a deep relief of more than eleven feet in height and ninety-three feet wide. The frieze that surrounded the Parthenon was 525 feet long, portraying the Pan-Athenian procession that was central to the Athena cult. This procession paid homage to the goddess who watched over the city for more than three thousand years.

The Parthenon rises from the Acropolis which sits high above Athens. Lesser temples of Nike (bottom left) and the Erechtheion with its group of caryatids (below). These are within that part of the monuments being restored since 1977 under archaeological supervision.

The awe-inspiring Hagia Sophia

For a thousand years it was the largest church of Christendom

It all started with arson. Early in 532 a rebellious mass set fire to certain Byzantine buildings in Constantinople, including the large cathedral or "Megale ekklesia." Within a matter of weeks the Byzantine emperor Justinian I had masons start building a new church on the ruins of the old one. It was to surpass anything else Justinian had previously ordained. The new cathedral of his realm was completed within five years. The emperor named it Hagia Sophia or the Church of the Holy Wisdom.

The master builders Anthemios of Tralle and Isidoros of Milete created one of the most impressive sacred buildings the world has ever known. Never before had a dome of such dimensions been constructed, purely on the basis of mathematical calculation. To the believers coming to worship, it seemed as if the dome was floating above them. With a rather squat appearance from outside, the interior of the Hagia Sophia is flooded with light from the many windows, making its interior a beautiful and most perfect spatial

arrangement in the history of architecture. "Praise God who found me worthy to complete this task," Emperor Justinian declared on the day of dedication, as he led the procession entering the high-vaulted nave.

A thousand years passed by before the Hagia Sophia was surpassed by the building of St. Peter's in Rome. Michaelangelo, who supervised its construction, devised even greater and higher domes. At about this time the Hagia Sophia, with its golden mosaics and artistic

marble arches, was lost to Christendom when the Ottoman empire conquered Constantinople in 1435. The city became Istanbul and the cathedral was turned into a mosque, known as the Ayasolya Camii. Four minarets were added around the dome, and inside the church, plaques were added citing passages from the Koran in golden script.

It was Kemal Ataturk, the founder of the modern Turkey, who prohibited Islamic use of the building in 1934 and opened it as a museum.

Blue mosque as counterpoint

A short distance from the Hagia Sophia is the Blue Mosque which provides visitors to Istanbul with an opportunity to compare this early example of Christian architecture with later Muslim efforts. Just across the Sultan Ahmed Park is the equally impressive domed structure of the Blue Mosque or Sultan Ahmed Camii. Sultan Ahmed was keen to surpass the greatness of the nearby unique Christian church, so he had the most famous Ottoman building erected in the early seventeenth century. The main dome of the Blue Mosque is actually slightly smaller than that of the Hagia Sophia but the exterior is certainly comparable and perhaps more harmonious. It is the only mosque in Istanbul with six minarets instead of the customary four. The interior is entirely decorated with tiles, predominantly of blue.

Another major tourist attraction close at hand is the nearby Topkapi Palace in the large park of the former sultan. At the time Constantinople was captured, most of the buildings here were constructed of wood. These were mainly pavilions which looked like a city of tents. When these buildings burnt down, as eventually they did, they were replaced by brick structures, and so gradually, an exciting row of palaces, domed halls, pavilions, courts, and minarets filled the view.

The Topkapi Palace today is primarily a rich collection of the riches from the Ottoman empire. Distributed through the various buildings, the collection includes weapons, porcelain, tapestries, miniatures and other paintings, antique clocks, calligraphy, and religious items, such as the tools used for circumcision. The harem is a realm of its own, with a dozen rooms, including those for the Nubian eunuch slaves, the court of the favorites, and the chambers in which the sultan would spend his time with them.

The Byzantine emperor Justinian erected the Hagia Sophia in the sixth century on the ruins of Constantinople's earlier cathedral. It was the principal church of his realm and a brilliant architectural creation. Under Ottoman rule the church became a mosque in 1453 and gained four minarets. The golden mosaic (top right) recalls the Christian origins of the building.

Mausoleum for a beloved wife

The Taj Mahal is famous as India's most beautiful building

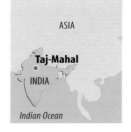

ASIA

Taj-Mahal

INDIA

Indian Ocean

ROUTE

Internal flight to Agra. By train from Delhi (125 miles/2 hours); coach tours to Taj Mahal

BEST TIMES

November–February

ACCOMMODATIONS

Hotel Taj View (luxury hotel with best view of the Taj Mahal)

ALSO WORTH SEEING

Fort Agra, mausoleum of Itimad-ud-Daulah

It is not just the architectural beauty of the Taj Mahal that enthralls people but the moving story of its creation. Probably one of the best-known of all beautiful buildings, its enchanting elegance in white marble rises majestically out of the plain of Agra. Its 236-foot-high structure seems so insubstantial that it has an ethereal quality. One large dome, echoed by seven smaller ones in a reflection of the female form are in turn reflected in a plain ribbon of still water for an image of perfect harmony.

The Taj Mahal's origin is a story worthy of the imagination of a romantic poet and legend has embellished the tale. The Muslim Mogul emperor Shah Jahan and his favorite wife Arjumand Banu Begum, whom he called Mumtaz-i-Mahal, "the pearl of the palace," are at the center of the story. The great Mogul was still a prince when he took a wife at the start of the seventeenth century. She was the beautiful fifteen-year-old daughter of a high official.

The ruler, who governed the country from 1628 to 1658 added her to his harem but left no doubt that all his adoration was directed at Mumtaz. It was she who sat beside him on formal occasions, and who accompanied him on his campaigns, and with whom he discussed matters of state.

Lamentation in stone

The favorite wife produced eight sons and six daughters for her lord and master. Soon after giving birth to her fourteenth child she died. Many moving stories are recounted of the Mogul emperor's grief, both as written by the court chronicler and suitably embellished in reworking by other writers.

It is said the emperor's dark mane of hair turned instantly gray at his wife's deathbed. Following her death he instituted a two year period of mourning. It was forbidden to feast, listen to music, wear jewelry, or perfume.

To express his sorrow "in stone" the grief-stricken husband promised

to erect a Taj Mahal or crown of a palace for his deceased wife. The emperor recruited architects, engineers, sculptors, and calligraphers from Persia, the Ottoman Empire, and the city of Samarkand. These people were put to the task of expressing his ideas for a mausoleum in the form of a mosque with four minarets.

To decorate the interior, a Venetian artist was commissioned, who also designed the sarcophagus that was placed above the sepulcher. A goldsmith from Bordeaux fashioned the silver entrance gate. It took 20,000 laborers twenty-two years to complete the building and to surround it with a Persian garden with ponds and rills. Its almost forty-five acres certainly meet the requirement for a "crown of a palace," presenting the eye with a vision of harmony that is truly a work of art.

The Taj Mahal remains the most beautiful and impressive example of Indo-Islamic architecture erected by the Mogul emperors during the sixteenth and seventeenth centuries. India has declared the shrine a national monument while the rest of the world views it as a magical example of Indian architecture.

The Mogul emperor Shah Jahan built the Taj Mahal as a mausoleum and expression of grief for his favorite wife, Arjumand Banu Begum, also known as Mumtaz-i-Mahal ("pearl of the palace"). She died in childbirth. An army of 20,000 laborers needed 22 years to complete the superb edifice and its gardens. Later Mogul emperors were also entombed there. For the interior decoration, artists were commissioned from Samarkand, Venice, Persia, Turkey, and France.

Home of the gods

Mount Everest is the world's highest mountain

ASIA

NEPAL • **Mount Everest**

Indian Ocean

ROUTE

One hour mountain flights from Katmandu in Nepal. Flight to Katmandu-Luka followed by a 10 day hike to the viewing point at Kala Pattar (Mt. Everest base camp)

BEST TIMES

October–December

ALSO WORTH SEEING

Thyanpoche Monastery, monastery and temple in Katmandu valley

Tibetans says that the world's highest mountain is best recognized by its "prayer flag." This is the name they give to the veil of ice crystals that swirl around the summit of Mount Everest on most days. Without its veil it is difficult to identify this famous giant among the eight thousand or so other peaks on the borders of the Hindu kingdom of Nepal and the ancient land of Tibet. It appears from a series of surveys of recent years with highly accurate satellite equipment that Mt. Everest is getting taller and also moving. Its current height is 29,035 feet, an increase of seven feet over the height recognized for the past forty-five years.

Long before westerners became aware of the mountain the people of Tibet worshipped the "goddess-mother" or Chomolungma as the holy abode of the goddess Tseringma. The people of Nepal, who have declared their part of the mountain as a reserve, call it Sagarmatha "whose top reaches the heavens." Its western name is derived from a British artillery officer and geodetic surveyor, Sir George Everest, who discovered in the mid nineteenth century that the peak which he listed as XV was higher than any other in the Himalayas.

Scientific expeditions experienced great problems finding the highest mountain peak of the world among the snowcaps of the eastern Himalayas, calculated by trigonometry. Early in the twentieth century Western encyclopedias still confused Everest with the Nepalese peak of Gaurisanker. This confusion arose through reports of the German explorer Hermann von Schlagenweit, who when journeying through Nepal mistook Gaurisanker—a mere slip of a hill at 23, 441 feet—perhaps because he was unaware of the "prayer flag".

Assaults on the top

British and Swiss climbers did find the right mountain the 1920s but failed to reach the top. After numerous failed attempts had been made, it finally fell to the New Zealander Edmund (now Sir Edmund) Hillary and his Nepalese Sherpa, Tensing Norgay to reach the top on May 29, 1953. They hoisted three small flags on Everest representing the colors of

Great Britain, Nepal, and the United Nations.

In the decade that followed, more than one hundred other climbers reached the summit of Everest, and in 1978, Reinhold Messner of South Tyrol and his partner Peter Habeler were the first to make the climb without oxygen. Two years later Messner repeated this alone.

Although everybody was climbing the same mountain, the precise altitude has not necessarily been agreed. The first measurements in the nineteenth century calculated the height as 29,002 feet and later a height was calculated of 29,160 feet but this was widely contested. Since 1954 the height stood officially at 29,028 feet, and Everest was even deposed in 1987 as the world's tallest mountain by a U.S. satellite survey by Prof. George Wallerstein which found that K2 was thirty-six feet higher than Everest.

The old ranking was restored a few months later by the Italian Prof.

Ardito Desio who calculated with a number of satellite measurements that K2 was 28,267 feet and Mt. Everest 29,107 feet, but this did not last long either. Scientists have now discovered that Mt. Everest grows by about seven inches each year. At this rate the mountain will grow to 32,808 feet 6,300 years from now.

On their way to the top of Mt. Everest (above), climbers were constantly battered by heavy snowstorms. The first successful ascent of this giant on the borders of Nepal and Tibet was on May 29, 1953 when the New Zealander (now Sir) Edmund Hillary and his Sherpa, Tensing Norgay reached the summit. Reinhold Messner from South Tyrol and his partner Peter Habeler were the first to climb Everest without oxygen in 1978. The smaller photograph shows Everest by evening sunlight. The Tibetans call the mountain Chomolungma, the "goddess-mother."

India's Seven Pagodas

The Temples of Mahabalipuram on India's Coromandel coast

ROUTE

Direct international flights to
Madras or via Bombay
(Mumbai); coach from
Madras to Mahabalipuram
(37 miles)

BEST TIMES

February–March

ACCOMMODATIONS

Temple Bay Ashok Beach
Resort

The small town of
Mahabalipuram, which
makes its living from
fishing off southern India's
Coromandel coast, may appear
somewhat sleepy at first but it does
invite a journey back in time. Its
history goes back to the fourth to
ninth centuries when this was a
religious center with ample gods to
worship. There was Shiva, the god of
destruction and procreation, Vishnu,
preserver of the universe, and his
beautiful wife Lakshimi, goddess of
beauty and fortune.

Not far from the beaches of the
Bay of Bengal, where tourists tan
themselves, to the south of
Mahabalipuram, great peaks of
granite soar above the green trees.
Almost all of these apparent rock

formations prove to be Hindu
pagodas and sculptural works of art
of considerable beauty.

The Pallava kings, the mighty
rulers of southern India, built their
temples here. The stories carved in
rock greatly enhance this temple to
the Hindu gods and provide them
with mythical events.

Heavenly chariot

The oldest of the temples of
Mahabalipuram are within caves such
as Vahara. Its walls have reliefs
depicting the various good
incarnations of Vishnu. As a wild
boar he battles a snake-headed
demon who would cast the earth into
the abyss of the world's oceans. One
entire wall is filled with the fifth of
Vishnu's manifestations as the dwarf

Vanana who suddenly changes into a
giant with one foot resting on the
earth, the other in heaven, thereby
liberating humankind from the
beast's reign of terror.

Impressive further development
of early Hindu architecture is
exemplified by the nearby cave
temples of the five Rathas or
heavenly chariots. These temples
have ornamental animals that are
each carved from rock by
generations of different sculptors.
The Pallava rulers had these rock
carvings made in the fashion of the
wooden processional chariots and
shrines on which Hindu deities are
borne by crowds of the faithful
during festivals. These were the first
free-standing stone temples of
southern India.

Hindus still visit the eighty-eight foot-long relief cut into a rock slope to a height of twenty-three feet, which depicts the source of the River Ganges, which Hindus believe sows seed in both the earth and the human mind.

The famous pagoda on the beach is not carved from a single piece of granite but built of pieces of stone which have been cut and dressed to shape. It dates from the seventh century and rises up picturesquely from the surrounding surf. The pagoda is surrounded by sculptures of bulls, representing Shriva's mount, Nandi. The pagoda is built from rectangular elements placed one on top of the other so that they taper to a point at the top. When Mahabalipuram still had a harbor, this pagoda also acted as an orientation point for sailors and a fire was lit on it at night. Today the shore is illuminated by the lights of restaurants and small hotels.

Heat, wind, and salty air have badly eroded the pagoda on the beach (7th century, top left). It is the best known pagoda of Mahabalipuram. Rock walls and caves near the town are also decorated with carved figures from Hindu mythology (top right). A heavenly chariot or Ratha was carved from a single piece of rock for the small pagoda shown left.

139

Thousand and one nights in Lahore

Art, architecture, and the cities too flourished under the Mogul emperors

ASIA

Lahore
PAKISTAN

Indian Ocean

ROUTE
By air to Lahore

BEST TIMES
November–February

ACCOMMODATIONS
Holiday Inn

ALSO WORTH SEEING
Fort Lahore, Jehangir
Mausoleum, Wazir Khan
Mosque, Maryam Mosque,
Shalimar Gardens

No matter which old gate, mosque, palace, or mausoleum you pause in front of, the people who live in Lahore will be able to tell you its story. The entire inner city, enclosed by a dilapidated wall, is like a stage set in brick for a tale from the *Thousand and One Nights*. The Muslim faith flourished more exuberantly in Lahore than anywhere else in Pakistan. Lahore sits on the Ravi River in the fertile Punjab, or "land of the five rivers."

Comfortable stronghold

The Muslim conquerors hoisted the green flag of their prophet in Lahore at the end of the tenth century. The mighty sultan Mahmud of Ghazni incorporated the city into his realm from the Punjab to Samarkand. Five hundred years later the powerful Mogul warlords enclosed this area

within a wall with twelve towers and built a town within the fortifications which already existed, complete with inner courts, palaces, bath houses, and the "pearl mosque" with its three domes. As with the Taj Mahal in

India, Lahore brought together the best of Mogul architecture and art. Beneath the long since disappeared Sha-Buri gate at the main entrance there was an inscription in Arabic: "The likes of this have never been

Colourful frescoes cover the walls of the Wazir Khan mosque from 1643.

seen and shall never be seen again." Gates of huge proportions were needed to allow the Mogul emperors to enter upon an elephant. The massively strong steps allowed an elephant to ascend to the famous Shish Mahal or "Mirror Palace" which reflects the artistic interior a thousand fold. On the walls mosaics of colored mirror shards produce a pleasing motif. Larger mirrors reflect gilded ornaments, while gems set in marble form enchanting floral patterns.

Enticing gardens of Shalimar

The "mirror palace" was the home of the ruler's wife. The Grand Mogul himself had a place of his own, complete with the "court of the harem maidens," and the "house of dreams" with the emperor's bedroom. Banquets were held in the "hall of forty columns." The residents of Lahore were also very active sportsmen as can be seen from tiles and murals. The best horsemen played polo, which originated in Central Asia. Other contests involved elephants, camels, and bulls.

In addition to the stronghold, the Moguls left mausoleums and buildings used for receiving visitors, plus the Badshahi Mosque, which is the finest religious building in Lahore. It was built of red sandstone in the late seventeenth century and set in its inner courtyard with minarets at each corner. It can accommodate 60,000 Muslims for prayer. The gate and the form of the three white domes echo the Taj Mahal. In common with that famous mausoleum, this mosque is also raised up on a plinth to emphasize its beauty.

Outside the city of three million people are the wonderful Shalimar Gardens with their green, flowering, and gurgling oriental park landscape, created in 1641–1642 on three terraces. Among the marvels of garden landscaping are a water basin of almost two hundred feet with 412 fountains, beautiful islets, bathing areas, superb pavilions, and marble walkways. The Moguls and higher nobility spent the hottest part of summer in the adjacent palaces and guest houses.

The courtyard of the 17th-century Badshahi mosque (top left) can accommodate 60,000 at prayer. The Shalimar Gardens (top right) and the miniature mosque (bottom right) are among the finest examples of Islamic architecture.

141

The palace of the Dalai Lama

Lhasa was home to Tibet's divine leaders

CHINA(TIBET)
● **Lhasa**

Indian Ocean

ROUTE
Internal Chinese flights from
Beijing and Chengdu or by
air from Katmandu

BEST TIMES
October–December

ACCOMMODATIONS
Holiday Inn

ALSO WORTH SEEING
Monasteries at Sera, Ganden,
and Drepung

Amid the mountain range known as the "house of snow" there is the "land of the calling deer" and its capital "the seat of the gods" in the valley of "happy rivers" that reflect the "palace of enlightenment." The names of these places are poetic when translated into English. We are talking of the Himalayas, Tibet (once known as Boyul), its capital Lhasa, the reflecting waters of the Kyichu River, and the Potala Palace.

Set at an altitude of 12,083 feet, the "seat of the gods" was one of the most isolated places in the world until the twentieth century, reachable only by difficult pilgrimage and caravan trails, and no strangers were permitted. In the final years of the nineteenth century the Swedish explorer of Asia Sven Hedin was not even permitted to glance at the objective of his Tibetan expedition from a distance. China, which occupied the mountain country in 1951, has also refused to grant visas to foreigners wishing to visit the "autonomous region" of Tibet.

Center of the world

For the inhabitants of Lhasa, the town has the same significance as Rome for many Christians and Mecca for Muslims. For this is the holy Jokhang Monastery of their spiritual and temporal leaders with its statue of Srongtsan Gampo, who introduced Buddhism into Tibet in the seventh century. The later Lamaism is a form of Buddhism with the addition of elements of Shivaism and the native shamanism. The divine ruler, the Dalai Lama, is believed to be a reincarnation of Buddha.

The twin spiritual and temporal leadership roles were first assumed in the seventeenth century by the fifth Dalai Lama, Lobsang Gyatso. This high priest built a kind of Tibetan Vatican on the Marpori or red mountain that skirts Lhasa, founded on the remains of the "Castle of

Immortality" of their leader Songsten Gampos. The fortress-like Potala Palace has since been extended by Lobsang Gyatso's successors. Until 1959, when the fourteenth Dalai Lama fled to the west to escape the Chinese, the Potala served as a monastic retreat, seat of government, and administrative center of Tibet's spiritual and temporal leaders.

Monastery as museum

When mist spreads out across the mountains, the Potala appears to hover above Lhasa to approaching visitors. Its architecture reaches upwards to the heavens, with walls that taper and angular towers. Most of the facade is a bright white honeycomb, although some of the upper layers are red. This is the red palace and former residence of the Dalai Lama. The building is now a

fine museum of Tibetan art with depictions of their deities, painted mantra scrolls, and incense vessels and other treasures of the Lamas romantically lit by oil lamps.

The Lamaist priests made certain in the past that noone entered, on pain of death. Today one might encounter more tourists than Tibetans in the course of the thirteen levels of the building. And instead of the chanting of mantras one hears the loud voices of guides as they drone their standard patter in English. The Potala contains one thousand rooms, supported by 15,000 columns, has 10,000 individual shrines, and 200,000 devout statues. Below, part of the cellar floor is of the reddish brown rock of the Marpori peak. The oldest wall of the over 1,300-foot-wide complex is thought to be that surrounding the "nuptial chamber" of Srongtsan

Gampo. The upper floor of the Potala contains the former private chambers of the self-exiled fourteenth Dalai Lama, who to the discomfiture of the government in Beijing does not let up in his struggle to regain Tibetan independence.

Communist ideology and the traditionally-minded and nationalist Tibetans do not gel well with each other. The historic center of Lhasa has seen many demonstrations against their occupiers. Under the suspicious eye of the Chinese police an almost endless procession encircles the main Jokhang Buddhist temple and its Buddha. Monks in colorful robes, sunburned nomads, and beggars in rags continue to chant their mantras as they did in the days of their spiritual leaders. The principal mantra is *o mani padme h'um* "O lotus jewel, amen."

Until the Dalai Lama fled the Potala Palace from the Chinese, this monastic retreat at 12,083 feet was also the seat of government of Tibet's spiritual and temporal rulers.

A glimpse of the Forbidden City

Beijing's old imperial palace opens its gates

Indian Ocean

ROUTE

International flight or 6-day journey on the Trans-Siberian railway. Emperor's Palace/Tienamen Square subway station Quiamen

BEST TIMES

September–October

ALSO WORTH SEEING

Heavenly Temple, Lama Temple, Confucian Temple, Summer Palace, Beihai Park

The people of Beijing used to marvel at the "purple city" hidden from them behind a forty-foot wall where their emperor lived. All they saw on a sunny day were the elegant purple tiled roofs. A Chinese person without either a job in the palace or an invitation was allowed no closer view. The emperor considered himself the self-evident center of the earth, and those who did not give his haven a wide berth could expect a savage beating. It is from these times that the foreigners gave the name "The Forbidden City" to the area of the palace.

Home to twenty-four rulers of the Ming dynasty

The palace compound that is rich in treasures of art was begun in the fifteenth century. The emperors of the Ming dynasty moved their seat of government from Nanking to the new capital of Beijing. A hundred thousand craftsmen and a million coolie slaves were engaged in the task. The 178-acre site reserved for the emperor was to accommodate the imperial palace, housing for the royal entourage, and formal halls for official functions. Most of these early wooden structures were eventually burned to the ground, and when

rebuilt, great changes were made, so that the current architecture of The Forbidden City mainly dates from the eighteenth century.

Twenty-four emperors lived in the palace before it was finally opened up to the public following Mao Zedong's Communist victory. Endless crowds of sightseers now shuffle through the Noon Gate to enter the palace compound where they enter the famed Hall of the Highest Harmony, a huge wooden building from the seventeenth century which is held together with wooden pegs rather than nails. The inside of the hall is 115 feet high and

the roof is supported by twenty-four pillars of hardwood, half of which are gilded. At the center of the hall is the imperial throne which is also gilded, on a dais of rosewood, with a dragon suspended above it from the ceiling. From here the emperor, as the self-styled "heavenly son," issued commands and decrees to his courtiers who had to prostrate themselves.

A second imperial throne is located in the adjacent Hall of Perfect Harmony, albeit somewhat less ostentatiously furnished. This served the rulers of the Middle Kingdom as a place for rest and meditation. A third Guardian of Harmony hall between heaven and earth was used for audiences and banquets. Today the People' Republic exhibits its archaeological treasures there.

Symbol of power

Quite apart from those items shown in this exhibition, there are more works of art on show in the Forbidden City than anyone can take in on a single visit. The interior has priceless room partitions and engravings, large statues of animals from Chinese mythology in stone and bronze—turtles and cranes to symbolize long life and lions representing imperial power. A particularly fierce lion raises a paw— the emperor will crush those who disobey.

There are 9,000 different rooms within the palace compound. New residences alone were needed for the countless eunuchs and concubines across the years. The emperors were by tradition permitted three wives, six other favorites, and seventy-two concubines, but this was not enough

for some of the emperors. China experts have discovered that some of these "sons of heaven" retained up to an unimaginable 2,000 concubines. To prove their status, the women wore golden chains engraved with their date and place of birth.

These ornaments can also be seen in the no longer forbidden Forbidden City. Sometimes such human touches attract more interest than the valuable works of art.

Thousands of woodcarvers, painters, and gilding experts, 100,000 other craftsmen, and a million slaves built the Forbidden City, Beijing's Imperial Palace. At left a beautifully decorated dome and above the Gate of Divine Courage or northern exit.

China's clay army

A terra-cotta army guards the tomb of the first emperor

ASIA
CHINA
Xian
Indian Ocean

ROUTE
Flight from Beijing or Hong Kong to Xian

BEST TIME
September

ALSO WORTH SEEING
Huaqing Hot Springs, Wild Goose Pagoda and large mosque in Xian

The shaft of the new well was quickly sunk for the members of a Chinese communal farm...but instead of water they found the fired earthenware heads of life-sized soldiers. The well diggers in the maize field between the Li Mountain and the Wei River, close to the northeastern provincial capital of Xian were replaced by archaeologists whose excavations turned a surprise into a sensation. They unearthed a complete army of life-size terra-cotta warriors, standing row upon row beneath the maize field.

That was in 1974, and today further battalions of this subterranean army are still being uncovered. This army, which stands

to attention as if on parade, guards the tomb of China's first emperor, Shih Huang Ti. In the third century BC the first emperor, who had conferred the title on himself, had a gigantic mausoleum built for his burial. History recalls him as a man who successfully united a divided land into a single realm, ordered the building of the Great Wall, reformed writing and legislation, but also burned down libraries and buried learned men alive because of his displeasure with them.

Monument to excess

Chronologists say that about three decades before his death, Emperor Shih Huang Ti had 700,000 forced laborers from all over the country

build a palatial subterranean mausoleum for him. A copper sarcophagus was made for the emperor and his treasure-filled sepulcher was protected against robbers by crossbows that were loosed automatically. When the emperor died, his son and heir buried him together with his childless concubines. Finally he buried alive all those who knew of the buried treasure.

Slaves heaped a mound of earth more than 160 feet high over the imperial grave and planted it with cypresses and spruce. It was close to this hill that the well diggers made their astonishing discovery in 1974. Subsequent excavations in the ensuing decades suggest the

emperor wanted a representation in clay of his entire army buried with him. To the east of the hill more than eight thousand terra-cotta soldiers have been unearthed, and it is probable that further ranks of warriors are standing to attention to the north, west, and south of the burial mound.

The entire area of the current archaeological dig is covered. The warriors are arranged in columns of four, forming parallel corridors which the archaeologist call shard spots. Some figures lead horses and wagons and thanks to the extraordinary attention to detail of the soldier's uniforms it is possible to assign them to their units.

There are infantry, spear throwers, archers with both longbows and crossbows, cavalry leading their steeds, charioteers, officers, and a six-foot-tall general who stands out above them all, wearing a well-modeled scarf and three ornaments on his breast plate.

No two faces the same

Thousands of skilled sculptors and dozens of potteries must have been pressed into service to produce the thousands of figures. The bodies may have been mass produced but the heads and many of the hands were separately modeled and attached later. Those who made the warriors were careful to copy hairstyles. There are twenty-four different types of mustaches and a rich variety of different headdresses.

Far more astonishing though is the often lively and widely different facial expressions on the faces of the terra-cotta warriors. One gets an impression that men from every tribe in the realm modeled for the statues. There are broad Mongolian faces, men with exceptionally high foreheads, or with pronounced noses. The faces of the officers are highly individual and the terra-cotta horses are also of great artistic merit. With their mouths usually open, nostrils flared, and ears pricked, these give a strong impression of untamed power.

The question remains what secrets still lie in the emperor's tomb itself beneath the burial mound? So far the Chinese have been terrified of disturbing the death rest of the first emperor, his concubines, and his unfortunate servants, who were buried alive.

The first emperor of China Shih Huang Ti ordered the building of the Great Wall of China in the 3rd century BC and the building of a mausoleum for himself close to the northeastern provincial capital of Xian. Since 1974, archaeologists have unearthed 8,000 life-size terra-cotta warriors (top left) who were buried with him for symbolic protection. The soldiers all have individual expressions on their life-like faces (above).

Old imperial city of Kyoto

Shinto shrines and temples amid a treasure-trove of Japanese culture

ASIA

JAPAN

Kyoto

Pacific Ocean

ROUTE

High-speed train from Tokyo (321 miles in less than 3 hours)

BEST TIMES

October–December

ACCOMMODATIONS

Miyako Hotel, Sanyo Keage (Higaslyama-ku district)

ALSO WORTH SEEING

Koyasan (holy mountain) 62 miles S

The year 794 is very significant in Japanese history for in that year the inhabitants of the Japanese islands created a new capital and seat of government for the new Emperor (*Tenno*) Kammu, with help from Korean immigrants. At first this city was known as Heianko but it later gained fame as the cultural and religious center of Japan under the name of Kyoto.

The new imperial city was modeled on Chinese examples in a grid of slightly more then three miles by just under three miles. Absolute symmetry was observed in the erection of the various districts. Each new street and alley within the walls and moat of the city was at right angles to those it intersected but this rigidity was quickly softened by the richness of form and color of traditional Japanese architecture which unfolded there during many centuries to make Kyoto one of the most fascinating places to visit in Japan.

Roofs that protect against demons

The imperial family moved from Nara to their new residence in the year the new capital was founded. The emperor's palace and the first temples were much influenced by Chinese-Buddhist architecture. This meant that elegant roofs were preferred which are upswept at their ends so that any demons sliding down the roof will be swept upwards and not fall to earth. The Tenno's palace was at first sited in the north of the new city but later was relocated to the northeast. It burned down completely in 1228 and was eventually rebuilt in its former splendor in 1856. Together with the Nijo Palace, it recalls the glorious times for the emperor of the feudal ages.

Central Kyoto—now a city of more than 1,500,000 people—still bears the imprint of its medieval temples and palaces.

The oldest surviving sacred building is the Tshionin Temple of

the Jodo sect which dates from the thirteenth century, although its impressive gate is an addition of five centuries later.

Buddhism was imported from China and adapted to Japanese thinking. It finds expression in Kyoto's architecture, such as the thirteenth-century Sanjusangendo Temple and the highly artistic Nishi-Honganji and Hagashi-Honganji Temples.

The cult of simplicity

The style of traditional Japanese tea ceremonies is associated with simplicity in design of living spaces that reached a high point in the imperial villa at Katsura near Kyoto. The basic design module used for all the rooms is the size of sleeping mats when spread on the floor. The smaller rooms can hold four mats while the larger ones accommodate multiples of four. There is also a

platform in the house for looking at the moon.

Further impressive examples of Japanese arts can be found in the gardens of the imperial city. Influenced by Zen, the miniature landscapes of traditional Japanese rock gardens originated here. These are not gardens designed to stroll through but to be interpreted like paintings or other works of art. The fourteenth-century Kinkakuji and fifteenth-century Ginkakuji are regarded as exceptionally success-fully examples of symbiotic relation-ship of architecture and sculptural "nature."

Nowhere else in Japan has there been such a density of cultural outpouring as the area around Kyoto.

Proponents of the city say that Kyoto is the richest treasure house of their country. The old imperial city has more than 1,500 Buddhist temples, monasteries, and gardens,

two hundred Shinto shrines, feudal pavilions, and palaces.

Japanese emperors ceased holding court in Kyoto in 1868 when Tokyo became the new capital and seat of the "kings of the heavenly realm."

The image of old Kyoto is one of carefully restored medieval temples and palaces. Shown (clockwise) are: the ornate roofs of the Helan Shrine, an animal sculpture at the Fushimi Inari Temple, Japanese garden art, and the Golden Temple.

The forbidden city of the Vietnamese emperors in Hue

Palaces and tombs along the perfume river remind of former might

ASIA

VIETNAM

Hue

Indian Ocean

ROUTE

Flights from Hanoi and Ho-Chi-Min City (former Saigon) to Hue. Rail connections with both cities

BEST TIMES

June–July

ACCOMMODATIONS

Century Riverside and Huong Giang Hotels, both in Le Loi Street with view of palace

Burial mounds and tombs come into view even when landing at Hue. The city is surrounded by graves, and the tombs of the emperors are closer to the palaces and pavilions of the former emperors. The other dead are buried by the thousand in circular mounds surrounded by stones. Alongside these there are smaller graves for children and even smaller ones for miscarriages. Rank and status were once observed even unto death in Vietnam's old imperial capital of Hue.

The city lies on the Huong Giang or perfume river, one of the most heavily fought over parts of the realm of Annam, which is largely the same as the present borders of Vietnam. Towards the end of the seventeenth century, Hue was created as a fortress town, then known as Phu Xuan, which was ruled by a succession of local strongmen until 1804 when the Emperor Gia Long made it the center of his Nguyen dynasty.

Emperor Gia Long had a "forbidden city" built on the site of the citadel as a personal residence along the lines of the Beijing model. Surrounded by high walls and a moat, the palace complex of Hue was a fortress within a fortress. Architects and garden landscapers went to considerable pains to create harmony between the structure and nature. When the emperor left his palace he could stroll through landscaped gardens with little streams and waterfalls, artistic islets, pavilions, fine residences, and temples.

The rulers had the main entrance to Dai Noi (the emperor city)

extended with a Noon Gate, the pavilions of which are two storeys high, with roofs covered in green tiles, except the middle one, which is golden. Immediately behind the gate one came to the throne room, or Palace of Ultimate Harmony, decorated with red and gold lacquered wood carvings. Three flights of steps lead via a colonnaded walkway to the throne of the emperor of Annam. The last member of the Nguyen dynasty to hold office was Emperor Bao Dai who was deposed in 1955.

Stone grave guardians

The six imperial graves of Hue are gems of architecture. The tomb of Emperor Gia Long and Empress Thua Thien Cao is sober in style: just two simple stone sarcophaguses that blend with the surrounding landscape. Other rulers had more ostentatious tombs built during their lifetime. The grave of Emperor Minh Mangs is guarded by stone elephants, horses, warriors, and civil authorities. Emperor Thieu Tris is entombed in a temple surrounded by water, and Emperor Tu Duc had himself placed in a burial pavilion spanning a brook, supported by columns. This had been his favored place for meditation, where he could find peace.

Many buildings and their artistic treasures were lost during the various Vietnam wars. In February 1968 the Vietcong hoisted their flag on the imperial tower in front of the Noon Gate but the Americans and South Vietnamese regained control of the city two weeks later, until the Communist regime eventually took it back. In the vicinity of Hue alone some 10,000 people lost their lives. Circular burial mounds that are gradually being covered with tropical lushness are a last reminder of them.

The main entrance to the imperial palace on its citadel site is through the elegant pavilion of Ngo Man (the Noon Gate). This leads to the Thai Hoa (Palace of the Ultimate Harmony, below). This is the throne room of the Nguyen dynasty where emperors received emissaries and guests.

155

The beauty of Angkor Wat

One of Asia's finest cities lies deep in the Cambodian jungle

The pagodas of the royal temples of Wat rise out of the landscape above the Khmer capital of Angkor like golden peaks. This once large and prosperous city lies in the northwest of Cambodia. At the beginning of the eleventh century the population of Angkor was one million, and the city boasted many pagodas and countless shrines to the Hindu gods. It must have been the most beautiful city in all Asia at that time. The Chinese diplomat Chou Takwan saw princesses riding elephants shielded from the sun by red canopies, caught the scent of jasmine in the air, and heard music played by cymbals, flutes, and gongs.

The Khmer king Suryavarman II surpassed all the existing buildings when he had a new temple built in Angkor between 1113 and 1150. In an area of about 240 acres surrounded by a 650-foot-wide moat, he had a new sacred quarter established. At its center are the five pagodas that tower like man-made mountains of sandstone blocks to a height of 213 feet. The pagodas symbolize the universe and the mythical mountain of Meru.

This enormous Asian sacred center was dedicated to both the Hindu god Vishnu and Suryavarman II, who permitted his people to worship him like a living god. As a symbol of his majesty he carried "the golden sword of Indra." Consequently, in reliefs around the temple compound, portrayals are found of mythical episodes from Suryavarman's life as well as the Hindu legends of holy men. It is said that he saw a nine-headed heavenly snake each night beneath the tallest pagoda of the temple, which took on the form of a beautiful girl so it could copulate with the king. According to his decrees, Suryavarman was buried at the temple.

The jungle takes over

The sophisticated city with numerous reservoirs for water and cleverly irrigated rice fields that were cropped two or three times each year flourished up to the fourteenth century. Angkor was invaded by Thai warriors and the king of Siam's soldiers set fire to the city, so that it was abandoned in 1431 and gradually forgotten. The jungle gradually reclaimed the land, covering Angkor Wat, together with the other temples and the ingenious irrigation system.

It was not until 1860 that the French researcher Henri Mouhot rediscovered the walls and pagodas in the Cambodian jungle. He described it as more impressive than any find in ancient Greece or Rome had ever been.

Later expeditions revealed new riches among the ruins spread over several square miles of jungle. Many of the buildings that were badly eroded were restored by French archaeologists and protected against further damage. When the German television journalist Hans Walter Berg visited Angkor in 1957 he considered the pagodas to be "more balanced, more harmonious, and more impressive than the Hindu examples." He also noted the fascinating way that lush vegetation was embracing the majestic art, damaging it, yet at the same time supporting it.

Much of the restoration work at Angkor was undone during the bloody Cambodian war in the 1970s.

Many of the statues and reliefs from the golden era of the Khmer were intentionally damaged at this time by their barbaric descendants.

In 1987, the restorers were able to return to work at the temple of Angkor Wat and the other important sites in the vicinity.

The holy site of Angkor Wat, surrounded by a 650-ft-wide moat (top left) was started in the 12th century in honor of the Hindu god Vishnu and the Khmer king Suryavarman II. He was worshipped by his subjects as a living god. In the past 100 years archaeologists have discovered numerous other temples in the vicinity of the palace temple compound, including Pré Rup (top right) and Bantea Srei (bottom right)

Where the Emerald Buddha changes his raiment

Bangkok's royal palaces and the temple of Wat Phar Keao

ASIA

THAILAND

Bangkok

Indian Ocean

ROUTE
Express ferry from Menam Quay in Ta Chang

BEST TIMES
November–February

ACCOMMODATIONS
Hotel Sukhotai 13/3 Sathorn Tai Road

ALSO WORTH SEEING
Wat Pho and Wat Saket temples, National Museum, Jim Thompson's house

Boats laden on the Menam River with bananas for cooking, golden pagodas aglow in the sunlight, white shrines to the spirits beside every road, gaggles of monks in saffron robes, blue and jade-green statues of the holy ones between scarlet columns—old Bangkok is a feast for the eyes of the beholder. Despite its population of seven million, expanding industry, and skyscraper hotels juxtaposed with the elegant temples, the Thai capital maintains its cherished traditions and retains its incomparable charm.

This metropolis on the banks of the Menam River was founded by the Chakkri dynasty which assumed power in the old kingdom of Siam through a coup by the officer corps of the army in 1782. The dynasty still rules and the present Chakkri king, who was crowned Rama IX in 1950 is King Bhoemibol. Together with his Queen Sirikit, this constitutional monarch has helped his country to become one of the major tourist centers of Asia.

For those visiting Bangkok who appreciate art, King Bhoemibol has opened up much of the royal palace. His ancestor Rama I started building it on the east bank of the Menam towards the end of the eighteenth century. The palace compound covers about 370 acres with a Buddhist monastery and temples and the Chedis pagoda that is gilded with gold leaf.

One of the older buildings, dating from 1783, contains a pagoda of five tiers. This was the first coronation chamber of the Chakkri dynasty and it contains the black throne of Rama I, decorated with mother-of-pearl, a second throne, and the king's bed. Angels are depicted on the green walls floating heavenwards from lotus flowers. The Thai call Bangkok, Krung Thep or "city of the angels."

Animals stand guard

Of the four additional palaces, the most impressive is the "great palace of the Chakkri dynasty." It is also the most curious architecturally, being built under British architects in 1876 during the rule of King Chulalongkorn as something of a replica Renaissance castle but with the addition of Thai elements such as pagodas from which heavenly green snakes emerge. These pagodas are in turn topped with smaller, more pointed ones.

The nearby sacred quarter of Wat Phar Keao or "monastery of the Emerald Buddha" is one of the most impressive examples of Thai temple building. Twelve enormous sculptures of Yaks guard the six entrance gates. These are partly harbingers of happiness but also act as guardians. Other buildings have other animal sculptures in bronze or stone of elephants, cattle, lions, and mythical creatures. A rectangular hall with external walls of blue and gold and tiered roof, decorated with small bells, contains the most revered spiritual symbol of the kingdom. The Emerald Buddha rests on a thirty-six-foot-high plinth. The Buddha is just over two feet tall and is carved from a single piece of jade.

In 1784, King Rama I proclaimed that the Emerald Buddha represented the holy guardian of the Chakkri dynasty. Devout Thai followers built the Bot, a special temple specially for the Emerald Buddha, which is enhanced with twelve symbolic animals adopted by Buddhism from the Hindu god Vishnu. To protect the Buddha a small golden and gem-encrusted home was created for him. The fortunate traveler may chance to visit during the three seasonal ceremonies attended by the Thai king. These festivities are for the rainy season, the hot season, and the cool season. It is at these times the holy guardian of Thailand changes his raiments.

To commemorate Buddha's death 2,500 years

A Buddha at Wat Phar Keao (monastery of the Emerald Buddha). The temple was built next to the royal palace of King Bhoemibol and Queen Sirikit in the late 18th century.

...go the temple roofs and golden Ghedi pagodas and the beautiful facades and the colorful guardians of Wat Phar Keao were carefully restored.

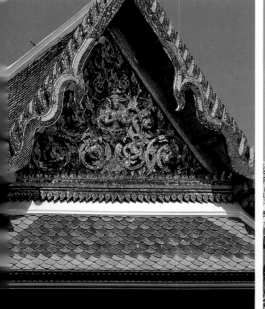

Java's temple of the many Buddhas

Borobudur is a major goal for pilgrims

SEA OF JAVA

JAVA
Borobudur

Indian Ocean

ROUTE

By air to Jakarta, internal flight or train to Jogyakarta. Bus to Borobudur (25 miles)

BEST TIMES

April–October

OPENING TIMES

6 a.m.–5 p.m.

ALSO WORTH SEEING

Prambaman Temple, crater landscape on the Dieng plateau

The court astrologers were commissioned to seek every spot in the kingdom where the male sun penetrates the female earth. Horoscopes were studied, calculations made, sequences strictly observed, and finally it became evident: the divine copulation occurs on a dome-shaped hill in a fertile region of central Java.

And so it was that midway through the eighth century the best possible site was found on which to construct a model of the mythical mountain of Meru, around which according to Hindu belief, the whole world turns.

Eighty years to build

Ten thousand coolies were needed to build the temple on the chosen hill with its nine different levels. For eighty years they piled the enormous volume of 74,082 cubic yards of precisely cut stone on top of each other without even a fistful of mortar until the original hill had been turned into a man-made mountain.

The form of this temple underwent even greater influence from Buddhism when this religion conquered Java. Buddhas in bronze, stone, and as reliefs were placed along the nine terraces. When completed in 830, this holy place was known by the Buddhists as

Borobudur, which means "many Buddhas."

To the many Buddhist pilgrims traveling to Borobudur the yellow-brown temple mountain seemed an unparalleled sacred wonder of the world. Ascending the nine levels in a clockwise direction they were told to climb the "three stairways of being" which lead from the earthly to the heavenly world. After this, pilgrims would pass thousands of relief tablets illustrating the life and teaching of Buddha. Beyond this many niches contain figures of Buddha and his disciples leading up to the three highest platforms of the temple where there are seventy-two stupas

(bell-shaped stone structures, each of which contains a stone Buddha).

At the top of the temple, pilgrims encountered the largest stupa and the only one that is empty, symbolizing the absolute peace and enlightenment of nirvana.

Until the middle of the tenth century, Borobudur was an important place of pilgrimage for Buddhists in the Indonesian archipelago, but later the faith became centered on eastern Java, where Buddhism enjoyed a new period of growth. When the Merapi volcano erupted in 1006 Borobudur was badly damaged, statues were toppled, and the temple was covered in a thick layer of lava. Soon the jungle reclaimed the temple and this great monument was lost for centuries.

Successful restoration

Its rediscovery in 1814 is entirely due to the British Governor-General of Malaya, Sir Thomas Stanford

Raffles who wanted to find out the meaning of the clearly carved rocks he discovered beneath the lush foliage. In the decades that followed, parts of Borobudur were uncovered. The temple had suffered greatly, most of the bronzes had disappeared, and many of the statues were headless.

From 1907–1911 the Dutchman Theodor van Erp organized the first systematic restoration. Meticulous

photographic documentation was made of the entire structure which aided its restoration in the twentieth century to its former condition. Once more as a thousand years ago, Buddhist pilgrims journey to the earthly representation of the heavenly mountain of Meru. It is said that if pilgrims stretch out their hand in the niches they may expect great happiness.

Hundreds of Buddhas adorn the 9th century holy shrine of Borobudur (many Buddhas). The larger Buddhas are housed in bell-like stupas (top left) while others are arranged in niches in the walls along the processional route up the temple mountain. Reliefs (top right) depict scenes from the life and teachings of Buddha. For centuries Borobudur was lost beneath the jungle before its rediscovery in 1814.

Samarkand – the paradise of the Orient

Under Tamerlane it was the great trading city between the Orient and Occident

ASIA

UZBEKISTAN

Samarkand

ROUTE

By air to Tashkent, local flight to Samarkand or by rail on the Trans-Caspian railway from Tashkent to Samarkand (approx. 190 miles)

BEST TIME

October

ACCOMMODATIONS

Hotel Afrosiab

ALSO WORTH SEEING

Oasis city of Tashkent, Buchara and Chiwa

On his campaigns against half of Asia, the Turkoman Mongol conqueror Timur the Lame surpassed even his famous predecessor Genghis Khan in ruthless destruction. He is better known in the west as Tamerlane, a corruption of Timur Lang (Timur the Lame). The list of medieval cities plundered and destroyed by his hordes is almost endless. Untold riches, but also skilled craftsmen were captured and returned to his capital Samarkand. His building lust reflected his megalomaniac tendencies, but he was determined that Samarkand should become "the paradise of the Orient."

In Tamerlane's time, the metropolis in what is now Uzbekistan was already 1,500 years old. Long before the first millennium, the routes of the caravans carrying silk from China met at this fertile oasis on the Zeravshan river. Paved roadways led to the great market where valuable cloth, hunting falcons, fur, tapestries, and gems were traded. In 751, the craftsmen of Samarkand made paper from rags, enabling the production of academic literature, dictionaries, and encyclopedias.

When Tamerlane chose Samarkand as his residence, the city was still recovering from the aftermath of occupation by Genghis Khan. To give the city a focal point, Tamerlane had a personal mausoleum built, the Goer-i-mir or royal tomb. The main part of this structure is still intact with its cylindrical boxed roof with grooved domes simulating flower buds. Travelers approaching Samarkand from any direction first saw the cobalt and turquoise main dome standing at 111 feet, so that it rose above the horizon like a gemstone lit by the sun.

Ostentatious entrance to Goer-i-mir

One of history's major architects, Muhammad bin Mahmud of Isfahan, built a thirty-nine-foot-high gate at the entrance to the Goer-i-mir, which is covered with a mosaic of glazed earthenware in bright colors. The motifs of the decoration represent the planets, sun, flowers, leaves, and fruit. Beyond this gate one entered the inner court bordered by the mausoleum on one

side and by a madrasah or Muslim college and accommodation for students on the other. The Goer-i-mir was completed in 1405 and established the central Asian style of architecture for the next century. When Tamerlane died shortly after this, he was laid to rest in his mausoleum.

The mother-in-law mosque

One of the finest pieces of sacred architecture in the Orient is the great Bibi Chanym Mosque, which Tamerlane had built for his wife's mother. It took ninety-five elephants four years to drag the blocks of stone from mountain quarries to be cut to shape by a team of five hundred stonemasons. Meanwhile artisans were forging the main entrance gates "from seven metals." When completed, the huge "mother-in-law" mosque possessed a large hall for prayers, and its four hundred domes were supported by hundreds of marble pillars and other supports.

Tamerlane drove people from their homes in the center of the city in order to raze them to create a large covered bazaar for merchants and tradesmen. Within a few years this new main market developed into the most significant trading center for the exchange of goods between the Orient and Occident, overflowing with riches from both hemispheres.

Under Tamerlane's cousin, Ulug Beg, an astrologer, the great bazaar was relocated and the area was transformed into a large open area known as the Registan. Later this was cordoned off on three sides with towers exuberantly decorated with mosaics.

Tamerlane's vision of "a paradise of the East" was fulfilled in part through his buildings and those of his successors, and the metropolis experienced a great period of flourishing trade. In 1941, archaeologists opened Tamerlane's tomb and found the skeleton of strongly built man with Mongolian skull, red beard, who was lame on the right side of his body.

The madrasah (above and bottom right) is on

three Muslim colleges. The towers denote the area of the Registan, most beautiful center of Samarkand where the great bazaar was held.

163

Arabia's first skyscrapers

High-rise building in Shibam along the Incense Road

ASIA

Shibam YEMEN
Indian Ocean

ROUTE
By air to Aden. Local flights from Aden or San'a' to Shibam

BEST TIMES
October–May

ACCOMMODATIONS
Shibam Guest House, Sam City Chalets (near Saiyun)

ALSO WORTH SEEING
Sultan's palace in Saiyun, San'a'

The view looks all the world as if someone has tried to model New York City in a sand pit. On closer examination you realize the scale is smaller and it is not sand but clay bricks from which Shibam's slender skyscrapers are built. But these buildings were withstanding sandstorms long before America had its first high-rises. Caravan travelers were telling tales as early as the third century of this town of "tall houses" sited at the south of the Arabian peninsula.

Building with clay bricks

Fugitives from Schwaba, that was put to the torch and razed around 250 AD, founded the town of Shibam in an area 1,300 feet by 1,600 feet on a hill in the Wadi Hadhramaut. Here they built five hundred dwellings close together to an unbelievable height for the age of almost one hundred feet. Perhaps they could have built even higher but they were not permitted to do so.

Of course some of the houses have been rebuilt over the centuries

but the basic form of the dwellings and town remained the same. Today's builders in Shibam still work in the traditions of their predecessors of the tenth century.

They continue to use sun-dried bricks of clay. If the walls lean too far because of sandy subsoil they just build a new upright wall. The narrow format of the homes has also remained unaltered.

The mud-colored or lime wash skyscrapers were often provided with a finely carved gate as the sole

form of ornamentation. The lower levels tended to be used for storage or as shops, the middle floors for the children and women, while the upper floors were reserved for the men and their guests. The roof gardens provide a fine view of the lush valley of the Wadi Hadhramaut, except during the rainy season. The valley is a thousand-foot-deep rift in the Dschol Plateau.

During the wet season the groundwater rises to the surface, enabling cultivation of date palms

and oasis cultivation of various types of cereal and vegetables. The town's wealth though was founded on its judicious position astride one of the major caravan routes of the Arabian Peninsula, the "Incense Road."

Incense trade

Around the middle of the third millennium BC caravans carried oliban along this route (a form of gum resin) from the gum olibanum tree, from Hadhramaut and Dhofar in the southern province of Oman. When heated, the yellow and brown resin emits an aromatic fragrance. This incense was used as part of death rites in Egypt, and the Greek and Jewish temples also burned oliban.

Both Roman and Byzantine ceremonies were inconceivable without the use of incense, and its aroma still wafts today through both Roman Catholic and Orthodox churches.

Besides oliban and the greatly valued myrrh, many other treasures were also transported from the Mediterranean along the "Incense Road," such as gold from the legendary Ophir in Africa, cloth from Yemen, and herbs and gems from India. Arab slavers probably used the route for their trade too. In the third century the wealth of Shibam made it the center of the Hadhramaut kingdom.

In the ninth century, the importance of the Incense Road waned and so too did the fortunes of the Hadhramaut kingdom. Shibam has barely changed in the past thousand years.

The center of Shibam with its white stucco mosque (top right) takes the traveler back 1,000 years, if you ignore the mopeds, power cables, and lamp post next to the small mosque. The 500 or so homes of the inner town are on six to eight floors. Houses are rebuilt in the traditional manner with sun-dried clay bricks , when they fall into decay. In the oasis gardens outside the town palms, cereals, and vegetables are cultivated.

165

ASIA

YEMEN

San'a' · Indian
Ocean

San'a' is still the "pearl of Arabia"

Dried sandstone and unique windows set the town's style

ROUTE
Regular flights from Europe
to San'a'

BEST TIMES
October–May

ACCOMMODATIONS
Al Gasmy Palace Hotel
(inner city), Rawdaw Palace
(8 miles N)

ALSO WORTH SEEING
Dar al-Jahar national
museum (former residence
of the Imam, 9 miles NW);
Shibam in Wadi Hadhramaut

Many a traveler on their first journey across the Yemeni highlands felt certain they were witnessing a mirage. Shimmering sandy forms rose up out of the dust clouds in the oppressive heat. Coming near it was possible for the traveler to see white ornamentation on the brown facades of buildings, arabesque trellis work, and window frames with stucco reliefs, and small brown and white-painted minarets.

The town that lay before him was San'a', rich in sages, pearl of the Arabia, a city of commerce, silversmiths, alabaster carvers, and weavers of fine cloths.

The origins of the town go back at least 2,500 years to the Yemeni kingdom of Sheba, of Biblical fame and renowned for its great queen, whose rulers selected a fertile area to create as a stronghold. The fortress, at a height of 7,700 feet, developed into a trading place for farmers and craftsmen who were protected by a wall running for over seven miles which was over thirty feet high and up to sixteen feet wide. It is from these defensive works that the name San'a' is derived, meaning "well-protected." An armed watch guarded the seven heavy timber towers.

In spite of a great deal of rebuilding and much new construction, the city has retained its medieval appearance, in part because the same

traditions have been retained for the facades of the buildings. The first step in construction is to create a foundation from large blocks of stone. After this the walls are erected to heights of four to six storeys, using blocks of sun-baked sandstone. The diversity in form of the windows is surprising. They are circular, arched, square, or vaulted. There are line courses of white masonry between each storey of the building.

Daylight filters through alabaster windows

The buildings of 65–100 feet still retain their traditional colors. Window frames are lime-washed white, in common with the decorative line courses and trellis of the upper windows. When lamps are lit at dusk the effect is magical. Colored glass in many windows shimmers and the traditional alabaster windows reflect a milky glow.

San'a' also reflects the various religions of the people who have lived here in the 2,500 years since it was founded, as conquerors overran the city's walls. The first temple was built at the time of the kingdom of Sheba when the Israelites, who were the kingdom's first silversmiths, built a synagogue. This was replaced in turn by a church for Coptic Christians, and ultimately used for

the brick mosque built by Arab conquerors in the seventh century. The Al-Kabir or "great mosque" has a stone recalling the Kaaba of Mecca. Today as capital of Yemen, San'a' has about one hundred mosques with forty-five snow-white minarets rising above them.

Apart from the city wall and the main Bab Al Jaman Gate of the seventeenth century, San'a' is a modern city with a population approaching a million. Medieval spinning and weaving shops have developed into modern cotton industries. There is a university with departments for Islamic law and education. There is an international airport and a radio station. The palace of the Imam reminds one of the occupation under the Ottoman Empire. It now serves as a Yemeni museum.

Tools fashioned from flint and obsidian demonstrate that humans hunted on the plateau enclosed within the walls of San'a' during the Stone Age.

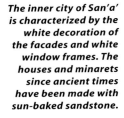

The inner city of San'a' is characterized by the white decoration of the facades and white window frames. The houses and minarets since ancient times have been made with sun-baked sandstone.

Mecca's most sacred shrine

Every Muslim must make a pilgrimage to the Kaaba at least once in his life

ASIA

SAUDI ARABIA

• **Mecca**

Indian Ocean

ROUTE

By air for pilgrims. Non-Muslims are not permitted entry to Mecca or Medina

BEST TIME

The hajj (pilgrimage) takes place during the 12th month of the Islamic calendar which shifts 11 days each year in relation to the Gregorian calendar

In the Islamic month of Dhul each year the same spectacle can be witnessed. Millions of Muslims from every corner of the world gather in the inner court of the great mosque in Mecca. They proceed around the cloth-draped tablet of stone that is the Kaaba. Their procession ends at the southeastern corner of the cubic structure where they kiss the Black Stone, said to be given to Abraham by the Angel Gabriel.

Long before the prophet Muhammad was born in Mecca and founded Islam in the seventh century, the long slab of basalt rock had been the focal point of religious worship. Arab tribes revered what is now presumed to have been a meteorite as a fetish sent from heaven and encased it for safe-keeping within the almost fifty-foot-high Kaaba (Arabic for cube), a windowless building with a flat roof supported by three pillars. Muhammad incorporated veneration of the Kaaba into his doctrine, which taught in common with Judaism and Christianity that there was only the one true God, Allah. From that time on he called the Kaaba "the house of God" and said the Black Stone was Allah's gift to humankind.

Islam unites Arabia

Before Muhammad ("the praised one") died, the new religion had spread throughout Arabia, uniting hitherto divided peoples, and so provided a political counterweight to the power of Byzantium and Persia.

When the prophet died at Medina in 632, a growing throng of pilgrims came to Mecca. Pilgrims from Egypt took to bringing black cloth with them each year as festive drapery for the Kaaba shrine.

In 700 AD the Caliph Walid I built an arcade surrounding the Kaaba, with marble pillars and mosaics of gold leaf. Gradual extensions led to the present-day two tiered promenades leading to the great mosque, beside seven minarets. The compound includes such sacred treasures as the Sensem springs and well which legend says the archangel Gabriel caused to gush water, taking pity on women. Elsewhere, at the Makram Ibrahim, a tile is displayed bearing an imprint of Abraham's foot.

Current Islamic doctrine requires that all adult Muslims shall undertake a pilgrimage to Mecca at least once in their lives. The only impediments that are recognized as appropriate excuses are illness or poverty. The ceremonies are strictly ordained. When the pilgrims arrive they must walk around the Kaaba seven times and kiss the Black Stone. Other rules require them to walk seven times between the holy hills of Al-Safa and Al-Marwa, which are connected by a long covered walkway. They must also make the longer walk to the Arafat Plateau, which pilgrims do from midday until the evening even in the burning sun in order to affirm their service to Allah. Pilgrims must also gather forty-six stones in a place called Musdalifa and take them to the three "pillars of Satan" at Mina the following day. The three pillars of different sizes are said to represent the devil in three guises. In the next three days pilgrims must cast stones at the pillars. Finally pilgrims sacrifice an animal such as a lamb and once more circle the Kaaba seven times before returning home.

The annual hajj poses major problems for Saudi Arabia and private enterprise was long since unable to cope. Today's pilgrims arriving by air, train, car, or on foot are catered for by the army which creates a temporary city outside Mecca for the millions of pilgrims who attend the hajj each year.

Around one million pilgrims visit Mecca each year for the annual hajj. On arrival and before departure they must walk around the Kaaba seven times. The Kaaba, which is hidden beneath black drapes, is located in the courtyard of the great mosque. The aerial photograph below sets the overall scene.

The second wonder of Ephesus

Archaeologists uncover a lost city port on Turkey's west coast

One of the original seven wonders of the world stood at Ephesus on Turkey's western coast but it was swallowed up by the earth. In the past century though archaeologists have been uncovering a new wonder that was once a thriving commercial port city. Ephesus is one of the largest and probably the most beautiful of all the ruined cities in Asia Minor dating back to the height of the ancient Greek and Roman civilizations at their peak.

The city's history goes back to the second millennium BC when vessels plying the Aegean could anchor in the harbor of Ephesus. The Lydians and later the Phoenicians established trading posts there. The nearby mouth of the Kaytros (now the Kucuk Menderes) and a caravan route leading to inner Anatolia stimulated the handling of goods through the port. Grateful for the improvement in their fortunes, the inhabitants erected a shrine at which they could worship the Earth Mother and goddess of fertility, Cybele.

Awe-inspiring Artemisium

Fertility rites were also central to the building by the Ephesians of the largest of all Greek temples in the sixteenth century BC. This temple

The Greco-Roman theater at Ephesus has space for 24,000 (above). The Hadrian Temple (right) was reconstructed by archaeologists from the original materials. Its fine entrance gates date from 130 AD. Next to it is a "house of pleasure."

was dedicated to Artemis, daughter of Zeus, who is represented as a beautiful woman with many breasts. The temple, which took 120 years to build, is praised by the Greek writer Plinius as "the noblest, greatest, and most wonderful sacred place on earth." The area of the Artemisium must have been at least four times the size of the Parthenon on the Acropolis of Athens. Its roof was supported by 127 columns and the temple was regarded as one of the seven wonders of the world. The temple was so impressive and famous in 356 BC that a psychopath named Herostratus, who wished to be remembered in history, set fire to it. A new temple on the site was eventually damaged by the Goths and the remaining stonework was used by stonemasons for other buildings.

Harbor silts-up

The majority of the superb Ephesian buildings that have been uncovered date from Greek, Roman, and Byzantine times. These are the remnants of an economic and cultural center that once housed 300,000 people but became doomed to decline as the harbor silted-up and the city was regularly plundered by marauders.

The center of the archaeological exploration has revealed a marble promenade over 1,700 feet long that is flanked by colonnades. Part of the city's most prominent building has been reconstructed by experts with the help of the findings they have made. The most advanced stage of reconstruction was achieved with the magnificent temple of Hadrian from

130 AD with its adjacent "house of pleasure." South of this marble walkway archaeologists have successfully reconstructed the famous Celcius library. About seventy percent of its two-storey facade with its 50-foot-high inner courtyard and parts of the gallery were rebuilt using the original materials. This fine example of Roman public architecture dates from the second century.

Nearby the library a Greek assembly or market-place has been unearthed. The square of 360 feet was bordered by a double row of pillar-fronted shops. Also close to the center are the impressive ruins of a Greco-Roman theater with seating for 24,000 in sixty-six rows.

Ephesus also contains early Christian structures. It was here that St. Paul the Apostle delivered his sermons and St. John the Theologian died there. There is a basilica above the probable grave of St. John where a council of the church declared Mary to be the mother of God in 431, making a strange link with the Ephesians' earlier cult of the earth mother. In the nearby Nightingale Hills, which provide a view to Selçuk, there is a small house that has been enlarged to form a chapel, where it is claimed St. Mary the Madonna died.

There is no proof of this claim but the Vatican did declare the "House of Mary" to be a place of pilgrimage in 1892. A Catholic Mass and Ascension of Mary is held there each year.

Artemis, daughter of Zeus, was worshipped in Ephesus as fertility goddess, represented as a many-breasted earth mother.

The white beauty of Pamukkale

In Turkey hot springs create nature's work of art

ASIA

Pamukkale

TURKEY

Indian Ocean

ROUTE

E87 for 150 miles S of Izmir

BEST TIMES

May–June, September

ACCOMMODATIONS

Pamukkale Hotel (with thermal baths, not exclusively for hotel guests)

ALSO WORTH SEEING

Ancient city of Aphrodisias

The mercury in a thermometer rises to more than 104 degrees Fahrenheit (40°C) on many summer days in central Turkey, so it is surprising to suddenly encounter a large area apparently of glacier ice. The blinding white expanse reminds the Turks of cotton fields ready to harvest, and so they call this strange phenomenon of nature Pamukkale—the cotton castle.

Chalk deposits create terraces

The sparkling white apparition is caused by hot springs. The water that drips and constantly flows down in countless gullies to the valley almost three hundred feet below is rich in calcium carbonate. As the water cools calcium carbonate is deposited, forming a white precipitate of chalky-flakes. In the course of thousands of years thick layers of calcium deposits have formed a series of terraces down the hillside to the valley below over an area of almost two miles into the valley.

The thermal pools that are supplied with mud from the springs and large pools of warm water were soon understood to have healing powers and this probably explains the establishment of the city of Hieropolis nearby in the second century BC. The residents of this city used the hot water in a Roman bath house. Perhaps those taking to the waters then also purchased souvenirs such as branches, leaves, and pebbles covered with layers of Pamukkale calcium carbonate.

As the water cools from 95°F (35°C) deposits of calcium carbonate are formed.

Thermal springs have deposited calcium carbonate that has formed stepped terraces of 300 feet in depth over thousands of years. People have bathed in the hot springs since ancient times for their health. Ancient buildings of the ancient city of Hieropolis were hidden beneath the snow-like chalk.

A less pleasant natural phenomenon near the hot springs was described by the Greek geographer Strabo in the first century. In his seventeen-volume *Geographica* he refers to a cave that produced toxic fumes that was fenced off to prevent people from inhaling the gases. Strabo also relates an account of the neutered priests who served the fertility goddess Cybele. They lowered sacrificial animals into the cave which were immediately asphyxiated. The eunuchs themselves were reputed to be immune to the fumes, thereby demonstrating their holiness.

Necropolis for craftsmen

Later the area around Hieropolis became prone to earthquakes and plundering. Parts of the ancient buildings disappeared beneath a thick layer of pebbles and flakes. In the 1880s German archaeologists began excavations, and this was later continued by Italians. A thermal building was uncovered close to an old bathing pool that dated from the second century. This is now the Pamukkale Museum. Not far from the poisonous caves, Plutonium, described by Strabo, archaeologists found the ruins of a temple to Apollo.

Among the objects from the classical period are the remains of an octagonal structure erected in the fifth century as a monument to St. Philip the Apostle who is assumed to have met a martyr's death at Hieropolis, an amphitheater with a frieze with mythological designs, and one of the largest ancient necropolises, with references on the grave inscriptions to weavers, dyers, and other craftsmen.

In recent years Pamukkale has become a significant Turkish tourist attraction. Numerous tourist coaches stop here and the white terraces are often thronged with people. Guests who can afford a longer stay will find comfortable hotels with their own thermal baths. Physicians recommend the steaming springs for rheumatism. The greater the flow of water that is diverted to the hotel baths the less there is to create further deposits on the famous calcium

carbonate terraces. Slowly the appearance of snow or ice will surely turn brown.

The pillars of Baalbek

Ruins retain grandeur

The Roman Temple of Venus is a masterpiece of the stonemason's craft. The horseshoe-form floor plan is unusual. The building dates from the first century.

A bronze statue in The Louvre in Paris shows the gold-helmeted god Baal. Other artifacts from early excavations in the Middle East depict Baal with bull's horns or armed with a club and spear. The god Baal, or Lord, once held sway among the Semitic divinities over the rain and fertility. Historians point to Baal rituals associated with Baalbek (city of Baal), the famous site of ancient ruins in the Lebanon.

More than thirty temples of the pre-Christian era must lie in the valley between the green hills and bare peaks of the Anti-Lebanon Mountains, buried beneath the ruins of later temples and places of worship. According to inscriptions in Assyrian, Baalbek was inhabited more then 3,000 years ago and then called Bali. The high god Baal was also worshipped as Hadad among the Phoenicians who turned Baalbek into a trading city. The Greek conquerors followed the Phoenicians, who identified Baal as their sun god Helios. At that time the city was known as Heliopolis, the sun city.

Around the time of the birth of Christ the city was occupied by the Roman legions of Caesar Augustus. The Romans regarded Baal/Helios as the same as their own god Jupiter. The Romans built an enormous temple to Jupiter upon an Acropolis which was already under construction by the Roman's predecessors. By bringing together the best of their architects and

sculptors the Romans created one of the most impressive sacred buildings of the Eastern Roman Empire. It was in harmony with Phoenician, Hellenic, and Roman styles and was hailed as a new wonder of the world.

Visitors to the temple, measuring 885 feet by 393 feet, entered via a wide set of steps which led to an entrance hall and a hexagonal inner courtyard with colonnaded arcades. This courtyard contained a multi-tiered altar flanked by two granite pillars, one pink and one gray. A further set of steps led to a larger temple set on a twenty-three-foot-high plinth covering an area greater than 8,300 square yards. The upper area rested on fifty-four pillars which were each seventy-two feet high. The temple was dedicated to a special local version of Jupiter,

distinct from the customary Roman Jupiter, nicknamed Optimus Maximus Heliopolitanus. Sometimes his image resembled that of his predecessor Baal.

The horseshoe-form Temple of Venus

Wars and earthquakes have left nothing but rubble of the area in front of the enormous temple complex, which was never wholly completed. Parts of the Jupiter temple were excavated by German archaeologists between 1900 and 1905 under the patronage of Kaiser Wilhelm II. Some of their finds were spirited away to the Pergamon Museum in Berlin. Of the fifty-four tall temple columns, only six are left intact, their capitals linked by a single slab of shaped stone. A few of

the pillars of the colonnaded arcade are also still standing.

The Roman Temple of Venus at the southern corner of the acropolis is astonishingly well preserved. Apart from its unusual horseshoe-form floor plan, this temple is a smaller version of the Jupiter temple. The high entrance arch is a magnificent example of the stonemason's craft in its own right with interwoven acanthus leaves, poppies, grapevines, and ivy. Here too Middle Eastern and Roman forms merge happily. The temple itself is bounded by two rows of Corinthian columns and a wall of the interior arcade contains a decorative niche.

Also worth seeing at Baalbek, which is now a minor town of about 20,000 people, are the smaller Mercury Temple, an amphitheater,

and the remains of the old city wall. The ruins in this historic place are still fascinating and evidence of the great beauty that Baalbek once was before earthquakes and wars, which have continued into recent times, destroyed so much.

Of the 54 huge columns of the Jupiter temple (top left) only 6 remain with their capitals joined by a single piece of crafted stone. Construction of the 886 feet by 393 foot temple started at the beginning of the Christian era. A row of pillars (bottom right) are part of the Temple of Venus.

Damascus the paradise

The story of this oasis city stretches back for 6,000 years

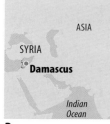

ASIA

SYRIA

Damascus

Indian Ocean

ROUTE

By air to Damascus

BEST TIMES

April–May, October

ACCOMMODATIONS

Cham Palace (Sh. Maisalun, about 20 min. to the inner city)

ALSO WORTH SEEING

National Museum, view from Mount Jabal Qassyun

Nothing is more like paradise as the Arabs imagine it than Damascus. Its old oriental quarters and beautiful location, surrounded by good soil for growing at the foot of the Anti-Lebanon mountain range have been praised by generations of poets. There is a story about the prophet Muhammad that he had experienced the city as so not of this world that he refused to enter. For humankind there is only one paradise and it is not on this earth. Hence the founder of the Islamic faith broke off his

journey to Damascus when he reached the southern suburb of al-Qadam, leaving his footprints, which long remained visible.

Damascus owes its well-being to the Barada River that created a natural oasis between the mountains and the desert. Six thousand years ago the first people settled here because of the water, and they in turn attracted others until a small village community grew into a city. No other place in the world has such a history of continuous human habitation. Arab historians regard

Damascus as the first city culture that arose. Its history is very much older than any European city.

Stage for biblical events

Countless stories associate this biblical place and holy Islamic city. Abraham, progenitor of all the Semites, is said to have been born here. Cain murdered his brother Abel, St. Ananias healed Saul of his blindness that happened on the road to Damascus and caused the unbeliever to become St. Paul the great apostle.

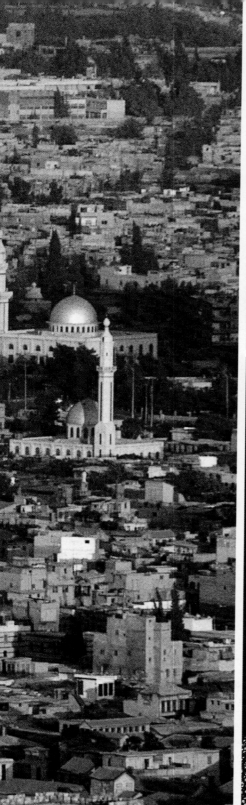

Major Mediterranean cultures helped to build the palm-shrouded oasis city surrounded by mountains. The Aramaeans built a temple beside the Barada to their god Hadad. The Romans constructed a temple to Jupiter. Christians added churches. If the core of the old city were to be excavated behind its wall with seven towers, traces would be found of Assyrian, Babylonian, Persian, and Greek origins among the many races that have been part of the history of Damascus.

From 636 on, the city developed into a spiritual and cultural Islamic center. The Byzantine churches of the Christians were outnumbered by the mosques and Muslims colleges of the new religion. A major peak in the development of their culture was the establishment in 1154 of the Maristan Nuri dar, one of the most modern hospitals in the world at that time. Europe's first hospitals were places where the dying found some comfort. Damascus had medical staff, medical literature, and wards for surgery, orthopedics, fever illnesses, and mental disorders. Unlike the practice in Europe at that time, the hospital was a secular organization, not under clerical supervision.

Among the Eastern-style bustle of the old inner city, where swords of the famed Damascus steel and golden ornaments are offered for sale, there are some thousand or so beautiful arabesque buildings standing shoulder-to-shoulder.

The Omajjaden Mosque is a leading example of Muslim architecture in Damascus. Built in the eighth century, it is enclosed by a wall extended from a Jupiter temple. In its inner courtyard there is a hexagonal structure resting on six pillars that is decorated in the Byzantine style. In former days, the state treasure was stored under the dome of this mosque. A triple-nave prayer hall contains a relic sacred for both Muslims and Christians: the skull of St. John the Baptist, revered in Islam as the prophet Yahua.

A number of major Mediterranean cultures left their marks on the Syrian capital of Damascus. At this site (top left) were once Aramaic and Roman temples, and Christian churches. The two photographs above show the decoration above the entrance and the entranceway to the Amajjaden Mosque, guardian of a relic of St. John the Baptist.

Pyramids of the pharaohs

World's largest tombs at Giza, near Cairo

ROUTE

Taxi or bus (line 9, 900, 901) to Giza, 6 miles SW of Cairo

BEST TIMES

October–April

ACCOMMODATIONS

Meno House Oberoi (at the foot of the pyramids)

ALSO WORTH SEEING

Sakkàra Cemetery 15 miles SW of Giza

Thousands of tourists jostle with each other year in year out, crouching through narrow and claustrophobic passageways, coughing nervously, all to view an uninteresting vault about 328 feet long, seventeen feet wide and nineteen feet high. The walls and ceiling are of polished granite, and there are no paintings or inscriptions. Just one simple unadorned sarcophagus in the western end without a lid. This is where Cheops, pharaoh of the fourth dynasty was entombed 4,500 years ago. It was from this resting place that the mighty ruler, preserved as a mummy, would ascend to heaven.

Marvel of the ancients

The Egyptian cult of the dead brought about the construction of a larger structure than humankind had previously attempted. The Pyramid of Cheops is a man-made mountain, erected in the desert as an act of faith. Cheop's subjects piled 2,400,000 blocks of stone averaging 2½ tons each, in the certain knowledge that this would render their pharaoh-god immortal and that they could follow after him. Once the peak of the pyramid—at a height of 482 feet—glistened gold against the blue sky as it reflected the sun, celebrating the sun god's daily fusion with the ruler of the earth. Today the pyramid is almost thirty-three feet lower. The pyramids were once sheathed in fine limestone, until this was removed in the thirteenth century to use as building materials.

To the southwest of the Pyramid of Cheops is another for his son Khafre (c. 2520–2494 BC), built on the same rocky ledge but with the addition of a Sphinx as guardian for the city of the dead with features resembling his own. The stern eyes are turned towards the east and the rising sun. A third pyramid for his son and successor Menkaure (2490–2471 BC) is further to the west. This is the smallest of the three pyramids.

From a distance these three pyramids look entirely intact, but closer up it is apparent that for hundreds of years they were regarded as useful sources of building stone. Yet the pyramids have withstood man and nature for thousands of years. The pyramids of Giza and the Sphinx are the oldest of the seven wonders of the ancient world and the only one remaining today.

For thousands of years people have sought secrets associated with these structures. In 820, Caliph Abdullah al-Ma'um was the first to

penetrate the interior of the Pyramid of Cheops. Legend has it that the chambers contained weapons that would not rust, glass that could not be bent, and priceless treasure. The caliph brought together a team of engineers, architects, and craftsmen to search the secret of the tomb. They carefully probed the entire structure but failed to find a secret entranceway so they forced a way in to the royal chamber.

They found no buried treasure. This had probably been removed by robbers within five hundred years of the pharaoh's death. The fact that they took everything, including the lid of the sarcophagus, gives rise to continued speculation down to our present age. Could the burial chamber be just a decoy? Was the pharaoh in reality buried elsewhere? Even the greediest of robbers tend to leave some traces behind them such as wreckage, scraps of wood or metal, removing only items of value or usefulness. Archaeologists found nothing in the pyramid of the ancient judge and the sarcophaguses were empty in other pyramids too.

It seemed at last as if luck had improved when the British Army officer Howard Vyse opened the Pyramid of Menkaure in 1838 and found a sealed sarcophagus. Curbing his curiosity, Vyse shipped it to England where its contents would be revealed. The ship ran aground on the coast of Spain and the sarcophagus was lost forever.

The great pyramids at Giza are just 6 miles from Cairo. These enormous structures were built 2,500 years before Christ by the pharaohs Menkaure, Khafre, and Cheops. The Sphinx still guards the eastern end of this city of the dead. This sole surviving member of the seven wonders of the world is Egypt's major tourist attraction.

Ramses II and Abu Simbel

UNESCO saved the desert temple from inundation

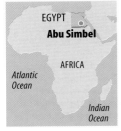

EGYPT
Abu Simbel

AFRICA

Atlantic Ocean

Indian Ocean

ROUTE
Internal flights from Cairo or Aswan. By rail (15 hours) Cairo–Aswan, then 169 miles by coach to Abu Simbel

BEST TIMES
October–April

ACCOMMODATIONS
Nefertari Hotel (near temple and out of sight of the Nasser Dam)

ALSO WORTH SEEING
Aswan, Luxor

Traveling by camel along the Nile through the Nubian desert, the Swiss explorer Johann Ludwig Buckhardt made a surprising discovery in May 1813. In a brief note in his diary he wrote: "My eye fell on the visible portion of four colossal statues...They stood in a deep hollow cut into the side of a hill. Unfortunately they were almost buried in the sand that the wind blows here just as if water dripping into a basin. The head and breast can be seen of one statue above the sand. The statue next to it can hardly be seen because the head is missing and the torso is covered up to the shoulders with sand.

Of the other two statues, only their headdress is visible." Buckhardt had discovered the temple of Abu Simbel.

Playing with the sun's rays
It was more than a century, in 1907, before the 101-foot-high facade of the temple in this remote spot could be cleared of the sand and seen in the full glory of which Buckhardt had seen such a small part. There are four figures, each portraying Ramses II seated on a throne. The pharaoh-god looks east across the shimmering waters of the Nile, towards the rising sun. Between his legs are the smaller figures of his mother, his favorite wife Nefertari, and some of his numerous children.

The interior of the temple has been carved out of rock to a depth of 164 feet. There are larger-than-life reliefs depicting Ramses slaying his enemies, riding in his chariot, witnessing the chopping-off of the hands of his enemies, and offering incense to the gods. On the rear wall of the temple, regarded as the most sacred part, are four giant figures of Ramses and three divine companions. Twice each year—usually before and after the winter solstice—the rays of the sun penetrate the front entrance to illuminate the statues on the rear wall.

A little north of Ramses' temple there is a smaller one which is cut into the rock; it is dedicated to Ramses' wife Nefertari and the god Hathor.

through the inner city, which is the true heart and soul of Fez, it is like traveling back to the Middle Ages, a pilgrimage for the senses.

Open-air museum

Submerging yourself in this lively "open-air museum" among the teeming souks, with people swarming and shouting, you find the alleys too narrow for motor vehicles, just wide enough for a donkey or hand cart. Each trade has its own section of the town, with each category of goods kept strictly apart. In one place you will find carpets, in another gold jewelry. Shoemakers work down one narrow thoroughfare, while the tanners are established next to the river.

The box-form houses of this ancient royal city are built on terraces on the hillside. For a thousand years this was the political, religious, and cultural center of North Africa, home to its kings, craftsmen, scientists, and artists. Visitors will still find some of the finest examples of Moorish architecture in Fez.

Ngorongoro Crater, paradise for wildlife

Wildlife in the tens of thousands inhabits the floor of this giant crater

AFRICA

Ngorongoro Crater

Atlantic
Ocean   TANZANIA

Indian
Ocean

ROUTE

Direct to Kilimanjaro
International Airport near
Arusha (Tanzania) or via
Nairobi (Kenya).
Tours start from Arusha

BEST TIMES

December–March,
July–October

ACCOMMODATIONS

Ngorongoro Wildlife Lodge,
Ngorongoro Crater Lodge

ALSO WORTH SEEING

Serengeti National Park,
Arusha National Park,
Kilimanjaro National Park

It is as if nature itself has created a special reserve for the animals of Africa. The forces of nature have created the enormous Ngorongoro Crater in northern Tanzania providing grazing of ninety-six square miles for countless herds of animals, breeding ground for astounding flocks of birds, and hunting ground for almost every kind of East African predator within this vast plain surrounded by steep hills.

This unique landscape was formed by several adjacent volcanoes. Millions of years ago, eruptions and lava flows created the cauldron-shaped crater about twelve and a half miles in diameter. Most of the vast plain of the crater floor is surrounded by the cliffs at the side of the crater rising to 2,300 feet above the bottom of the cauldron, and a height of 7,480–7,906 feet above sea-level.

The fertile crater floor of the Ngorongoro is covered with acacia

trees, tall grasses, an area of swamp, and a salt lake and flats called Magadi. The living conditions in these surroundings are ideal for

Flamingos feeding in the saline waters of Lake Magadi

almost every animal indigenous to East Africa.

The numbers of mammals such as elephant, rhino, hippo, gnu, water buffalo, zebra, antelope, and giraffe living in the crater is estimated at 20,000–30,000. This number varies because many of them also live outside the Ngorongoro for part of the time. The big cat predators roaming are chiefly lions, cheetahs, leopards, and a few of the smaller cats also.

Traces of the first inhabitants

The saline waters of the Magadi are frequently the feeding grounds of thousands of flamingos. Flocks of Nile geese and various types of duck also land on the water. Cranes too find plenty of cover to hatch their eggs as do plovers, hoopoes, coursers, and great bustards. On the more solid ground one finds ostrich, always ready to take flight, wandering around in the world's most densely populated volcanic crater.

The paradise-like conditions of the Ngorongoro attracted upright

man as far back as 3,600,000 years ago. These hominids were four to five feet tall. In 1978, the American anthropologist Mary Leakey discovered footprints of these early Africans about twenty-five miles from the crater wall. They have a species name like animals: *Australopithecus afarensis*. Because of their prominent lower jaws they have been dubbed the "nutcracker people."

Much more recently, the verdant crater floor was pasture for 10,000–15,000 Masai with their herds of around a million cattle. When the Ngorongoro Crater and nearby Serengeti National Parks

were created, the Masai were restricted in their use of this habitat. Today they are permitted to graze their animals on the crater floor but not to live there.

Both the Ngorongoro Crater and the Serengeti would be seriously threatened without the strong protective measures that have been put in place. There is a small stone cairn at the entrance to the Ngorongoro Crater National Park as a memorial to the zoologist Bernhard Grzimek and his son Michael who died in an aircraft crash in 1958 while filming the legendary film *The Serengeti Shall Not Die*.

Volcanic action formed the vast and fertile Ngorongoro Crater in the north of Tanzania, covering 96 square miles. The crater walls also act as a boundary. Just about every indigenous species of East African wild life can be encountered here, such as hyena, and water buffaloes (bottom right).

The thundering Victoria Falls

The Victoria Falls on the Zambezi stride the border of Zambia and Zimbabwe

AFRICA

Atlantic Ocean · **Victoria Falls**

ZIMBABWE · Indian Ocean

ROUTE

International flights to Harare (Zimbabwe). Local flights to Victoria Falls or via Lusaka (Zambia) to Livingstone/Maramba

BEST TIMES

May–September

ACCOMMODATION

Victoria Falls Hotel

ALSO WORTH SEEING

Lake Kariba, Hwange National Park, Matoba Hills National Park near Bulawayo (Zimbawe)

Mosi oa Tunya: the Smoke that Thunders. The Zambezi separates Zambia and Zimbabwe.

The British explorer David Livingstone was lyrical in his description. "This is the most marvelous sight I have ever beheld in Africa," he jotted in his notebook in November 1855 as he stood on an island in the river gazing in awe at the thundering mass of water of the Zambezi as it cascaded into a narrow gorge. Deep below he saw two rainbows against a backdrop of a dense white cloud with a "column of vapor two or three hundred feet in height" rising aloft, "the upper portion of which took on the color of dark smoke."

Crossing Africa from the Atlantic to the Pacific, the Englishman was the first European to reach the legendary falls on the Zambezi river, the largest in Africa. The sound of falling water was deafening to the point that the natives, fearful of the mighty spirits at work, dared not draw near. They called this wonder of nature Mosi oa Tunya, "the Smoke that Thunders." Livingstone had already noticed five columns of apparent smoke from a distance, as if the savanna was burning.

Falls into nine canyons

David Livingstone named the falls Victoria Falls in honor of his queen and later the town that grew up a few miles away was named after him. Today's map of Zambia uses the African name of Maramba for the town once known as Livingstone.

The Zambezi is 1,287 miles long and the longest river in southern Africa. At the border between Zambia and Zimbabwe (once North and South Rhodesia), at the place described by Livingstone, the Zambezi's mass of water, more than a mile wide, drops 360 feet over a basalt ledge into a narrow gorge that is linked to a further nine canyons which were once receiving basins for the cascading water. The Victoria Falls consist of five separate falls: the Eastern Cataract, the Rainbow Falls, the Horseshoe Falls, and the Devil's Cataract on the western side of the geological fault.

Since Livingstone's time the falls have remain largely unaltered except for luxury hotels such as the Mosi-oa-Tunya Intercontinental and a new highway almost to the brink of the falls. A railway bridge has also crossed the narrower section of the falls since 1904 linking Zambia and Zimbabwe. A picturesque jungle track in Zambia leads to Knife Edge, a slippery rock path between the first and second canyon of the Victoria Falls.

Although the "columns of smoke" described by Livingstone are rarely seen today, and enormous mist cloud still hovers above the falls which is at its largest during the end of the rainy season when around 84,500,000 gallons of water pour over the falls each minute. The volume of water reduces to a mere "trickle" of some 4,800,000 gallons per minute at the end of the dry season.

Exceptionally lush vegetation still surrounds much of the Victoria Falls as described by Livingstone. Clouds of mist cause fine rain to fall over an area with a radius of more than eighteen miles from the falls, creating a great wealth of plant life. The entire area on both sides of the Zambezi are now protected National Parks. On the Zambian side the Mosi-oa-Tunya and the Victoria Falls National Park on the Zimbabwe side.

The tourist center for Zambia is Livingstone (Maramba), less than five miles from the falls.

With deafening roaring, millions of gallons of water cascade into a narrow gorge 360 feet deep and 165 feet wide. The rising clouds of foam cause a fine mist to descend in a radius of 20 miles.

Photo credits